Praise for the works

Thursday Afternoons

A fun and sexy book that will tug at your heartstrings. The pace of the book is excellent, and at no point are you left feeling uncertain about Ellis and Amy. The chemistry between them is there in spades. I loved the way Tracey Richardson amped up the tension when everything is revealed and the chapters that follow. This made it really easy for me to connect with the story line and the characters.

-Les Rêveur

There's no manufactured conflict here that can be resolved with a frank discussion over a cup of coffee. Ellis's and Amy's careers have them at odds and they both have so much at stake. The side characters gave me even more reasons to become invested in the book and their plotlines are seamlessly woven together. Good stories always make you want to go back to the beginning and start again, and this is definitely one of those. It has everything from steamy, lust-filled sex, to dramatic tension and a great slow-burn romance between two amazing, beautiful women inside and out. If you're looking for a book that gives you everything you're craving at once, then this is positively the book for you.

-The Lesbian Review

I'm Gonna Make You Love Me

Claire and Ellie might just be my favourite couple that Tracey Richardson's written so far. There are some great side characters between Claire's best friend Jackson, and Ellie's roommate and cousin Marissa, plus her family. They help us get to know the leads better and are integral to both of the women's character arcs. Richardson's writing is easy to sink into and this book was no exception. The romance has a nice burn to it that's slow, but not too slow, and I marveled at how natural Claire and Ellie's journey from former boss/employee to happily ever after was. If you're a fan of contemporary romances, especially those with age gaps or opposites attract pairings, I recommend picking up *I'm Gonna Make You Love Me*. I thoroughly enjoyed it and will be reading this one again (especially if a spinoff happens!).

-The Lesbian Review

What a fun story with lots of fantastic music to read along to. One of my favourite tropes is age-gap romance and this did not disappoint; I really enjoyed this unraveling of the romance. The pace was perfect and I hadn't realized I had read so long until I had finished the book in one sitting. It was easy to like both characters and the chemistry for both Ellie and Claire was there from the moment Claire returns Ellie's pup home. This story had happily ever after written all over it from that moment on.

-Les Rêveur

Heartsick

This was such a sweet story of heartbreak turned friendship turned love. I knew I'd enjoy the story from the get-go because it's a Tracey Richardson book but I was really drawn to the characters over and above the storyline itself.

-Les Rêveur

Delay of Game

There are so many things to love about this book. There are great characters working to be together in a seemingly impossible situation. The scenes on the ice were wonderful and visceral, but without slowing down the story. I've heard it said that in some sport romances, the sport scenes can get in the way of the plot, which is definitely not the case here. The action on the ice is as important as what happens off the ice, both in terms of character and plot development.

-The Lesbian Review

With a story set around the very real rivalry between the Canadian and US women's ice hockey teams, this book has a realistic edge to it to go along with the romance that is the main focus of the tale. Although the romance is given slightly more weight, there's enough of the hockey story to keep sports fans truly interested. Richardson clearly knows hockey, and all the scenes around practice, training, and actual matches come across as very authentic.

-Rainbow Book Reviews

Ten Days in May

Other Bella Books by Tracey Richardson

Blind Bet
By Mutual Consent
The Campaign
The Candidate
Delay of Game
Heartsick
I'm Gonna Make You Love Me
Last Salute
No Rules of Engagement
Side Order of Love
The Song in My Heart
Thursday Afternoons
The Wedding Party

About the Author

Tracey Richardson is the author of thirteen previous novels, all of them lesbian romances with Bella Books. Her best-known novels include *No Rules of Engagement* and *Last Salute*, both of which were Lambda Literary Awards finalists, along with bestsellers *Thursday Afternoons*, *The Candidate*, *By Mutual Consent*, and *Delay of Game*. She's also written several short stories, one of which won second place in an international competition. Tracey worked for nearly three decades as a daily newspaper journalist, but now writes fiction full time. She lives in the Georgian Bay area of Ontario, Canada, with her wife, Sandra, and their dogs. Visit www.traceyrichardson.net for more information about her books and to connect further.

Ten Days in May

Tracey Richardson

BELLA
BOOKS

2022

Copyright © 2022 by Tracey Richardson

Bella Books, Inc.
P.O. Box 10543
Tallahassee, FL 32302

All rights reserved. No part of this book may be reproduced or transmitted in any form or by any means, electronic or mechanical, including photocopying, without permission in writing from the publisher.

This is a work of fiction. Names, characters, businesses, places, events and incidents are either the products of the author's imagination or used in a fictitious manner. Any resemblance to actual persons, living or dead, or actual events is purely coincidental. The publisher does not have any control over and does not assume any responsibility for author or third-party websites or their content.

Printed in the United States of America on acid-free paper.

First Edition - 2022

Editor: Medora MacDougall
Cover Designer: Kayla Mancuso

ISBN: 978-1-64247-357-5

PUBLISHER'S NOTE

The scanning, uploading, and distribution of this book via the Internet or via any other means without the permission of the publisher is illegal and punishable by law. Please purchase only authorized print or electronic editions, and do not participate in or encourage electronic piracy of copyrighted materials. Your support of the author's rights is appreciated.

Acknowledgments

When the pandemic fell from the sky like a hundred-pound hammer, it took me awhile to figure out how I wanted to tackle this gnarly topic in my fiction writing. None of us has a crystal ball as to when and how the pandemic will (finally) end nor what might come after, but I wanted *Ten Days in May* to be different. I wanted it to reflect the seismic internal shifts many of us have been experiencing over the last two-plus years. Whether we wanted it to or not, the pandemic (as well as climate change, war, and the ever-worrisome political landscape) has us all looking inside a little more, reflecting on what is important, on what kind of person we want to be, on what we want our future to look like. These are universal themes that have never seemed so relevant and so pressing, and I wanted to reflect those themes in this novel. Ultimately, this is a novel not about dying, but about living, about finding our way. People save people. And love saves us all.

Thank you to my wife, Sandra, for sharing my life. Thank you, dear readers, for letting me indulge in my creative outlet this way. And thank you to Linda and Jessica and all the wonderful staff at Bella Books. As always, a special shout out to my editor Medora MacDougall, who always helps me make my novels better and who never fails to teach me a few things along the way. We make a great team, and I am so grateful!

Finally, a special thank you to my friend Joan, a psychologist who also happens to be a writer. Lucky me, I get the benefits of her knowledge and experience to help me "analyze" my characters and make them (and the book) better.

CHAPTER ONE

Camryn Hughes clicks open her email at the notification sound—an annoying squawk that sounds like a flock of birds in crisis. She doesn't want to miss an email from a client or a potential client, because to them, time is everything. In the hourglass that is their life, there are only a few grains of sand left.

The whole mortality thing is the part that makes most people so uncomfortable when they hear what Cam does for a living. Just the other night at book club, she started to recommend *The Needs of the Dying* after they'd all read Joan Didion's *The Year of Magical Thinking*. There was polite tolerance for a moment or two before someone suggested they talk about something "lighter." So typical. As if on cue, one woman launched into gossiping about her neighbor's affair with a married man, while another couldn't wait to update the group on her niece's boyfriend's cousin's awful Covid saga. So much for "lighter" topics. Cold shoulders are as common to Cam as cracks in the sidewalk. *You do what for a living? Oh, I see, well, I'd better not be needing your services anytime soon, ha ha.*

Cam does so much internal eye rolling that if she were rolling her eyes that much for real, they'd have fallen out of her head by now. But she wouldn't trade her job for anything, no matter how much social awkwardness she has to endure, because the work makes her feel more real, more connected, than anything else she's done in her life. Akin to how a midwife or birthing coach helps prepare a woman, a family, for a baby's arrival, Cam, as a death doula, helps her clients and their loved ones prepare for a soft landing to wherever it is that their soul is going after their body dies. Sort of like getting ready for a trip, is how she thinks of it. If her clients want help cleaning their house or putting their legal affairs in order, no problem. If they want help communicating with health care providers or even estranged family members, she will do that too. She'll read out loud to her clients, take them to appointments, fetch them a milkshake to satisfy a sudden craving if that's what they want. Spending time with the dying has been a gift to Cam—a daily reminder that not only is life fleeting, but that it's meant to be *lived*.

These days, Cam doesn't have to advertise. Word of mouth, after putting in the legwork of getting to know local social workers, clergy, doctors, and nurses, has given her more work than she can handle. She can afford to be selective about her clients and her workload, and so she hesitates after reading the email from a dying man who wants to hire her.

Landon Ross is a professor at Northwestern Michigan College, here in Traverse City, and he isn't a total stranger to Cam. He used to walk the cutest, friendliest little dachshund a few streets over, and Cam would sometimes stop to chat with Landon and Harvey. She even started carrying treats in her pocket for Harvey, but the dog must have died because, now that she thinks of it, she's only seen Landon walking alone over the last few months. Actually, she hasn't seen Landon at all in probably two months now, maybe longer. She's sorry to learn that this friendly stranger is dying of pancreatic cancer.

There's a snag, though. Landon Ross not only wants to hire her as his death doula but also to make a trip out of town on an undisclosed errand. The request raises a red flag, because Cam can't simply take off for days without a lot of planning and organizing. She's had clients before who seem to think she's a genie who can grant them wishes before they die or can complete their bucket list vicariously. It's awkward, because her work isn't supposed to be about *her*. It's why she's learned to become quite adept at setting boundaries, at saying no, though sometimes she says yes. It all depends on the client and on the task. The last line in his email grabs her attention: *My budget has no ceiling.*

Visions of a new furnace tempt her, so Cam hits the reply button. It can't hurt to sit down and talk with Landon. Maybe she can talk him out of his road trip request. Or maybe she will like him enough to feel compelled to do it. She's learned not to judge clients before she gets to know them, and even then, the prospect of death can be a lightning rod to change.

Take Jim Duffy. He was an elderly curmudgeon who screamed at the poor paper carrier daily for not taking the time to set the newspaper exactly so on his doorstep. He threw snowballs in winter or tennis balls in summer at stray cats who dared step a paw on his property. The man was despised. And yet by the time Cam visited Jim in hospice, he was the sweetest, most polite old man she'd ever met. Holding *her* hand, asking *her* how she was doing. It is the biggest misconception of all that people don't change, because in her experience, people change all the time.

Cam walks to Landon's for their first meeting; his house is not far. It's a two-story English Tudor with vines crawling along its exterior walls of brick and stucco, which seems to make it the perfect house for a professor (his email signature line says he teaches economics). A middle-aged woman with one of the most disarming smiles Cam has ever seen opens the door. She is tall, willowy, not gorgeous exactly, but pleasant-looking. She looks like someone you can count on to tell you the truth but in the least harmful way possible. Cam likes her right away.

"Hi! How do you do? You must be Camryn Hughes." The woman's handshake is warm, firm, her gaze direct.

"I am. It's very nice to meet you."

"Likewise. I'm Tenley Sutton. Come on in. Landon is expecting you."

This is always the part Cam is most eager—and nervous—about. What shape is he in? And most of all, will she like him? If there is anything about his demands or personality that aren't a good fit, she'll decline the job. She always tells prospective clients the same thing—that if they too feel it's not a good fit, she will help them find an alternative.

Tenley leads her toward the back of the house and knocks softly before opening the door to a spectacular library with floor-to-ceiling bookshelves, stained glass windows, a leather sofa and a couple of comfortably worn wingback chairs facing a gas fireplace. *I could lose myself in a room like this, with its scent of leather and books,* Cam thinks with a trace of envy. Landon is sitting in one of the wingback chairs, looking gaunt in sweats with a fleece blanket wrapped around his shoulders like a shawl. He is obviously chilly even though the ambient temperature is comfortable enough. Cam notices that he is markedly thinner since she saw him on a walk in early winter, and his skin has the pallor of the sick. His brown hair, gray at the temples, is thinner too. He half pulls himself out of the chair to greet her until the effort proves too much and he sinks back down with a smile that's more a frown.

"Hello, Camryn Hughes. I'm so glad you're here."

Cam shakes his hand; his fingers are dry as twigs. "Just Cam is good."

"Okay, Just Cam. You already know I'm Just Landon. And this is my partner, Just Tenley. Though you already met her at the door." He lowers his voice to a whisper, mischief alight in his eyes. "I keep trying to marry her, but she doesn't believe in the grand institution. Even now that I'm dying she won't marry me. Have you ever heard of anything so grievous?"

Cam breaks into a smile. She likes Landon and his dry sense of humor. "Well. I'm a little shy about the grand institution myself."

"Not me," Landon proclaims. "I already tried it. It's not half bad, you know. Though it helps if you have the right person to walk down the aisle with."

Tenley rolls her eyes as she lays an affectionate hand on her partner's knee. "Even a divorce wasn't enough to dull the incurable romantic in him."

"That's because I actually like my ex."

"Unfortunately, I can't say the same about mine," Tenley says on an aggrieved sigh. "Which is why I won't walk down the aisle again. But I'd go anywhere else with this big goof." She squeezes Landon's bony knee. "Please, Cam, have a seat. Can I get you anything? I've got tea on."

"Tea sounds perfect." It will give her a few moments alone with her prospective client.

Cam sits on the leather sofa and watches Tenley switch on the gas fireplace before clicking the door shut behind her. It is already warm enough in the library, but Landon needs the warmth and winter hasn't entirely yielded to spring yet.

"Let me look at you, Cam," he says. His gaze is scrupulous. "You look exactly like your photos, you know."

"My photos?" Cam absently runs her hand through her thick hair, a life-long habit of trying to tame it.

"From my Google investigation. When I used to see you in the neighborhood, I had no idea what you did for a living, until I needed...well, the services of someone like you. Can't hire a death doula who might, I don't know, rob me blind or take advantage of my body, you know."

She laughs politely, but a small pit lodges in her stomach at the knowledge that Landon Ross has been *investigating* her. And while it makes her uncomfortable, she can't blame him for wanting to be confident in her credentials. When he next mentions her mother, it throws her for a second, and she wonders exactly how deeply he's been looking into her background. "You knew my mom?"

"I did. I remember her well. Ruth was a wonderful veterinarian. I'm sorry she's...no longer here. Is she the reason you came back to the place you grew up?"

"She was. I was looking for a fresh start and she needed my help. I came back here nine years ago, after her diagnosis. I never left."

"And that's what convinced you to become a death doula? Looking after your mother?"

"It was. I already had a social work degree that I wasn't putting to good use, so it seemed natural to segue into this. Plus, I think I'd forgotten how nice it is living so close to the lake. When you spend years landlocked, you forget the power and beauty of water." Earth with air but no water has always made Cam feel incomplete.

Landon nods thoughtfully. He's taking everything she says and storing it in his memory, she can tell. Little files alphabetically labeled in his mind. She understands because she does the same. "You fled after high school."

"Doesn't everybody flee their hometown as soon as they can?"

"Good point. I sure did. Couldn't get out of Indiana fast enough. But I love it here. Tenley's originally from here. I moved here over a decade ago after we met because I couldn't stand the idea of living without her." He chuckles to himself. "Tenley has a habit of getting what she wants, but moving here wasn't a tough decision for me. And for the record, I'm glad you stuck around after your mom passed." His eyes pierce her as though by merely staring he can suck out every scrap of information about her. "No career or spouse or kids you had to leave behind?"

"It was the right time for me to make a change." It's a dance, sharing personal information. Cam likes to share enough about herself to put her clients at ease, to make sure they understand their arrangement is unique and special. Too much sharing and intimacy can make it emotionally tough on her when her client dies, though emotional aloofness and an overabundance of formality aren't productive either. She walks a line with her personal feelings. She and Landon will get to where they need to be with one another, but it won't be today. Today they're simply feeling one another out.

Landon takes her answer and seems to roll it around in his mind for a minute before breaking into a crooked smile. "Any regrets?"

"None that would put me anywhere else right now."

Tenley is back with the tea.

To her, Landon says, "I like her, Ten." To Cam, "When can you start?"

"I...well...once we're sure that we're all on the same page and that we think we can work well together."

"I see. So have I passed your test yet? 'Cuz you've passed mine."

Cam laughs and sips her tea. Landon Ross seems like a good guy, like someone who genuinely seeks the truth and who doesn't spend a lot of time bemoaning things or looking for trouble. And that is good enough for her. "Yes, you've passed my test."

His smile splits his whole face, giving Cam a glimpse of how he looked as a younger man. Tenley looks pleased too. Relieved, more like. Clients and their loved ones always exhibit relief when Cam agrees to take them on, as though their burden has been instantly lightened. Handshakes all around are enough. From this day forward, they are a team, the three of them.

They spend the next several minutes going over her rules (she doesn't give medical assistance, but is there to talk and listen, to run errands, to liaise with medical professionals and anyone else he wants her to, to help plan his funeral, to fetch groceries, to give whatever emotional, spiritual, and holistic support—to both of them—that she can). Then Landon and Tenley outline what they expect of Cam, which isn't a long list and includes the enigmatic little "trip" they want her to go on. She wants to press them on it, but Landon is starting to nod off.

"More on that some other time," Tenley says, clutching Landon's hand to wake him up. "I think this is probably good enough for today."

Landon's voice halts Cam as she is about to get up. "Tell me something, Cam. You came back to Traverse City. You came home. Does that mean you believe that you *can* go home again?"

Immediately she recognizes the old saying "you can never go home again," straight from the title of a 1940 Thomas Wolfe novel. How many millions of times have people asked that question? she wonders. "I think…" She pauses to watch him, to gauge whether he is teasing her or testing her. In any case, it's pretty clear that Landon Ross is the kind of man who, when he asks a question, expects to receive an answer. "I think you *can* go home again, whether home is a physical place or a place in your mind. But what you find may not be what you expect."

He nods once, his eyes drifting toward the windows that look out onto a lovely perennial garden whose shoots are emerging from the receding crusts of winter. Purple and yellow crocuses timidly poke their heads out of the cool soil. "So then…what *do* you find when you get there? Home?"

Her shrug is noncommittal, but Landon's eyes, a shade of blue that match the still-freezing-cold lake a few blocks away, swing her way and pin her like it's the big final *Jeopardy* question he's waiting on. "Your homework," he says pointedly. "To be discussed further, next visit."

This client, Cam knows in her gut, will challenge her. Not only challenge her, but quite possibly change her, as some clients do. Second thoughts creep in like a bad dream and she is tempted to make her excuses, to reject this job. But she loves a challenge because they keep her fresh, engaged, and because the last thing she wants is for her job to feel, well, like a job.

Plus, she likes Landon and Tenley.

"Yes, Professor. I'll get on that."

"Good," he answers, his eyes drifting shut. The meeting is adjourned.

At the door, Tenley gives Cam a brief medical rundown of where Landon is at with his illness and promises to email more details later.

Walking home, it feels to Cam as if she's just stepped off something surefooted and predictable and into something that is neither of those things.

CHAPTER TWO

Another email, the second one in three days. Brooke Ross punched the reply button, ready to give Jason Whitaker a piece of her mind. *For the millionth time, I'm not selling the restaurant so stop bugging the shit out of me ab—*

Delete delete delete. She slammed her laptop shut, filled the coffeemaker, and switched it on, then commanded herself to calm down. Whitaker wasn't a wolf, and he wasn't trying to insult her or take advantage of her. He was a decent guy, even if his persistence was on the annoying side. He already owned a Mediterranean-style restaurant in town as well as a takeout pizza joint, both with good reputations. Brooke's jazzy little Italian eatery in Ann Arbor's university district could be, as Whitaker described it, the crown jewel in his collection of restaurants if only she would sell it to him. *Blah blah blah.*

Okay, so she couldn't deny his offer was fair, but selling the restaurant would be like selling a kidney or something. She'd put everything she had into it over the last twelve years...all her money and some of her ex's, her aching back, her time, and most of all, her heart. She'd stuck it out during the sledgehammer otherwise known as the pandemic, even dipping into her meager retirement savings, and when that wasn't enough, she took out a loan to keep her employees on the payroll and the rent paid so she could at least offer takeout service during the merry-go-round of lockdowns. Selling now would be like driving through a blistering snowstorm only to give up right on the doorstep of her destination. Because Mangiare Roma was bouncing back and gradually approaching pre-pandemic levels, a reward for Brooke's patience. Customers were steadily returning, but the small loan remained. Brooke's financial health had taken a body blow, and there were no guarantees for the future. The restaurant business remained one giant roulette wheel.

She poured herself another cup of coffee and returned to the kitchen table and her laptop. She knew exactly how much money she had in the bank and what she owed. She shouldn't outright reject Whitaker's offer, her head knew that at least. But dammit, how could she even *think* about letting it all go so easily? What if she sold it and Whitaker ruined the best little Italian eatery between Detroit and Chicago? And what would she do with her life anyway? She'd be directionless, bereft. No. She'd give it more time, see if the next few months restored her energy, her resolve, and most importantly, brought in more revenue. Summer was coming. She couldn't give up on the place. Not yet.

"Hey." Rachel shuffled in, her purple hair wet from a shower and sticking straight up, like a field of cornstalks. She beelined for the coffeepot, dumping what remained of it into the largest mug Brooke owned. Rachel didn't start another pot, but then, she never did.

"Hey," Brooke answered with a discreet eyeroll, loathing *hey* as a greeting, but it was Rachel's go-to. She hated Rachel's purple dye job too. Not that she'd ever voice such a thing, because World War Three didn't hold much appeal.

Rachel pointed at the laptop. "What-cha doing?"

"Going over work stuff."

"Want to go out tonight? The new Bond movie's finally here."

Brooke hated James Bond movies. All violent action movies, for that matter. She could turn on the news for free if she wanted to see violence. "Can't. Jessica called in sick tonight." Jessica was her best server, and it was too late to find someone else. Brooke had been racking her brain trying to come up with a solution, but now she didn't need to. Now she had a handy reason to avoid going to the movies with Rachel.

Rachel slammed her half-filled mug down on the table. Black liquid sloshed over the sides, and she made no attempt to clean it up. "Dammit, Brooke. When's the last time we did anything together?"

Brooke quirked an eyebrow at her.

"Fine, but I'm not talking about sex."

Sex was the only thing they didn't fight about these days. Rachel was a nurse at the children's hospital (her purple hair was for the kids, she claimed, but Brooke knew better). She kept her own apartment, but usually spent two or three nights a week at Brooke's townhouse. When the pandemic first hit, they barely saw one another. Between extra shifts at the hospital and her fear of contracting Covid and passing it on to Brooke, Rachel insisted they see each other only a couple of times a month— something Brooke quickly began to realize she enjoyed. But now Rachel was back to staying over regularly, to wanting "to do things" together. Social things that were always Rachel's ideas and never held any appeal for Brooke.

"Rach, I can't find anyone else to cover the shift. It's only for a few hours. Why don't you come over later and we'll watch a movie or something?"

"So you can fall asleep halfway through it? No thanks."

It was the same fight, episode number ninety-nine. Rachel always claimed Brooke worked too much. She didn't, if you considered fifty-five hours a week a normal amount of work. Rachel was almost as bad, never turning down a last-minute shift at the hospital. But Rachel got to go home at the end of her shift and tune out. The restaurant followed Brooke wherever she went because there was always something to do or solve— work out a new menu, try a new dish from her chef's constant tinkering, train a new server or sous chef, get a plumber in to fix a sudden leak. And then there were all the bills to pay, fresh food and wine to order, advertising and marketing to conduct, and cleaning. Always, there was something to clean.

"I'm sorry," Brooke said simply. She didn't want to fight, really she didn't. But Rachel had that tight jaw and the death stare that said she was spoiling for one.

"You've been zero fun now that the worst of this pandemic is over. We were supposed to go on a trip, remember? Whatever happened to that?"

Brooke took a breath and counted to ten. "I don't have the time or the money for a trip right now, you know that."

"So I'm supposed to wait a couple more years for the restaurant to get back on its feet and start running itself or something?"

"The restaurant *is* getting back on its feet. It won't take much longer." She hoped.

"Whether it takes a week or a decade, you never make *us* a priority."

Brooke passed her lover a look that said she was making a big deal out of nothing, but Rachel wasn't wrong. It was true that Brooke didn't make their relationship a priority, but Rachel's idea of how they should spend time together was nothing like what Brooke wanted. Rachel was big on them going out Saturday nights with her friends or to one of her friends' houses for a backyard barbecue where the booze and the pot flowed endlessly. It was at these gatherings that Brooke felt all of her forty-eight years, while Rachel carried on like the thirty-two-year-old she was, saying that partying was her time to decompress and, oh, Brooke's favorite, that it was *self care*.

"Look," Brooke finally said, on the verge of pleading, because she was drowning in the frustration of being pulled in so many directions. "I just want things to be simple between us for once. The restaurant is complication enough, and so is your job. I want something—*one thing*—to be easy in my life."

Rachel, her hair brightening a shade as it dried, gave a furious shake of her head. "You should sell that damned restaurant, is what you should do. *That* would simplify your life, like, a whole lot. Maybe you'd have more time for us then."

Regret tugged at Brooke for telling Rachel about Jason Whitaker's offer. She should have kept it to herself, because to Rachel, the restaurant was like an old bicycle or sofa to be sold—an annoying thing Brooke should simply dispose of. She didn't understand Brooke at all, couldn't see how owning a restaurant was the biggest part of her, the one and only thing she had wanted to do with her life. The sacrifices, the hardships but also the joy that came with owning her own restaurant—it was all incomprehensible to Rachel.

"Sell it and do what?" Brooke countered. Her ire was up, but even if she warmed to the idea of selling, what the hell would she do with her life? The sad truth was, she had no idea how to reinvent herself. The one thing she did know was that she did not want to spend more time with someone she wasn't in love with. The idea of going on a trip with Rachel was a misery she could barely fathom. In fact, she'd rather pull out her hair one strand at a time.

Rachel made a tsking sound. "Do I have to come up with all the ideas around here? Okay, fine. Sell it and let's go on that trip."

Shoot me now, Brooke thought. With both Rachel and Jason Whitaker bugging her to sell, the ambush was on. But it was her decision, dammit, and she would not be railroaded into anything. Especially not if Rachel thought that the pot of gold at the end was going on a trip together. Ugh. "I'm not selling it, Rachel. I don't care if Whitaker offers me a million dollars. It's not happening." There. That ought to end the discussion.

Rachel stood and stared at her for a long time, her mouth and jaw as fixed as a plaster statue that might crack at any minute. The only emotion in her eyes was anger. Another minute ticked by before she stalked to the door, a decision having been rendered. From the coat hook near the door, she grabbed her backpack. "I'll make this real *simple* for you, since that's what you want. Goodbye, Brooke. Don't call me, all right?"

The door slammed behind her. Brooke didn't move. Her gaze fixed on Rachel's spilled coffee on the table—a Rorschach testimony of their relationship—and she felt nothing. For an instant, it occurred to her that maybe she should cry or something. Hell, she cried the other day when she dropped her phone on the street and it skittered down a drain hole. This time she waited for the prick of tears or at least a tickling in her throat. Nothing. *Okay. Fine.* She opened her laptop again, clicked on the folder that contained the spreadsheets of her bank accounts and pored over them. Things weren't great on the black side of the ledger, but they were much better than they were a year ago when the pandemic still had them all in its ceaseless grip. She was sure that if she hung on a little longer, the restaurant would get out of this hole for good and be more successful than ever. She knew how to stay the course, how to do whatever she needed to do to make things work.

She also knew a thing or two about walking away.

CHAPTER THREE

Cam has had other clients with pancreatic cancer. The disease is a bitch, claiming more than 40,000 lives every year in America. With little in the way of known causes, it can be difficult to catch the disease in its early stages. Most patients, once diagnosed, face a condensed terminal illness. Landon Ross is no different.

Cam knows what to expect, or rather, what her client can expect. At her second meeting with the couple, she makes sure they have a solid understanding of everything about his diagnosis—his symptoms, his treatment, how the progression of the disease will play out. Most of her clients want to know everything they can about their disease, because doing so can make them feel less helpless, more empowered. But the mind-numbing details can be too much for some.

Early in Cam's training, when she was working at a hospice, there was a patient named Marion Banks. She was in her early fifties and refused to admit to herself or to anyone that she was dying of the ovarian cancer that was the very reason she lay in a hospice bed, her life ebbing away. There were periods where she would constantly chatter, sing, bounce around the room, claiming that she was fine, that she merely had some benign fibroids on her ovaries that caused her pain, the same issue scores of women lived with every day. Even when her illness finally prevented her from getting out of bed, she insisted she would get better "one of these days." It drove her family mad, until Cam finally counseled them that if Marion didn't want to face reality, it was her choice and that they should support that choice. She died believing she was not going to die, because she clearly could not cope with the fear of such a disastrous outcome.

Landon and Tenley are nothing like Marion Banks. They're realists who seem to acknowledge that they will play this losing hand as best and as long as they reasonably can. Cam confirms that their legal work is in order before asking Landon about how he came to be diagnosed. It's important to learn her client's history before, during, and after their diagnosis.

Landon recounts the symptoms he first began to notice months ago, right as summer gave way to fall—abdominal pain, weight loss, loss of appetite. There were other causes to blame his symptoms on: pandemic depression, anxiety about the new school year starting and all the work that meant for him. By the time he (or rather, Tenley) began to notice some jaundice in his eyes, he was ready to consult a doctor. "I had so much work to do to get ready for a new semester," he explains sheepishly. "So I was stubborn about it. And stupid, as it turns out."

"Not that it really would have made any difference," Tenley adds. "But at the age of fifty-four, pancreatic adenocarcinoma wasn't something we expected. Maybe ulcers or IBS, but not this. We weren't prepared, not like we are now."

"I understand. No one expects such a diagnosis at that age. And there's the medical system to navigate." Cam watches Tenley nod emphatically. Sympathy for the couple comes easily. They've been thrown into the deep end of disease and death, hospitals and doctors, so quickly and with so little help in the beginning. "So, two rounds of chemotherapy. Are you planning to do more?"

Landon glances at Tenley before shaking his head. "I've been given three to six months. My oncologist says chemo won't change that significantly. So, no. I'm not willing to put myself or Tenley through that again."

"Fair enough." Many times, she has wondered if she'd have the same courage as her clients were she in their situation, but no one can really know until it happens to them. Her mom was the first to show her bravery in the face of death, choosing not to think of death as an end but as a transition, a moving into something else that may not be known but wasn't, to her at least, formidable. "I didn't know," her mom said at the time, "how it was going to be once it was clear I would need to raise you on my own. But it wasn't scary, Cam. It was the most gratifying thing I ever did. And I don't think this will be so scary either. In fact, I'll be going back into the soup." Ruth Hughes's favorite soup was cream of mushroom, so Cam teasingly asked her if that was the kind of soup she would be going into.

Now she swallows the lump in her throat—the same lump she gets whenever she misses her mom—and forces herself to concentrate on Landon's list of medications in the binder she's made for him. A photo of Landon and Tenley graces the front of the binder. It's where she'll keep all her notes on their visits, on the progress of his illness, her observations, and she will offer it to Tenley after Landon is gone, if she wants it. A final journal, so to speak, for his final journey. "I see you're on medication for pain and for the jaundice. What about for nausea? For sleep? And are you taking anything for the stress, to help you cope?"

Landon clears his throat as if he's stalling, then announces almost defiantly, "Cannabis for all three."

"All right, glad to hear it." Tenley and Landon seem surprised by Cam's reaction. She's taken a few seminars on medical cannabis because many of her clients use it. The drug is recreationally legal in Michigan, though she confirms with Landon that he has a medical prescription for it. Next they discuss his fatigue, his pain level, what he can and can no longer do.

"What happened to your dog? Harvey?" Cam asks suddenly.

"He died soon after I got sick. Oral cancer. Another damned thing on top of my diagnosis."

"I'm sorry." Pets can be a fantastic diversion, as well as a comfort, to cancer patients. Landon and Tenley have been through so much, perhaps they need another dog. "Thought of getting another one?"

"I have but…" Landon glances at Tenley. He does this a lot, Cam notices, before he speaks. It's almost as though they're one person. "I think a puppy would be too much work at this point."

"I understand." Cam makes a note to check with dachshund adoption agencies for an older dog for Landon and Tenley to consider. The couple might flat out say no, but she'll at least make some inquiries and see if it's an option. "Okay, now that we have all the medical stuff out of the way, can we talk a bit about your thoughts? Are you up for that?"

Tenley gets up, says she's got some errands to do, but cautions Cam not to let Landon talk for too much longer because he needs his rest.

"She has a hard time when I talk about, you know, what's going on in my head," Landon says after she's gone. "I don't blame her. She's a chemistry teacher at the high school. She's a science and facts kind of gal. Emotions are tricky."

"And you're an economics professor. Aren't you a numbers and facts kind of guy, too?"

"I am. But I can't keep this stuff inside all the time. I try but…" His hands are bony, the skin papery, as they fall into his lap.

"No, you can't. And that's why I'm here. You can unload on me all you want." Cam makes a note to get Tenley alone at some point, so she can figure out what's going on with her. Loved ones and caregivers suffer too. Ideally, the couple is able to talk about any aspect of Landon's disease, but it doesn't always work that way. Cam had a client once, Donna, who was a widow dying of complications from breast cancer. Her only child, a grown daughter, refused to discuss her mom's feelings, even when her mother begged her to talk about it. "I'm dying," she told Cam. "It's all I think about, all I want to talk about, because that's my life now. But people don't want to talk about it." Cam suggested counseling, separate and joint, but the daughter refused. Her mother not only died of cancer, but of a broken heart, because they'd let her impending death come between them and forever lost that final chance to grow closer. She'll keep an eye on how Landon and Tenley communicate as a couple.

"Can you light that lamp for me?" Landon points to an antique oil lamp on the fireplace mantle. Cam has noticed it before. It's gorgeous, with an etched blue glass base and a clear glass chimney with a beaded design ringing the top of it. Another oil lamp, this one less spectacular, sits on a side table nearby.

"That's a gorgeous lamp. Is it a family heirloom?"

"Used to belong to my great grandparents. It's from the turn of the last century. I love those old things. I have a couple more of them. I find they're kind of like a thread that connects us to the past." He walks her through how to light the lamp, which is actually a pretty simple process. Its glow is soft and warm.

"Landon, how did you feel when you first got your diagnosis?"

"Devastated," he says simply.

"Can you elaborate?"

He closes his eyes, maybe to blunt the sting of the memory. "I thought they must have got it wrong, mixed me up with another patient. And then I thought I'd be lucky and it could be cured, but it was too advanced. Accepting it has been…a process. You realize it's too late to start over in life. You know? With your career, a relationship, travel, whatever. That's one of the biggest things. It's like the train is kicking you off at the next stop whether you planned to get off or not."

"How does that make you feel? That what you've accomplished in life so far has to be enough?"

Landon shrugs. "Maybe that's exactly our problem, you know? We're always running around trying to *accomplish* something, trying to be someone or something, acquiring things. Anyway." Landon takes a long, slow breath and pauses for a few minutes. "If the train is kicking me off at the next stop, so be it. I have everything I need."

"Regrets?"

"Not really. Nothing big."

"Well, that is something not a lot of people can say." She certainly can't. She has one giant regret. And there's not a damned thing she can do to fix it, not after almost two decades. "Nothing left unsaid? No loose ends to tie up?"

"Oh, there's definitely a loose end to tie up." He eyes her intently. "And you're going to help me with that. But not quite yet."

"The mystery trip?"

"Yes. But you won't have to go too far and I'm pretty sure you're going to enjoy the scenery. It's a truly lovely place."

"I'm intrigued. Can you tell me more?" Cam hasn't officially said yes to the trip yet, but she hasn't said no. If it's not far, as Landon says, and it's brief, then she really has no objection.

He shakes his head. "When the time is right. Hey, weren't we supposed to discuss the question of whether a person can ever go home again?"

"Absolutely. Is going home something you want to do, Landon? Go back to your hometown?"

"Naw, I'm already home here with Tenley."

"So, figuratively, then."

"Yes. I'm talking about that feeling inside of familiarity, of feeling like you belong, of knowing you're accepted unconditionally. It's a place where you can exhale and just be. Of course, it's not only a place where you physically exist, but a place where your soul can rest. That's my dying man's take on it. And that's where I am. Home."

A place where your soul can rest. Cam likes that saying and plans to remember it.

"Have you ever had that feeling, Cam?" His eyes won't let her off the hook.

"Well, I'm home now. Here in Traverse City."

He waggles his finger accusingly at her. "Not what I mean."

"Let's see." She pretends to ponder but knows she won't answer entirely truthfully because it's too personal. Even remembering that time when she felt at home is bittersweet—

pain and joy woven so tightly together, they're two halves of the same feeling. *But I was young then*, she tells herself. Young and full of piss and vinegar and so fiercely dedicated to exploring her own path that she let everything else go with barely a fight. Moving on became more important than fixing where she was. "I feel at home with the work I do. I feel like I was meant to do this work."

Disappointment flashes across Landon's features, but he recovers quickly. "I'm so glad you enjoy your work. Is it very hard on you? I mean, it's not like you get repeat clients." He laughs hollowly at his own joke.

"It can be hard on me at times, yes, because I like my clients. I come to really care for them. But I know what comes with the territory and I'm okay with it."

"Well. Thank you for helping me out."

"Of course, Landon. I'm honored to be here for you."

"Good. Because I have a favor to ask. Besides the trip."

"Anything."

"I think I'm...ready soon to have a hospital bed instead of the bed I share with Tenley upstairs. It's getting difficult to get in and out of it, plus I wake up a lot and..."

"It's fine, you don't have to explain. If you're ready, I'll make arrangements to lease a bed. Where would you like it placed?"

"Here. In the library. Surrounded by my books." He looks worried instead of relieved. "But I'm not sure Tenley will be happy about it."

"I understand. I'll talk to her about it."

Landon brightens. "Will you?"

"I think I hear her coming in the house. Why don't I go talk to her about it now?"

He nods gratefully. His eyes are beginning to droop.

"Good. I'll see you tomorrow, but don't hesitate to call me if something comes up in the meantime, okay?"

Cam finds Tenley in the kitchen, where she is putting away groceries.

"Can I get you anything?" Tenley asks.

"Why don't I make us both a cup of tea?"

Tenley's mouth is a straight line of worry as she nods and shows Cam where the tea bags and mugs are. "Things are progressing, aren't they?" A minute later, she and Cam sit at the kitchen table with their mugs of tea clasped tightly in their hands. It's as though each of them needs something solid to hang on to for this conversation.

"Yes, they are." She knows Landon's type of cancer will metastasize to his liver and probably his bowel, if it hasn't already.

"And how are you doing, Tenley? Really doing?"

Tenley stalls, seems to search for answers in her tea. Caregivers can be so busy trying to keep the boat afloat, they don't even notice the new leaks springing up every day. "It's... hard. But I'm okay. I plan to do everything I can to make sure Landon is...you know." She can't raise her eyes to Cam's.

Cam does know. Tenley is committed to helping her life partner on his final journey, but she's overwhelmed sometimes and probably exhausted. In Cam's experience, the ones who seem to be the strongest, to have it all together, are mostly just good at disguising their weak moments. Both Tenley and Landon are strong people, Cam can see that, but it's as though they're afraid to show each other any cracks, any doubts. It's like both are doing their best to hold up their end, but if one collapses or drops their side of the load, the whole thing falls apart. *That's what they're afraid of. They're afraid to show the other that they're faltering.*

"How did you two meet?" It isn't idle conversation. Knowing their history together will help Cam better understand them both.

Tenley smiles, instantly lost in the memory. "It was outside a bookstore in Petoskey. I'd gone there for the weekend with my now ex-husband, whom I was on the cusp of divorcing. We'd gone there for one last try at our marriage. Stupid ass. Me, I'm talking about, thinking we could save that disaster. Don—our marriage—was already a lost cause. I pretty much spent the whole weekend doing my own thing...hunting for the famous Petoskey stones on the beach, hanging out at the bookstore, the museum." She rolls her eyes. "I was doing that while Don planted himself at the same bar Hemingway used to frequent. Anyway, it was outside the bookstore that I dropped a book on the ground and Landon happened to be walking by. He stopped and picked it up, but not before commenting on how much he loved the book and had read it many times."

"What was the book?"

"Jack Finney's *Time and Again*."

"Ooh, that is a great old classic."

Tenley sinks her head into her hands and begins sobbing. Tears streak her face as she takes great gulps of air. Cam grasps her hand to help ground her, urges her to take her time, says that it's okay.

"I'm sorry," Tenley says haltingly. "It's so hard some days. I—"

"Hey, you don't need to explain. I understand."

"I'm so glad you're here." Tenley manages to smile through her misery. "It really helps."

"Good. Because I'm not going anywhere. You, on the other hand, why don't you go somewhere for a couple days? Take a break?" It didn't take more than a few weeks for most caregivers to desperately need a break, and Tenley has been looking after Landon, alone, for months.

"Really? You think I should?"

"I do. Go somewhere and enjoy yourself. It's important to get out of the land of the dying and into the land of the living for short breaks. I'll stay with him as much as he wants. And he's stable enough for you to go." Cam can't remember the last vacation she took. Even with her intentionally lighter caseload these days, she hates being away from her clients for long. It feels too much like letting them down. Giving Tenley permission to go away, however, seems to be exactly what's needed.

"You would do that? And he'll…" She swallows. "He'll be okay while I'm gone?"

"Yes and yes. Do you want me to talk to him about it?"

"No, it's okay. I'll do it. And thank you. I would love to go visit my brother and his kids for a few days. They're in Chicago.

I could fly from here to Detroit and go on from there. If you're sure it's okay." Already her entire body is less clenched, more relaxed, and there's relief in her face for the first time.

"It'll be okay, and it will do you good to get away." Landon's disease is progressing, but he won't die in the next few weeks. What Cam doesn't say to Tenley is that now is her best and possibly only chance if she wants to get away. "I do want to talk to you about one other thing. Landon would like to have a hospital bed brought in for him and placed in the library. And I agree. Stairs are getting too much for him. The hospital bed would be much safer."

"Plus he loves that damned library." Tenley sniffs back the remainder of her tears. "Tell you what. I'm fine with it as long as we can add a second bed in there for me. I don't want him down here alone all night. Hell, who am I kidding? I don't want to be up there…" She points at the ceiling. "By myself, knowing he's down here."

Cam clinks mugs with Tenley. "Atta girl. Now, do you want me to make arrangements for you to get to Chicago?"

Tenley closes her eyes and says yes.

CHAPTER FOUR

Brooke scanned the crowded pub to be sure Rachel wasn't there, since it was one of her regular stops. She hadn't seen or heard from her in a week, but it would be just her luck to stumble across her tonight. Especially since Brooke was meeting her sister Marcy for a drink. Marcy hated Rachel, which made for interesting family get-togethers. Last Christmas at Brooke's, Marcy "accidentally" dropped a plate of cranberry-covered brie on Rachel's lap after Rachel made a snarky comment about Marcy's work as a naturopath not being "real medicine." Brooke could laugh about it now, but it had nearly resulted in a massive food fight. As it was, there was much swearing and at least two door slams.

"Hey, baby girl, there you are!" Marcy swept in with all the subtlety of a freight train, her wrists jangling with bracelets, her long silver hair a bubblegum shade of pink today. You never knew what color of the rainbow would end up on her head. Funny that she and Rachel had that part, and only that part, in common. "Come here and give your big sister a hug."

Marcy was a hugger. Brooke was not, but there was never a choice when it came to Marcy's demonstrative affections. She'd grab you and scoop you into a hug whether you were willing or not. Throughout their youth, Brooke would have bet money that one of them was adopted, because they were nothing at all alike. They didn't look alike either. Where Brooke was tall and slim and blond, Marcy was short, stocky, and her blond hair was more ash than gold. When Brooke was seven years old, she made her parents swear on some dusty old bible that they were, in fact, biologically related.

Marcy, as was her habit, wanted a table in the middle of the room where she could see everybody and everybody could see her, but Brooke managed to talk her into a cozy table in the corner…better for keeping an eye out for Rachel. They ordered a drink: wine for Brooke, a vodka and soda for Marcy. Marcy was vegan and a keto freak, and who knew what other letters of the alphabet she was practicing now.

"So, Brookie, what's on your mind?"

"Who said anything was on my mind?" All her life, Marcy had had a sixth sense for when things weren't going well in Brooke's life, pinning Brooke like a bug until she spilled the beans. Annoying as hell…except for the times Brooke really did need to talk to someone. She supposed this was one of those times, except she wasn't sure how much she wanted to say or where to start. Especially when it came to Rachel, because already she could hear Marcy in her head shouting, "Well, Christ on a cross, you should have ended that excuse for a relationship ages ago!" Marcy was always that voice in her head giving her shit about something.

"Come on, spill it." Marcy flashed her a look that said she wasn't going to stop until she knew everything. "Even for you, you look tighter than a bull's asshole in fly season."

Oh God. Brooke did a quick scan around the room to make sure no one had overheard the crass remark. Most of the time, she never knew what was going to come out of her sister's mouth. "I'm fine. Just worn out from all the pandemic lockdowns and getting the restaurant back to where it was."

Their drinks arrived and Brooke took a merciful sip of her pinot grigio. Maybe Marcy would chill for once and they could have a normal, sisterly interaction. Though come to think of it, there wasn't exactly a normal interaction with Marcy. Ever. Oh, well. Her sister was different, but her honesty and her loyalty toward Brooke never wavered. Nor did her self-directed over-protectiveness of Brooke, which sometimes—no, almost all of the time—translated into bossiness. It was due in equal parts to their four-year age gap and their diverse personalities.

"Do you think it will ever get back to where it was? I mean, Jesus, that pandemic has wiped out a hell of a lot of businesses. It's been an absolute tidal wave of disaster. I feel for ya, hon."

Brooke gave an exasperated shrug; she was done trying to find a crystal ball. Mangiare Roma was holding its own on its climb back to profitability, but if revenue didn't keep improving, she would have to make a hard decision in the next year or two, especially with her outstanding loan. If the pandemic dragged on or some other disaster befell her restaurant, that'd be it. There was no more wiggle room. "It's slow going. People are coming back, but not like they used to. Takeout is fine, but it's not really paying my overhead." Nor did takeout provide the cozy, familiar environment she strove for. If takeout was all she cared about, she could have opened a food truck. Having people eating in, enjoying the specialty wines she kept in storage, chatting romantically or amiably, celebrating occasions, asking for staff's recommendations—none of that came with takeout. The fact was that diners hadn't fully embraced returning to indoor eating, not after more than two years of Covid's constant clobbering. Brooke had lost count of the number of restaurants that had gone under.

"How much longer can you carry on?"

"A year or two, I suppose. Longer if things keep trending up. I've actually had an offer."

Marcy's eyebrows disappeared into her hairline. "A decent one?"

"Yes, more than fair."

"What are you going to do?"

Brooke shrugged. She hated the idea of quitting the restaurant after working so hard to bring it to where it was. She'd done all the redecorating herself a few years ago, had built a regular clientele from the ground up, loved her staff. Her finger was in every pie there, and yes, maybe Rachel had a point that she was a workaholic, but when it was your baby, it was your baby. "What else can I do but keep plugging away?"

"That offer might disappear while you dither."

It likely would, meaning she faced the risk one day of walking away empty-handed. Jason Whitaker wasn't going to chase her forever, wasn't going to give her the luxury of taking months or a year to make up her mind. "It's…so hard to think about actually doing this. It would be like abandoning my dream. Like cutting off a hunk of myself."

"I know, sweetie. But sometimes cutting bait is the smart thing to do, and we all know that emotions often block us from making the smart choices. And you can, you know, reinvent yourself. Grow another part of you that's passionate about something. People do it all the time."

But Brooke wasn't *people*. This was her passion, running the restaurant. Perhaps Marcy had a point, though. Maybe she should be seriously considering the offer. Maybe she really could find something else to do that filled her heart that didn't feel like running on a treadmill, going nowhere. She was exhausted. And maybe even at the end of her tether. "So you think I should sell it?"

"Newsflash. I'm not *only* talking about the restaurant."

Oh goodie. They were going to talk about Rachel now. Not that it came as a surprise because Marcy liked to pick at the biggest sore, no matter how hard Brooke tried to bandage over it and hope that Marcy wouldn't notice. "The restaurant *is* kind of a big deal in my life."

"Ah, yes, but you've got that look."

"What look?"

"The one that says the restaurant is not actually your most immediate concern at the moment."

Brooke could stamp her feet and deny and try to distract, but it was futile when Marcy fixated on something. She was a vulture and she was about to pick over the carrion of Brooke's shitty romantic life. "Fine." Brooke downed the rest of her wine for a shot of bravery before signaling the server for another. She didn't need to be at her restaurant until tomorrow. "I think Rachel and I are done, since you insist on knowing the truth."

"You *think* you're done?"

Brooke winced. "She sort of left in a snit a week ago and I haven't heard from her since." A bit too succinct a summary, but she didn't feel like dredging up every crappy detail. Nor did she feel right now like analyzing their almost three years together. Poking her eyes out with the fork in front of her would be more fun.

"Do you *want* to hear from her?"

It took the question to be thrown in her face for Brooke to decide that she did, in fact, know the answer. "I don't think I do, no."

"Wow. Okay." The wind gone from her sails, Marcy silently sipped her drink in rare contemplation while Brooke accepted her second glass of wine from the server, in no hurry to restart the conversation. Except the silence was starting to get to her, and there was no way Marcy was going to leave until Brooke told her more. She sighed loudly. Might as well get this over with. "Honestly, I think our relationship ran its course long before this. I wasn't seeing her much in the thick of Covid, so it wasn't so bad, and breaking up seemed like one more crappy thing to add to the mountain of crap last year. I guess it was easier to plod on."

"You're not the first person in relationship jail during Covid. I get it."

"You do?" Since when did Marcy ever pass up an opportunity to trash Rachel?

"Of course. We've all been in a holding pattern with our lives. Holding our breath, more like. Holding on financially, trying to hold onto our sanity. Languishing, they call it. But anyway, she was never right for you. You're better off."

"Thanks," Brooke mumbled.

"For what, sweetie?"

"Not giving me the third degree over Rachel."

Marcy waved her hand in the air like a white flag. "It's kind of nice not having to spend any more of my mental energy on her. Don't get me wrong, I'm all for you having some fun in your life, but you're not the play-the-field type and we both know that Rachel wasn't long-term material." She rolled her eyes. "Me, on the other hand… I like my men and women hot and then cold. As in gone before the heat has a chance to cool."

They chatted about Marcy's active love life while Brooke nursed her wine. The distraction from talking about the restaurant or Rachel was welcome, and Brooke clung to it the way a wallflower at a party clutches their drink with both hands and hopes nobody notices them. Marcy was on her second vodka and soda when she suddenly blurted out, "You ever, like, think about your ex anymore?"

Brooke felt her mouth form an O of surprise. She and Landon emailed each other once a year to catch up, but there wasn't anything more to it. They'd remained distant friends, a sort of pen-pal relationship. But Marcy already knew that. "Why would I be thinking of Landon?"

"Not Landon, silly."

Everything stopped for a minute…the noise in the pub first, followed by her heart. Jesus, why would Marcy bring *her* up after all these years? It was almost two decades ago since they'd parted. "Why would I be thinking of her?"

"Don't tell me you've finally stopped." Marcy wagged a condemning finger at her. "She'll never be out of your system, that one. And do you want to know why?"

"Matter of fact, I don't."

Oblivious, Marcy prattled on. "Because Erica Foster was the one that got away and you will forever haunt yourself with thoughts of what might have been. Plus, she's the only one you've ever really loved. Sorry, Landon," she whispered at the ceiling, "I know you're a good guy. But it's true. Landon was the consolation prize, and who wants a consolation prize after you've had the real thing?"

She was right, of course, but that didn't mean Brooke wanted to admit it. Or even talk about it anymore. It was old news, after all. Ancient history. "So what? I'll never see Erica again and that's fine. We had something once, but it was a long, long time ago. I don't know about you, but I barely remember my twenties and early thirties anymore."

There, that should have ended the conversation, claiming she could barely remember that time. And never admitting (even if Marcy instinctively knew anyway) that for years, Erica was the first thing Brooke thought of when she woke up each morning and the last thing she thought of before falling asleep. And was very likely the reason that every romantic relationship she'd since had had gone up in smoke. But if she was going to talk about all *that*, it wasn't going to be in a damned noisy pub and it wasn't going to be with Marcy. And it sure as hell wasn't going to be over a couple of glasses of wine—it would be the whole bottle.

Marcy blinked with an intensity that meant, in her mind at least, the topic was far from over. "So weird how she went from being on the cusp of fame and success to practically disappearing off the face of the earth. I mean, I can't even find a trace of her on Facebook or anything. Nobody seems to know what happened to her. Do you think she's still alive? And if she is, why did she go underground? Something must have happened."

Heat infused Brooke's cheeks and her hands went there naturally to soothe them. It sucked that she wore her emotions so visibly. It was a curse.

Marcy's finger stabbed the air in triumph. "Ah-ha. You've Googled her too, haven't you?"

"Not in ages. And no, I don't know what's happened to her but I'm sure she's still alive. Somewhere." *She has to be,* Brooke thought with urgency, because the alternative hurt too much. The thought of Erica being out there somewhere, looking at the same stars at night, breathing the same air, made Brooke feel like maybe, possibly, they might find one another again. A distant beacon in a raging storm was how she thought of Erica... there, solid, safe, and beckoning, should Brooke need her again. But it was only a fantasy—the kind of self-indulgent reverie you allowed yourself after too many drinks or after a shitty day. No, she wouldn't need Erica one day, even if the idea gave her some crazy measure of comfort.

"Enough of the walk down memory lane. I need to figure out where the hell I'm going, not where I've been, okay?" Close to tears suddenly, Brooke held the stem of her wineglass in a death grip.

"You're right, sweetie, I'm sorry. Let's talk about something else." Marcy reached across the table to stroke her hand. It was just like her, lobbing an emotional grenade and then telling her to forget it, that everything was fine. "Did I tell you I've been asked to teach a class on hypnosis next fall?"

"Right here at the U of M?"

Marcy nodded and spent the next twenty minutes extolling the virtues of hypnotherapy until Brooke yawned and said she needed to get to bed. Tomorrow would be a long day at work.

"It won't kill you to relax for an evening, you know. Or you could have just told me I was boring you to death."

"All right. You're boring me to death."

"Yeah, yeah, I probably am. But you're a workaholic who obsesses too much about the restaurant."

"Ooh, we're trading insults now. I'm going to need another drink if we're going to go a few rounds of that game."

"Nah, not really in the mood tonight. Come on, Brookie, I'll take you home before you turn into a pumpkin."

Brooke retrieved her jacket from the back of her chair. "It was the coach that turned back into a pumpkin. Pumpkins are highly underrated as a fruit, by the way. Did you know they originated in Mexico thousands of years ago? And they're a great source of Vitamin A? And—the coolest part—they produce both a male and a female flower."

"All right, all right. A plant that can actually go fuck itself." Marcy cackled at her own joke.

"Oh, Marcy," Brooke said on a sigh that was more affection than exasperation. "What am I going to do with you?"

CHAPTER FIVE

Cam heats up minestrone soup and fresh bread for herself and Landon. Tenley won't be home for a couple more days, so Cam is spending three or four hours each day with Landon and then a couple more hours in the evening. Already he's getting a little weaker, eating a bit less each day, sleeping a bit more. He's on a predictable downward trajectory, but he's holding his own.

"For your strength," she says, bringing into the library a tray of soup and bread and glasses of water for them both. The room has become Landon's nest. His new hospital bed is there, along with his comfy and worn recliner chair. A single bed for Tenley has been set up as well. Everywhere there are signs of what's important to Landon—photos of places he's traveled, photos of him and Tenley and his dog, Harvey, his framed college degrees, a few antiques. And books. Mountains of books.

There are important things she and Landon need to discuss and get out of the way, so she begins before he grows too tired. What does he want his final weeks and days to look like? Who does he want visiting? What things, both temporal and spiritual, will he want for comfort? The library is clearly where he wants to die, so she asks him to make a list of special books he'd like read aloud to him, music he would like to hear, even if he's at the stage of being unconscious. Is there any special lighting he desires? What are his most favorite things to smell and touch, to eat and drink? She jots down his answers, then asks him to think about his funeral or memorial service, if he hasn't already, and, when he feels up to it, to write out his own obituary.

It's a lot for him to take in at once. "I don't know about all this. Will I feel better or worse, planning my own funeral and all that stuff? Because I definitely don't feel good about it right now. It depresses the hell out of me, to be honest."

"I understand that. But it may help you feel like you have some control over the situation. Participating in your death preparations can give you comfort later, even though it feels overwhelming and weird right now. But don't force it if the time doesn't feel right." It's part of accepting that he's dying, but Cam doesn't come right out and say it. She's pretty sure he understands.

Cam remembers one of her early clients, Helen Forester. The day after her terminal diagnosis, she made a list a mile long of things she wanted to do to prepare for her death, with hiring a death doula as her first priority. Each day, Cam and Helen ticked off the chores Helen wanted out of the way before she got sicker, and within five days, she had everything done. "Now I can relax and die," she said with a serene smile. And she did die, three weeks later.

But Landon isn't there yet. He might never see this with the clinical detachment such a list requires. It's hard for Cam to tell at this point. "Nothing feels right about this, Cam. It's like I'm watching this happen to somebody else."

Cam pushes her empty soup bowl aside and notices that Landon has a decent appetite today—he's eaten most of his soup and half his bread. "Tell me more about what you're feeling."

"I'm angry most days."

"What or who are you angry at?"

Landon's jaw turns to granite. "I'm angry at the cancer for choosing me, for ending my life. I'm angry at myself because obviously my body is a failure, which makes *me* a failure. I'm pissed off at the universe because I feel like I'm being cheated. I'm only fifty-four. This wasn't supposed to fucking happen yet." His anger is a fist around his throat, making him choke out his words. It's all part of the emotional baggage that comes with dying.

"All right. Let's unpack this. Do you feel you did something to deserve your cancer?"

"No, of course not. Just unlucky, I suppose."

"You feel that your body has let you down?"

"Yes." Tears carve tracks down his sunken cheeks. "I thought I'd looked after myself, tried to exercise and eat well, didn't drink too much, never smoked. No family history. I don't get it. It doesn't make sense that this is happening to me."

"But this is not your failing or your fault, Landon. Sometimes there isn't a reason, or at least, none that fit into our preconceived template of acceptable reasons. You see, we're not raised to see death as a natural event. Death, when it comes, should not take us by surprise. It should be part of the full expectancy of life. If we understand that we are born, we get to flourish and live our lives, then we die—if we can accept that, we can live our lives in a meaningful way and live our death in a meaningful way."

He shakes his head. "I don't know what you mean."

"What I'm saying is, if we've lived our life in a meaningful way, then there is nothing for death to steal or rob from us. We have lived a complete life, no matter the chronological number of years. If we accept the completeness of our life, there is nothing to feel cheated about."

"So you're saying I haven't lived my life in a meaningful way? That's why I'm feeling so sore about it all?"

"You tell me. Are there things you've wanted to do but didn't get to accomplish? Have you been honest and genuine with people you care about? Do you have any big regrets? Things you wish you could take back, things left undone?"

He thinks for several minutes while they sip their water, the silence broken only by the ticking of the antique mantle clock. "I've done everything I wanted to do with my career. I found my life companion. I guess I've been a pretty happy guy most of the time. As for things left undone, there's always something, isn't there? I've never been to Rome. Or Paris, for that matter."

"Do those cities matter to you? Do you feel your life is less meaningful for not having visited those places?"

There is a trace of laughter in Landon's eyes, but the effort is too much to involve his mouth. "Nah. They're just places. It felt like it was something a dying person should say."

"Ah, yes. The great marketing campaigns of the world that tell us we don't have enough or haven't done enough. You haven't *lived* until you've been to Paris. Or Rome or wherever. Now, what about your ex-wife? Any regrets there?"

Cam is surprised her question is met with a smile and not a frown. "My ex is lovely. I still love her, but not romantically. She's…not always as brave as she needs to be." He shakes his head lightly and wipes a stray tear from his cheek. "Like, I'm one to talk, blubbering baby that I am."

"Did her lack of bravery affect your marriage?"

"Sort of, but not in the way you might think. She actually can be very brave when she wants to be. Started her own business and everything…that takes guts. But in her heart, she's sometimes scared to go after what she needs. Maybe she thinks she doesn't deserve to be happy. Hell, I don't think I deserve to die. I guess we all think we know exactly what we deserve and don't deserve."

"What if nobody *deserves* anything? I mean, we've been conditioned to thinking that if you work hard and do good, you will earn your rewards in life. Or in the afterlife. But what if the only true reward is that you get to live another day? What if we can learn to accept that we don't control everything? That someday…it ends, whether we are ready for it or not."

Landon thinks for a few moments. Cam has noticed that he likes to think before he speaks, consider each word before he breathes life into it. "It's a lot to accept…some days. I guess… no, I know I struggle with when to fight and when to let go. Mostly I'm stuck at the fighting part right now."

Cam meets Landon's gaze fiercely. "You're going to die, Landon. What happens between now and then is largely up to you, but it won't change the outcome." She's seen too many dying people cling to denial or get stuck in fight mode until the very end, which leaves no time for processing and accepting what's inevitable. It's an ugly death to die bitter and angry.

Another tear gathers in his eye, wobbles there, but doesn't fall.

"I know that's hard to hear," she adds quietly.

"Actually, I think what you just said is one of the most useful things anyone has said to me since my diagnosis."

Cam nods. At this stage in Landon's death journey, the sooner he accepts his fate, the sooner he can get on with living the way he wants to live for his final weeks or months. She reaches over and squeezes his hand. "Landon, you might not be able to go on a trip anymore or dance on an ocean beach at sunset, but there's still a life to be lived. Your life. And I will help you do that, if you want."

"Yes," he says simply. "I would like you to help me do that."

"All right, let's start with this. Are you willing to try a meditation exercise with me?"

He examines her as if he's peering into her soul. She knows instinctively he's gauging whether he can trust her with his life. He finally nods, gives a thumbs-up signal.

She gets him to move to his recliner chair but asks him to leave it an upright position. "You want to be comfortable but not fall asleep, so sitting is best. Now, relax into a balance that's both alert and soft. Feel your sitting bones rooted to the earth. That will be your anchor. Do you feel heavy?"

Landon nods, his eyes closed. He's going along with it beautifully.

"Now, I want you to imagine yourself as a newly born infant. Can you see yourself as a little baby? All the earthly noises and sensations are new...bright, loud, things smell and taste funny. Even the air against our skin feels new and different."

She leaves Landon to his imagination for a minute. "Think about your earliest memories of being in your mother's arms." She watches his facial muscles relax. His eyes roam behind his eyelids, a wisp of a smile forms at the corners of his mouth.

"Now follow the trajectory of your story... Your first day at school, your friends, your early jobs, people you fell in love with. Mistakes are there too, both mistakes that were made by others that hurt you and mistakes you made that hurt others. It's all there.

"Now I want you to feel great loving kindness and compassion for yourself. Hold that. What is happening to you at this stage in your life is very similar to your earliest moments, where things felt different and foreign and scary. Picture yourself as that child, because we never truly shed that inner child; he is always there inside you. Using your imagination, embrace that child. Hold that little baby that is you, in your cupped palm. Do you have him in your hand?"

"Yes."

"Hold your other cupped palm over the top so you are holding the image of your infant self safely in a loving nest. You are safe, you are protected, you are loved, you are forgiven. Hold yourself in this same loving nest as you take yourself through childhood, adolescence, and adulthood. Hold yourself in this nest of kindness throughout all the stages of your life, especially through the challenges in your life. And understand that your life is a story for which you can hold great, compassionate love—even through your mistakes or any unkindnesses you may have inflicted on others. Know that you are basically good, that you have had obstacles, heartbreaks, fears, and traumas, just like everyone else. Hold yourself gently and kindly. Feel the light pulsing through yourself." To Cam, it comes down to forgiving oneself for being human.

After several minutes of silence, Cam tells Landon he can open his eyes. "How do you feel?"

"Surprisingly calmer. Less anxious, less fearful." A shadow of surprise lurks on his face.

"Good. You can try that exercise any time you're feeling anxious or upset."

He drags out a long, exhaled breath. "I've never tried anything like that before."

Cam attempts a joke because she is pretty sure Landon can handle it. "Dying is a lot of work, you know."

There's a sparkle in his eyes when he grins back at her. "I'm beginning to see that."

CHAPTER SIX

It was officially over with Rachel. And Brooke hadn't shed a single tear. Oh, her ego was taking a bruising, but she'd get over that. The two met at a café after Brooke caved and texted that they should talk. Call her crazy, but she wanted some closure.

There was zero drama. It was a clean, unemotional transaction that saw Brooke's stress sliding off her like rain on leaves. It mattered little more to her than crossing off an important item on her to-do list: ~~Rachel~~ . It beautifully summed up everything she needed to know about the relationship.

Should I feel bad about this? Sad? She asked herself that over and over, and the answer never changed. No, she was not sad. She practically danced down the street, grateful for a newfound sense of freedom and the lift it gave her spirits. It was as though she had a whole smorgasbord of choices now that she hadn't noticed before. It wasn't that she actually possessed any more freedom—the restaurant continued to demand most of her time and energy—but at least Rachel was no longer an obligation.

That alone was enough to make Brooke feel like she had a new lease on life.

Walking to her restaurant to check on the pre-dinner hour preparations, she decided Rachel would be her last relationship. Just like that. Done, with a capital D. Her success rate was shit, and it was time to admit it and to stop trying to pound a square peg into a round hole. Erica was her one regret, and she'd blown it all those years ago. Landon was a rebound mistake, although a nice rebound mistake that, luckily, hadn't resulted in either of them being hurt too badly. There were a couple of others she'd dated after Landon and before Rachel, so she was long past the three-strikes-you're-out rule. Still, there was no need to mourn her relationship failures; if nothing else, she was pragmatic about love...or the lack thereof. From now on she would keep her focus on herself and her business. Or herself and whatever came after her business, if she decided to sell.

The second she walked through the door, her assistant manager pounced on her. But instead of the looming disaster she expected to be told about, Tara Kessler bounced up and down on the tile floor like a rubber ball before grabbing Brooke by the shoulders and giving her an excited shake.

"You'll never believe who ate lunch here a couple of hours ago! Not in a million years, but go ahead and guess."

"Hmm, is this someone I would recognize?"

"Maybe. I mean, I didn't recognize her at all. I think she was incognito 'cuz she had this bright silk scarf around her head and wore these huge sunglasses that she never took off, not even once. And she hardly spoke, just sat real quiet with some older gentleman. Oh!" Tara did another little impromptu spin. "She had the polenta fritters for lunch."

"Wait, aren't you going to let me finish guessing?"

"Oops, sorry, boss. I'm so frigging excited! And pissed that I didn't realize who she was at the time or I would have gotten a selfie or an autograph or—"

"Someone famous ate here? Like, what, the governor or something?"

Tara had the nerve (*the nerve!*) to laugh. "No, silly. Not some boring old governor."

"Hey, our governor's not boring. Or old. She's quite hot, actually."

"Okay fine, she's hot, but it wasn't her."

"Jeez, Tara, I have no idea. Wait! Lily Tomlin." She was from Michigan originally, so maybe the mystery woman was Lily.

Tara gave her a face that said Brooke was way off base. "All right, all right. I can see you're terrible at this. The name M. Ciccone was what the reservation was made under, like, duh, I guess I should have figured it out, but I didn't. It wasn't until she started tweeting about the restaurant after she left that I realized who she was. Tweeting and Instagramming about how much she loved it! How the food is among the most authentic Italian food she's ever tasted, and the best polenta she's ever had. She's been all over the world, Brooke, so she knows food! She—"

Brooke held up both hands like a giant stop sign. "Wait. Are you actually going to tell me who this person is?"

"Madonna!" Tara squealed. She pulled out her phone and clicked on her Insta app. "We're already booked solid for the rest of the week now—the phone has been ringing nonstop for the last hour."

Brooke had to sit down. Madonna? Here in her restaurant? She pulled out her phone and clicked on her Twitter app while Tara, as if on cue, raced to answer the restaurant phone. Holy shit, she hadn't been kidding. There was Madonna's official Twitter account, tweeting about Mangiare Roma in Ann Arbor, Michigan. *Her* Mangiare Roma! And there were about a million likes and retweets. She clicked next on Instagram, and there Madonna praised her restaurant as well. It was almost impossible to believe that one of her favorite childhood singers had sat right here and eaten her food. Memories of dancing to "Like a Virgin" when she was ten and her sister was fourteen came to mind…they'd throw a Madonna album on the family phonograph when their parents were out of the house and crank the volume. Oh, God, Marcy was going to flip.

Her thoughts flew to Erica before she could rein them in. Erica had loved Madonna too, the later stuff especially—"Like A Prayer," "Beautiful Stranger," "Don't Tell Me." One night after a romantic dinner of lasagna over a bottle of Amarone they could ill afford, Brooke had put on a Madonna playlist, and they danced in their tiny living room, Erica holding her close and taking over from Madonna, singing the familiar songs in a voice far richer and more layered than Madonna's. That voice purring in her ear had given Brooke goose bumps. Goose bumps she could almost feel now if she tried hard enough, because Erica had a voice that burrowed right into your soul, gave you no choice but to fall in love with it. It was deep, thickly intimate, yet tonally as clear as a perfect bell. She could have been the love child of Karen Carpenter and Ann Wilson.

Wherever Erica was now, was she still singing? From a distance, Brooke had followed her music career until Erica abruptly "retired" from singing a decade or so ago. No real explanation, just an announcement on her Facebook page and in a couple of trade magazines that she was leaving the music business for the ubiquitous "exploring other opportunities." Maybe by her late thirties, she got tired of chasing her dream in crowded bars and rundown arenas and in that broken-down old van she'd painted up for touring. Maybe she met someone and wanted to settle down and have a family. Hell, for all Brooke knew, maybe Erica had moved to Costa Rica or Thailand or something, where the sun and sand were wall-to-wall and the living was cheap. An ache lodged in her throat as she thought about Erica throwing away such a gift, depriving the world of such a magnificent voice. It was a tragedy really, and it was a tragedy that in spite of the years of hard work she'd put into it, for most of her career, she never really became known outside of the Midwest. From Detroit to Chicago to Buffalo to Toledo, Erica could work as many nightclubs and music festivals as she wanted, but outside of those regions, it was a struggle. And then, like, months before she left the business, she was suddenly hotter than she'd ever been. Radio stations had started to pick her up, and she'd even made *Rolling Stone* magazine…well, so what if it was at the back of the magazine in a single column of future-stars-in-the-making. It was something to build on. Except…she went and did the exact opposite and left it all behind. Such a mystery. Such a loss.

Brooke's cellphone rang. It was Jason Whittaker.

"Hello, Jason," she said into the phone with bold confidence and an assassin's smile. "I take it you've seen Twitter or Instagram this afternoon?"

The conversation went predictably, with Jason—again—offering to buy the restaurant. Only this time he increased his offer by twenty percent. And good thing, too, because if he was going to insult her with the same old offer again, she was going to tell him to go screw himself.

"I won't wait long, Brooke. Not gonna keep chasing you. It's my final offer and it expires in one week. If you say no, I promise I can handle it. But you can't keep me on a string. I'll move on if you say the word."

A twenty percent increase was not to be sneered at. That part alone would leave her totally debt-free. The offer was probably as good as it was ever going to get, and she knew it. "A week, huh?" A throbbing had begun in her temples and her right hand couldn't stop quivering. Even before her mind recognized it, she knew her body was a step ahead of her; yes, she was seriously considering doing this. First Rachel was out of her life, and now, possibly, the restaurant. Things were rushing toward her at blinding speed. Funny how you could live your life for years with barely a ripple of change, and then, bam! Suddenly everything is upside down.

She dry swallowed and sat down. More like collapsed into the nearest chair. "All right, Jason, I promise you I will seriously think about your offer this time and get back to you, okay? Within the week."

She rang off and immediately called her sister. Marcy had made no secret of the fact that she thought Brooke was in a rut and massive changes were not to be feared at this juncture, but welcomed. "I think I'm actually considering blowing up my entire life," she announced to Marcy, leaving her sister nearly speechless. Brooke promised to meet her tomorrow for breakfast to tell her all about it, though getting Marcy to agree to wait until tomorrow was like making a kid wait on Christmas morning.

Brooke set her phone down and stared at the ceiling. *What in the hell am I doing? Can I really pull an Erica and just...stop?*

CHAPTER SEVEN

"Can you come over for dinner tomorrow night?" Landon asks Cam over the phone. "And dress up. I want the three of us to have a nice, fancy dinner, maybe even a little dancing and music."

"That sounds awfully romantic. You sure you want me as a third wheel?"

"Yup. We're going to have a good time. No more moping for me. I want you to see that I'm taking your advice and living my best life. So…not exactly a celebration, but something close to it. Nothing else is going to matter except having a good time."

Cam can feel her heart expanding in her chest. "All right, in that case, I look forward to it. What time? And can I at least bring the wine?"

"Six sharp. And yes, bring the wine. Everything else is being catered. Tenley's already set it all up, God bless her."

Cam notices the transformation immediately. Tenley has the glow of an early spring tan—Chicago is always a week or two ahead of Traverse City this time of year—and her face is relaxed instead of fraught with worry or exhaustion as she greets Cam. She's had her hair streaked while she was away, and it has the effect of instantly shaving about five years off her age. She looks good, and it gives Cam a glimpse of how she might look down the road when Landon is gone and she emerges from her shell of grief to live her life again. She will be fine, Cam knows, even if Tenley doesn't yet know it.

"You look smashing, Tenley." And she does, in her long-flowing, off-the-shoulder gown the color of a deep, red wine. So does Landon, in spite of the fact that his blue suit hangs on his frame. He beams with pride like he is heading to a gala or a ball, instead of attending a party for three at his home. "As do you, Landon. Very handsome." His face has a nice bone structure, she can see. And he has a gentle smile, along with blue eyes still as sharp and bright as a noon sky. She's not lying when she calls him handsome, because the imprint of his handsomeness remains, like the watermark from a glass left on a surface. He will always be a handsome dude.

"You clean up nicely yourself," he says.

"Thank you." She'd dug around in the back of her closet for her tuxedo shirt and creased black trousers, plus an emerald green, silk jacket—souvenirs from her earlier career. Beyond funerals, which goes with the territory of being a death doula, she rarely dresses up these days.

Landon produces a bottle of Veuve Clicquot with a hearty "ta-da." Tenley has to pop the cork though, because Landon isn't strong enough, but seeing him actually happy is such a surprise that Cam can't speak.

After another minute, and not really caring about the answer, she says, "What are we celebrating tonight?" Any reason to pull them out of the cocoon of the dying—even for a few hours—is good enough for her.

Landon grins back. "Life. We're here, we're alive. Nothing less, nothing more. Now, let's have an evening, shall we?"

Cam can't keep the smile off her face as she watches Landon play the part of the impeccably mannered host, shepherding them out to the back patio, where the weather is exceptionally nice for a May evening, and she can tell that he's excited to leave his prognosis behind for a while. The subtle scent of a budding lilac bush makes the evening even more perfect.

"Oh, this is lovely," Cam says, meaning the champagne, but then she notices the trays of appetizers that are enough to feed at least twice their number. "You two are lovely hosts, thank you for inviting me. This all looks fabulous."

"It wouldn't be the same without you here," Tenley says as she lights the propane fire column. "You're part of our journey now."

To Cam, it's an honor and a privilege to accompany someone to the end of their journey. But it wasn't always so. She'd barely given a moment's thought to death and dying until her mom's terminal diagnosis. But the experience—not only of losing her mother but of accompanying her on her final journey—changed Cam in profound ways. How could it not? Endings are usually more of a catalyst to change than beginnings, and Cam has found that the dying, and those who care for them, have taught her more than anything she ever read in a book or learned in a classroom. She certainly would never have predicted that she'd go on to use her old college degree to help the dying, yet she can't imagine doing anything else.

They sit around the propane fire pit on comfy chairs and chat. When she closes her eyes, Cam can imagine that they are simply three friends enjoying an evening of drinks and food and chitchat. It's a nice change from talk of death, but she's here for that too should the conversation meander in that direction. She eats a mushroom cap dipped in a creamy garlic sauce, and it's the most delicious thing she's eaten in weeks. She's not much of a cook.

"Tonight isn't only a celebration of being alive," Landon cautions before glancing at Tenley. Cam almost expects him to propose marriage (again), but instead he says to Cam, "We want to discuss the errand I'd like you to do. It involves my ex."

Ah, the ex he still loves in a nonromantic fashion. And whom Tenley doesn't seem to mind as a presence in their lives, even though it's at a distance.

"Does she know you're terminally ill?" One of the many things Cam has learned as a death doula is to never ignore the fact that someone is dying. The thing about death is that everyone is terrified of it happening, is devastated when it does, and goes out of their way to pretend that neither is true.

"No. She doesn't." Landon winces in pain. He's on a fentanyl patch but sometimes the pain is too much. "I thought I was feeling pretty good today. Dammit."

"It's okay," Cam says. "Give yourself a minute. Or lie down for a bit if you need to. You're in charge here, Landon. Tenley and I can wait."

He shakes his head a little, closes his eyes. After a few minutes, whatever was taking a bite out of him recedes. "What you should know about my first marriage is that it was never going to work. But it doesn't mean she and I don't have a bond. You see, my ex-wife's heart made the choice to fall in love with someone else a long time before she met me. I thought she could eventually love me like that too, that I had some control over that, but it was no use. Her heart made the choice for her, and my choice was to get out of the way before anybody got hurt further. We divorced ten months after we married. It was a long time ago now, and I walked into it with my eyes wide open. It was amicable, believe it or not. We still write to each other once or twice a year to check in."

There is a tug at Cam's heart for Landon having to experience the hollowness of unrequited love. "Is she someone you and Tenley would welcome here, for you to share some time with in your last days or weeks?"

Landon shrugs. "Maybe. It depends on...how things go, I suppose."

Cryptic, but okay.

"Anyway," Landon says. "I want you to tell her."

"Me?" The surprise of his request sends Cam mentally reeling for a moment. "This is the errand you want me to go on?" Unusual, but not unheard of, she decides. She'll let Landon explain things further in his own time. She once had a client, Rosie was her name, who insisted that Cam drive to her cottage two hours away to retrieve a treasure trove of old books that she wanted near her deathbed. At the last minute, she inexplicably decided to give all the books away to a neighbor. Cam has learned to give her clients a lot of latitude in making decisions, because too often they change their minds.

"Yes. But right now there's something more important to do." He looks at Tenley with a glint of mischief. "Fire up some music, honey. I want a couple of slow dances with my honey before the sun goes down."

Tenley disappears, returns again with a boom box that plays CDs. They're still in the nineties, with their antiquated technology, but it's somehow quaint. At least the thing plays CDs and not cassette tapes, so there is that. Al Jarreau's "We're in This Love Together" starts up and Tenley and Landon sway together on the patio, him leaning a little on her, her arms securely around him. Their cheeks are touching, their eyes closed. They don't need to speak, they are both remembering happier times, and it's almost enough to make Cam cry. She knows the power of music, how it can heal, rejuvenate, tap into buried emotions that can produce joy, sadness, nostalgia, hope, regret, comfort. She considered becoming a music therapist—even took some courses on using music therapy to treat traumatic brain injuries and autism—before deciding that helping the dying filled her heart more or was perhaps more needed. Besides, her complicated relationship with music is a Pandora's box she'd rather not open.

She watches her new friends in their own little world, knowing that as a couple Landon and Tenley need this. They need to feel they are still a couple, a couple in love, and not a couple whose relationship is defined by her caretaker role and his illness. At least for a few minutes or hours, Cam knows this will make them feel part of something normal again.

Sipping her champagne as the song segues into "Hello Stranger," Cam thinks about the last time she was in love and had someone to hold onto as if it were a last dance. Oh, she can try to convince herself that the nineteen months she spent with

Nora was the last time she was in love, but she knows better. Nora was lovely, but she wasn't Bette. And neither were the dozens of women she slept with back in her thirties, when she thought the world was her playground and it was her duty to try every toy offered to her. Bette ruined her for anyone else, but Cam doesn't fight it anymore. There's no point. That time in her life is a distant memory, and Cam is doing fine on her own. More than fine. She loves her quiet walks along the shores of Lake Michigan, the fact that she can make last-minute decisions about what to cook for dinner, watch whatever she wants on television, read in the silence if that's what she feels like. She thinks about getting a dog one day, and she will, dammit. Nora was allergic to dogs, but there's nothing holding back Cam now.

"Oh, shit," Landon says. The music has stopped abruptly and he's desperately stabbing at buttons on the boom box, trying to restart it. "I think it's jammed or something." Tenley tries to help, their combined actions becoming more frantic until Landon looks like he's about to cry.

"Wait," Tenley says. "I'll be right back."

"I can go home and get my Bluetooth portable speaker if you want," Cam says to Landon. "It would only take me a few minutes." But before he can answer, Tenley is back, proudly holding a guitar in her hand like it's a trophy.

Landon's eyes light up. "You can play this, Cam, can't you?"

Cam feels the breath catch in her throat and considers her options—one of which is simply to bolt. Calm down, she tells herself. *This isn't about my former life, about which Landon can't possibly know anything.* "What makes you think I can play the guitar?" she says innocently.

There is a note of alarm in Landon's distraught gestures. "Sorry, I mean… I don't know, sometimes the fentanyl gets me confused. I thought… I don't know why I thought that. Hoped, maybe?"

"Neither of us can play it," Tenley adds. "I found it one day. Someone had put it out to the curb with the trash, and I couldn't fathom why they would throw out a perfectly good guitar, so I brought it home."

"It's okay," Cam says, averting her gaze so she doesn't have to see the tears in the corners of Landon's eyes nor the distress behind Tenley's smile. "Let me take a look at this thing."

The guitar is in good shape, and it only takes her a moment to tune it, the memory of how each string should sound coming back to her as though she's done it a million times. Which she has, but a lifetime ago. She plays a few notes, finger picks a slow jazzy piece she can't remember the name of. It's awkward at first, but it isn't long before her fingers know what to do. They'll hurt tomorrow. Her calluses are long gone.

"Could you sing us something?" Tenley asks meekly. "Anything?"

How much do they know? Cam wonders, the kernel of panic taking root in her stomach again. *Are they messing with me? Why are they doing this?* But they're looking at her with the kind of fragile hope that will shatter with a simple no, and she doesn't want to be responsible for that, so she begins to pluck out the notes to "You Were Meant for Me." It's all right there, at the tip of her memory, and one note leads effortlessly to the next, and it's only a moment before she's singing the song. Singing the way she used to sing it for her ex. The first time was at a folk festival in some little town by the water in Ontario, Canada (she can't remember where anymore). As newly minted college grads and only a year into their relationship, they hit as many little festivals as they could in a beat-up old minivan with its missing hubcap and rusted wheel wells that looked like sloppily drawn eye shadow. "You Were Meant for Me" was at the top of the charts then, so Cam played it on the stage at an open mic slot. She was really playing it for Bette, as Bette sat on the grass in the front row, gazing back at her with such love and admiration in her eyes that Cam had to sing the rest of the song through the blur of tears. Every song she sang then came from somewhere in her being that she never had to think about, never had to coax or question or bargain with. It was always right there to access, whenever she wanted. And then one day it got harder. And then harder yet as the weeks, months, years piled on top of one another. When Bette walked out, that artistic well or reservoir or whatever secret sauce had inspired her music gradually and irrevocably ebbed away. It was as though Bette had sliced opened one of Cam's veins on her way out the door, and the bleeding didn't stop for years.

"Jesus," Landon mutters in astonishment. "Don't stop. Please."

Cam sees their mouths frozen in a perfect O, so she stops mid-note, fearing something's wrong.

"Your voice," Tenley says in astonishment. "Where did you learn to sing like that?"

"I…I don't really…" Cam can't seem to find the words to put an end to all this and go home. She should have played dumb and never picked up this stupid guitar.

"Please?" Landon pleads. "Finish the song so Tenley and I can have one more dance?"

Anger at Bette swamps Cam again, an emotion she hasn't felt toward her ex in a very long time. The music has brought the old feelings to the surface, punctured the amiable feeling in the air. She's not sure if she can ever forgive her ex for the fact that music went from something she adored to something that became a yoke around her neck. It was Bette who decided Cam's music career was too much. It was Bette who made the choice for them both.

"All right," she says quietly and resumes the song. Landon and Tenley finish their dance, ending it with a kiss and a few whispered words.

"That was absolutely beautiful," Tenley says to Cam. "Thank you. Would you like to sing another?"

"No," Cam says, a little too sharply. "Thanks. I think I've worked up an appetite. How about some more of these incredible dishes before they go to waste?"

Landon only nibbles around the edges of the food, Cam notices, but at least he's trying. After dinner, as she and Tenley are eating fresh strawberries dipped in warm chocolate and sipping the pinot grigio Cam brought, Landon announces that it's time to talk more about Cam's errand.

"Are you sure you're up to this?" Cam asks Landon because his skin has paled and he's clearly tired. "We can talk about this another time if you'd like."

"No, now is good."

"Okay." Her clients usually have very good reasons for asking her to do something. Knowing that your life is quickly receding can give birth to some odd requests. One client asked her to look into human cloning before he died. Another, a woman who "missed" the rebelliousness of the 1960s because she started a family before she was barely out of her teens, asked Cam to get her some pot to try because she wanted to know what it was like before she died. "Can I ask why you want the news to come from me and not you?"

"Simple, really. I don't want it to be over the phone or in an email and I'm not strong enough to travel. I want her to hear it from someone in person, and for obvious reasons, it shouldn't be Tenley. So that someone is you."

Sensing little more is forthcoming other than the fact that her task involves traveling, Cam asks, "Where am I to do this task?"

"It's just up the interstate. Mackinac Island."

Cam has never been to the island before even though she grew up only a hundred miles away. Correction: She went there once for a school day trip when she was about ten, but it was only for a few hours and she can barely remember anything about the island, except that there are no motorized vehicles. She remembers the clip clop of horses and their grassy, musky scent, but little else. Oh, wait, there was a choppy ferry ride that nearly made her throw up. And there was fudge on the island. Lots of fudge.

"All right. The island is special to you and your ex?" It's not unusual for the dying to want to go back and relive a particular memory.

Landon shakes his head. "It's where Tenley and I went for romantic holidays."

"So…let me get this straight. You want me to tell your ex-wife that you're terminally ill in the place where you and Tenley went for romantic vacations?"

Tenley, clearly sensing Cam's puzzlement, offers an explanation. "The island is such a beautiful, peaceful place, and we both think this kind of news should be delivered in a setting that has given us such joy and comfort over the years. We really think it's the perfect spot."

Landon chimes in. "Did you know I've decided I want my ashes scattered there?"

Tenley confirms the news with a nod, and it makes more sense to Cam now. Mackinac Island has played a significant role in Landon's life. She won't question it again, though it still feels like there's something they're not telling her. "When do I leave?"

"The third week of May," Landon answers.

That gives Cam almost two weeks to plan her schedule. She currently has only one other client, a woman in her sixties in the residential hospice who, unfortunately, likely won't be alive in two weeks. "All right." She pulls out her phone and taps the calendar app. "How long?"

"A few days."

"Will it really take that long to deliver the news?" A day, two maybe depending on the ferry schedules, would be more than sufficient.

Tenley replies. "It's all booked. We have you staying at a hotel near the water."

"What about you?" Cam says to Landon. "I need to be here for you, and I can't do that if I'm a hundred miles away for a few days."

Landon's eyelids have begun drooping and his voice is weakening. The fight should be leaving him, but he's not relenting an inch. "We can talk on the phone, text, email while you're gone. We'll be okay, right, Tenley?"

Tenley nods, squeezes his hand. "We've already spoken to Landon's doctor and to the hospice for backup help. We'll manage while you're away."

"Don't worry," Landon adds. "I'm not going to die while you're gone. And besides, you were hell-bent on Tenley getting away for a few days. Now it's your turn. Call it a work vacation, if that makes you feel better."

It doesn't. Attending to Landon is her job, and she doesn't need breaks the way a twenty-four-seven caregiver does. But she won't keep arguing with him. "As long as you're stable when I go." Her hesitation recedes because she knows someone in Landon's situation doesn't have time for others to dither, deciding whether or not they approve of his wishes and motives. It's his life, and when Cam took him on as a client, she signed up to be there for his final journey, wherever that takes them. "I feel like I'm deserting you, if you want to know the truth."

Landon takes her hand in both of his and looks her in the eye. "You're going to love it there, it's so beautiful and peaceful. And I have a whole list of things for you to do and places to see, so it will almost be like a vicarious trip for me. You'll send me photos and email me about it every day. That's all I need. Well, that and to tell my ex the news, of course."

"You should be in sales, not teaching," Cam teases.

The joke plants a new glint in Landon's eyes. "Nah. I'd rather stand up and pontificate in front of a classroom in my ratty old tweeds."

Cam pictures Landon doing exactly that. "With elbow patches and everything? A bow tie perhaps?"

Landon shakes his head, but the smile hasn't left his face. "If you want to know for sure, you'll have to snoop in my closet."

"I'd rather keep the image in my head, if it's all the same to you. Even if it's only a fantasy."

On the walk home, Cam supposes that a mini-vacation on a beautiful island isn't exactly the worst thing she's been asked to do. But it's certainly among the strangest.

CHAPTER EIGHT

Brooke and Marcy had barely ordered their omelets (vegetarian for Marcy, ham and cheese for Brooke) before Marcy was all over her about her news. Brooke had so far managed to avoid saying the words out loud to anyone, because as soon as she did, she knew it would be a done deal. It might take her an inordinate amount of navel gazing and pondering, but once she made up her mind about something, her word was gold. She was ready for this.

She took a deep breath, let the heft of her decision center her. "I'm doing it. I'm selling the restaurant."

Time seemed to slow down as Marcy's facial expressions went from shock to cheerful acceptance…the same tsunami of feelings swamping Brooke since yesterday. Well, except for the cheerful acceptance part. She was still a bit stuck within the shocked part.

"Wow, I can't believe it. And why aren't we doing this over some bubbly instead of coffee and eggs and cheese?"

"Because I figured you wouldn't want to wait until tonight to hear what I had to say and it's too early to drink."

"Fine, you win." She clinked coffee cups with Brooke. "So what made you finally do it?"

Brooke felt the catch in her throat that was usually a precursor to self-doubt. "I… I don't know for sure, except that there won't be a better time than now to sell it, not with the offer I've had. And…I think I need a change in my life. Something different. Which scares the shit out of me, if I'm honest. But with Rachel gone and the pandemic mostly over, maybe it's time to start fresh."

Marcy clapped a hand over her mouth in mock amazement. "You hardly ever swear. Wow. There's hope for you yet, sister. So tell me what scares you about it."

"Because I haven't a clue what to do next."

"Ah yes. The worrier of the family doesn't have a plan, a safety net." Marcy's smile was a little too excoriating for Brooke. "Well, it's about time you took a blind leap."

"You act like having a plan for your life is a serious personality flaw."

"Don't be so dramatic." Marcy took a massive bite of her omelet. She always ate like it was her last meal. "You're just like Dad, plodding along with your plans and scared to try something different. And look where that got him."

"Come on, not this old crap again. You can't blame his heart attack on the fact that he worried about everything and was a planner. That's just dumb." Kenneth Avery had been a chemist who worked for a large pharmaceutical manufacturer. He was the opposite of spontaneous, with his shirts and socks neatly lined up in rows in his dresser drawer, organized by days of the week. He was a man who scrimped and saved for a pension that he would never collect, because a heart attack killed him weeks after his fiftieth birthday, when Brooke was a freshman at college.

"I'm not blaming the heart attack on his personality. I'm blaming his personality for the fact that he never enjoyed life while he had the chance. Remember that trip they won to Costa Rica back when we were teenagers? And Dad wouldn't go because he would have had to ask for time off work?"

"And Mom went instead with her cousin."

"And came back with that weird bug bite that made her sick for weeks. But she didn't care. She said it was worth it."

"Yup, that's Mom. Consequences were a dirty word to her."

Marcy shot her a look of warning. Their mother, Abigail, was most definitely the opposite of their dad and so much like Marcy, it wasn't funny. The two even looked alike—twins born twenty-two years apart. When their mom discovered the women's lib movement in the 1970s, she stopped wearing bras and dresses and went to work at a bookstore that specialized in self-help books. By the 1990s, after their dad died, she was off to Israel and northern Africa, Bangladesh too, working with Oxfam International. Abigail Avery never much worried about anything beyond the day in front of her. At the age of seventy-four, she was currently living in an ashram in India—something Brooke wouldn't put past Marcy to do one day too.

"Just don't be like Dad."

"But I *am* like Dad." She certainly wasn't like her mom or sister. And what was wrong with plans and order anyway? Plans and order piloted her life.

"What I mean is, don't miss out on life while you're playing it safe with all your *plans*."

Brooke pushed her half-eaten omelet aside. "Look, I'm sorry, but not having a plan is so…weird and nerve-wracking for me." Her vacations (when she took them) were planned a year in advance, buying a car took her months, and even long after the worst of the pandemic, she had enough hoarded toilet paper to last her a year.

"It's not like you haven't been there before. What about when you first took a chance on the restaurant? That had to be scary."

"It was, but not totally. It was already an established Greek restaurant, which is close enough to keep a lot of the same clientele. And I'd been thinking about and planning on owning a restaurant for years. So no. This isn't that."

"Don't short yourself. There's a difference between thinking about something for a long time and actually doing it. You did it and it was a success."

Brooke hated blowing her own horn. Always had, which drove Marcy nuts and made her proclaim that Brooke needed to be less humble and more demanding. "I simply made it stand out from anything else that was around here. And it didn't happen by magic. I had a plan, which, if you'll recall, included hiring the best Italian chef in these parts. I had the time and the money from friendly investors to make it happen." Well, one friendly investor. The rest came out of the money she'd squirreled away for years. Plus it was a good thing banks liked to lend money.

"So, you'll make something happen again, that's all. You're totally capable of it."

If only, Brooke thought, she had Marcy's bottomless confidence. But at forty-eight, starting over again felt like jumping from a plane without a parachute. "I don't know. Maybe it's too late to chase new dreams."

"No." Marcy pointed her fork at Brooke, and if it wasn't for the fact that Marcy was a pacifist, Brooke might have been alarmed. "Every time you're on the precipice of something big in your life, you choke. That's all this is, history repeating itself."

"I do not choke!" *The nerve of her*!

"Yes, you do. You bailed on Erica right before she was going to ask you to marry her."

Brooke had to grind her teeth to keep from saying that Marcy was full of shit. There was never any proof that Erica was going to ask her to marry her, only a feeling on Brooke's part...a feeling she never should have shared with Marcy.

"Just don't, okay? My life is not a chess game that you get to pick apart and criticize or analyze or whatever you want to call it. And stop bringing up ancient history. Jesus!" Marcy seemed to think that birth order gave her some preordained right to meddle and dole out unsolicited advice. And yet from decades of habit, Brooke went along with it, pouring out her troubles to Marcy in exchange for her advice. It was a transaction that had become stifling of late rather than beneficial.

Marcy patted her hand on the table like a mother consoling a child. "There, there. Didn't mean to ruffle." They ate in silence, Brooke seething with every chew. It wasn't her fault that she couldn't bring herself to jump blindly into things, that she needed the comfort of order, of plans. Erica had been incapable of giving her the stability she craved when they were together. Which wasn't Erica's fault either, and yes, she'd been an idiot to do what she'd done to Erica. *I'm not that person anymore*, she wanted to scream. And yet…maybe she was. Maybe that scared little reactionary girl was still inside her. She was scared then and she was scared now, and yet something she couldn't explain was pushing her to be brave, to strike out on a different path, to take all the pieces blown to bits by the pandemic and put them back together into something completely new and unrecognizable. Because as much as she wished for things to go back to the way they were before the pandemic, she was a realist.

Marcy broke the silence. "I'm not trying to bust your balls, Brooke. I swear I'm not. I know you're capable of doing anything you set your mind to. That's what I'm trying to tell you."

"Well, forgive me for not being quite as convinced as you."

"Can I give you one more piece of advice?"

Brooke speared a piece of omelet with her fork, then with equal vigor speared her sister with a glare. "Not if it comes with more veiled criticism."

"It doesn't." Marcy waited until the fight receded from Brooke; she always waited for the right moment for maximum drama. "Trust the universe. It really is that simple."

"Oh, I don't think there's anything simple about the universe."

"No, but you trusting it can be simple. Try it. Please."

The universe could kiss her ass, but Brooke sketched a *whatever* sign in the air. Getting Marcy off her back was all that mattered at the moment. "I don't need saving, you know."

Marcy cackled. "Honey, everybody needs saving. Don't you know that by now?"

CHAPTER NINE

Landon pushes his rollator along the sidewalk at a painfully slow pace, but Cam doesn't mind. However long it takes them to circle the block is fine with her. The mid-May sun is warming by the day and the air is faintly redolent with the perfume of blooming lilacs. She could stay out here all day, she thinks, turning her face to the sun.

They're talking trivialities when Landon interrupts with, "Did you know I almost died once before?"

"No. What happened?"

"It was twenty-three years ago. I'd always wanted to learn how to fly a small plane, so I started taking the courses and working on my pilot's license. I was on my fourth solo flight, a little Cessna 172 that I was leasing for the day. Right after takeoff, I knew I was in trouble. The engine sputtered and began to die on me. I fought with it, tried to bring the plane down safely, but I knew deep down that it was futile. I knew I was going to crash."

"And how did that feel?"

"Remarkably peaceful."

"Really? I would have thought there'd be panic involved."

"Oh, there was, while I was fighting to get control. Once I realized I wouldn't be able to, that I was going to crash into the trees I was quickly gaining on, I felt suddenly resigned to it. It was the damnedest thing. In an instant my brain recognized there was nothing more I could do and that I was going to crash and probably die."

Cam has tried to imagine what it might feel like when catastrophe is imminent, what her final thoughts and feelings would be, but it's impossible to know for sure. Would fear take over? Disbelief? Anger? Or would she be okay with it? Not that she is anxious to find out, but because she counsels people who are dying, she's tried to place herself in many different hypothetical scenarios. "What went through your mind when you resigned yourself to crashing?"

Landon is quiet for a moment. "I was surprisingly okay about it once I realized I had no more choice in the matter, that there was nothing more I could do."

"So you were content to leave it with God or the universe or whatever?"

"Yes. It was out of my hands, and once I gave myself over to that thought, there was peace."

"Since you obviously didn't die, what happened?"

"I crashed into some trees. Woke up dangling from a limb that my jacket had caught on. I was rescued but had two broken legs, broken ribs, and a punctured lung. I was in hospital for over three weeks."

"Wow. Did you ever fly again?"

Landon laughs. "Nope. But I should have. I mean, look at me now, I don't have much time left. We're all going to die of something, whether it's a plane crash or cancer. But that doesn't mean I don't feel panic creep up on me...like you saw recently. I guess it's the long, drawn-out part of this disease that makes it so hard to reckon with. It's hard to compare it to crashing a plane, even though I've tried."

"So, it's more about having time on your hands to think so much?"

Landon nods. "Too much time to think and worry. And suffer."

"What's your biggest worry right now, Landon?"

They resume their walk, slower yet because Landon is distracted. "Can I be blunt?"

"Please."

"All right, my death expert. What's going to happen to me after I die?"

"You won't be alone and we'll make sure Tenley isn't alone either. A coroner will be called to—"

"No," he snaps. "What happens to *me*? To the person I am inside. My brain, my thoughts, my memories. Where the fuck does it all go?" He wipes a tear from his cheek, then another. "I hate not knowing what's going to happen. I'm sorry." He chokes out a sob, and Cam takes his arm for a moment and rubs it soothingly with both hands.

"The fact that you're thinking about it and questioning it means you're becoming more self-aware. You're starting to figure out that you're a partner with fate rather than its victim."

"I'm sorry, but what the hell does that mean? That I'm on my way to resigning myself to it like I was in that plane?"

"Yes. But I also think it means that you're willing to learn the lessons this is teaching you. That you're realizing you're more than you think you are. That…now don't laugh…but you're eternal. Or at least your soul is. You're part of something much bigger, as are all of us. That each of us is a soul with a body, not a body with a soul. The body dies, the soul goes on. At least, that's how I like to think of it."

"But how do I really get there? I mean, to really come to peace with…what's happening to me? There's got to be a way to feel more…" Landon throws up his hands in frustration. "Maybe it would be better if it was just…over."

Cam shakes her head. "No, don't ever wish the time away. Time is precious. Every day you have is precious. Each day, try to shed something that's weighing you down or that you're unhealthily attached to. Whether that's a specific worry, or anger toward something, or even a physical thing that you've been attached to that you don't really need. Try letting it go. Once you have fewer things to lose, your burden will be less… burdensome."

Cam thinks about her career choices, about how it took her so long and cost her so much heartache before she let go of the music career that was no longer making her happy, that had begun to hurt her. You're not supposed to give up—that was life's constant refrain. You're supposed to fight for everything you want and never let go, consequences be damned. Well, life wasn't that black and white. Not for her, not for anyone. Yet only when she stopped forcing things, stopped fighting, was she able to finally figure out what really mattered to her.

"You know," she adds, "we never really are in charge of our own future, much as we try to convince ourselves that we are."

"You're right. I couldn't get control of that damned plane."

"And look at what the pandemic has taught us about who's in control." She knows enough people who lost their businesses, their homes, their health, because of the pandemic. And too many who lost their lives. A nurse she used to do yoga with every week succumbed to the virus last year. Same with her auto mechanic, who not only wielded a magic wrench, but who seemed to possess an endless collection of jokes. She missed them both.

"True. That damned thing has sure knocked the stuffing out of us all."

"We don't get to control as much about our lives as we think we do. But we can control our thoughts. We can control our behavior. Only you are responsible for what you do with what life throws at you."

"Forget that I'm dying and enjoy each day, right?" His words are sharp with a mocking edge. This isn't the Landon from the little backyard soiree the other night. This Landon is bitter and angry—all part of the roller coaster of emotions the dying experience.

"No and yes. You can't forget you're dying, Landon. It's the biggest thing that will happen to you besides being born. Don't hide from it, but yes, dammit, don't let go of what living has to offer while you're still here." She wanders over to a lavender-colored lilac bush hanging over the sidewalk, its blossoms soft as velvet and its scent as strong as perfume. "Like this. Isn't this lilac bush wonderful?"

Landon sticks his nose right into the pretty petals and takes long, deep inhales. "God, that smells good."

"Touch it."

He does. "Soft. Like velvet."

"Remember the other night, when you and Tenley were dancing in your backyard?"

The memory lights up Landon's face.

"You actually managed to push living to the forefront and dying to the background. You have the power to be content or the power to be pissed off. It's your choice. What's it going to be, Landon? How do you want to spend your final weeks or months?"

Landon tears himself away from the lilac and smiles. "I don't want to be bitter, I can tell you that much."

"Don't get me wrong, I'm not suggesting it's easy. I've got a couple of audiobooks on the subject I'm going to set you up with. Oh. I almost forgot to tell you. I'm bringing a visitor around the day after tomorrow."

Landon makes a face of displeasure. "I'm not up to visitors. I don't want to see anyone but you and Tenley right now."

"I promise you won't mind this one." She's already squared it away with Tenley. Through her hospice contacts, Cam found a ten-year-old dachshund named Wendy whose owner has recently died; Wendy needs a home and Landon needs a dog. But the decision will ultimately be Landon's.

Landon shakes his head, but Cam senses that behind his hesitation lurks hope. "You don't like to take no for an answer, do you?"

"Nope. Not when I know you trust me."

"Well, that I do. I'll miss you while you're on the island. Are you packed yet?"

Cam will leave in four days. "Not quite but I'm getting there. And before I go, don't forget Becky Neerhof from the hospice is coming over to your house tomorrow to meet with us all."

"She won't be you."

"Aw, thanks Landon. But she's good. You'll like her, I promise."

"All right. And while you're away, you're going to take some of your own advice, right?"

"I'm not sure what you mean."

"Every day is precious, and you'll make the most of it. All that jazz you keep reminding me about. Right?"

She checks to see if he's being facetious, but he's deadly serious. And then he winks and cracks a smile that's heavy with something she can't decipher.

"Fine," she says with a self-deprecating laugh. "I promise you that I will take my own advice." But she knows Landon and Tenley won't be far from her mind. And it's only for three or four days, at most.

"Atta girl, Cam."

CHAPTER TEN

Brooke leaned over the steering wheel of her Subaru and let the tears flow. She'd come from a meeting at her lawyer's office with Jason Whitaker and his lawyer, and the deal was done. The restaurant was no longer hers. She should be happy to escape the rut she'd been in. First Rachel was out of her life, now the restaurant. *This*, she thought, *must be the feeling of freedom*. And yet it felt...weird. Confining rather than liberating, confusing instead of uncomplicated. When every choice was in front of you, it was somehow easier to wallow in indecision.

Through a curtain of tears, she gazed out the windshield, and after she'd emptied her emotional well, what filled it was something close to bliss. She was floating, a kite without a string, following the streams of wind and air wherever they chose to take her. She could make her own life. She could start over (*gasp!*) without a solid plan. Look at her mother. And Marcy. They flitted around like butterflies from flower to flower without much of a plan, and they were doing okay for themselves. They were...happy, Brooke supposed.

Am I *happy?* No, she decided quickly. Happiness was something she hadn't truly felt in years. The restaurant had satisfied the yearning in her until the pandemic hit. Then everything—the restaurant, life itself—became a chore, became something to be endured. It was enough, back then, to plod on until things got better. Now, plodding was no longer enough. She wanted more. Christ, she wanted to be happy. *So, what do you want to do that would make you happy?* she asked herself. And came up empty. *How can it be so hard at my age to figure out what makes me happy?* There had to be something. Was she overthinking it? Did she need a goddamned *plan* on how to be happy? A shrink to tell her what to do? A book or ten? It was a mystery, and she had no key with which to unlock it.

She got out of the car and headed down the walk to her townhouse, the loneliness of her predicament choosing that moment to almost knock her on her ass. She'd never wanted a dog because of her hours at the restaurant. What if she got a dog now? Or, wait, what about a trip to Europe? She'd always wanted to go and now she had the time and the money. Well, *some* money. Her debts were resolved, but she couldn't go spending her savings like a drunken sailor, not without having another job lined up. Maybe she could go to the West Coast for a few weeks? Or take a trip down the Eastern Seaboard. She'd put on her to-do list to look at some travel sites, see what deals were out there. A vacation might help her get her head on straight.

The first thing she noticed when she opened the front door was the sound of running water. Then she looked at her feet. Water was everywhere, soaking her new heels and flowing down the stairs from the second floor. *Holy shit, what did I do?* Brooke thought as she raced up the stairs as fast as her wet shoes would allow. Had she been distracted enough this morning to leave the shower running or...? Nope, it was the toilet. A crack in the tank. Cursing, Brooke closed the shutoff valve beside the toilet and watched with relief as the gushing water trickled to a stop. Hands on her hips, she stood and watched her bathmat float away. She wanted to float away too, on a wave of new tears.

On this, of all days, right when she was on the verge of feeling like figuring out how to start over was at her fingertips. What superb goddamned timing!

For about three seconds she was tempted to send out a distress signal to Marcy. Then she gave herself a mental kick. It was time she stopped relying on her sister to help her run her life. She loved Marcy. Marcy had been the coolest, hippest older sister who was always quick to supply her with a reefer or a pint of whiskey on the few occasions Brooke had dared to be rebellious. And Marcy knew more about sex pre-Google than anyone Brooke ever knew. But this wasn't a job for Marcy. This was a job for an adult who was endeavoring to be treated like an adult by her overbearing, older sister. She needed to figure this out herself.

With her cellphone, Brooke left a message for a plumber. Then she Googled local damage restoration companies and called the first one that popped up. They could be there in an hour, they said. Oh, and be prepared to move out for two or three weeks, they advised, because of the risk of mold and the time it would take to do the repairs. The floors would probably have to be refinished. *Great. Jobless and now homeless.* Her next call was to her insurance company. She sat afterward on the small stoop that only had room for one chair and stared at her phone, trying not to think about the mold spores multiplying in her home. An email notification popped up. It was from Landon, of all people. They usually only exchanged emails around Christmas and sometimes birthdays. What could he possibly want?

Dear Brooke:

Let's skip all the preambles and get right to the point with this email. I need you to do something for me, and I know it's a huge ask, what with your restaurant being the best little Italian eatery in the state (yes, I saw Madonna's post on social media! Yay you!) What I'm asking is a long shot, but I don't have the luxury of beating around the bush or of you saying no. So here goes. The thing is, I need you

on Mackinac Island next Wednesday for about ten days. I know you're probably thinking I've lost my mind, but I promise you I haven't. And please don't ask what this is all about. I know your mind will be buzzing with about thirty questions right now, but please, just do whatever you need to do to make it happen and come. I'm calling in that old favor, and this is the only thing I will ever ask of you. Don't worry, you might even find it fun. The arrangements have all been made and I've attached them to this email. Thank you, Brooke. Know that this means everything to me.

Landon

Brooke read the email again. What reason could Landon possibly want her on Mackinac Island for? It was, like, a seven-hour drive just to get to the ferry crossing. Jesus, this was no small favor. Her fingers hovered over her phone. She was about to reply that what he was asking was impossible and way over the top, that there was no way she could jump in her car with no further explanation than this inadequate email. Did he not care that she had responsibilities? A life?

Oh. Wait. She actually didn't have a life right now. Or responsibilities. Her restaurant was now Jason Whitaker's and her townhouse was out of commission, thanks to a leaking toilet. Brooke's shoulders slumped in defeat.

Well, Mackinac Island was a far better option than couch surfing at Marcy's for the next couple of weeks. She didn't need an endless litany of life advice from her know-it-all sister, which is the price she'd have to pay if she bunked there. Could she do this thing for Landon? Jump in her car and head north for ten days with no idea what the hell he wanted? Yes, she could, she decided, though the spontaneity of it was annoying. Spontaneity made her break out in hives, but she did owe him. More than a decade ago he'd given her a hefty interest-free loan toward buying the restaurant, and although she'd managed to pay it back in full before the pandemic hit, it'd been pure blind faith on his part to lend her that money. She supposed she could show him some blind faith, too.

All right, Landon. You know I'd do anything for you. See you there.

Brooke slipped her phone back into her pocket. *Okay, universe. I'm taking Marcy's advice and trusting you. Time to show me what you got.*

CHAPTER ELEVEN

Though the wind tosses Cam's hair in about forty directions, she stays on the ferry's upper deck, not wanting to miss the view as they close in on Mackinac Island. The chop in the Straits of Mackinac is significant, pitching the ferry enough to keep Cam planted in her seat and one hand clutching the railing beside her. Landlubber that she is, if she were to get up and go below decks, she'd be about as steady as a drunk, swaying and trying to feel her feet below her. No thank you to that. But outside of finding a small plane on which to hitch a ride, twenty minutes on this hell ride is her only option. Her face to the sun and to the slight mist released from the churning of the boat against the waves, Cam squints at the distant white spec on the rocky cliffs still some distance away. It's the island's crown jewel—The Grand Hotel.

It feels as though they're only inching their way toward the island, but when she peeks at the waves passing below, she sees that the ferry is traveling at a decent clip. When she looks up again, the hotel isn't as tiny anymore. She can now make out the green roof and the massive veranda across the entire front of the structure, almost seven hundred feet long—the longest porch on a hotel in the world. Cam is a history nut. Not in terms of career choices or even much in the way of her college course load when she was a student, but more in her way of looking at things. Not one to charge headfirst into something she knows nothing about, she instead finds comfort in learning about things first. Only then does she allow herself to feel the tug of new discovery, to feel free enough to immerse herself in the experience of it. Her mother used to scold her constantly for having her nose stuck in a book instead of being outside and playing with other kids, but there was always so much to *learn* about the world. "How can I know what words mean or what happened in the wars or why people are the way they are if I have to be outside playing?" she would counter. When she was too young to stay home alone after school, she'd hang out at the vet clinic where her mom worked, sitting in a quiet corner with a book in her lap. There was never enough cajoling or enough quarters in the receptionist's pocket to convince her to take some of the four-legged in-patients for a walk—not when there were written words to pore over. Then came her love of music when she was a teenager, and then her nose was stuck in sheet music or tucked up against an instrument. Cam is still that kid with an unquenchable thirst for learning, except now she tempers it with *doing*, because she understands how short life is, understands that doing is learning too.

Her one visit to the island as a school kid consisted of little more than the pursuit of fudge and marveling at all the horses and carriages. She wasn't allowed to wander the grounds of the great hotel or spend hours in museums or go off and read about the island's history. This time she'll do it her way because, without noticing, she's slipped headlong into vacation mode—a welcome if unexpected surprise. Early in her training, her mentor, a serious-looking man who walked with the slouch of those encumbered by too many unpleasant things, made her promise not to ignore her own needs. "You won't have the stamina and the strength to help others if you don't help yourself first." Her enthusiasm for her work, her loyalty to her clients, meant she sometimes went months—no, years—without taking a vacation. It was somehow easier to keep going than to stop, to ignore her mentor's advice. But now that she has stopped, it's... not so bad, she decides, and into the wind she whispers a thank you to Landon. A few days doesn't make for a real vacation, but this little break is as close to one as she's going to get for the foreseeable future.

Watching The Grand Hotel loom bigger on the horizon, Cam selfishly wishes Landon had booked her to stay there, but it's awfully expensive. Built in 1887, it was a summer playground for wealthy visitors who arrived on steamers from Chicago, Milwaukee, Cleveland, Buffalo, Detroit, Toronto, Montreal (she is still tired from staying up late reading about the island). Its guest book is supposed to be littered with names of presidents and other world leaders, actors and authors and athletes, the famous, the wealthy, and the anonymous. Movies have been filmed on its famous promenade, which is stunning with its massive white columns and crisp American flags snapping in the breeze. Cam yearns to plant her feet on the island as quickly as the ferry can get her there.

Then she remembers the envelope from Landon for his ex, tucked safely in her messenger bag, waiting for her to deliver it. He'd scratched B. Ross on the front of it—she didn't think to look at it until later. *I think you better tell me more than just her first initial*, she texted Landon before jumping in her car for the trip north this morning. She pictured greeting the woman with the embarrassment of having to ask her what her actual name was. *Brooke*, Landon texted back. Okay. So Cam will have lunch with Brooke Ross to hand her the envelope and answer any questions about Landon. Then she can go on her merry vacation ways for a couple more days. She'll offer this woman her support, of course, should she need it, but Landon and Brooke Ross have been divorced for well over a decade, and after a marriage of only ten months, she's not expecting a big scene. Hopes, anyway, because she won't be happy if Landon has saddled her with a needy, grieving ex who will allow her not one minute of solitude. It's not that she doesn't want to help, but death is her specialty, not being a human crying towel for distraught ex-spouses from years ago.

In any case, Landon hasn't mentioned anything about her being a head case, and Cam trusts him. He seems to trust her too, but yesterday she wasn't so sure. After receiving Tenley's permission to explore the possibility of the couple adopting a dog, Cam got busy searching for a dachshund in need of a home. She found Wendy through a hospice contact. Wendy is ten years old and was recently left orphaned after her owner died.

Man, was Landon pissed at her when she brought the dog over. "I can't look after a dog, Cam, you know that. I'm dying for Christ's sake."

"You're living," she retorted. "Until one day you won't be."

"I'll be dead long before this thing is. You want her orphaned again?"

Tenley had Cam's back though, gently reminding Landon that she won't allow Wendy to be orphaned. "You're kind of forgetting about me in all this, love. Wendy and I can take care of each other when we need to."

Landon grumbled about getting too attached to Wendy or Wendy growing too attached to him, but before they knew it, he was petting the dog and squinting into her big, moist, brown eyes. He needed to decide for himself if he was willing to give his heart to this dog, and so Cam let him take his time. When he continued to make noises of objection, Cam reminded him that Wendy needed a soft landing spot right now. "We all need those safe and gentle landing spots at times in our lives. Including dogs. Be her landing spot, Landon. At least for now."

"Did you even try to find someone else for her?"

Tenley had had enough. "You love dogs, Landon, and so do I. Your heart is big enough for this, I promise you. And I'll be right here too to help look after her. And so will Cam. Right, Cam?"

"Of course," Cam replied. "I'll help walk Wendy whenever I can, and she can stay for sleepovers with me when I get back from the island if you need a break."

The dog licked Landon's hand and it was only a few more moments before he was talking baby talk to her.

"Anyway," Cam said, pretending not to notice that Landon was quickly turning to jelly over the dog. "After I get back from the island, if you don't want her, I'll find another home for her, okay? You can consider it a week-long trial if that helps."

"Fine." He gave the dog a menacing look that was anything but scary. "You got a week, Wendy. You hear that? You'd better be on your best behavior, or you'll be out on your ear."

The dog's tail wagged as though it knew Landon was full of crap. Which he was. By the time Cam returns to Traverse City, she's positive that Landon and Wendy will be inseparable. That's her hope, anyway. Why not fill your heart with as much love as you can before you go, she thinks. *Better to leave this world with a full heart than an empty one.* A dog would definitely help fill Landon's heart.

And yet... What about her own heart? It's not empty, but it's not full either. She loves her work and she loves the handful of friends she's acquired since moving back home, but that's the easy part, the safe part. By design she's walled off a big chunk of her heart, the most important chunk of it. No one has been inside those walls since Bette all those years ago. No one has had the power to hurt her like that again, because along the way, avoiding pain became more important to Cam than accepting love. Papering over the hurt took priority over seeking joy, because doing so was the only thing that allowed her to survive, to move forward. She did what she had to do.

The ferry nudges up to the dock and a deckhand leaps off and begins looping its massive ropes around the thick, cast iron tiedowns. *That wasn't so bad,* Cam convinces herself, standing and strolling down the metal stairs to the lower deck like there's nothing to these water crossings. She takes her first step onto terra firma and wonders how many others have washed up on this island looking to heal, to start over again. That's the thing about islands. They can be a last-ditch place for the lonely or the suffering, and yet, it's so beautiful here in this place that catches people. There's nothing depressing or suffocating with all the open air and the expanse of blue water. On the contrary, the place feels soul-nourishing, safe. And maybe even a breeding ground for hope. Hope for what, she doesn't know. She's been spinning in place lately, nearing some sort of a precipice perhaps. She knows enough to pay attention to the signs of impending change, and it feels like something in the distance is gathering, readying itself to sweep into her life.

Cam fumbles with a foldout map of the island, sees that her hotel is a short walk from the dock. She shrugs her oversized backpack onto her back, smiles, and nods at the other tourists as she makes her way to her hotel, a yellow-clad, four-story Victorian affair with a covered porch and gardens brimming with red, yellow, purple, and white annuals.

She checks in at the reception desk and is handed an actual key, not a digital key card. Is everything here about stepping back in time? "Enjoy your stay here for the next ten days, Ms. Hughes."

"Excuse me. Did you say *ten* days? I believe there's a mistake. My booking should be for three nights."

The clerk, a young woman who might be a college student in the off-season, checks the computer again. "Nope," she says with a smile. "The booking was made for you by a Mr. Landon Ross. It's been paid for the next ten days."

"Well," Cam says, trying her best to remain cheerful in the face of Landon and Tenley pulling a fast one on her. "I'm pretty sure I won't be here that long, but thanks."

The clerk shrugs. "As you wish, but we'll keep the booking as it is, just in case."

Up in her room, Cam keys in Landon's number on her cellphone. "Landon, you made a mistake with the booking," she tells him, giving him the benefit of the doubt.

Calmly he replies, "I didn't."

Her blood pressure pounding in her ears, Cam says, "I can't possibly stay here for ten days. That wasn't what we agreed on at all. You said a few days, and I don't appreciate you keeping this important piece of information from me."

"Look, I'm sorry." There is not a shred of remorse in his voice. "I'll get Tenley to have more of your stuff shipped to the island. But three days isn't a vacation, Cam, it's a timeout. I want you to have a real vacation. Is that so wrong?"

"It's wrong of you to not tell me, Landon. It's wrong of you to deceive me." *Manipulate* is the word that keeps repeating in her mind. *What are you up to, Landon?*

"Oh. Kind of like how you deceived me about Wendy?"

Cam presses her hand to her forehead. He has a point. "All right, all right. We're even. But just so you know, you can't actually make me stay here for ten days." She is free to leave whenever she likes.

"Fine. *I* don't need to make you stay there that long. The island will do that. Trust me."

Whatever, Cam thinks. "I need to call Becky Neerhof to make sure she can sub in for me longer than I'd planned."

"Already done."

"You mean she's in on your little scheme?"

Landon chuckles. "You underestimate me."

Clearly, she has, but she will not make that mistake again. "How's Wendy?"

"Acting like she owns the place, the little bugger."

"Good. Somebody needs to keep you in your place."

"Nah, I got Tenley for that."

"She doing okay?" Three days before Cam left for the island, Tenley broke down in tears privately with Cam, admitting that she'd been trying to replicate Landon's homemade spaghetti sauce, to no avail. "I need to be able to make it exactly as he does after he's…gone. I need to be able to do this, Cam, and I can't get it right."

Anticipatory grief is a thing with loved ones—grieving before the dying person is even gone. So the next day, Cam went out and got all the ingredients and got Landon to make the sauce with Tenley, all while Cam videotaped it, so that Tenley will not only have a great memory to look back on, but so she can make the sauce exactly as Landon makes it.

Landon lowers his voice. "Honestly, I think she adores Wendy even more than I do, Cam. I hate to admit it, but you were right about us needing a dog. Just like I'm right about you needing a holiday."

Cam rolls her eyes. "Goodbye, Landon. I'll be in touch after I deliver your envelope."

CHAPTER TWELVE

Brooke stepped off the ferry and was immediately thrust back in time nearly two centuries. Ah yes, no motorized vehicles—only horses and wagons and bicycles. *Lots* of bicycles. Crossing the street on foot meant constantly dodging two-wheelers. There was no denying the place was charming. More than charming. Pheromones practically wafted in the air, the place was so romantic. Well, romantic if you were in the right mood and you were with the right person, she supposed. Who wouldn't want a cozy horse and buggy ride with their lover? Or lounging together, holding hands, on the front porches that seemed to grace every hotel and inn and house. There were walking paths and bicycle trails, patios for drinking cocktails, kayaks to rent, plentiful benches along the shoreline on which to read or sunbathe, restaurants that could undoubtedly meet Brooke's picky standards. She'd done her research over the last few days because, well, what else did she have to do? The island, the online sites gushed, was a newlywed's paradise. Or in her case, a newlywed paradise for one. Perfect.

What she didn't understand was why Landon wanted her here, of all places. He had to know this would be torture for her. The romance part of their past union, or rather, the lack thereof, was no secret. In fact, Brooke wouldn't call any of their short time together particularly romantic. Being with Landon had felt like walking through the pages of a romance novel and feeling only a sense of otherness, of floating along the margins, like she didn't belong. Like *they* didn't belong as a couple. Landon tried. Brooke tried too, though her heart had never really been in it—again, not a surprise. During their first weeks together as newlyweds, he constantly fussed over her, as if such fairy dust might convince her to fall in love with him. He'd pull out her chair, ask her if she was okay, was she happy, could he get her anything, could he run her a bath, pour her a glass of wine—when all she really wanted was to be left alone with her private misery. Marrying Landon had been like marrying her brother, and she'd known it with a desperately sinking heart the minute she said, "I do."

That was sixteen years ago. Now here she was, the specter of romance smacking her in the face everywhere she looked. She was shipwrecked on Romance Island. Jesus, Marcy would have a field day with what that was supposed to mean.

Brooke ground her teeth as she bumped her luggage along the wooden dock. She could almost believe Landon was trying to torture her, exact a little revenge, except he didn't possess a spiteful bone in his body. He'd given her nothing in the way of hints about the purpose of this little trip, even though she'd begged him for more details. She would have to wait until tomorrow's official lunch date for the mystery to be revealed, and with luck, she could get out of here in a couple more days, cut this little impromptu "romantic" vacation, or whatever it was, short. Oh, wait. She was still homeless, thanks to her stupid townhouse being out of commission. Her groan attracted the attention of a young man in a bellhop's uniform.

"Help you take that to your hotel, ma'am?" He pointed affably to her suitcases. "I can throw those on my bike and take them for you."

Ma'am? Though she was old enough to be his mother, she was no ma'am. She brushed aside her bruised ego and told him the name of the inn she'd been booked into, then followed on foot because he'd promised it was only a couple of blocks away. A bicycle nearly ran her over and she swore after it, her cuss floating harmlessly away on the breeze. A horse attached to a wagon stood perfectly still, snorting occasionally as it waited for direction from its master. The streets saw a steady stream of pedestrians pointing at signs, hurrying into the endless fudge shops, carrying oversized shopping bags stuffed with T-shirts and hats and beach towels they'd probably never use once they got home. Couples of all ages strolled by holding hands, taking no notice of her.

The current of life flowed past her, as if she were only a minor obstacle to dodge. She stopped for a few seconds, turned her face to the cloudless blue sky, and breathed deeply. Everything smelled fresh around her, even the horse dung in the streets. Perhaps it was the water surrounding them that was responsible for the cleansing breezes in every direction. *In through the nose, out through the mouth.* She breathed deeply a couple more times and allowed herself, in all this expanse of air and water and humanity, to understand that she might be alone but she was not lonely. That she had no real plans but she wasn't aimless. What was she, then? Besides being here. She had no answer, no insight. Not yet. "I'm here," she whispered into the breeze and told herself that it was enough.

Her inn was majestic with its classic Victorian charm and bright yellow siding, its back facing the water, its front only steps from Main Street. A massive porch wrapped around the front as well as the water side of the building. The scent of lilacs was everywhere. The island was practically overrun with the sweet pink, white, or lavender shrubs, their swollen bounty drooping heavily over fences and sidewalks.

Her suitcases awaited her in the hotel's lobby. She felt a sliver of expectation, as though Landon might stroll through the double front doors any second, but there was no sign of him. So she checked in, pleasantly surprised that her stay had been entirely paid for in advance. What could Landon possibly be buttering her up for? What did he want from her? He said he was calling in a favor, and he had every right to. She owed him. But…ten days? What was she to *do* here? Although staying here versus continuing to crash at the Days Inn in Ann Arbor was no contest.

Her room was gorgeous. A king bed, a loveseat, and two chairs facing a gas fireplace, a fainting couch near the French doors that would be perfect for reading. Outside the French doors was a balcony that was big enough for two or three people and offered a partial view of the lake. Well, okay then. She'd be happy to hang out right here for ten days with her books, her wine, her balcony, her fireplace. What better place to hide from the bombardment of happy couples, with their handholding and their bicycles built for two and their candlelit dinners in the cozy restaurants. It was bloody well Noah's Ark here, everyone strolling around two-by-two.

Brooke checked her stash of books to make sure she hadn't accidentally slipped a romance novel in there. If she found one, she'd toss that sucker straight into the lake.

CHAPTER THIRTEEN

It's too early for dinner, so Cam walks the four blocks or so to the general store, which has the sheen of something that's been around forever. Distressed wooden floors that look original, an antique cash register she presumes is only for looks but probably still works. The place is called O'Doul's and has pretty much everything anyone might need in a pinch. Wine, beer, apples, bananas, bread, bacon, chips, juice, eggs. It's a bottle of wine and some crackers she's after for later in her room.

"Hello there." The voice that greets her is cheerful, guileless, and belongs to a woman with soft brown eyes and silver hair cut on an angle that barely grazes her shoulders. "The pharmacy area is in the back corner if you need it, love."

Cam is affronted for about two seconds before she laughs. "I look bad enough to need a pharmacy, do I?"

"You look wonderful, dear." The woman smiles. There is only kindness in her eyes. "But you do look a little green. Difficult ferry journey in this wind?"

"You could say that."

"Ah, well, those boys and girls on the boats know what they're doing. I'm glad you made it over safely. Welcome to the island. And to my store, of course."

"Thank you. You're the owner?"

She comes out from behind the antique glass and oak counter to shake Cam's hand. "Maggie O'Doul." Her accent says she hails from somewhere on the British Isles.

"Camryn Hughes. Cam is my preference."

Maggie regards her with a raised eyebrow. "That's a lovely name either way. You do look the tiniest bit familiar. Have we met before?"

Cam stiffens. "I doubt it. I don't seem to leave Traverse City very often these days."

When someone recognizes her, or thinks they do, from her former life of belting out tunes and strumming her guitar, it throws her for a moment. She has never thought of herself as famous or semi-famous. Even the tiny write-up in *Rolling Stone* magazine was buried so far in the back pages, she swore only her mom saw it. So, she was really only known to Michiganders and other Midwesterners who happened to like lesbians who sang folk and soft rock and blues. Which made for a pretty small pool of people. Maggie O'Doul is probably one of those, although she hasn't placed Cam yet and might never. There was a time when Cam would lie, deny she'd ever been that person, that she must have a double somewhere out there. Nowadays she usually shrugs, gives a vague answer, and changes the subject. But Maggie continues to squint at her, scanning her memory like her life depends on dredging up where she has seen Cam before.

Don't bother, Cam wants to tell her, because I'm not that person anymore. And maybe never was. Helping people, not entertaining them, is her bag now. The singing, the performing, she was good at it, and for a long time it meant everything. But it was a hard life, a nomadic life, and the rewards grew less and less satisfying. Strangers buying her drinks, women elbowing other women out of the way to get her attention...or the attention of Erica Foster, as she was known then. Each performance ignited the adoration she craved, but when the cheering vanished and the fans melted away and went back to their lives, there was nothing. Nothing but an emptiness that a few drinks or a few tokes of marijuana fell short of filling. The intoxication that success and one-night stands gave her had vanished long before she finally pulled the plug on it all. And then there was the instability of her bank account. The life of a performer was feast or famine. When the famines hit, she'd play backup for somebody else or find some session work, but one too many times it was a bag of microwave popcorn for supper.

Maggie, thankfully, changes the subject. "So, this is your first time here, love?" *Ah, okay, she's Irish.*

"School trip when I was a kid, but first time here as an adult. Somehow, I think I'm going to discover I like a lot more about this island than all the fudge."

Maggie laughs a full-throated, deep laugh. "Ah yes, the fudge! What would we do without all the fudge, eh? Well, you're excused for your childhood infractions, but some of the fudgies, as we like to call the tourists, never really get past that part. Fudge and horses are all they remember about the island."

Cam laughs too, loosened by Maggie's honesty. "Yup, that's about all I remember. Please tell me there's so much more than that."

Maggie retreats to the counter and pulls out a sheaf of booklets, hands them to Cam. Even though Cam has already researched the island online, she'll pore over these later tonight. "These are a start. Are you here alone?"

What am I, an open book these days? Maybe, but...meh. She has no reason to conceal or disguise anything from Maggie O'Doul. She likes Maggie and won't see her again after this trip. Funny how much more confessional people are when they think they won't see someone again. "I am. Sort of a working vacation, but light on the working part." Hopefully.

Maggie's smile is so wide that her eyes almost pinch shut. "Good. Come over for dinner tonight and meet my wife and we'll tell you everything you could ever want to know about Mackinac Island. And everything you probably didn't want to know, too."

"Do you always invite strangers to dinner?"

"Oh, at least once a week. Jane's used to it after all these years."

"How many years, exactly?"

"Oh, let's see. I came here forty-three years ago from Ireland to work the summer. Jane grew up in Mackinac City. We met working at the same hotel here. We never left."

"Wow. That's a long time you've been together." Cam doesn't know any gay people who've been coupled that long. And on a little island like this? People must have talked, must have given them a rough ride early on. Maggie and Jane are a walking, talking history book, not only because they've been pioneers as a gay couple, but in their knowledge of the island. Cam wants to soak up every bit of wisdom these two women have to offer.

The bell over the door tinkles and a young couple with a toddler stroll in, blinking with that slightly stunned look of disappointment, like they can hardly believe there's only one brand of diapers to choose from and not six. *Wait*, Cam thinks to herself with a chuckle only she can hear. *I'm already judging other tourists?*

Maggie winks at her. "Come by tonight, seven o'clock. We live upstairs and have a nice little garden out back. I'll tell Jane to throw an extra steak on the smoker. Unless you're vegetarian?"

Cam's mouth is already watering. "I would adore a steak. Thank you."

Well, this is quite a turn of events, Cam thinks. She makes friends this easily, well, almost never. But it is an island, and she imagines what it must have been like decades or centuries ago—everyone stranded together, relying on one another, communing together. Yup, she can do this. Besides, it might make the stay more enjoyable if she has a couple of friends here.

Maggie squeezes her shoulder before turning to the young couple. "Hello there. Can I help you folks find anything?"

"So what brings you to our lovely island? Besides the annual lilacs display." Maggie's wife, Jane Fielding, winks at Cam as if to say she knows something much deeper than lilacs must have brought her here. And she's right. Although Cam's olfactory receptors appreciate the lilacs' perfume, she's not exactly an avid gardener. Not that she has anything against flowers and shrubs. During her performer years, her nomadic lifestyle never allowed for that kind of interest, and since then, well, other things have taken priority. Or rather, inertia about things like gardening crept in and never left.

"I'm on vacation for ten days. Well, sort of a working vacation—heavy on the vacation part, light on work."

Her gaze slides around the small but quaint backyard of Jane and Maggie's home, with its ivy-covered outer walls, lattices of honeysuckle and rose bushes and other perennials she can't name, and Cam longs for a place she can call home that isn't her childhood home, but *hers*. Maybe even hers and a partner's. Like what Maggie and Jane have here. Is it possible? Well, of course it is, she tells herself, though she's under no illusions that it will actually happen. She's grown accustomed to being alone, the way one grows accustomed to eating more veggies because they're good for you. But not sharing her life with someone has become two-dimensional, a bit lonely these days, if she's honest. Before she moved back to Traverse City, there were always people around her: other musicians, fans, stagehands, concert promoters, record producers when she got lucky enough to record. But since then, other than the brief interlude with Nora, it's mostly just her, the occasional outing with a friend, and monthly book club. The solitude and quiet have been her antidote to all those crazy years on the road. Is it time to pop her head out of the gopher hole she's been hiding in? Maggie and Jane make her feel like maybe it is. And that it's safe to do so.

"Maggie said you're here by yourself?" Jane asks without judgment. She's scrutinizing Cam so intensely that Cam almost squirms.

"Yup, just me."

"Well," Maggie adds. "You'll love it here, and if it has to be a working vacation, there really is no better place."

"You won't get an argument from me." To Cam, island life conjures images of viewing endless sunsets from a chaise lounge with a cocktail in her hand. But she also knows that for thousands of people in the summer and several hundred in the winter who live and earn their wages here, the island is not one long vacation. She's confident that Maggie and Jane aren't drinking cocktails from a chaise lounge all day. "I can certainly see the appeal of calling this home. No wonder you two stayed. It's lovely here. I think I'm in full envy of you two."

Jane gets up from her patio chair to flip the steaks on the smoker. "Well, hopefully the *work* part of our relationship with the island will come to an end soon and we can enjoy it more like the tourists. Goddess willing, of course."

Maggie gives a little gasp and shoots a warning glance at her wife. To Cam, she says, "We haven't exactly made an announcement yet. So please don't mention to anyone that we're going to be putting the store up for sale soon."

"Oh," Cam says. "I promise I won't tell a soul. Easy to do since I don't know anyone here anyway. That's got to be a big decision for you both, I imagine. What will you do?"

Jane takes her seat again, takes a swig from the sweating bottle of beer in her hand. "We'd like to enjoy some retirement years while we're still able to do stuff. Don't get us wrong, that store has been like our child and it's not easy to let it go. Well, *if* we find a buyer. We won't leave the island without a general store. It's too important, especially for the full-time residents. But if we do find a buyer, we'd like to spend winters in Florida. Winters around here are back-breakers."

Winters on the island sound intriguing to Cam. She pictures snow-covered streets, the grand homes adorned with Christmas lights, snowmobiles zipping around instead of horses and bicycles. But if she had been enduring island winters into her sixth decade, she'd probably have had enough of them, too.

Maggie looks like she's near tears. "We've put everything into it. Our hearts, our time, our money. It's really been the center of our universe and we've loved it, all of it. It's going to be so hard to give it up."

"It sounds," Cam says, "like the store has given as much back to you as you've given it." Maggie seems like a textbook example of an extrovert who thrives on chatting up strangers, shepherding them into her circle, sprinkling them with her Irish fairy dust.

Maggie grins her agreement, the ghost of any tears banished. "Oh, I've loved meeting everyone who's walked through those doors, folks from all over the world. It's been so fascinating hearing their stories. And one of our summer employees ended up becoming a famous actor. Well, famous if you like television soaps. But…" She reaches for Jane's hand. "It's so much work and we're, well, not exactly young anymore. Change is hard, that's all."

"It is," Cam agrees. "The only thing that's permanent is change, as they say. Adjusting to change is the hard part, at least for most of us."

Jane plants her fist under her chin and looks Cam up and down. It's only another minute before she bounds out of her chair with that look on her face of having connected the dots. "Wait a minute, I know why you're here now. You're playing in that little music festival they're putting on at Mission Point next week, right?"

"Um, no, actually. I didn't know there's a music festival next week."

Jane wags a triumphant finger at Cam. "Come on, you're holding out on us. I saw you at the Michigan Womyn's Music Festival. We both did, remember honey? It was sometime in the late nineties. I'm sure of it. You were wonderful!"

Maggie looks unconvinced. "I'm not so sure. And the name Camryn Hughes doesn't ring a bell, though when I first saw you today, you did look a wee bit familiar."

"No, no, not Camryn Hughes," Jane proclaims. "It was Erica something. Erica…Foster. Yes, Erica Foster! Either that or you're a dead ringer for her."

For some reason she can't really name, Cam doesn't obfuscate. Maybe it's because she doesn't want to lie to these two lovely and generous women. Especially Maggie, who reminds Cam so much of her mom. Ruth Hughes never met anyone who didn't become her friend, whether she met them through their pets at the vet clinic or in the grocery store. Cam feels her face warming, and for once, she doesn't care. "Guilty as charged. I'm afraid you got me there. But it was a lifetime ago."

Maggie and Jane grin in unison before Maggie asks sweetly, "Why do you say it was another lifetime ago? And how come it's Cam now and not Erica?"

Cam lets Jane top up her glass of wine as she summarizes the last couple of decades—how the minute she graduated from college (because she had promised her mother she would earn a degree before pursuing her music), she devoted all her time and energy to singing and writing music. For years after graduation the road took up an inordinate amount of her life, with fame and fortune always beyond the next hill to climb. She finally stopped believing her own hype, that one more album or one more concert would be all it took. By her mid-thirties, exhausted and disillusioned, she returned home to lick her wounds around the time her mother was diagnosed with cancer. Her manager thought she was nuts, swore she was on the cusp of being discovered, but Cam had heard those empty promises too many times before. Besides, her mom needed her. "I never looked back after that. I'd come to the end of the road because I didn't have anything else to give to that part of my life anymore."

By the end of her story, the steaks are done. While they pass around the homemade bread and a garden salad and pour more wine, Cam explains how she changed her last name to her mother's birth name and started going by her middle name instead of Erica. The name change wasn't hard, she tells them, having no affinity with the name Foster because her father left when she was little more than a toddler. "I wanted a fresh start, a new life. The life of a grownup. Erica Foster's time was up. Cam Hughes is the person I was really meant to become."

"And what," Jane asks, "does Camryn Hughes do, if not singing, for a living?"

Ah, yes. The part where the air gets let out of the room, but Cam does a mental shrug because she knows they expect an honest answer. Plus there's the thing about never seeing them again after this trip. When she tells them she's a death doula, neither woman flinches.

"I think it's marvelous," Maggie announces. "The world needs more people like you. Death and dying are so damned scary to most of us. If someone like you can take the mystery out of it or at least ease some of the fear and pain, why, I'd give you everything I have to help me when *my* day comes."

"I'll drink a toast to that," Jane says and raises her glass. "Though I sure never would have guessed such a talented singer would transition to that line of work. But wait, you said you're here on business? Don't tell me you're here to help someone die?" Her free hand automatically drifts to her throat and her voice tightens. "Oh jeez, is it anyone we know?"

Cam shakes her head. "Nothing like that. I'm here to tell my dying client's ex-wife that, well, that he's dying."

"Oh, dear," Maggie says. "That sounds hard. Maybe? You said it's an ex, so maybe it won't be so bad."

"I hope it goes okay. Guess I'll find out tomorrow." Cam's stomach clenches at the thought of tomorrow's lunch date at the Iroquois Hotel with Landon's ex. She is completely unprepared for meeting Brooke Ross and delivering his news. Well, his envelope, which hopefully explains everything so that she doesn't have to. He was so stubborn about providing details or insight into this woman. She should have demanded he share more, because ambushing her with his news might be easier if Cam knew more about her. "Actually," Cam amends, "maybe you better top up my wine again."

CHAPTER FOURTEEN

Brooke followed the cobblestone path alongside the Iroquois Hotel to its patio restaurant nestled behind it. She stopped to take in the view of the Straits of Mackinac before her, watched the big freighter lumber by while diners chatted over the clink of utensils. The lake was that shade of dark blue that looked cold, too cold for swimming yet. A maître d' showed her to the table reserved under the name Ross, but the back of the head already seated there most definitely didn't belong to Landon. It belonged to a brunette with luscious, shoulder-length hair shot through with fine threads of gold highlights.

"I'm sorry," Brooke said to the young man escorting her to the table. "I think this is the wrong table."

At the sound of her voice, the mystery woman's head snapped around as if a gun had gone off. Brooke's heart stopped. She blinked. Blinked again in case her eyes were deceiving her. Even in sunglasses, the woman uncannily resembled Erica Foster. But no, Brooke thought. It must be her memory gone haywire. Not in a million years would Erica be sitting at a table on Mackinac

Island—the same table where Brooke was supposed to meet Landon. The two women stared at one another, paralyzed by their surprise, both looking like they'd tripped suddenly and couldn't figure out what or who had tripped them.

Holy crap, it *was* Erica! A whole ocean of questions flooded Brooke all at once, dizzying her. Where the hell was Landon and what had Erica done with him? Like, how was it possible the two of them even *knew* each other? Brooke didn't meet Landon until more than a year after she and Erica broke up. What the hell was going on? Was this some kind of a setup? A cruel joke? What the actual fuck?

Erica's mouth didn't seem to be working either. To her credit, she seemed as shocked as Brooke, although Brooke wasn't ready to give her ex-lover the benefit of the doubt. She had no idea whether seconds or minutes had passed, but the maître d', coward that he was, had scurried away to let them sort out the problem themselves. *Wait*, Brooke wanted to scream at him. *There's been a terrible mistake here! Help!*

Erica was the first to speak. "Bette? Bette…Avery?" She seemed to roll the name around in her mouth, as if getting used to the feel of it there again. "I… I'm supposed to meet Brooke Ross."

"And I'm supposed to meet Landon. What the hell is happening here?"

Erica went mute again, so Brooke grilled her, the questions tumbling into one another like dominos. Where is Landon? How do the two of you even know each other? Who did you think you were meeting today? And why? Why are you here at all?

"Bette, please. Sit down. I…I didn't know it was you."

"It's not Bette anymore, in case you haven't figured that out. Hasn't been since… Well, you know."

Bette had been Erica's pet name for her, dating back to the early years of their relationship. They were devotees of *The L Word* show, as were their friends. Erica began teasingly calling her Bette as a play on her full name, Brooke Elizabeth, and soon their friends began calling them Bette and Tina after the famous lesbian television couple. And it fit, because the truth was, she and Erica, while they didn't look like *The L Word* actors, did resemble a real-life version of Bette and Tina. Totally in love, totally committed, ridiculously, nauseatingly sweet with one another. They were meant for one another, just like the fictional Bette and Tina, and the whole world knew it. Except, well... Bette and Tina weren't real and there was no happy ending for Brooke and Erica. No one had called her Bette in years.

"I had no idea you... I haven't thought of you as Brooke in forever. And Ross? You kept your married name all this time?"

"I did, not that it's any of your business."

Erica ignored the little dig. "I really think you need to sit down, Be...Brooke."

Sit down? Was she nuts? There was no way she wanted to sit and suffer through any more of this...whatever this was. Except her legs, as numb as the rest of her, couldn't be depended upon to carry her away. So she sat. And forced herself to look at Erica, really look at her. Wow, had it been almost eighteen years since they'd laid eyes on one another? Erica had hardly changed—another annoying thing about today. The least her ex could do was look lousy after all this time. But no. Those same dimples that used to stop Brooke in her tracks, the smile that was actually brighter than the spotlights on the stage—all still there and as dazzling as ever. God, Erica was no less pretty. Heart-stoppingly pretty, actually. She looked fit in her cream chinos and mint green scoop neck tee, and while time had added maybe a dozen pounds to her frame, it suited her. Erica pushed her sunglasses onto her head now, and it was clear that her eyes hadn't lost any of their swirling depths of green and gold, a rare combination that reminded Brooke of a precious gem left out in the sun. *Stop it*, she commanded herself. *Stop drooling over her!* "What do you mean you didn't know it was me? Talk to me, Erica. What are you *doing* here?"

"I..." Erica shook her head a little, paused before starting again. "First of all, in the name of full disclosure, it's Cam now."

"What's Cam now?" Brooke's brain was sludge. Little about this was making any sense.

"My name. Camryn Hughes. I started using my middle name and took Mom's birth name after I...left the music business."

The change to her last name made sense, since Erica never had a relationship with her biological father. It also explained why Brooke had never been able to find anything on the Internet about what had happened to her. The confirmation now that Erica had ditched her music career made Brooke's heart sink a little. All Erica had wanted to do was perform. She was born to sing, what with that voice and her songwriting talent and her stunning looks. She had that whole trifecta of can't-miss going for her. And she had *loved* it. She adored being on stage, adored singing and playing her guitar, loved the crowds, loved everything about music. *What happened, Erica? What happened to you? How could you quit something you loved so much?*

No, no, no. This wasn't some happy little reunion, where they got to reminisce and catch up. "All right, then. Cam, since that's what you go by now. And as you can see, I'm all grown up now and going by Brooke. But forget all that. Where the *hell* is Landon?" She was almost tempted to peek under the table.

"He's not here."

The server materialized and asked what they wanted to drink.

"Then I don't think I'll be staying," Brooke said, half rising.

Cam (boy was it going to be difficult getting used to her new name) reached across the table and gently touched her wrist. "Please stay," she whispered. "It's important."

Well, then. If it was so important that they talk after almost two decades, Brooke was damned well going to have a drink. Or two. "I'll have a glass of prosecco," she told the server.

"Make that two," Cam added.

Brooke might have suggested splitting a bottle, except she had no intention of staying long enough for that. After the server departed, she said, "Do we really have to go through the pretense of having to eat lunch?"

"Yes. Landon insists. It's on his dime and we have to eat anyway." Cam raised one shoulder in a shrug, a gesture Brooke always found endearing. *Used* to find endearing.

"So how do you know Landon?"

"Let's order first."

"Fine," Brooke huffed. She forced herself to look at the menu. The Cobb salad looked good. She closed the menu again, determined to get this whole thing over with as quickly as possible. Cam, though, was taking her sweet time, studying the damned menu like it was a textbook. When she finally set it down with a tiny thunk, Brooke said, "So if Landon's not joining us, please tell me what the point of all this is. Because I'm not really in the mood for..." Any of this, is what she wanted to say.

"Landon sent me in his place. To talk to you."

"To talk to me? I can talk to him myself, thank you very much." Why in the hell were her two exes—the only two exes who'd ever mattered to her—conspiring with one another behind her back? A shadow settled over her. She didn't like this at all. It was like being a kid all over again and having your two best friends gang up on you.

"Landon and I have become friends. We—"

"*What?*"

The server returned, and it took all of Brooke's self-control and the gritting of her teeth to get through placing her order.

"We both live in Traverse City, as coincidence would have it," Cam said. "A few blocks from one another."

God, she was being so annoyingly calm, but then, not surprising. Erica—or Cam—was the kind of person who, the more stressed or upset she got, the more self-possessed she became. "Wait, what? You both live in Traverse City?" Cam's mom was from there, so it made sense that Cam might return, but the city wasn't *that* small. Was it? "And you didn't know I was his ex-wife? Forgive me, but my bullshit meter is through the roof right now." Working in the restaurant business had sharpened Brooke's cynical side. If you didn't grow thick skin, the industry steamrolled you.

Cam raised one eyebrow, her only display of expression. "You've changed."

For all but the first year of their almost eight years together, Brooke worked part-time as a kindergarten teacher while moonlighting in the evenings at a restaurant, learning the trade from the ground up. Her view of the world, of everything, really, had evolved into something far more jaundiced. But that was age and experience too. Being in your twenties, when you actually believed the world was your oyster, was nothing like your forties, when you finally realized there were so many obstacles, so many detours on the way to your dreams, that there was no straight, ascending line from here to there. And none of it was simple. "Of course I've changed. Haven't you?" No way was Cam still that eternally optimistic singer who knew, *knew*, her ship would come in one of these days if she just kept at it hard enough and long enough.

"I've changed, yes."

Cam was so in control of her emotions, so smooth. Smooth as creamy peanut butter that melted in your mouth. And just like that, Brooke needed to torch that coolness with a little fire.

"I'll say you've changed. Conspiring with Landon to...what exactly? What are you two up to? I feel like I'm the game and you two are chasing me. Everything about this is wrong, and you damned well know it."

The food arrived, the Cobb salad for Brooke, whitefish and fries for Cam. Brooke took a long sip of her prosecco, hoping it would cool her temper, knowing it probably wouldn't.

"You're angry with me." With agonizingly slow deliberation, Cam squeezed fresh lemon evenly over her fish.

"Of course I'm angry with you." Brooke stabbed a hunk of tomato with her fork. What she really wanted to do was put a fork straight into Cam's composure. "You and Landon pulling a fast one over me. Oh, wait until I get my hands on him!"

"Brooke, calm down, please. Nobody is doing anything to you. In fact, this whole thing isn't truly about you."

"All right, now I'm completely confused. As well as pissed off." Brooke's fork clanged against her plate after she practically threw it down, prompting other diners to glance their way. "Landon practically begs me to come here for some secretive mission. Instead I find you here and no Landon and no answer to the goddamn mystery of what I'm doing here. What gives,

Eri—Cam? Because my patience is literally hanging by a thread right now."

"I know. I'm sorry—"

"Stop saying you're sorry and tell me what the hell is going on."

Cam ran a hand through her hair, still as thick and wavy as ever. Brooke had always envied Cam her hair. Brooke had cut hers short a couple of years ago to disguise the fact that it had begun to thin a little. Damn menopause had her in its sights. "Maybe this was a mistake."

"You think?"

Cam sipped her drink with the tiniest tremble to her hand. Finally, a crack in the veneer of her self-control. She followed that up with a shaky inhale. "Landon sort of pulled a fast one on me too. He said his ex-wife's name was Brooke Ross, and he wanted me to deliver some news on his behalf. I didn't... I assure you, I had no clue Brooke Ross and Bette Avery were one and the same. Like, even when I first learned his ex's name was Brooke...why would it occur to me that it was you?"

Brooke shook her head, incensed all over again. "Jesus, the nerve of him! Why would he play a sick joke on us like that? Not that I thought he was the type to do such a thing, but people change, apparently."

It was impossible to fathom why Landon, after all this time, would choose now to exert some kind of revenge on her for continuing to be in love with Cam while she was married to him. And what had Cam done to deserve getting mixed up in this? Other than she was the person who'd stolen (and kept) Brooke's heart all those years ago. Maybe this was his way of screwing them both over. Who knew?

"I-I really don't think it was a joke."

"Maybe not, but it was still intentional on his part. He knew about us, knew about our past." Brooke had shed many tears crying on Landon's shoulder over Erica. The fact that he would betray her in this way was beyond hurtful.

"I'm not sure how I feel about...what he's done." Cam's self-assurance seemed to be slipping another notch. "I mean, he never breathed a word about you being *my* Brooke, about knowing we'd been a couple." Her brows knitted in fierce concentration. "Why would he withhold that from me? I don't get it. And I don't get how he figured out that I was Erica Foster. I never told him anything about that part of my life." The color in her face left her, as though she were only now acknowledging the complexity of Landon's scheme.

Brooke bit the inside of her cheek. They'd definitely both been played. But why? "I can assure you that I'm going to call him and let him have it. That's for starters. And then I'm going to pack up and—"

"No, Brooke, please. There's a reason for this, I promise, even if I don't truly understand all of it myself. And I don't. I don't get a lot of this."

For a moment, Brooke felt sorry for Cam. Then she took one last bite of her salad, swallowed the rest of her drink, and nearly tipped the table over as she hastily stood up. Another sea of annoyed glances washed over them. "I think I've had about enough of whatever game Landon's playing. I'll see myself out. And I'll…see you around, Cam. I'm sorry you got hurt by this too."

"No, wait. Don't… Not like this. Look." Cam scratched something on a napkin and handed it to Brooke. It was the room number and name of the inn she was staying at. Of *course* Landon had set them up at the same inn. Across the hall from each other, no less. *Jesus.* "Come to my room this evening. Doesn't matter what time, I'll be there. We need to talk. I need to tell you what Landon—"

"Landon," Brooke hissed. "I'm going to kill him!" Steps from the table, she halted and turned around. She couldn't help it. She wanted to look at Erica/Cam one last time before she walked out on her. Again. "Goodbye, Cam."

CHAPTER FIFTEEN

Cam can't shake the sting of feeling like she's been slapped across the face. Seeing Brooke—*her* Brooke—turned the mental script she'd been prepared to verbalize about Landon's terminal illness upside down. The fact that she'd managed to remain mostly calm in Brooke's presence was no small miracle. But blowing up isn't Cam's style, and now she can't reach Landon. He's not answering his phone, probably deliberately. He'd know by now that she and Brooke had met for lunch, and if he had a brain about him, which he did, he should be able guess at how poorly it had gone. How could it not? Throwing two people together unexpectedly after almost eighteen years, when the last time they laid eyes on each other was during an epic breakup that would have made Hollywood film writers green with envy. Of course today was going to be a disaster. It never had a chance.

A long walk along the water and past the island's small but quaint library helps Cam shunt aside the emotional detritus from seeing Brooke again. But she can't help but be puzzled by the whole Brooke and Landon thing. How and why did they get married? How did they meet and why did they call it quits? And more importantly, is Brooke bi now? She never showed any sexual interest in men back when they were a couple. So, like, the minute they broke up, she decided to double her dating pool? If she did, it's fine with Cam, but it's another thing about Brooke she thought she understood and clearly didn't.

Other things are different about Brooke too. There's a streak of fierceness about her, an unapologetic bluntness. Long gone is the youthful, afraid-to-open-her-mouth neophyte kindergarten teacher Cam had once been in love with. When something used to anger Brooke, or, say, she'd stub a toe, a yelp of "oh fudge" was her F word. Not that Brooke had been an angel, mind you. There'd been nothing sweet or angelic about the way she ripped Cam's heart out and stomped all over it. But maybe she had always been a jumble of contradictions and Cam simply hadn't noticed before.

Another thing about Brooke that Cam can't wrap her head around is how she looks. She is stunning and she shouldn't be. Considering what she did to Cam, Brooke should look a hell of a lot worse—like karma had bitten her in the ass. Hard. But no, she hasn't lost her looks at all. If anything, the years have only made her more beautiful. The short hair is a youthful touch, and Brooke carries herself with the confidence of a woman who knows what she wants and doesn't need anyone's help. She's a force now.

Back in her room, Cam opens her laptop, clicks on her email program, and types a message to Landon, her fingers stabbing the keys:

I do not appreciate the ambush you set Brooke and me up on. And please don't insult me by telling me you didn't know the two of us have a past. These are peoples' feelings you're playing with. I think you have some explaining to do and I deserve honesty from you. I'm feeling used.

She hits send. What she'd like to do is pack up and catch the ferry back to the mainland—exactly what Brooke is probably doing right now. Or has already done. It's clear that the animosity between the two of them hasn't waned much, if at all, over the years, but they're right to uniformly turn their anger on Landon. He's placed them in the middle of a rude, hurtful, even dangerous game. She can't begin to reconcile in her mind why he would do it. And now she's torn between letting her emotions run wild and cutting him loose as a client or finishing the job she started.

Sitting at the little table for two on her balcony, Cam eats half the penne a la vodka she'd picked up on her walk for supper, then pushes the container away. There's nothing wrong with it, but her appetite is almost nil and, frankly, the bottle of pinot grigio she's opened holds much more appeal. She takes a sip and considers that Brooke is probably on the mainland by now, gone from Cam's life. Again. And so be it. Clearly they have little to say to one another, even after their wounds should have long ago healed. Cam takes another sip of wine and stares at the lake, its hue growing darker by the minute in the diminishing light. Brooke has left without hearing Landon's news—a failure on Cam's part. She'd been too rattled by seeing Brooke again, and too pissed off at the turn of events, to remember why she was there at all. For his part, Landon hadn't exactly set the table for success. She ought to fire him as a client; she'd be totally justified in doing so after his little stunt. But then what? Landon will still be dying and Brooke will still be oblivious about it, and Cam will still feel betrayed. How were they all going to navigate this miasma of feeling wronged?

Well, if Brooke has left the island, so be it. Landon will have to tell her his news himself. She never even got to hand Brooke the letter—it's still in the messenger bag that she'd tossed on the bed when she got back to her room. *Okay, calm down.* Landon's plan has blown up in all their faces, and it's no wonder. It was impossible under the circumstances. What had he been *thinking*?

A knock on her door almost makes her jump. *Let it be Brooke, don't let it be Brooke*, repeats in her head as she gets up to answer it.

It's Brooke, holding up her phone, in a trembling hand, like it's a weapon. "What the hell is going on here? Landon just sent me an email telling me to calm down and not to leave in a huff. Does he have a bloody camera on me? Or are you reporting to him everything I say and do? Like…what are you, a *spy*?" She spits out the word with accusatory venom.

Oh, Bette, Cam thinks, finding it difficult to think of her as Brooke. *Why are you so angry at me?* "I'm not a spy. Come in. Please. We need to talk. Plus I have something to give you."

"Oh, I definitely have some things to say. Mostly to Landon. But to you as well." Brooke is a coiled spring ready to snap as she follows Cam into her suite. Hands on her hips, she blinks in surprise when Cam suggests she join her for a glass of wine on the balcony.

"We can do this in a civil fashion, I promise," Cam says. "I'm as much a victim in all of this as you are, so let's figure things out together, okay?" *Somebody has to be the grownup around here if they're going to get to the bottom of this.*

The offer of wine and conciliation pokes a hole in Brooke's fury. "Come on, Cam, you must know *some*thing. All I'm asking for is a little honesty, at the very least. It took me all day to drive up here yesterday from Ann Arbor. I'm too old and too tired for games, and Landon won't tell me anything. I'm to talk to you."

"How come you didn't leave the island this afternoon?"

Brooke blushes. "I was going to, but… I don't really have a place to stay at the moment."

Cam raises her eyebrows in question, but Brooke has clammed up, and it's none of Cam's business. "Anyway," Cam says, "you're right, you do deserve honesty." *As do I*, she thinks as she pours a glass of wine for Brooke, tops up her own, and escorts Brooke to a rocking Adirondack chair on the balcony, its cushions whimsical swirls of blue and red and white. "And I agree. Games suck."

Cam takes the identical chair next to Brooke, a small, round café table between them. For a moment she does nothing more than breathe and take in the inky, violet streaks that have begun to swallow up the sun's last rays. Raising her glass for a sip, Cam closes her eyes and is struck by the memory of lying next to Brooke, watching her sleep, watching that perfect profile of delicate nose and full mouth in repose. She used to wonder what Brooke was dreaming about when she slept or whether she dreamed at all. Cam doesn't dream much at night. Dreams are for the daylight. Dreams are for doing, for accomplishing. They aren't an abstract indulgence to her.

She waits until she's sure Brooke is ready to listen. A couple more sips of wine for lubrication, then: "I meant it earlier when I said I had no idea it was you I was meeting. Landon sent me here with a message for his ex-wife. You, as it turns out." It is *so* not the time to ask how Brooke became Landon's wife, even though the thought is like a stone rattling around in Cam's shoe that she can't discard. "I sent him an email a little while ago, telling him off, but he hasn't written back. He's not answering his phone either, so I'm pretty sure he knows he's in trouble and is doing everything he can to avoid us. He's probably hoping it will blow over, that we'll magically be okay with what he's done."

Brooke blows out an exasperated breath. "Why on earth would he send *you* to deliver a message to me? Like, can he not call me? Text me? FaceTime me? I don't get any of this."

"It's not that kind of message. It's the kind of message that needs to be delivered in person." *But by me? Why, Landon, why of all people did you task* me *with this?*

"All right, so why isn't he here?"

"Because he can't. He's…physically incapable."

Surprise flares in Brooke's eyes, followed by puzzlement. "I don't understand. What's going on?"

Cam darts to the bed and retrieves the envelope from her messenger bag, smooths the crinkles, and hands it to Brooke. She has no idea what's in the letter, but she watches Brooke as she reads it. Watches as her brow furrows, notices the quick sharpening of the crow's feet around her eyes, the tightening of her lips. For a moment, Cam quietly panics. She doesn't know how Brooke will feel about the news, mostly because she has no idea how close she and Landon were or might be, plus there's the tiny detail that she doesn't know Brooke at all anymore. She is vastly unprepared for this. Delivering Landon's news to a stranger, which is what she thought she would be doing, would have been so much easier than this.

Brooke scrunches the letter into a ball, stuffs it in her pocket. Her face is completely devoid of emotion as she says, "You never told me why Landon wanted you to tell me this. Like, he could have mailed me this letter."

"He could have, but I think maybe he didn't want you to be alone when you got the news. You see…" Cam takes a breath, unsure how Brooke will react to her confession. "I'm his death doula. The rest of his reasons for choosing me to do this…" She lifts her hands in a gesture of futility. "I'm not so sure about."

"His… Wait, what?"

"Death doula. A sort of end-of-life midwife. I'm helping him die, to transition to what's next. It's what I do. Now."

Brooke squeezes her eyes shut, shakes her head with the kind of vigor that says everything is simply too overwhelming right now. "My ex-lover is a death doula helping my ex-husband die. Jesus Christ, Cam. I mean, what am I supposed to do with this information? How am I supposed to feel about all…this?"

"That's up to you," Cam answers softly.

A minute of silence passes before Brooke rises, with nothing in her tone or facial expression or actions to suggest what she's thinking or what she's going to do next. She's flipped a switch on her emotions, which only intensifies Cam's discomfort over how things have shaken out.

"Thanks for the wine, Cam. And thanks for sharing Landon's news. Now if you'll excuse me." Without looking back, she marches through Cam's room and to the door.

"Wait, Brooke. Are you going to be okay?" Brooke has suffered a double shock—seeing Cam as well as hearing that Landon is dying. Cam can't help feeling sorry for Brooke.

"Do you care if I'm going to be okay? Or is this all part of the job?"

The verbal jab hurts more than it should. "Of course I care." She shouldn't, but she does. Cam knows she has always cared too much about lost causes. There was the stuffed monkey, torn to shreds accidentally in the laundry, that she dutifully repaired, the lost dog she took in for a week while she walked for miles posting signs until she found its owner, the teen suicide help line she volunteered with all through college. Is Brooke a lost cause too? Is that the only reason she cares? Maybe.

"Well," Brooke says, one foot out the door. "I'll probably leave the island tomorrow." She rolls her eyes. "But thanks for telling me. I'll write or call Landon again. Eventually. When I'm not so pissed off at him."

"Don't leave until I check in with you tomorrow, okay? Did you notice that bench along the water? Beyond my balcony?"

Brooke nods.

"I'll meet you there in the morning at nine sharp." She swallows before lying. "Landon will want me to make sure you're all right before you leave."

Brooke nods once and is gone. Cam closes the door and leans heavily against it, wishing like hell she'd never agreed to this assignment. Well, at least she's now accomplished what she was sent here to do. After one final check-in with Brooke tomorrow morning, she can relax—alone—for a few days before heading home.

CHAPTER SIXTEEN

A twenty-minute shower did little to invigorate Brooke following a night of tossing and turning. Even focusing on brushing her teeth took effort, and she most certainly didn't want to think about meeting up with Cam in a few minutes. Cam the death doula. The fact that Cam was helping Landon die was a cruel irony. The only two exes she'd ever given a damn about. And now one was dying, the other was helping him die, and she was…what was *her* role in all of this? Were the three of them part of some sacred triangle, connected by pathways of old feelings that had long ago been paved over? Was this a test, making her witness her ex-husband's death journey with the only woman she'd ever loved as the bridge between them? What was she supposed to *do* with this? What did it all *mean*?

She closed her eyes and counted to ten. Then twenty. None of her questions mattered at the moment. What mattered was that Landon was dying, with only a short time remaining. That he was only fifty-four really, really sucked. Maybe she was naïve or weak, but she wasn't ready for contemporaries to die of illness or natural causes. Nor was she ready for someone she'd once loved and still cared about to die. Was that the sort of thing Cam helped with? Coming to terms with dying, not only for the person dying, but for their loved ones as well? And why Cam, of all people? How the hell did someone go from gutting it out on stage to becoming a death doula? How did that kind of segue even make sense? This certainly wasn't the Erica—Cam—she once knew. As for Landon, she barely knew him anymore, either. Even though they'd kept in touch periodically all these years, and he'd given her an interest-free loan to start her restaurant, they didn't talk, not for real. She knew that he loved his college teaching job, that he loved a woman named Tenley, that he had a dog that had died in the last year. What else? She racked her brain but when it came down to it, Landon had become a stranger. The things she knew about his life could be compacted onto one very small piece of paper.

Tears dripping onto her hand caused Brooke to put the toothbrush down. Every relationship in her life, except for the ones with Marcy and her geographically distant mother, was superficial. Every. Damn. One. She had no friends, at least not any that weren't on her payroll at the restaurant. The few people she'd dated were simply for something to do—an occasional distraction from the hours she spent at the restaurant. She never really gave her romantic partners a chance, because it was too much work to let them in, to really try, and the restaurant sucked away about everything she had to give anyway. Rachel was the aberration in terms of longevity, but Brooke would have ended it with her long ago if the pandemic hadn't happened. Stuck for months at home while the restaurant was shuttered, Rachel was the only thing that kept her from becoming bored out of her mind. Not an excuse, but the only one that came anywhere close to being an acceptable one.

In the mirror she stared at her pale face, at gray eyes that looked weak as rainwater, thanks to fatigue and tears. *The only people you've ever loved are so far in your past, they don't even resemble the people you once knew. And they're only back in your life briefly because one of them is dying.*

Brooke sat on the bed and cried into her hands. She cried for Landon—a sweet man who'd only ever been good to her. She didn't want to cry for Cam, but dammit, she was crying for her too, for what they'd lost. What *she* had lost. It was the needle skipping on the record all over again. Why had she given Cam up all those years ago? What had she been so scared of? The years have flattened the contours of her memories, at least the difficult ones, but she could still remember how Cam's drive to be one of the best singers in the world had paralyzed her with fear that Cam would leave her behind once she glimpsed the greenness of other pastures. Paralyzed her with fear, too, that there wasn't room for both of them to pursue careers. She successfully convinced herself that she would be better off on her own, because then she could focus on her own dreams. Dreams that didn't include living a nomadic life, of not knowing where their next dollar was coming from, of having to arrange herself and her needs around Cam's road trips, Cam's crazy late nights, the strangers who always wanted something, the plentiful booze and weed that were hallmarks of the lifestyle. She never wanted any of that; it was not *her* dream. Afterward came Landon, sauntering into the restaurant where she was working evenings at the time, asking her to choose her best dish for him, asking her what she thought of the news of the day, about politics, about travel and distant places. Those kind blue eyes of his had settled on her like she was the most interesting person in the world, and he listened to her as though her dreams were already a reality. He asked her to go walking with him when her shift was over, and by the end of that walk, they were holding hands and she was telling him everything, including her devastating breakup with Cam a year-and-a-half earlier.

Oh, Landon. Why did you even bother telling me your news? I never deserved you, and I don't deserve to be in your life now as it comes to an end. His letter was still scrunched in a ball on her nightstand, but she'd committed every inadequate word to memory. Inadequate because a one-page letter about a topic like this could never be enough.

"Brooke, please don't shoot the messenger," it had started out with. *I want to shoot* both *messengers*, she thought.

And please understand why I am not able to come myself to tell you my news. Cam will do a splendid job of being there for you, and I trust her, just as I know you once trusted her too. She's a good person, Brooke, I like her very much.

But enough about Cam for now. I have a terminal illness. Pancreatic cancer. It's a son of a bitch, Brooke, and it's going to kill me soon. I wanted you to know, because I still care for you. I will *always* care for you, and I'm sorry we weren't right for one another. But I've had a good life. I've known great happiness. I'm a lucky man in so many ways, and I wanted you to know that I have no regrets. I hope you don't either, at least not about us.

Now. Back to Cam. Lean on her if you need to. She's a great listener and smart as a whip...but you probably already know that. Be kind to one another. I will be in touch again soon.

Brooke's phone chimed a reminder that she was to meet Cam in ten minutes. She didn't want to go. Cam's job was done; she'd delivered Landon's news. She couldn't possibly give a crap about how Brooke was handling it. Checking her phone for the ferry schedule, Brooke saw that one was leaving in an hour. She would be on that ferry, even if it meant Marcy's couch or more nights at a Days Inn room that smelled of stale cigarettes and wet dog. She should pack right now. But she pictured Cam sitting on that damned bench, alone, waiting for her, wondering what had happened to her until the realization sunk in that Brooke had walked out on her. Again. No, she wouldn't do that. She would at least say goodbye.

Cam was waiting on the bench, two cups of coffee beside her. Brooke couldn't explain it, but Cam's thoughtfulness only made her feel worse. She wanted this to be done, wanted them to go back to their lives and not see one another for another seventeen or eighteen years, because her grief for Landon, her grief for the way things had ended with Cam—they were two sides of the same crappy coin. And it wasn't something she wanted to deal with right now. Maybe she could find some sand to bury her head in for, oh, about a decade or so.

"Hi," Brooke said softly and sat down, pulling her light jacket tight against the morning breeze off the water.

"Hi. I'm glad you made it."

"You didn't think I would."

"No."

"I wasn't sure I would, either."

Cam handed her a coffee. She'd remembered exactly the way Brooke liked it. Funny, though, because Brooke couldn't remember for the life of her how Cam took her coffee. "I'm glad you did."

"Are you?"

The smallest raise of a finely shaped eyebrow. God, Cam was still gorgeous. No, she was more gorgeous in middle age than she ever was in her twenties. A calm intelligence resided in those green-gold eyes, not the slightly wild, raw ambition of a wannabe rock star who was always pumped for the next big thing, whether it was a concert, a contract, an adoring fan who wanted an autograph. Cam looked...settled now. And not in an unhappy way, not as though she had *settled*, but rather in that contented, confident way of accepting things as they came, of being at peace with her life. Brooke couldn't say the same. Not even close.

Cam sipped her coffee and looked away, causing Brooke to immediately feel the loss of that warm gaze. "How are you feeling this morning?" Cam asked.

"Does it matter?" The sting of seeing Cam unexpectedly, the shock of Landon's news...of course she wasn't okay. A wave of petulance overcame Brooke, and she directed it at Cam. Not because Cam deserved it, but because she was there and Landon wasn't and somebody was going to pay. "You have the power to kiss it and make it all better or something?"

"I did. Once. But I'd like it if you answered the question."

Brooke bit back a sarcastic retort. "Maybe I'd rather drink my coffee and watch the lake."

"All right. We can do that too."

A lake freighter crawled its way through the straits, the distant rumble of its engines carried on the breeze. Brooke's anger was not nearly so measured. "Why are you being so nice to me? Why are you doing this?"

"Doing what?"

Brooke sipped the coffee that was damned near perfect. "This! The coffee, checking on me to see how I'm doing. You're off the clock, Cam. You can go home, back to Landon and his… his…dying." The tears almost pushed their way out until Brooke bit her tongue to hold them back. She did not want Cam to see her this way, to be her consoler. Landon had consoled her when she was drowning in regret and pain from irrevocably sending away the one woman she would ever love, and now Cam was trying to console her over Landon. It was fucking weird and cosmically pathetic, and she didn't like it one bit.

Brooke's phone vibrated in her pocket at the same time Cam's phone chimed.

Brooke's hand automatically slipped into her pocket. "I guess we should—"

"Yes. We should."

They both pulled out their phones. It was a text from Landon.

"Finally! Should we…"

"Yes," Cam said, quickly glancing at the screen on her phone. "Let's read it together."

CHAPTER SEVENTEEN

First, I ask your forgiveness. And then I'm going to ask for a crap load of blind faith from you both.

Okay, so I get that you're both pissed off at me. I don't blame you. And I'm sorry. But please hear me out.

Cam, I didn't know you were Brooke's Erica when Tenley and I first looked into hiring you. It was through our research into your background that we figured it out (as I told you, Cam, I knew your mom, though not very well). When I saw a picture of you on our Google search, you looked so familiar I knew I'd seen you somewhere before (and not just from meeting you on walks in the neighborhood). Brooke used to have a picture of you she kept hidden in her nightstand drawer (sorry, Brooke, I snooped!). I also remembered, when Brooke would talk about you, that you originally hailed from Traverse City. I didn't say anything to you because I knew you would be uncomfortable if you figured out our mutual connection to Brooke, and to be honest, I really wanted you as my death doula (everyone says you're the best and I agree). I liked you right away.

Brooke, I know you've been buried neck deep in your restaurant. But if the pandemic has taught us anything, it's never to take life (or life the way we know it) for granted. My illness has more than driven that point home to me. Don't wait until you're in my shoes to realize what you've missed or what you might regret. I don't want that for either of you. I want you both to be happy. And so I'm simply giving you two a nudge toward one another.

Cam glances up at the symphony of sighs and murmurings from beside her. Brooke's brows form an angry V as she reads the text, her right hand clenching into a fist occasionally.

In an accusatory voice, Brooke says, "What?"

"Nothing."

"Nothing? How dare he make assumptions about my life! Our lives! What is he, a genie granting wishes? The angel in *It's a Wonderful Life*? Do you actually think this is a good idea?"

Still impatient and angry is Brooke. Cam remembers when they were living in a tiny attic apartment and the kitchen water tap sprang a leak. The landlord ignored their calls and they couldn't afford a plumber, so Brooke marched down to the nearest hardware store, bought a soldering iron, and figured out how to fix the thing herself. She didn't like not being in control.

"I'd like to see where he's going with this, Brooke. What can it hurt now?"

"I don't like being a puppet in someone else's show."

"Come on, it's not like that. We have our own free will. He's not making you or me do anything. I think he just wants us to get to know one another again. To be friends."

"So you don't mind that he secretly dug into your past?"

"Clients have a right to vet me."

"But this is personal, Cam. He's straying a long way into your personal life here. That's okay with you?"

It isn't, not really. She likes to keep her personal life separate from her work, but she also understands that the act of dying can revolutionize relationships. Those that are distant can magnify into something close, and sometimes close relationships fall apart under the strain. Landon saw an opportunity to hire her as his death doula and at the same time, to mastermind a meeting between her and Brooke. The secretiveness behind his plan isn't cool, but really, can she fault him for trying?

"The thing is, Brooke, dying is personal. So is helping someone die. You can't do that in a place devoid of authenticity and humanity. And yes, it gets emotional sometimes. And personal. And even ugly. I can't say I'm ecstatic about any of this, but I don't believe he's trying to hurt me. Or you. I think that for him, this—us—closes some sort of circle for him."

Brooke stares out at the water, where tiny whitecaps bob on the waves, until another incoming text chimes.

The only thing I want from the two of you is this: to spend ten days on the island. Together. As in doing things together, discovering one another again while you're discovering the island. I want you both to see if anything still exists between the two of you before it's too late. I don't know you very well, Cam, but I know you were Brooke's first and only love. She won't ever love anyone the way she loved you (it's okay, I'm over that now, lol). And Cam, I know you must be lonely inside. You need someone with whom to share that big heart of yours.

I'm going to email you both a list of things I'd like you to do there. Send pictures, say hi when you can and update me. But don't yell at me. I won't read those texts or emails. I have no expectations and neither should you. That's not the point. I simply want you to try one last time. For me. Because I do know this: if I didn't have the love of a good woman, I wouldn't be trying so hard not to leave this world.

Please don't reply yet. Take the day and evening, go over my email later, and think about the possibilities. What's the worst that can happen? You're in a gloriously relaxing, beautiful place. Enjoy it, become friends again. To be honest, I'd like you both to discover more than friendship, but friendship would be marvelous too.

Oh, and if you say no, Tenley's going to cry and I hate it when she cries, because then I cry too and then we're both a blubbering mess. And then Wendy will get upset, and that will break my heart so... Just give this a try, okay? For me? Please?

"Who is Wendy?" Brooke asks.

"His new dog." Cam smiles, relieved that Wendy has wormed her way into their hearts already.

"Well, we can't have the dog upset, now can we?" Brooke's tone is sarcastic, but there's the barest trace of a smile at the corners of her mouth.

"Good point. We don't want to add to their drama. But... I'm not so sure we can actually do this. What he's asking of us." One thing Cam knows for sure is that she won't spend time and energy on this little mission if Brooke isn't going to meet her halfway. She'd rather be alone, thank you very much, than spend ten days—well, nine counting today—with someone who's determined to be uncooperative and unpleasant.

Brooke is gazing at the water again, her expression unreadable. "I don't know either. I'm not even sure I want to try. I mean, what right is it of his to try to force something like this on us? Shouldn't it be our choice?" A blush sweeps up her neck and over the constellation of faint freckles on her cheeks. "I mean, *if* it was something we wanted to do. And I'm not saying it is." She holds up her hand like a stop sign, shakes her head with new determination. "The idea of him or anyone trying to manipulate me into a relationship or even a friendship is absurd. I'm sorry he's dying, I really am. But what he's asking... I think I'd slap his face if he was standing here right now."

Cam winces at the vision. Of course Brooke has no idea of how sick the man is, how weak he is. "He *is* asking a lot. And he has no right to ask it. But...would it be that terrible to hang out for a few days? I guess that's really all he's asking when you get down to it." It isn't, but Cam doesn't want to argue the finer points right now. A friendship with Brooke, maybe. Anything more is inconceivable and unworthy of further discussion or even thinking about. She and Brooke had their chance a long time ago and it ended dismally. There's also the small detail that she's never forgiven Brooke and Brooke has never apologized. A request from a dying man can't paper over that gigantic chasm.

Brooke's voice wavers as she says, "So you're...okay with going along with his idea?"

Cam shrugs. She knows, thanks to her work as a death doula, that she has the ability to shove that old hurt aside for now and get on with what needs to be done. "I suppose it would be okay. Without a tour guide, we'll have to muddle our way around the island."

Brooke gathers up her empty coffee cup and squashes it in her hand. "Thanks for the coffee. I need to think about this for a bit. I'll let you know."

She gets up and begins to walk away, anger heavy in her gait.

"Hey," Cam yells after her. "Don't forget he's going to send us an itinerary at some point."

Brooke throws two exasperated arms into the air before she stomps off again.

God, Cam thinks, *she's still got the best ass.*

CHAPTER EIGHTEEN

No way was Brooke going to hang around the hotel all day, not with Cam's room in such close proximity to hers. Distance and perspective would help her figure out what she should do next. Her life was a snow globe that had been shaken and turned upside down; it was impossible to recognize it anymore. The restaurant was gone, her townhouse was a disaster zone, and now her dying ex-husband thought he could somehow engineer her into a romance with her first love. For someone who prided herself on her ability to shape and control and plan every aspect of her life, it was as though the fickle finger of fate had pressed the nuclear button. With glee.

Brooke nabbed her windbreaker off the hook and jogged down the two flights of stairs, hurrying to avoid Cam. She didn't know who she was angrier at: Landon for trying to manipulate her, Cam for seeming to think Landon's antics were okay or maybe even sacred, or the damned universe for deciding Landon's life was over.

Without a destination in mind, Brooke walked, barely paying attention to her surroundings. Tourists, jubilant after a couple of pandemic summers, strolled past her in happy chatter with ice cream cones dripping down their hands, but she kept her head down in silent rage. The pandemic had nearly wiped out her business and her savings, and the stress had obliterated much of her confidence. Over the past year, she'd built the business back into a reasonably healthy state again, but she couldn't seem to shed the constant state of weariness that left her with an aching back every day, regular headaches, an inability to sleep more than a few hours at a time. Her physical self had remained in a constant state of bracing for life's relentless battering, while her thoughts too often turned pessimistic, her voice too many times shouting the chorus of a victim. She was not okay and she didn't know how to become okay again. Her future was a giant question mark, and she had no idea where to begin. She had to begin somewhere—she knew that much, because nothing stood still, especially not her future.

She couldn't stop thinking about Landon, the fact that there would be no more beginnings in his future. At least she had a future. *Oh, Landon. Why do the good ones always die young?* He'd never asked anything of her. Well, except to try and fall in love with him, as he was with her, but she couldn't. Wanted to, tried for months, but she was only going through the motions, thinking that wanting a thing to succeed was enough to make it happen. Maybe she could have loved him if he'd come first, if that kind of love was the only kind she'd known. But her heart knew the difference. The truth was, the familial love she'd felt for Landon never stood a chance against the passion she'd known with Cam.

By the time she stumbled into the general store, tears blinded her. She didn't need anything in the store, but browsing here seemed like a better idea than trying to walk down the street while crying her eyes out, running into people, tripping over curbs, and having strangers staring at her with concern.

"Oh, dear!" A silver-haired woman with soft blue eyes and who wore an apron that said "O'Doul's General Store" in cheery script, rushed to her side. "Are you all right, love?"

"I…" Brooke's shoulders slumped. A gush of tears burst from her. Unable to speak, she let the kind, older woman guide her toward the back of the store while calling out for someone named Jane.

"I'm Maggie. Maggie O'Doul. My wife Jane is…ah, there you are. Honey, can you woman the store while I make a pot of tea? Here, sit down, you poor thing. No, wait. Jane, show Ms. …" Brooke blubbered her name. "Show Ms. Brooke to the garden and I'll bring the tea."

A few minutes later, Brooke's tears had run dry and she was sitting on a slider adorned with comfy, flower-patterned cushions and had a warm cup of tea in her hands. "I'm sorry. Really, you didn't need to go to any trouble. I'm fine, honest."

"I don't doubt you, love, but there's nothing wrong with taking a load off for a bit. When I'm feeling poorly, sitting out here does something to restore my soul. And you don't have to say a word. Just sit and enjoy the peacefulness if that's what you need."

Brooke sipped her tea, touched by this stranger's empathy and generosity and ashamed that she didn't share that same generous spirit. Or did she? And if she didn't, why didn't she? She could see now how she'd made a life pattern of surrounding herself with people who were empaths. Cam was one, so was Landon. Even Marcy, kooky and opinionated as she was, had chosen a life of helping others. Had she learned anything from them?

"I think," she said in a voice she hardly recognized, "that I… that I…want to finally be the person I was meant to be."

If Maggie was surprised or confounded, she didn't show it. "All right. In that case, I have two questions for you: why now and what's stopping you?"

Astonishing herself, Brooke spoke before she had time to reconsider or self-edit. "My ex-husband is dying and my ex-ex has unexpectedly popped back into my life and I sold my business and I don't really have anywhere to go right now."

"Oh, Mother of Mary, that's a lot all at once. And the answer to my second question?"

"That's easy. I don't know how to change. I don't know where to start."

No judgment from Maggie, just a long moment of pondering before she spoke. "Well, if you want to change, I mean, I'm no expert, but I think the best way is to trust others. Trust that the people you're with are safe for you to invest your emotions. Trust that they will care for you and encourage you no matter what. And most of all, be authentic and honest."

"But that can get you hurt."

"Yes. But you have to be strong enough to take that chance with people."

Being strong wasn't a problem. And honesty didn't scare her, but trust did. Trust was a gamble that could go badly. "I don't think I know how or where to start."

"You already did. By taking a chance to sit and have tea and open up to a stranger." Maggie's blue eyes twinkled. "Do you feel better, dear?"

By God if she didn't. But she wasn't naïve enough to believe that sharing tea with a stranger would open up a whole new world to her. Maggie didn't possess all the secrets of living a happy life. No one did. But maybe this could be a miniscule start. "I do, Maggie. Thank you for this."

"You're welcome. And I'm sorry about your ex-husband. Are you close?"

"Yes and no. We haven't seen each other in a long time, but we've stayed in touch. He's a nice man, Maggie. He doesn't deserve this."

"No, I don't imagine he does. Maybe for his sake, you can start making those changes in your life so that something good can come from his passing. When it comes down to it, the ways we impact other peoples' lives is ultimately what matters most. That's what my mam back in Ireland taught me, that it's the little things. And I believe it more and more, the older I get."

"But don't you ever get...angry? Bitter? Pissed off? Let down?"

Maggie laughed. "Of course, I do. And when I feel like that, I make myself stop it by holding the things I love even closer.

My wife, my books, the food I love to cook, this store, the island and its people. They're all gifts. You just have to accept them. And then appreciate them."

Brooke had never been good at accepting things, gifts or otherwise. "I'm not sure it's that easy."

Maggie waved her hand in front of her face. "You're right about that, dear. Nothing is easy, not now. But at other times it wasn't, either. Look at wars. People survive horrible things, Brooke. And they do it by relying on each other. People save people."

Brooke thought for a minute. Maybe the older woman was right, but it felt like only part of the picture had been revealed. How exactly did people come to rely on each other in tough times? What did she mean by people saving people? How did that work exactly? Because she didn't have it in her to save anybody, of that she was sure. Oh well, the missing pieces, she'd have to figure out herself. She set her empty cup down and stood. "Thank you so much, Maggie. Your kindness has really helped. And you've given me a lot to think about."

"I'm so glad." Maggie took her elbow and escorted her to the gate that opened onto an alley at the back of the property. "Start small, my child. Don't try to change too much too soon, okay? Rome wasn't built in a day."

Brooke smiled. "You're a real treasure, you know that?"

"As long as my wife thinks so, I'm good."

Walking back to her hotel, Maggie's words repeated in Brooke's head: *People save people.* And she made a decision. If Maggie was right and people were the key to everything that mattered, then she'd start small, like Maggie said. She'd start with one: Landon. She couldn't save him, obviously, but if Landon wanted her to hang out here for ten days, then fine, she'd do it. She'd do almost anything for Landon, except fall in love again with Cam. That was *never* going to happen.

CHAPTER NINETEEN

"All right, I'll do it."

At the sound of Brooke's voice, Cam looks up from the novel she's reading, her legs tucked under her on a rattan love seat positioned in a quiet corner of the hotel's front veranda. She can't keep the twitch of a grin from her mouth as she takes in Brooke's pose: hands on her hips, mouth tight, dark sunglasses that try but fail to look menacing (they make her look more like a big bug, truth be told). She wants to tell Brooke to chill, to stop being so serious all the time, to take things in stride, the way life is meant to be. But she's not so stupid as to offer her head up on a platter. "All of it?"

"What do you mean, all of it? I've thought about it, and spending a few days on the island isn't exactly a hardship. So... I'll do it. As long as..."

Cam produces her most innocent, wide-eyed look. It's fun seeing Brooke all worked up. "Yes?"

"As long as Landon doesn't expect something ridiculous, like you and me getting back together again."

"Ridiculous?" *Ooh, this is fun!*

Brooke avoids Cam's eyes, but her sigh is as loud as a gust of wind. It's as much of an apology as Cam can expect. "You know what I mean."

"I think he just wants us to be friends, Brooke. For his sake. Are you sure you can do that?"

"I guess. I mean, if you can. Eight-and-a-half more days, right?"

Jeez, what does she want, a notarized document spelling out every eventuality as well as the end date? Cam understands that Landon expects a reconnection between the two of them to last more than the duration of their stay on the island. It should be obvious to Brooke that he wants to leave this world knowing that his ex-wife is happy again with someone she should never have walked out on. But Landon, she reminds herself, doesn't know all the sordid details. Or if he does, he's only heard Brooke's side. What he doesn't understand is how much effort it's going to take Cam to be okay with his little pipe dream. She'll do it for him, or at least try, but the unpleasant reality is that for this to work she will need to forgive Brooke and Brooke will need to be honest, because, dammit, they're going to have to see if there are any pieces left and if their hearts are strong enough to examine the wreckage of their relationship. And that's just for a friendship. She is skeptical that Brooke is up to such a monumentally emotional task. For that matter, Cam isn't sure she's up to it either. She looks skyward. *This is not a small thing you're asking, Landon.*

"To be precise, yes. Eight-and-a-half more days," Cam repeats. "But I think we need some ground rules."

"Great idea. Absolutely. Like no holding hands or kissing or anything that couples would do."

"Who said anything about that stuff?"

"Fine. Good." Uninvited, Brooke sits down beside Cam, causing Cam to shift her legs to create more space. "As long as nobody gets the wrong idea about any of this."

"Fine. Good." If Brooke keeps acting like she hates her, there'll be no risk of getting the wrong idea. "So how about we be civil toward one another. You know, polite? Respectful?"

Brooke pushes her sunglasses onto her head, revealing red eyes and cheeks moist from crying. Cam resists the urge to ask if she's okay.

"All right," Brooke says. "Is that Rule Number One?"

"Yes."

"Fine. And the second rule should be that neither of us has to do anything we don't want to do."

"Okay. What else?"

"That we're not spending all our time together. I need my own time too."

"Fine. So do I." *Well, that's a relief.* Brooke's company so far isn't exactly irresistible. Cam feels her phone vibrate in her back pocket with a notification. It's an email from Landon, his itinerary for them. She glances at it quickly, sees that Brooke has been copied on it. "I think you better check your email."

Brooke pulls out her phone and silently reads the identical email, her face a parade of comical expressions. "Holy shit. Dancing under the stars? Horse and buggy rides for two? Jesus, Cam. Has the cancer gone to his brain?"

"Brooke!"

"Sorry. It's…a lot to take in. A lot for him to ask, I mean."

Cam has had it with Brooke's negativity. Not because Brooke isn't right to feel outrage at Landon's manipulation, but because her black mood is starting to rub off. "It is a lot. And in case you've forgotten, I'm the one who should be waving the white flag here. If anyone's unhappy about this little social experiment, it should be me."

Brooke pinches her eyes shut as though she's tolerating something painful. "Fine. I get it. And I don't want to talk about any of that right now."

If Brooke thinks she can continue to evade that little ripper of a conversation, she's got another think coming. But okay. It doesn't have to happen today.

Brooke stands up, in a hurry suddenly. "So, he wants us to do a fancy dinner tonight at the Grand Hotel. I'd better see what I have to wear. Meet you there?"

"It's only a ten-minute walk from here," Cam says with fake cheerfulness. "We might as well walk there together, don't you think?"

Brooke crinkles her nose like an unpleasant smell has wafted her way. "All right, I suppose we might as well. Meet you in the lobby at seven?"

"Or you could just knock on my door when you're ready to leave."

"Do you always have to be so…so…"

"What?"

"Annoyingly cooperative?"

Cam smiles. *Oh, the next eight-and-a-half days are going to be memorable.*

CHAPTER TWENTY

Brooke had packed only two dresses for the trip, and for dinner at The Grand Hotel, she chose the sexiest one because, well, it was The Grand and because part of her wanted to show Cam that she still could look good in a dress. Being in your late forties didn't have to mean Frump City, and there was definitely nothing frumpy about the green strapless dress that almost made her gray eyes look green or the vintage lacy white shawl across her shoulders that, without being too obvious, drew just enough attention to her cleavage. Her hair she'd coiffed and teased a little, and she wore only the amount of makeup she needed to accentuate her eyes and mouth. Classic with a side plate of sexy was the look she was going for. *I can be forty-eight years old, single and jobless, and still look hot, dammit.*

When Cam answered her door, Brooke did a mental *whoa* that might have been auditory. She was too busy listening to her own pounding heart to be sure. Dammit, if Cam didn't look her own brand of fantastic in black slacks and low-slung heels, a cream-colored tailored jacket that broadened her strong shoulders over a blindingly white collarless shirt unbuttoned part way down her chest. The passage of time had not diminished Cam's hotness one bit. *Unfortunately.*

"You look…" Cam's eyes skittered over Brooke, as if to blunt her reaction, but her nostrils had flared at the sight before her. "Really nice."

"Thanks. So do you."

"Thank you. Shopping excursion today, since I thought I was only going to be here a few days. Shall we?"

The walk was filled with small talk and by the time they reached the steps leading up to The Grand's portico and main doors, Brooke felt Cam's hand drift to the small of her back. But only until they got through the doors, then the hand fell away. As the hostess seated them, Brooke noticed heads turning in their direction and wondered if Cam was aware of it too. They always did make a spectacular-looking couple. Not that it mattered since they weren't a couple, hadn't been in a very long time, and never would be again. But the fantasy was a momentary and pleasant diversion, the overlapping of a memory onto the present.

"Excuse me," Cam said to the hostess, holding out her phone, "Do you mind taking a picture of us?"

Brooke was about to protest before she realized it was part of their agreement with Landon to text him the occasional photo as some sort of proof or something. Proof that they hadn't killed each other, she supposed. *Yet.*

"Of course," the hostess replied, smiling a row of gleaming teeth that reminded Brooke of toothpaste commercials from her childhood. "Why don't you two move closer?"

Chairs annoyingly scraping the floor, Brooke and Cam moved closer for the photo and pasted on smiles that probably wouldn't fool Landon, but so be it. He wanted them to spend time together, and that's what they were doing. Anything else was not his purview. Photo snapped, Brooke hustled her chair back to its spot. Menus were placed before them, and Brooke studied hers as though an exam would follow. Menus from other restaurants always fascinated her. She kept a small collection of them in a shoebox in her closet back home.

"Wow, the prices!" If they were going to charge fifty dollars for a steak, it had better be the best steak in the Midwest, she thought. Otherwise it was pretentious, and people would see through it and not return. *Okay, stop. You're not a restaurateur anymore. You're here to enjoy a meal. And...okay, so they're charging extra for the unique ambience of the place.*

"I know, but Landon's picking up the bill and he wants us to have a good time."

A server in black tie and crisp tuxedo shirt materialized, cradling a bottle of Dom Perignon and two flutes.

"Oh!" Cam said. "I'm afraid we didn't order this."

If an eyeroll could be transformed into a thin smile, the waiter had the trick down pat. "I'm afraid it's part of your tab. From your friend, Mr. Ross."

After the bottle was opened and champagne poured, Brooke took a quick sip and set down her glass. "It feels wrong."

"What? Being out for dinner together?"

Awkward yes, wrong no. "No, the Dom. It should be for celebrating something, and I don't feel much like celebrating."

"Do you want to talk about Landon?"

"Nope." What the hell, the Dom was open and it'd be a damned shame to waste it. Brooke took a long, pleasurable sip. "Wow, this is good."

Cam took her own sip, then another. Brooke liked the new gleam in Cam's eyes that came courtesy of the wine. She always did have the most adorable wide-set eyes that managed to look innocent, even when they weren't. And those dimples in each cheek only added to her allure. Cam had to know the power her looks gave her, but she had the unique talent of appearing unaware of it. Even when women used to chase her backstage, it always seemed to take Cam by surprise. Brooke assumed a parade of women had continued to chase her through the years. Like, why wouldn't they? And had she finally learned to give in?

Brooke squared her shoulders before diving in. "You...must date a lot?"

Cam looked at her like she'd grown a second head. "Why would you think that?"

Because you're still too damned gorgeous for your own good, Brooke wanted to say, but didn't have the guts. She shrugged instead, cleared her throat to dislodge any emotion. "You're a nice-looking woman, that's all. You've aged well. You would be, you know, good dating material." Okay, so the wine was loosening her lips.

Cam's face softened at the compliment. "Thanks, but…no. I don't really date. Not in many years."

"Why not?" The question flew out of her mouth before Brooke could catch herself. She took another sip of bubbly. They had an entire bottle to kill, after all.

"Honestly?" Cam's eyes studied her.

"Honestly."

"Because I hate the whole getting-to-know-a-stranger thing and suffering through the dating dance. I guess if I could fast-forward myself into a healthy, loving relationship with someone, maybe I'd do it. But being alone isn't so bad. Let's say I've grown accustomed and prefer it that way."

Suffering through the dating dance. Brooke wondered if Cam had dated anyone during the last decade and a half. She hoped Cam had. For Brooke, the thought that she might have ruined her for anyone else wasn't something she wanted to think too hard on. It was certainly something she'd never intended. Actually, she'd never given it a thought until now. *Huh.*

"I think," Cam whispered, "we're getting the hairy eyeball from our waiter. We should probably figure out what we want."

Brooke picked up the menu and quickly perused it. "Easy. I'll have the pistachio-stuffed chicken."

"And I think I'll have the salmon," Cam said.

Food ordered and delivered, Brooke and Cam made their way through the bottle of Dom as they ate, making small talk about the island. More substantial topics would take some careful navigating.

"After-dinner drink?" the waiter asked. "We have some of the finest scotches, bourbons, and brandy from around the world."

Brooke wasn't going to, initially. The champagne was already making her warm and tingly all over, slightly tipsy. Ah...why the hell not? She wasn't driving (there was nothing to drive here anyway except horses and bicycles), and had no other responsibilities tonight. Plus, Cam would never try to take advantage of her. She was safe with Cam. "All right. How about a mint julep?"

"Of course," the waiter replied and swung his gaze to Cam. "And you, ma'am?"

"I'll take the same, please."

"Absolutely. It's a lovely evening. You ladies are welcome to take your drinks outside on the veranda. Unless you want dessert first?"

Both Cam and Brooke shook their heads. Their dinners had been delicious and there was no room for anything else.

"Shall we?" Cam said after their drinks were delivered. She took Brooke's elbow as they strolled out to the massive porch with the oversized flags snapping in the breeze. It wasn't horrible, Cam's touch, which could have been viewed as possessive or old school, Brooke supposed, but she liked it. She hadn't been out with a gentlewoman, or gentleman, who treated her with such respectful attention in a very long time. So long, she couldn't even remember when. Landon was probably the last.

"I'm not tipsy, don't worry," Brooke said, instantly regretting her words when Cam removed her hand.

"I know. Old habit, I guess."

And not a terrible one, Brooke thought. They sat in rattan rockers and set their drinks on the café table between them. Lights twinkled around the perimeter of the pool on the expanse of lawn below them. Potted geraniums were everywhere, and roses of peach and crimson climbed trellises. Beyond the grounds was the lake, pitched black now. Brooke could imagine sitting out here for hours watching the lake, watching people stroll by, just as thousands of people on this very porch had done for over a century. She closed her eyes for a moment, the alcohol making her sleepy.

"This is nice," Cam said on a sigh, sipping her julep. "I could get used to this, I think."

"Did I ruin you?" Brooke blurted out. So much for careful navigating. "For anyone else, I mean?" Oh God, it was the alcohol talking, but the question burned. Nothing at the moment was as important as the answer.

Cam took her time answering. "No one has that kind of power over me. Not even you, Brooke."

"So don't flatter myself, right?" Okay, Cam's words hurt. And she deserved it. But she also didn't believe Cam.

"Right."

Brooke cradled her drink in her hands, pleased by the combination of smoke and sweet with the bourbon and the fresh mint. All this time, she'd never apologized to Cam. Not for the breakdown of their relationship, which they'd both contributed to, but for the shitty way in which she'd broken up with Cam. She couldn't explain then—or now—why she'd wanted to hurt Cam so badly. It might have been jealousy. Cam's career path had been steadily trending up at that point, all her hard work and sacrifices, sacrifices they'd both made, beginning to pay off, while Brooke's career hadn't even gotten off the ground. Plain and simple, she felt left out. It was all about Cam and Cam's music, and Brooke had grown weary, impatient. And, okay, jealousy couldn't be overlooked either. She'd been resentful enough, selfish enough, to inflict grievous emotional injury on Cam. It was not something she was proud of, not then and not now, but her pride had never let her apologize. All that water under the bridge. Really, what was the point in apologies now?

"Cam, just so you know, I'm not ready to—"

"Earlier today," Cam interrupted, her expression thoughtful. "You looked like you'd been crying. Why?"

Nice evasion tactic, Cam. Well. Two could play that game. "I don't have to answer that..."

And just like that, the walls she'd erected around her emotions came tumbling down, like a tent folding in on itself, collapsing, cutting her down in two seconds flat. A sob rose in her throat, snuffing out any more conversation. Her hands flew first to her throat, then to her eyes. She couldn't catch the tears fast enough. She cried for having broken Cam's heart and she cried for her own broken heart and she cried for Landon, who'd they'd soon lose. The landscape of her life looked awfully barren at the moment. A wasteland.

Wordlessly, Cam reached over, took her hand in hers, and set their joined hands on her own thigh. She squeezed Brooke's hand lightly—a kind gesture Brooke didn't want to read too much into. She was grateful Cam didn't pressure her to talk.

"You're good at this," Brooke said, her throat dry as a desert and her tears finally exhausted. It was the only thing she could think to say to show her gratitude.

"What?"

"Listening. Consoling."

"It's what I do."

True, and it shouldn't be a shock, seeing her this way. Cam always had a knack for finding and helping people who couldn't help themselves. People who were lost. People who needed a north star, a guiding light. As a performer, Cam shone brightly and boldly on stage. She could whip up a crowd with her smile, her sexy dance moves, her honeyed voice. She was more luminescent than any star in the sky, but that's not what this was. This was a different kind of light. This light was strong but tranquil and gentle. This star was not showy, not garish. It was the opposite of all that, the antithesis of ego, and it took Brooke's breath away.

Brooke cleared the last of her tears from her throat. "Cam?"

"Yes?"

"I don't want Landon to die. He's a good guy."

"I know." Cam sipped her drink, her eyes firmly riveted on the blackness of the horizon when she said, "Did you love him?"

"Yes." That part was easy. "But not enough."

Cam nodded.

CHAPTER TWENTY-ONE

"You want us to ride this thing? Together?" The look on Brooke's face runs the gamut from astonishment to annoyance to doubt as she gapes at the tandem bicycle Cam has just rented for them.

Is it bad that I kinda like seeing her uncomfortable? Cam smothers a chuckle behind her hand. "Not my idea, remember?"

"If Landon wasn't dying, I'd kill him."

"That's the second time you've said that in as many days."

Brooke's jaw drops in a look of horror. "I didn't mean it, I swear!"

"I know. It's okay. Even dying people like a good joke, you know."

"Huh. Really?"

"Really."

It's obvious Brooke hasn't yet come to terms with Landon's news, but of course she's only known for such a short time. The shock probably hasn't worn off yet, though it's impossible to understand Brooke's feelings without knowing more about her relationship with Landon. Cam's curiosity about their marriage is more than clinical—she can't stop wondering how deep Brooke's feelings run for her ex-husband. It's clear she's fond of him, but her admission last night that she hadn't loved him "enough" hinted at the source of their marital discord. She hadn't loved him enough to stay married? If that was the case, why did she marry him at all? And who made the move to end it?

The questions in her head lead her straight down the path of recalling Landon's words in his email to her and Brooke. He'd said Cam was the only person Brooke had ever really loved. How the hell did he figure that out? Did Brooke *say* that or was he intuiting it? Either way, it made no sense, because if Brooke really had loved her, she wouldn't have betrayed her in the devastating way she had. No. Brooke was the one who'd made sure they were unequivocally done.

"All right, you take the front," Brooke orders. "If I recall from the one time Marcy and I tried a tandem bike as teenagers, the heavier person sits on the front part."

"You're calling me fat?" Cam mumbles. It's tempting to push Brooke's buttons, and Cam is definitely in the mood to push. All those nights she used to lie awake, thinking up hurtful and spiteful things to say and do to Brooke if she ever saw her again. The anger, red-hot, led her down self-destructive paths that only time and a career change would eventually diminish. She still has half a mind to retaliate in some way, to see Brooke suffer. The old grievances are advancing again, alluring in their dark, poisonous way. But Cam doesn't want to sink into the useless emotions of misery and blame. She cusses under her breath.

"Did you say something?" Brooke hikes up her sunglasses and rakes her eyes over Cam. Her gaze tries so hard to be detached, but Cam can see the curiosity there, the stamp of memories slowly surfacing. They're both thinking of those years, whether the memories are welcome or not.

Can't you apologize, Brooke? Can't you say you're sorry just once?
"Nope, didn't say a thing."

Brooke shrugs, pulls a map of the island from the back pocket of her Capris. "Let's do the circumference of the island. That way we won't have to kill ourselves pedaling up those treacherous hills on this thing."

"They do have a medical clinic here, you know."

"Uh-huh. And there's probably a cool ice bar in Siberia, but it doesn't mean I want to have a drink there."

Cam climbs on the front of the bike. "Come on, Daddy Long Legs. Let's see what you got."

"Daddy Long Legs!" Brooke is all pretend outrage at the old nickname Cam has dredged up, from back in college when Brooke used to run long distance track. Her legs were so long and skinny, that Cam, when she wasn't calling her Bette, would call her Daddy Long Legs. "You better worry about keeping up, Shorty."

They set off, more than a little wobbly at first, as Cam sings out, "Sticks and stones, sticks and stones, na na nanana." She's not short. Sheesh, Brooke's only a couple of inches taller.

"Yeah, yeah, I know. Nothing bothers you. Water off a duck's back, huh?"

If only you knew, Cam thinks. Holding grudges is all about ego. Ego and misplaced pride. No, she decides, she will not go down that rabbit hole. Not because she doesn't want to hold Brooke accountable for the past, but because of the simple fact that it won't change a thing.

They pedal in a gawky fashion that eventually levels out, though Brooke keeps trying to steer from the back. Her handlebars are fixed, welded right behind Cam's seat. Only Cam can steer, and the periodic jerking of the handlebars behind her confirm that it's driving Brooke nuts that Cam is at the controls.

Cam calls out behind her shoulder with a grin Brooke can't see, "Okay back there?"

"Of course. But I think we need to stop up ahead at that lookout spot so we can appreciate the bridge."

"Ah, the bridge. We wouldn't want to miss that!" Like, how could they miss the longest suspension bridge in the Western hemisphere looming ahead at more than 26,000 feet in length.

It's impossible to miss from pretty much anywhere on the island. Ah, now she gets it. It's Brooke's way of asking for a rest. Brooke may be skinnier and have been a long-distance runner in her youth, but she's not nearly as fit as Cam if she needs a break already.

They let the bike coast to a stop but neither gets off. Cam takes a drink from her bottle of water, passes it back to Brooke.

"Thanks. Sorry, I forgot to pack one. But I did pack some apples and cheese for later."

"Forgiven."

"Whew! Wouldn't want you to leave me here and ride off."

It would serve you right, Cam thought. "You're only a couple miles from the hotel. The walk wouldn't kill you. Didn't you used to run track in your youth?"

Brooke smacks Cam's shoulder. "A hundred years ago."

"Rested now, old fart?"

"I'm not resting. I figured this might be a good spot for a selfie for Landon. You know, with the bridge behind us."

Cam climbs off the bike. "Good recovery."

Brooke smiles dumbly and takes out her phone, while Cam steps behind her to pose. She snaps a photo, careful to capture the bridge in the distance. "There. Perfect." She swipes her phone and presses a couple of buttons. "On its way to Landon as we speak."

They climb back on the bike and continue along the paved path, which hugs the shoreline. It's quiet this far from the hotels and restaurants, and they come across only an occasional cyclist or jogger. When they reach the north part of the island about twenty minutes later, Cam feels Brooke trying to steer again.

"Need another break?" she teases Brooke.

"Lunch, silly."

The vision of food in her head prompts a deep belly growl. "I could handle that."

They stop and dismount from the bike. From her small knapsack, Brooke retrieves a beach towel, three kinds of cheese and two apples that have already been sliced. "Oh, wait, there's some summer sausage too!" She roots around in her pack for it, and to Cam it's nothing short of a feast. They find a spot on the beach called British Landing, which, to no surprise, features an old cannon and some historical plaques. Brooke lays the towel down with a flourish and bids her to sit.

As they munch on their food, Cam reads out loud from the pamphlet she stuffed in her shorts pocket that explains the historical significance of the spot. It was the place where, in July of 1812, a British invasion force of several hundred landed and ultimately took the island without much of a fight because the Americans didn't realize a war had started. "Imagine that," she says. "A war was declared a month earlier and they had no way of finding out until the enemy landed at their door. Ha, in today's world we would know within minutes."

"I miss the water," Brooke says suddenly, hiking up her sunglasses. Her eyes are an alluring shade of blue-gray, a reflection off the water.

"You live in Ann Arbor?"

"That's right." For Brooke, Lake Erie is at least an hour's drive, and Lake Michigan about three times that. "You're lucky, living in Traverse City and being so close to all…this."

Cam stares out at the horizon, the sky a couple of shades lighter than the dark blue of the water. A few clouds scud by and there is only the sound of a seagull screeching as it dive-bombs toward the water in search of lunch. "I am. Being close to water keeps me grounded, you know? It serves as a reminder that we're all just passing through. That none of us has been around as long as that water. We're borrowing Mother Nature's gifts."

"You've changed," Brooke says simply.

"Yes." Would she have changed if Brooke hadn't dumped her? Would she still be grinding out a career in music? Perhaps not performing as much anymore, her body wouldn't be able to take it, but there's a decent career to be had in songwriting, session work, producing. But when Cam walked away, she walked away from all of it.

"You really enjoy your work, don't you?"

"I do, weird as that may sound."

"Well, it does sound weird, being a death doula. But somehow you make it…not so weird and scary."

"Thanks, I think. What about you? Owning your own restaurant is no small accomplishment."

"You can say that again." Brooke's voice is reflective, but sad too, as she admits, "I put my heart and soul into that place. I loved it, though. The adrenaline rush, the sense of accomplishment at seeing others enjoy the thing you put your whole self into, you know? It was—is pretty cool."

Cam nods, flashes Brooke a knowing smile. "I get it. I was a musician, remember?"

"Right. Not like I'd ever forget that. Or that voice of yours."

Two compliments in the last couple of minutes. She wants to tease Brooke, saying something to the effect that her shower of compliments is giving her a big head, but she doesn't. "Thanks, Brooke. Hey…is everything ok?" Something about the way she talks about her restaurant isn't sitting right, plus all her hints about having nowhere else to go. Something is clearly wrong in Brooke's world, and while Cam really, *really* wants to know the details, she will be patient. "You kind of were using the past tense talking about the restaurant."

"Oh, right, sorry. I guess it's the sun getting to me. Or maybe this grueling bike ride."

Cam laughs at the word *grueling*, but she's covering for Brooke, who seems to be papering over something that makes her sad. Something other than Landon's news, but Cam isn't ready to push into any more serious personal territory. Not yet, and she expects Brooke feels the same. "Hey, remember that time we went tubing on Lake Michigan?"

"Oh God, how could I forget? And you're still in the doghouse over it."

A friend with a powerboat had taken them tubing one summer. Brooke had been reluctant to try a tube ride until Cam promised her it would be gentle. Once they got going in gentle, lazy circles, Cam, who was spotting, urged the driver to go faster. "I thought Brooke wanted a gentle ride," their friend at the wheel said. "No, she wants a faster ride now," Cam insisted, mischief behind her actions. They only stopped after Brooke flew off the tube from the vigorous cross-cutting over waves and the boat's wake.

"You said it'd given you an enema that would last a decade."

"Believe me, that's not something I'll forget."

"Well, did it?"

"Did it what?"

"Last a decade?"

Brooke smacks Cam lightly on the arm. She's been doing that a lot lately, smacking her in an affectionate, familial way. But there's no mistaking the little gestures or the strolls down memory lane for anything meaningful or romantic. This reconnecting is nothing like that. They're simply taking the first tentative steps toward becoming friends again, and Cam is okay with the idea...or at least, she will be. Being with Brooke was always comfortable. And fun. She can feel them sliding back to that place where it was easy to be around one another. Yes, Cam decides, she can do this for the next eight days. She pictures cutting out the rotten bit of an apple and throwing it away, imagining Brooke's long-ago betrayal as that discarded piece.

"You know," Brooke says as she begins packing up the remnants of their lunch. "This—hanging out with you—isn't as bad as I thought it'd be."

"Wow, yet another compliment. Sort of. Careful or you'll end up taking Landon at his word and fall in love with me all over again."

Brooke laughs before her smile dissolves into a frown. Maybe she's remembering that she's not supposed to be enjoying any of this. She fastens her knapsack, slides it onto her back, and heads toward their bike.

Cam mentally rebukes herself until Brooke yells out, "You coming, oh Humble One?"

"Yup. Just packing up my humility in case I need it again."

"Hmm." Brooke pretends to examine the frame of the bike. "Think this thing is strong enough to support the extra weight from that big head of yours?"

Cam climbs onto the front of the bike. "Smart-ass."

CHAPTER TWENTY-TWO

Finally they were on their last mile of the bike ride, much to Brooke's relief. Her ass hurt from the seat that felt like concrete, and her legs were as heavy as if they'd cycled a bloody marathon. Who knew that cycling eight miles would be such a hardship. Perhaps joining a gym was called for. She could no longer use the excuse that she didn't have the time. In the seat ahead of her, Cam, as usual, seemed no worse for the wear, hardly even breaking a sweat for the last two-plus hours. The woman had a knack for landing on her feet, for grinding through the unbearable without scars. *Lucky her.*

"Oh, look!" Brooke yelled. "To the right! It's Arch Rock. Isn't that cool?" The big limestone arch loomed four stories high on the cliff above the water, a natural rock formation that almost resembled a giant donut. It played a feature role in all the pamphlets about the island.

"What? Where?"

Brooke hauled on her useless handlebars to turn the bike so that Cam could see the rock. The bike bucked and wobbled in response and began to tilt. "Oh, crap!"

The tilt turned into a full-out topple. Both women tumbled to the ground, the bike landing on top of them. Cam was the first to get to her feet and pull the bike away.

"Jesus, are you all right, Brooke?"

It took a minute for Brooke to notice her skinned, bleeding knee. Tiny pebbles adhered to the raw flesh. "I think so. Though my knee isn't looking so pretty."

"Let me see." Cam took her elbow and helped her up. "Can you move it okay?"

Brooke gingerly bent her knee. "Yup, it seems okay. Stings though."

Cam gently placed her fingers on either side of the abrasion, her touch cool and soothing. "We need to clean this up. You don't want an infection getting in there."

"Yes, Doctor, but I'm sure it will be fine." Brooke smiled at Cam's concern. Concern that she didn't deserve since she was the one who'd crashed the bike, but she'd gladly take it. "How's the bike?"

Cam stood it up and gave it a quick once over. "It seems to have fared better than you. Do you want to walk the last half a mile, or are you okay to ride?"

"I can ride." *I hope.*

"Hop on. I'll do the pedaling."

Like hell, Brooke thought. She did her best, but if there was such a thing as limping while pedaling, she had it down pat, leaving her little choice but to let Cam do the bulk of the work. Minutes later, they pulled up in front of the general store.

"Hi, Cam! Hi, Brooke!" Maggie said. "What are you two—oh." She frowned at the sight of Brooke's knee. "What happened?"

"We, um, sort of crashed and burned," Brooke said.

"Yup, that's us," Cam grumbled. "We seem to be experts at crashing and burning."

"Wait." Maggie's grin nearly ate up her face. "And here you each told me you were on the island alone. Had a fight and needed some space before getting back together, huh? Ah, I can understand that." She shook her head, but the smile hadn't left her face. "A long time ago, I was in a snit and went back home for a couple months. To Dublin, and yes to feel sorry for myself, but my heart grew tired of letting my ego and my pride run the show, so I came back with my tail between my legs."

Brooke worked her jaw, but nothing would come out.

"It's... We're..." Cam looked from Brooke to Maggie, a flash of uncharacteristic panic in her eyes. "Not like that. We're each here alone. We're just...hanging out. Sometimes."

"Ah, relationships," Maggie said with a subtle roll of her eyes. "Sometimes it's hard to tell if things are on or off. You'll get past that part and sort it out. Now, let's get you cleaned up, young lady."

Brooke's stomach dropped. Oh God, she'd put two-and-two together and figured out Cam was the "ex" Brooke spoke to her about earlier. She should set Maggie straight on the fact that yes, Cam was her ex, and no, they weren't back together, but Maggie's attention was on her knee as she carefully wiped it with soap and water before applying some antiseptic. She hustled away to find a bandage.

Cam whispered, "I didn't know you met Maggie already."

"And her wife, Jane. They're lovely. When did you meet them?"

"A couple hours after I got off the boat. Wow, it's like this place is the center of this little universe."

"I don't think I've ever been in a store so genuinely charming." Brooke lowered her voice. "She assumes we're a couple."

Cam shrugged a what-can-you-do before Maggie returned, holding up a bandage. "We'll get you good as new again, Ms. Brooke."

"You're too kind," Brooke replied. "Patching up clumsy cyclists is above and beyond the call, Maggie, but I appreciate it."

"Ah, it's nothing. Happy to help, that's all. Did the cycling help take your mind off ...things?"

"Things?" Brooke repeated.

"You know." Maggie gave her a quizzical look. "What you told me about. What you're struggling with."

Feeling her eyes grow wide, Brooke glanced from Cam to Maggie. It'd been so easy to confide in a stranger, but maybe it hadn't been such a good idea. "Um, yes, all good," she said quickly, which only seemed to add to Maggie's confusion. "I really appreciate this, Maggie. Give my best to Jane, too. Sorry to run, but we better get the bike back to the rental place."

She had to practically drag Cam out of the store.

"Don't worry," Cam said. "I won't ask what that was all about. Actually, I lie. I will ask you, but how about over a drink?"

"Will it help my knee heal faster?"

"No, but it might help you forget that your knee hurts. Isn't that almost the same thing?"

"Oh, right, yes. I do believe a drink might be exactly what the doctor ordered." A drink with Cam... Wait, that wasn't even on Landon's to-do list. "On the other hand, maybe we..."

But Cam was already on her way across the street to hand the bike over to the rental guy. When she jogged back, she hooked her arm through Brooke's and flagged down a horse-drawn taxi. "I know just the place for that drink."

"You're being too nice to me," Brooke countered, but she was no longer protesting the drink.

"Probably, but you'll get over it."

CHAPTER TWENTY-THREE

The Jockey Club sits across from the Grand Hotel and on the doorstep of the first tee of the hotel's nine-hole golf course. Cam helps Brooke hobble to a table for two on the patio; if conversation stalls, at least they can watch the golfers or the horses, buggies, and cyclists meandering up the hill to the Grand.

They settle into their seats and each order a glass of sparkling wine along with a simple cheese platter.

"I may get fat over this trip, so be warned," Brooke jokes. "Might need to look for some stretchy pants while I'm here."

"So noted, although I think you will be absolutely fine. Say, how does a restaurateur stay so thin? Aren't you tempted to constantly graze at your restaurant?"

"Nope. Well, within reason. If I ate everything in sight, it would affect my bottom line. And my bottom, if you get my drift."

Oh, she gets the drift, all right. Brooke has been blessed with a nice bottom. A nice everything, when it comes to looks.

Pretty isn't the word to describe her because pretty suggests a certain banality, and there's nothing run-of-the-mill about Brooke. Never was.

Cam's gaze drops to Brooke's left hand, ringless where Landon's wedding ring had once been and long after Cam had entertained the idea of placing a ring there herself. She once longed for tangible evidence of their connection for everyone to see. She'd even imagined the perfect proposal spot (a private beach at sunset), had begun saving for a nice ring because a proposal only happened once, and it had to happen right. She would get down on one knee, tell Brooke she was the love of her life and that she couldn't imagine spending the rest of her life without her biggest inspiration, her biggest support, her one love. She'd memorized the script, had written a song around it that she planned to sing to Brooke, a cappella. It was all for nothing.

Cam hadn't known a thing back then about marriage or even how to make a relationship last beyond a few years. The whole proposal idea had been a child's fantasy. When their relationship ended, it was almost as though Brooke had retained the end of some vital thread between them, a thread that stretched and untangled slowly through the years until it finally ran out. There had been no way, until now, to wind herself back to Brooke. Somehow, miraculously, they've managed to reach back through time, through the darkness, and find each other again. But why? What are they meant to do with this? What *should* they do? There are no answers, not while the sting of Brooke's betrayal all those years ago remains imprinted in her DNA, the way a body manufactures antibodies in response to an invading virus. Antibodies that have stayed with her and are ready to fight Brooke off again, because, dammit, she can't go through the same kind of hurt Brooke inflicted on her all those years ago. She almost hadn't survived it.

"Sorry, what?" Cam hasn't been listening.

"I said I think the wine is helping my knee. Or at least helping me not to think about my knee, so you were right. Thank you for suggesting it."

Cam takes a sip of the wine, enjoying its crisp citrus notes. A golfer in the distance shouts, then laughs in frustration, as his ball lips out of the cup. "Maggie said something to you about taking your mind off things. You told her about Landon?"

"Yes. I mentioned him…I mean, not his name, but what's happening to him. I met her in the store when I was, well, a bit of a mess. It was right after I'd learned his news."

"How are you feeling about it now?"

"Sad. Confused. His letter didn't say much."

"What are you confused about? Can I help?" If they're going to spend the next eight days together, there's no sense in ignoring the reason they're here. Or rather, the person behind the reason.

Brooke plays with the stem of her glass before she responds. "How is he doing? I mean, with handling his prognosis? Is he… okay?"

"He's handling it pretty well, overall. He's scared but courageous. It's a journey that's new, so he's discovering new feelings, new questions, every single day."

"Is he philosophical about death?"

"Yes. At times. Other times he's angry and frustrated and sad."

Brooke is silent for a long moment. "Has he been happy? I mean, before his diagnosis? I haven't had a huge amount of contact with him over the years, mostly superficial stuff. In his letter he says he's been happy. I hope it's true."

"He has, yes. He and Tenley have had a pretty good last decade, I think."

Brooke begins to cry softly. She doesn't try to hide it, nor does Cam try to console her. She can't. She doesn't know Brooke anymore and knows nothing about her relationship with Landon. Maybe it's time to find out.

"What is it about Landon you're grieving most about?"

"That I hurt him and he didn't deserve it. I seem to have a knack for hurting people who love me very much."

Cam can't disagree. "I'm pretty sure he's over it." Did Brooke cheat on him too?

"Well, maybe *I'm* not."

"Then that's your journey, your issue to resolve. Not Landon's."

Brooke's eyes brim with more tears. Her mouth trembles. Cam knows what's coming next, and she doesn't want to hear it. Not right now.

"Cam, I've done some things I'm not proud of. I hurt you too and—"

"No, Brooke. This conversation is about Landon, not me."

"I know that. But, I mean, shouldn't we talk about what happened between us? At some point?"

Cam draws in a nervous breath. She can feel, with every word her memory summons, the press of the shock against her chest, squeezing her, urging her now to replay the scene like some elaborate injury one has to relive over and over until its power to hurt expires. For years, all she wanted from Brooke was an acknowledgment of how much she'd hurt her. Well, an apology too, of course. But now that Brooke is sitting before her, looking sad and vulnerable and perhaps even ready to confess her contrition, it's no longer what Cam wants. There is nothing Brooke can say that will change anything about how the last eighteen years have played out and nothing she can say that will have any impact on the next eighteen. The very thing she wanted from Brooke doesn't matter anymore, and the epiphany unlocks something in Cam. "Sorry, Brooke, but no. I've moved on. I no longer need to know or care why you did what you did. So you don't need to address it for my sake, okay? In fact, I'd really rather you didn't."

The surprise of Cam's declaration slowly registers on Brooke's face. "Fine. As for Landon and me, I cared about him an awful lot, but I didn't love him enough to be married to him. He knew it from the start but thought things would evolve. They didn't. He asked me for a divorce a few months after we married, and I agreed."

"So, I gather it was amicable?"

"Yes. We stayed friends."

Cam is helpless against the stab of jealousy in her gut. There was nothing amicable about her and Brooke's split, no common ground on which to forge a friendship. It doesn't matter anymore, she tells herself. *You've moved on, remember?* "So why did you marry him if you weren't in love with him?"

"Because I was in love with someone I thought I would never get a chance to make things right with again. So I figured, okay, I can't be with the person I'm meant to be with, so why not be with someone who's good to me? Who loves me? I told you, I wasn't proud of it. I was stupid. I've been stupid a lot when it comes to relationships."

Cam swallows. She understands that Brooke is talking about her, about them, but it will have to remain the elephant in the room. She has lost the desire to talk about their breakup, and it's because she doesn't want to revisit the lowest point of her life. What if it unlocks all that pain again? What if it sends her into another tailspin? She has survived Brooke, and she's been doing just fine since. More than fine. She's a plant on a rock that doesn't need much sun or water to survive.

"Well, it sounds like Landon has forgiven you, so there's nothing for you to feel guilty about."

"I didn't realize you still hate me so much." Brooke hisses, her words having the effect of a stone that has been flung into calm waters, sending ripples far beyond. "You were being nice to me here, so I thought, maybe after all this time, you—"

"I don't hate you, Brooke."

"But you don't much like me, either. And it's not that I blame you, really—"

"Don't do this!" Cam says, converting her personal desperation into anger. So much for comparing Brooke's betrayal to that bruised piece of apple that could so easily be discarded. That apple, rotten bits and all, was lodged firmly in the back of Cam's throat at the moment.

"Fine," Brooke huffs, her gaze sliding away. "Maggie O'Doul said something to me yesterday. She said people save people. Do you think she's right?"

"Are you saying you need saving?"

"I don't know." She's squinting at the empty fairway in front of them as though she's trying to locate something through a dense fog. "Maybe?"

Well, Cam thinks, *it's not going to be me who saves you, Brooke.* "You know what? I think we should keep our conversations less personal from now on."

"New ground rule for the duration?"

I may not survive it otherwise. "Yes."

Brooke pulls her expression into something neutral, but it's not fooling Cam. "All right."

They finish the rest of their wine and cheese in silence, Cam silently tapping her fingers against her thigh, Brooke stealing glances at her phone in the way that bored people do.

CHAPTER TWENTY-FOUR

Brooke couldn't be happier about the next item on Landon's list: a spa afternoon. Relaxation, more like healing, was what was needed after yesterday's disastrous drink by the golf course with Cam. Cam's refusal to discuss their breakup all those years ago, the bitter edge to her voice when she'd said, "Don't do this," had hit Brooke squarely in the chest. Cam was the reasonable one, the unbreakable one, the genial one who didn't hold grudges. But it must be an act, because clearly Cam hadn't forgiven her and never would. And now Brooke was forever stranded alone with her feelings of guilt, remorse, shame, confusion. It had been so stupid to try to talk about their feelings. Embarrassment and fury pulsed through her all over again.

It was Maggie O'Doul's advice that was to blame: be honest, be genuine, trust others. The mantra had shone like a beacon in Brooke's brain, so she took the chance to trust that Cam would accept her honest attempt to talk, rather than trampling all over it. Well. Cam clearly didn't want to talk about the past, which meant there would be no future friendship, either. This little charade they were playing for Landon's sake was just that, a charade. A charade that was getting harder and harder to endure, for both of them. Brooke's patience was down to the size of the head of a pin, and she imagined Cam's was too.

A pedicure and a hot stone massage would occupy their afternoon. Saunas and steam rooms were a no-go since Covid, which was fine because steam rooms made Brooke claustrophobic anyway. All that thick steam was like a wall that made her feel like she couldn't breathe. Cam was getting her own pedicure and massage in a separate room, but afterward they were to enjoy a special smoothie at the spa "bar"—all part of the package Landon had paid for. The massage and pedicure she looked forward to. The smoothie later with Cam, not so much.

Before she undressed for the massage, Brooke took her phone from her bag and started texting Marcy that she'd made a mistake coming to the island. Delete delete delete. She hadn't told Marcy that Erica—Cam—was here too. She usually told Marcy everything, but for the first time in a very long time, she wanted to keep the information to herself. She wanted to figure this out. Alone. Wanted to figure out everything about her life without Marcy's input, which was a new and weird feeling, but it was long past due. Marcy was more of a crutch than a support, and that was the truth of it. *It's time you grew up, Brooke.* Her fiftieth birthday would be here before she knew it, and if that thought wasn't enough to scare her into being an adult, she didn't know what was.

The massage, the hot stones, and the warm hands, left Brooke feeling like she was floating in warm, thick water. For a blessed hour, nothing mattered. Not Cam, not her jobless future, not Landon's illness, none of it. It was pure, unadulterated bliss.

"How's your knee today?" Cam said from her perch at the smoothie bar. A safe topic, Brooke supposed.

Everything here was made of sleek bamboo and other types of wood, little reminders everywhere that the spa used only natural or renewable resources. The lighting was dim, meant for soothing, and the quiet gush of a waterfall filled the air from invisible speakers.

"Fine. Better." Brooke still wore a Band-Aid on her knee, but it didn't hurt as much. "How was your massage and pedicure?"

"Good. Relaxing. How was yours?"

Brooke cringed at the formalities. What was the point of all this? Cam looked miserable, in spite of the tepid smile and the innocuous questions. They were both miserable. In that instant, she made up her mind. She would pack her bags and leave on the first ferry tomorrow morning. Yes, she would be bailing on Landon with a week to go. Landon would be disappointed that his little fantasy wasn't coming to fruition, and for that, she was sorry. Who wanted to disappoint a dying man? Not her, but that wasn't enough to hold her here for another week, and it wasn't reason enough to keep making Cam miserable. Cam wouldn't bail on Landon, that was clear, so it was up to Brooke to cut them loose from this dysfunctional and downright unpleasant commitment. Or, well, mostly unpleasant.

Sipping on her spinach and avocado smoothie, Brooke ignored the churning in her stomach and turned to face Cam, who was busy sucking on her straw and looking for the answers to the universe in her identical smoothie. "I'm going to leave the island first thing tomorrow morning. I'm sorry, Cam. I'll contact Landon and explain, but I think it's for the best."

Cam continued to stare at her drink until Brooke began to repeat herself.

"I heard you the first time, Brooke."

"So that's all you have to say about it?"

They spoke in near-whispers. There was no need for histrionics…that ship had sailed a long time ago. At least now there'd be no more wondering what would happen if she ever found Cam again. No more indulging that secret space in her heart where love for Cam had staked its claim and never left. There was ice in her chest where there was once hope that Cam would forgive her or at the least they would come to a peaceful understanding between them. But it was no use. They were over. There would be no going back, no closure where her heart was concerned.

"Yup," Cam said simply.

Brooke wiped her cheek with the back of her hand and was surprised by the confirmation of tears. She half expected Cam to protest or at least try to convince her to stay. But no. Cam too was apparently eager to end this charade. She thought back to that moment of the gut-wrenching declaration she made to Cam almost eighteen years ago and how the second it was out of her mouth, she wanted to take it back, admit the truth. But such folly was like stuffing spent bullets back into a gun; the damage was done. Oh, what a freaking coward she'd been. Had continued to be, but no longer. This, she told herself, was what it was like to own up to your mistakes. It didn't always end with a hug and a smile and forgiveness. Sometimes it hurt like hell and continued to hurt like hell, the way it did now. Perhaps, she thought with a sliver of hope, this epiphany was the missing link all along that had stunted her from moving on with Landon or anyone since. Cam was never going to forgive her, and there was not a damned thing Brooke could do about that.

She swallowed the last of her silent tears along with her smoothie. If what Maggie said was true about people saving people, then she was saving Cam the heartache of having to be around her for another week. Saving herself too, from continuing to see in Cam's eyes evidence of the hurt she'd inflicted on her all those years ago.

CHAPTER TWENTY-FIVE

Cam is unreasonably angry with herself. She was so sure that for this little social experiment with Brooke she could put aside the past, ignore the slightly sick feeling that has been in her stomach ever since that lunch date at the Iroquois Hotel. They're both adults, and what happened between them was a very long time ago. Too long ago to let it poison the present. And yet she's allowing it to do exactly that. Why? They could talk, without a flurry of emotions, about their breakup, couldn't they? It should be easy, and yet, when Brooke—Brooke!—tried to steer them there, Cam had cut her off at the knees.

I'm the coward, Cam thinks. *I'm the one who blinked first*. She's letting Brooke have all the power…the power to hurt her, the power to manipulate her feelings, the power to call off Landon's plans, and now she doesn't know what she's more upset about, being afraid to talk honestly with Brooke or allowing Brooke to call all the shots.

She decides to call Landon and Tenley to fess up that while she and Brooke gave it a try, their little fantasy for the two of them is over. Tenley answers and puts the phone on speaker so Landon can hear too. They talk first about Landon's condition before Cam drops the bomb. Landon and Tenley are predictably disappointed. And then the pleading comes, but it basically comes down to: surely the two of you can talk out your differences and come to a truce, if not an understanding, and start fresh.

They aren't getting it. Cam has no choice but to tell them the truth. And so she confesses the thing she's never told anyone—that Brooke betrayed her eighteen years ago by having an affair. How that betrayal had ambushed her out of nowhere, how it was the one provocation for which there could be no reconciliation, no way forward for them. What she doesn't explain now is how the breakup gutted her, how it ultimately led her to choose a different path for her life—one without the stage. *That* confession is far too personal.

Landon and Tenley are stunned into silence. Finally, Landon says, in a voice cracking with emotion, "I'm sorry, Cam. I didn't know, or I never would have arranged this trip. I never would have... I didn't think... *Brooke?*"

"Brooke."

"Jesus," Landon says. His shock at hearing that Brooke would do such a thing, and to someone she professed to love, is impossible to miss. "Why? I mean, why would she do that? To me, okay. She wasn't in love with me, but *you?* Why would she do that to you? It doesn't make sense, Cam. I know how much she loved you. She carried a torch for you the entire time I knew her, and I suspect she still does. It doesn't make sense."

Cam squeezes her eyes shut, pinches the bridge of her nose—as if these tiny acts will make this conversation disappear, make all this renewed heartache over Brooke evaporate into thin air. "I can't speak for Brooke," she finally says. "But she's leaving tomorrow morning on the ferry. That's all I know."

Tenley says, "But she can't."

"She can and she will," Cam says. "She's pretty determined, and frankly, I'm good with it."

"No," Landon interjects. "What Tenley means is that she can't go because there's a big storm coming your way any minute. The ferries are all canceled for tomorrow. In fact, I just saw on social media that the last one is leaving the island any minute now."

Cam looks at her watch. 7:20. Brooke won't make that final 7:30 ferry, not unless she leaves her luggage behind and sprints to the dock. "I'll let her know. And I'm sorry about this, Landon. I know you had your heart set on a nice reunion for Brooke and me."

"Hey," he says, his voice sounding far away. "I'm the one who let *you* down."

"I'll come back as soon as the ferries are up and running again." *Well, on the one* after *the one Brooke takes.*

Tenley won't hear of it and says, "There won't be refunds at this late date anyway, so somebody might as well enjoy it. Please, Cam, we want you to stay and enjoy a nice long break. And Becky Neerhof isn't you, but she's doing a good job filling in."

Cam relents, if only for the sake of making them feel better, and says her goodbyes. Next she touches base with Becky, the hospice outreach worker for Landon. He's doing okay, she reassures Cam. No changes to speak of.

From the credenza in her room, Cam takes out the bottle of bourbon she purchased to bring home, but what the hell. This is a job tailor-made for bourbon—the job of getting good and well drunk. She finds a glass, extracts an ice cube from the ice bucket she'd filled a short time ago, and pours a few fingers of whiskey over the ice. Smoke and heat hit the back of her throat. Then she remembers she hasn't told Brooke about the ferries shutting down. A second sip and she decides there are other things she hasn't told Brooke that maybe Brooke ought to hear.

With her glass in one hand and the bottle in the other, Cam gathers her courage and strides across the hall. She knocks on Brooke's door.

CHAPTER TWENTY-SIX

The staccato knock on her door stopped Brooke from stuffing things in her suitcase. First thing tomorrow morning, she'd blow this joint, and while it was a small detail that she didn't have anywhere to go, Marcy's door would be open as usual. There was also the dreaded Days Inn, which was probably a better idea, since more independence from Marcy was on her to-do list. She'd be okay.

Maybe it was Cam at the door, here to beg her to stay, and the thought was enough to make Brooke laugh out loud. She opened the door and promptly clamped her mouth shut at the sight of Cam with a glass in one hand and a bottle of something in the other. By the look of her pinched expression, she was most definitely not here to beg Brooke to stay. More like her foot was ready to help Brooke out the door and down the stairs with one swift and well-placed kick.

"Uh…come in, I guess?"

Cam's eyes pinned her. "You can't leave."

Brooke emitted a sound of disbelief. "I most certainly can." There were only a few more things to pack; she'd be on that first ferry in the morning.

"Nope."

"What do you mean, 'nope.' Are you drunk?"

"No, but I will be by the time this night's over."

She watched Cam take a sip from her glass. The bottle in her hand was whiskey, mostly full. Cam didn't strike her as much of a hard liquor drinker these days. "Suit yourself."

There was no hesitation as Cam marched into Brooke's bathroom and returned with an empty glass. She poured a few fingers of whiskey into it, handed it to Brooke.

"Oh no no no no. What do you think you're doing? I'm not getting drunk ten hours before riding a bouncy ferry back to the mainland. No thank you to that hangover hell!"

"Bring your glass with you and come out to the balcony with me. There's something you need to see."

Reluctant but also curious, Brooke followed anyway after taking the proffered glass. Though she had no intention of drinking with Cam, she didn't have it in her to kick her out either. Not until she got a read on what she was so hell-bent on.

"Look at the sky," Cam said. "To the northwest."

Clouds—thick and angry and black as night—scudded across the straits at a wicked clip. The wind was up too, swirling and whistling. Droplets of rain had begun to tick against the balcony railing. "Hmm. That doesn't look so good."

"The last ferry for today left five minutes ago," Cam said. "Tomorrow's ferries are all canceled because of the storm."

Brooke's stomach dropped like an elevator car without a cable. "That can't be. They can't just cancel all the ferries." There was no way off the island except by boat. Well, there was an airstrip, but it was only for private flights. "Can they?"

"They can and they did." She nodded her head at the glass in Brooke's hand. "Might as well drink up."

"You mean drown my sorrows?"

"Any better suggestions?"

"Not a single one." *Well, shit.* Stranded here for probably another twenty-four hours with the last person on earth she wanted to be stranded with. Correction. *She* was the last person on earth that Cam probably wanted to be stranded with. Oh, Marcy would call this fate or divine intervention or black magic or God knew what, but it sounded like purgatory to Brooke.

"I don't think it will kill you to stay a little longer. I won't get in your way. We'll be strangers, okay?"

Brooke wanted to laugh. They'd never be strangers. She knew every inch of Cam's body, knew it as well as her own. They had shared their most intimate thoughts and dreams, their weaknesses and doubts. Shared a bed, a home, a life, for almost eight years. Almost two decades had passed, but when she looked into Cam's eyes, even now, it all came speeding back: the passion, the joy, the love, the disappointment, the arguments, the long talks. It was all there, lodged deep in every cell. Oh, they might be a lot of things to each other, but they would definitely never be strangers.

Brooke finally took a sip of the liquid fire. It burned and she coughed like an amateur, but the heat smoothed out as it hit her stomach, enveloping her instantly in a warm blanket of tranquility. Another sip and she almost forgot why she was so eager to get the hell away from here as fast as she could.

"I suppose I can survive a couple more nights. Not like I have anywhere to go, anyway."

"What is that all about, by the way? What do you mean you have nowhere to go?"

The rain fell harder, sending Brooke scurrying back into her room with Cam hot on her heels. "I... My house had a big water leak and is undergoing repairs and..." Brooke dropped into one of the two wingback chairs facing the gas fireplace. What was there to lose in telling Cam how screwed up her life was? If Cam wanted to judge her, so be it. She probably deserved it, and anyway, she'd be gone from the island, and from Cam, before she knew it. "I sold my restaurant, too, so I don't really have anything to get back to."

"Wow, really?" Cam plopped down on the matching chair and set the bottle of whiskey on the small round table between them. "You sold your restaurant? I thought you loved the restaurant business? I mean...I guess I assumed you love it."

"I did love it, but the pandemic took such a big bite out of the hospitality industry. Took a big bite out of me too, emotionally and financially." The worries and stress of the last two-plus years hadn't yet released her, even with signing the papers that had made her a free woman. She had one foot in the past and one in the present, which left her feeling more than a little unbalanced. "I sold it a couple of weeks ago."

"Why didn't you say anything?"

"Because, honestly, Cam, do you even give a shit?"

"Of course I do."

Brooke leveled her best I-don't-believe-you look as a crack of thunder shattered the momentary silence.

"All right, I'm sorry. I haven't been very pleasant to you lately."

"Understatement, but thank you."

"What are you going to do?"

"Right now? I'm going to turn on the fireplace." Brooke found the remote control for it on the mantel and switched on the fire. Flames leapt to life, instant warmth replacing the cool downdrafts from the storm outside that had chilled Brooke.

She thought she caught a glimpse of a smile as Cam sipped her drink. "And after that?"

Brooke shrugged. "I thought I might humor you and drink with you for a little bit."

"Ah, taking pity on me?"

"Well, call it what you like, but it's no fun getting drunk alone."

"True that. Though I haven't done it in years."

Brooke took a deep breath and decided to crawl out onto that limb again…the one Cam had so quickly sawed off a few hours ago when she'd refused to talk about their shared past. "You sure you want to drink with someone you can't stand the sight of?"

Staring at the fire, her lips pursed, her voice thick, Cam said, "Who said anything about not standing the sight of you?"

"Well, earlier, you—"

Words shot out of Cam's mouth with the velocity of bullets. "Why did you do it, Brooke? Why did you fuck around on me?"

Everything stopped. Even the breath Brooke was about to expel stalled in her chest. All she could see in her mind's eye was the look of horror and pain on Cam's clenched and ghost-white face all those years ago when Brooke told her that she'd been unfaithful—twice—with a fan of Cam's that had followed them around from gig to gig that summer. The look in Cam's eyes—disbelief, hurt, rage—had pierced Brooke with a sharpness she instantly knew would be impossible to recover from. Cam had turned from her without a word and walked away, walking the walk of the defeated, of the unforgiving, and Brooke hadn't tried to stop her. The permanence of their undoing was evident in that moment, and they would never see one another again. Until this week.

Brooke took a long, burning sip of her whiskey. She'd need it for what she was about to say. Well, it was more the fallout she was bracing for.

"I didn't fuck around on you, Cam. It was a lie."

CHAPTER TWENTY-SEVEN

Cam stares at Brooke for a long moment while she tries to think. Because Brooke isn't making any damned sense. Of course Brooke screwed around on her. It was the proverbial stake through the heart of their relationship, the thing that had ended them for good. Brooke had admitted it. Like, who would admit to such a thing if it wasn't true?

"Wait," Cam finally manages in a voice that's jumped a couple of octaves. "Now you're saying you didn't sleep with that girl?"

"I didn't sleep with that girl. Or anyone else."

God! She's just confessed to being a liar except now *she wants to be believed?* "So you want me to believe that you're the only person in the history of the world who's confessed to having an affair when they actually didn't?"

"Yes." Brooke's face is flushed. "I know it sounds unbelievable, but I swear it's true. I was never unfaithful to you."

Cam takes a slow sip of whiskey. The bumblebees are starting a chaotic dance in her forehead and behind her eyes. Making sense of this conversation has entered the realm of painful. No.

Remembering is painful. The conversation is just fucking weird. "Why on earth would you confess to something you didn't do?"

Brooke is silent, and in the silence, the pain swamps Cam. Every word of their conversation has opened the dam of emotions a little more until sweat has begun to break out on her hairline, her neck. She remembers how Brooke's confession had filleted her, exposed her, left her unfathomably hurt, because Brooke turning to someone else for the most intimate physical exchange between two people was the ultimate rejection, the ultimate fuck you. Brooke had never even apologized. With that one clean and mortal slice, they simply stopped being a couple.

"Forget I asked," Cam mutters. There is no point in this. She worked so hard to pull herself out of that devastating depression, to figure out what mattered most, to discover how to nurture herself, how to be happy, how to move on with her life. It took an astronomical amount of work and time to heal. What could going backward now possibly accomplish?

"No." Brooke sips her whiskey, but she seems completely sober. "I'm going to answer."

"It's so long ago. Let's leave the past right where it is." Cam begins to extricate herself from her chair until fingers close gently, pleadingly, around her forearm.

"Please," Brooke whispers. "Don't you dare run from me now, Cam. This is our one chance—our only chance—to sort this out once and for all."

"I don't want to." It's the damned whiskey that made her bring up their past. She should have stayed in her own damned room.

"Well, I do. I need to." Brooke releases Cam's arm. "You're not the only one who was broken. Why do you think I married Landon?"

Cam doesn't want to hear this. It's not her business. In fact, she can't even picture Brooke and Landon together. It hurts her brain to do so. "Brooke, listen—"

"No, *you* listen. Please."

She's not doing this for me, she's doing this for her. It really has nothing to do with me, not anymore. Brooke can't hurt me now. It's that thought that allows her to calm down and let Brooke continue. *Let her speak her truth if it's so important to her.* "All right, fine."

"I married Landon because I was scared. And lonely. And hurting. I knew I'd made a huge mistake with you. But I also knew you'd never take me back, that you would never trust me again, even though I didn't do the things I said I did." Brooke's shoulders fold into themselves. "I was so ashamed of myself for everything. I was like a lost kitten and Landon found me. He was solid, he was patient, he was kind, he was my rock. I could heal with someone like that. With him, I could gather the bravery I needed to open my own restaurant. He was a safe port in the storm."

"And I wasn't?"

Brooke pours more whiskey for herself. Cam shakes her head at the offer of more. She is already on her way to getting drunk, but it's not a fun drunk.

"Honestly?"

"Is that what we're doing? Being totally honest now?"

"Yes. I wasn't before. And I'm sorry, Cam. I'm sorry I wasn't brave enough to tell you the truth, that I had to lie instead."

"And what was the truth?"

Brooke takes another drink, the booze coarsening her voice. "You weren't there for me. At least, not as much as I needed you to be. You were always on the road, or you were recording, or you were giving interviews, or you were writing songs, rehearsing. It got to be that there was no room for me, no room for what I needed. I had my own dreams, you know."

"I know that. You were teaching kindergarten and working nights at a restaurant so you could eventually open your own restaurant someday. I supported that dream, Brooke. How can you say I didn't?"

"Because nothing changed for you. You kept doing your own thing. There was nothing for you to 'support' because you didn't have to sacrifice a goddamned thing. That last year we were together, we hardly saw one another, we were both so busy. Don't you remember? We went eleven weeks once without laying eyes on one another while you were on the road. Eleven weeks! That's not normal, and it's sure as hell not healthy. I was lonely all the time. And if I wanted to pursue my own goals, I couldn't be following you around the country for weeks or months at a time. I couldn't go on being your groupie. I was much more than that."

"Come on, of course you were much more than that. You were my partner."

"Being a partner is a two-way street, Cam. And there were a lot of one-way alleys in those days."

Cam closes her eyes against the fog of the booze, the haze of their argument. It's a conversation they should have had seventeen-and-a-half years ago. "What do you want from me? An apology? Fine. I'm sorry I was so absorbed in my career. I was trying to…" *Fuck.* Now tears are pressing behind her eyes. "What the fuck, Brooke? You want me to apologize for pursuing my music career, for giving it everything I had? I was supposed to give it up or not try very hard because you wanted to chase your own dream? Why did it have to be either/or? And you never goddamned answered why you made up an affair!" *I'm not going to cry, dammit.* Cam sniffs back the tears collecting in her throat. She's already cried an ocean of tears over Brooke. Does Brooke want her blood, too?

Brooke is shaking her head and fixing her gaze on the flames in the fireplace. "It didn't feel like there was room for both of our careers in that relationship. I think you knew that, too. Everything was dandy as long as it was me following you around, making all the sacrifices."

"That's not fair." Cam hates the way her voice is shaking. None of these old wounds should matter so goddamned much, and yet here they are, fresh and raw and stinging like a bitch. *Fucking hell.*

"Remember my thirtieth birthday?" Brooke asks.

"Not really, no."

"Exactly. Because you weren't there. Your tour van broke down in fucking Gary, Indiana, or something, and you couldn't make the party that Marcy had organized for me."

"That's what this is all about? Missing your birthday party?" *After all these years?* Incredible. Ridiculous.

"Missing the party was only one example, but it was a last straw for me. It made me realize that your lifestyle, your career, meant I'd spend a lot of big moments without you. And I didn't want that. I needed you and you were never there. You couldn't give me what I needed."

"Why didn't you tell me any of this before?"

"Because you were never there! Don't you get it? We never talked any more. When I saw you, it was only for a few days, and then you were off again. And I did try. I remember going out for dinner, and I was going to talk to you about how I needed you to cut back on your tours, on your work, so that you could be there for me with *my* work. And then these fans kept interrupting to ask for your autograph. And then your manager, Danny, and your drummer Stephanie found us because you'd told them which restaurant we'd be at. They sat down and joined us like it was expected, like they belonged. And they didn't belong, Cam. They didn't belong in our relationship. We stopped knowing how to be a couple, how to be Brooke and Erica. Or...or... fucking Bette and Tina."

Like the ocean's tide receding, the fight begins to leave Cam. Because Brooke is right. She'd given Brooke the leftovers, the crumbs, after her career demands were met. She couldn't see then that they were just going through the motions while she obsessed over achieving fame and fortune. Though why shouldn't she have tried to put everything she had into her dream? She was good, she was crazy good, everyone told her so. It was supposed to be a matter of time, she'd come to believe, if only she continued to put in the work. All Brooke had to do was hang in there with her, because later, after Cam got what she wanted, she'd make time for Brooke. She swore she would. Except it didn't happen that way. Brooke, it dawns on Cam, stayed for as long as she could, until she needed to save herself, save her own dreams. *I was a selfish idiot who was wrong about everything. Jesus Christ.*

Cam clears her throat roughly. "So you needed a way out."

"I needed a way to make things different," Brooke says. "I thought that making up a transgression would not only get your attention, but that it would be like some giant reset of our relationship. I figured that if I blew it all up, we could rebuild. Start fresh, build something that addressed both our needs. Except…"

"Except I took what you said at face value, that having an affair meant you didn't want to be with me anymore."

Brooke pours more whiskey, borrowing against one whopper of a hangover tomorrow, Cam is sure. "I knew as soon as the words were out of my mouth—the lie—that we were finished. That you would never give us another chance. I made a mistake, Cam. A huge mistake."

And so the handful of years after that—the ones filled with too much booze and pot, with too many tears, with the nameless women that visited Cam's bed for a time or two before she cut them loose, and with the other self-destructive behavior that saw a coinciding backslide of her career at an alarming speed—were all premised on a lie. She'd nearly let the pain destroy her; it had certainly changed the course of her life.

"I hated you for a long time," Cam says quietly.

Brooke stares at her searchingly, as if trying to locate her through a heavy fog. "Do you still?"

Do I? Cam wonders. She could argue that it was Brooke's bombshell that unraveled her singing career, that forced her to change her entire life, that made her reject long-term relationships, or any close relationships, for that matter. Even during the nearly two years she spent with Nora, she hadn't truly given herself to the relationship. God, it had been so easy to heap all the blame onto Brooke while letting herself off the hook.

But Cam isn't that indignant, in-denial young woman anymore. Relationships don't fall apart without good reason, and the *victim* is seldom devoid of blame. Yup. She's woman enough now to admit she was a shitty partner, that she didn't take responsibility when she needed to. Brooke had had every right to have an affair…except she didn't.

"No," Cam says on a long sigh. "I don't hate you. I was a selfish idiot. But you were…dumb to do what you did, too."

Laughter, deep from her belly, explodes out of Brooke. It's only another moment before Cam is laughing too. "Selfish and dumb. Yup, perfect descriptions of our thirty-year-old selves. Thought we had the world by the tail without having to do anything to earn it."

"And we thought we knew everything. Don't forget that one."

"And that tomorrow would fix everything."

"Or if it didn't, well, we'd worry about it later."

Brooke's laughter vanishes as quickly as it came on, and in its place, a tear drips down her cheek, leaving a track. And then another chases the first one. "For a while, after I lost you, I thought someone else would come along. Someone I would love as much as I loved you."

"Landon?"

"Yes, Landon. Except he wasn't you and I didn't love him like I loved you. So…no."

Poor Landon. He didn't deserve to get mixed up in their drama, but then again, he went into it with his eyes open, Cam supposes. And, miraculously, he doesn't hate them. Somehow, in all this wreckage, they've discovered the thread that binds them all together. Hours ago, Cam had been ready to pull that thread, to let everything unravel. To hell with it all. But maybe letting things unravel is the wrong thing to do. Maybe in some crazy way, they all need one another.

When Cam looks at Brooke again, she sees that she's nodded off. As quietly as she can, she reaches over and removes the whiskey glass from Brooke's hand and sets it on the table between them. She stands and carefully picks Brooke up under her arms, her limp arms. Brooke might be a bit taller than Cam, but she's probably a good twenty pounds lighter. In her drunkenness she's like a ragdoll, but Cam is strong and pulls her up and against her, holding her so she doesn't fall, and half carries her, half walks her the short distance to the bed. She lays Brooke down on her side, tosses a blanket over her sleeping form. Before she leaves, she fetches a glass of water from the bathroom and sets it on the nightstand beside the bed. Just in case she wakes up thirsty. She shuts off the lamp and the fireplace, flips the lock on the door so that when she closes it from the outside, it will lock.

Funny, Cam thinks as she closes the door with a soft snick and steps across the hall to her own door. She doesn't remember ever tucking Brooke in like this before. She doesn't remember taking care of Brooke, not when she was sick or hurting or when Brooke simply needed her. *Probably because I never did.*

The landscape of Cam's past has changed into something unrecognizable. *She's* the culpable one, not Brooke. *She*, who always gave everything she had to her two careers, had barely given a damn thing to the one person who mattered the most.

In her own room, in the dark, Cam undresses and sits on the edge of the bed. Numerous times, she's counseled Landon and others to forgive themselves, to forgive others, for being human. Maybe it's time for a dose of her own advice. Maybe it's long past time to forgive herself. And Brooke.

CHAPTER TWENTY-EIGHT

Her head pounded with the worst headache she'd had in years. And then Brooke realized that at least some of the pounding originated at her door. *Ugh. What was I thinking, drinking like I was twenty-one?* Her forty-eight years felt more like about eighty right now. She'd have been happy to stay in bed all morning and sleep off her hangover, except—*dammit!*— whoever was at the door remained intent on torturing her.

"Coming!" *Ouch.* Regret at using her voice was immediate.

It was Cam at the door, with something more valuable than gold—hot, fresh coffee. "Sorry to disturb, but I thought you could use one of these."

"Could I ever." Brooke grabbed the cardboard cup of steaming goodness out of Cam's hand like it was a life ring. "Thanks."

"You're welcome. You feeling okay this morning?"

"Do I look okay?"

Cam's smile was of the cocky, sober variety. "Not really, but it will pass."

"You say that now, but I don't believe you. Ugh. Thank you for putting me to bed last night. I'm assuming you did, because I really don't remember doing it myself."

"It's okay. You'd have done the same. Actually, you *have* done the same for me in the past, if I recall."

"True that. Do you want to come in?"

"Sure. I won't keep you long. You, um, probably want to go back to bed."

Understatement of the year. Most of the previous night's conversation found its way back into Brooke's foggy brain. It had to have been the alcohol that prompted her to confess everything—the fake affair, the feelings of inadequacy, the resentments, the hurt—all of it she dumped onto Cam's lap without warning. *Oh, what have I done?* In the blink of an eye, she would take it all back if she could, because hoping Cam was too drunk to remember wasn't a likely option. And yet, here was Cam, not angry, but smiling and genial and...nice. Had they stumbled their way to some sort of truce? Were they actually taking the first steps toward healing? Toward actually becoming friends?

Brooke didn't trust her brain's nebulous ability to make sense of it all. "Come and have a seat. Finish your coffee with me?"

"Sure."

Brooke took her first sip once they were seated. Talk about manna from heaven! After another brain-soothing swallow, she found her courage. "Are you upset with me? About last night?"

There was a long pause before Cam answered. "No. But it was tough to hear. I was hurt, confused, shocked. It's not much fun looking in the mirror and not liking what you see."

Brooke nodded. She didn't like what she saw in the mirror lately, either. Maybe Cam was the selfish one when they were together, but what had Brooke been all these years since? Selfishness had been her building blocks to get the restaurant going and then to be successful. She really did understand what it took to make dreams come true, but now she finally understood the cost. It meant she hardly had any friends, had

had no meaningful romantic relationship since Cam (if she didn't count her failed marriage to Landon). She couldn't even make time for a dog. And the worst part? None of that selfishness had ultimately made her happy. She was alone. And damned tired of it.

In a voice she barely recognized, Brooke said, "I really fucked up. And I'm so sorry."

"I really fucked up too. And I'm sorry, Brooke. We really blew it, didn't we?"

Amazing that they could sit and talk about this now, Brooke thought—something they were far too stubborn and sanctimonious to do before. "I wonder if anything would have been different if we'd had this conversation a long time ago?" Would she still have gone on to open her own restaurant? Would Cam have gone on to the kind of success on stage she'd so desperately desired? Would they still be together? Landon would be dying, that part wouldn't be different, but Cam would never have met him.

"I won't pretend that it would have saved me a lot of heartache and that I haven't wondered myself what might have been different if we'd stayed together. But I don't regret leaving the music industry. It never gave me the kind of purpose that my work as a death doula gives me. I mean, there's no comparison, Brooke. I used to entertain people. Now I help the dying. I feel like I'm actually doing something meaningful with my life now. Something that *matters*."

"Joy is meaningful too, not just death. You gave people joy when you sang to them. You were pretty spectacular on stage, you know." Brooke could still picture a sweaty, flushed Cam—Erica Foster then—strutting across the stage in kick-ass boots, tight leather pants, a silk jacket that showed a tantalizing amount of cleavage, the microphone an extension of her body. Hot as hell, she owned the stage, the audience, with a powerful voice that was at once gravel and silk and a bossy, chin-out attitude that made her untouchable but soooo desirable. A raised fist, a pointed finger, a drop down to her knees, a leap and a kick into the air. Cam was a ball of wicked energy on the stage, devouring everything in her path. A raging inferno then, Cam was more like the warm and guiding light of a lantern now—something Brooke would never have imagined. Where there was anger, there was now understanding. Where there was capriciousness, there was self-possession. Cam had become a beautiful woman inside.

"I don't know. I don't think about those things anymore. It's almost like that life wasn't really me. Like it happened to a different person. But I get what you're saying."

Brooke didn't have a clear dividing line between who she was then and who she was now. Not like that. But maybe all of this... The island, seeing Cam again, learning about Landon, selling the restaurant rather spontaneously... Didn't it all reinforce that it was time to reinvent herself? To discover who she really was inside? To make a new future for herself? This, right now, was her line in the sand.

"I'm sorry that part of your life is something you don't want to think about," Brooke said. "But it is still part of your history." The world had lost something when it lost Cam's songs, her voice. "You know something? I was never alone when I was with you. It's since we've been apart that I've been lonely."

"I feel the same. I realize now that I was a shitty partner. Actually, I think somewhere inside I knew it all along. That's probably why I've never really tried again with anyone else."

"Really?" Brooke would have guessed Cam had a long string of relationships behind her.

"I tried once but...she wasn't you."

The admission brought a lump to Brooke's throat. She and Cam were two sides of the same coin, unable to make a relationship work with anyone else. Cam didn't deserve to be alone, and the thought saddened Brooke. Cam wasn't a terrible person, not by any stretch. In her twenties, she'd made her career her one and only priority. Who didn't at that age? It didn't make her a bad person or a terrible partner. It made her human. The problem was Brooke hadn't allowed Cam to be human, to be imperfect. The awareness of her own shortcomings was razor sharp now, and it stung.

"Jesus, Cam, how come we didn't try harder to make us work?"

Cam shrugged, her body language in total contradiction to her eyes, which swam with unshed tears. "I guess we weren't strong enough. I guess we figured it had to be either the relationship or our careers. We couldn't figure out how to make room for both."

"So our careers won." The irony wasn't lost on Brooke that currently neither of them was now employed in those precious, burn-everything-else-to-the-ground careers. "Do you think… that maybe we were just a case of bad timing? That we needed to grow up away from one another?"

Cam's gaze fixed on the far wall, then returned softened, more at peace. "Maybe. Thanks for this, Brooke. I'm glad we talked." Cam rose with her empty coffee cup and made for the door. "Want to meet for lunch later? We need to talk about what we're going to do about Landon and…all this." She spread her arms to encompass the room, the hotel, the island. "Landon thinks you're leaving the island in a snit as soon as the ferries are running again."

Brooke rolled her eyes. "Right. I was in a pretty big snit, wasn't I?" She wrinkled her nose at Cam in apology. "Meet you at the Yankee Rebel around two o'clock?"

"See you there." Cam's eyes were bright and warm and teasing. "Unless you need another day to recuperate from your hangover."

"Smart-ass."

CHAPTER TWENTY-NINE

The tavern is no different from a typical pub. A long wooden bar along one wall features mounted televisions above shelves of liquor bottles lined up in tidy rows like glass soldiers. There are wooden booths along the other walls for those who want privacy, plus a few tables in the middle for the uninhibited. Cam and Brooke claim a booth after hanging their wet raincoats on a nearby hook. Cam orders a Pepsi with her club sandwich, Brooke orders iced tea with her chicken and Caesar salad. She looks a little more alive than she did a few hours ago, but only a little. Food should help.

Cam tilts her chin at Brooke's iced tea. "No hair of the dog for you?"

"Nope. God, I don't even want to think about how much whiskey I drank last night."

"Don't worry. We didn't finish the whole bottle."

"Thank you, Lord. So I might survive this?"

"You will."

"Not sure I want to," Brooke grumbles.

Their food is placed before them, and Cam can't wait to dig in. She's famished. It's as though their conversation last night has busted through a wall in her mind. Things are still tumbling around in there—questions, musings, regrets—but the hurt that has felt like a weight on her heart all these years is gone. She's featherlight inside for the first time in a long time, though she knows there is still some wreckage to pick over, some feelings to sort through. There is time for that later.

"So," Cam says carefully between bites, nervous for the answer. "Are you going to leave the island tomorrow?" The storm has moved out; only a light rain remains, but the ferries won't resume operation until tomorrow morning.

Brooke shakes her head, stabs half-heartedly at her salad. "No. I think I want to sort some things out first."

Cam quietly expels the breath she's been holding in. "What kind of things?"

"Me. I want to take the time while I'm here to sort out my life. There's that thing, you know, the part where I no longer have a job, a career."

"You have some time to figure it out, though, right?"

"I do. There's no rush, but it feels…weird. The thing I worked at, dreamed about, for so many years, it's gone now. It's been a big part of my life. The biggest part of my life, really. I feel sort of…untethered."

"I get that. Music was everything to me for over a decade. I couldn't imagine not doing it. And yet, well, here I am, *not* doing music in any way, shape, or form. And yes, it is weird for a while. But you'll figure things out, Brooke. Just give it time."

"But how did you do it, Cam? How did you make that transition to something else? I mean, how did you figure out that you wanted to change your life?"

"I realized my music career was hurting me." Her words can't adequately describe that monumental realization, and she's still ashamed of her behavior—the booze, the pot, the one-night stands. But that was the external stuff. The stuff people didn't see was her exhaustion, the bitterness that ground her down, the sadness that made her not want to be around others. All of it ended at one destination: loneliness. The stage was home, sure, and the crowds made her feel loved, wanted, appreciated. But when the lights faded and the audience went home, there was nothing. It was like walking from bright sunshine into the dark. Over and over again. The highs and lows never left, like a never-ending, bad roller-coaster ride.

"I realized one day—I think I was around thirty-four, thirty-five—that I was depressed. I mean, okay, I was depressed when we broke up." She's minimizing, because Brooke doesn't need to hear all the gory details. "The music would lift me for a few hours or a few days. But then it no longer was my refuge. It got…hard somehow, a chore that wasn't fulfilling me. I wasn't moving up the pecking order the way I wanted. I felt like I was standing still. I finally figured out that I was only doing it, going through the motions, because it was all I knew how to do. And that wasn't enough for me. Which means it probably also wasn't enough for audiences. People know when you're not really into it. They hear and feel the shortcuts, the lack of passion, the absence of fun. It's a vicious circle. As soon as you start acting like you don't want it anymore, it becomes a self-fulfilling prophecy."

"But weren't you about to hit it big? Weren't you almost there when you quit?"

Cam shrugs. The industry is so fickle, she might have finally enjoyed recognition and money if she'd persisted a bit longer, but for how long? A year? Two? Then it would have been back to obscurity. Cam knew she was good, but she also knew she was no superstar. "I reached a point where I was no longer willing to pay the price, whether the reward was there at the end of it or not."

"So you quit? Just like that?"

"Not quite. I spent another year fulfilling all my contracts and obligations, then couch surfed at friends' around the country for another year like some teenager their parents have kicked out. I guess I wanted to disappear." Waking up in two-day-old clothing stained with your own vomit isn't anything to be proud of. Just thinking about it fills her with shame.

"I'm sorry your music career didn't work out. I really wanted it to. For the record." Brooke rolls her eyes with embarrassment, and it's cute. "I sort of followed your career until you dropped off the face of the earth."

"Really?" A little river of pleasure runs through Cam. She'd always assumed Brooke had hated her in her eagerness to discard her like an old, broken shoe. It was the gospel on which she mapped the next destructive phase of her life. And yet she'd been wrong. Brooke hadn't hated her, hadn't betrayed her, hadn't truly rejected her. Brooke had been lost, unhappy. And in her desperation to fix herself, to fix them, she'd made a crap decision and lied about having an affair. Brooke had pulled the fire alarm, but Cam had been the one playing with matches.

"Really, Cam. I never stopped caring about you."

The truth catches up to her at the speed of her galloping heart. Brooke had never stopped loving her. It was Cam who'd given up on them first. "I failed you, Brooke. God, did I ever fail you. Can you forgive me?"

The moment seems to uncork something important. There is both astonishment and absolution in the look Brooke gives her. "Thank you for saying that. I mean it, Cam. But we both screwed up. We're both equally to blame. We should have been a team. But we were two individuals who thought we were a couple."

Cam's tension falls away. Maybe it's not forgiveness she needs, but rather, to be understood. "I know we can't change the past, but I'd like to be friends. I mean, if you think you'd like that, too."

Brooke smiles, and the effort lightens the color of her eyes at least two shades. "I'd like that. Very much. Oh, wait." Brooke's smile freezes, then wobbles. "What about you? Are you going to leave the island? Go home?"

"Do you want me to?" Cam doesn't want to go, because Landon is right, it is beautiful here. And peaceful. And yes, probably romantic too, but that's neither here nor there. She'll go if Brooke wants her to, because frankly, she can see that Brooke needs the time and space to figure out her future, while

Cam doesn't. They can stay friends whether Cam remains on the island or not.

"No, I don't want you to go. I sort of like having you around. And besides, who's going to look after me if I get another hangover? Not that I plan to." Brooke face-palms herself. "Never again."

"I won't hold you to swearing off hangovers forever, but okay. If you're sure. What are we going to tell Landon?"

Brooke pushes her half-eaten plate of salad away. "I'm sorry for what's happening to Landon, but I can't keep going through with his little plan."

Cam's heart stutters a beat. She'd begun kind of liking this little pretend dating game thing, but it's better knowing where she and Brooke stand: friends who don't need to pretend to Landon or anyone else that there's a chance for something more. They can just be Cam and Brooke from now on, with as much or as little baggage from the past as they choose to drag along with them.

"All right," she says. "We can tell him…" What? The truth? Yes, Landon deserves the truth. And even if it comes as a disappointment to him, he must realize that he can't simply snap his fingers and make this little romantic fairytale come true. He is not responsible for her or Brooke's happiness. "We can tell him the truth. That we're working on being friends, but in our own way and not as part of some script. And I think he'll be more than fine with it."

"Perfect."

Cam pays the bill. They step out onto the glistening sidewalk. The fierce winds are beginning to die down.

"You haven't told me," Brooke says, "what made you choose your second career. I mean, why a death doula? I'm curious."

"Let's get out of here," Cam says and hails a cab—a horse and buggy—before Brooke can object.

As they climb in, Cam instructs the driver, "The cemetery please."

CHAPTER THIRTY

Kurt was the horse's name. He was big and gray, with the softest brown eyes Brooke had ever seen. A gentle giant. At the direction of his driver, Kurt trudged them slowly up the main hill that bisects the island, past the old fort with its cannons and pretend soldiers in their replica blue uniforms. The buggy swayed gently, the clip-clop of Kurt's hooves rhythmic and reassuring, steady. Nothing on the island was ever in much of a hurry, something that would have irritated Brooke if she weren't in vacation mode.

Part of her wanted to ask Cam why they were going to the cemetery, but she resisted. Learning to give up control, to take things as they came, wasn't exactly her nature, but she sensed that trusting Cam, trusting whatever was to unfold, was the right thing to do. Huh. Maybe Marcy's wacky blathering about the universe and meditation and inner peace had some merit after all. Or not. All Brooke knew for sure was that the old threadbare habits hadn't been making her happy. Happiness, for her, was always a fraction out of reach, pityingly undeserved, or elusively unobtainable. Was that discontent to blame for her poor relationships over the decades? For turning her into a workaholic? For making her less-than-fun to be with? For hardening her shell a little too much? Probably.

She had a million questions for Cam, as the buggy trundled up the gravel laneway to St. Ann's cemetery. They crossed under a lane-wide stone archway with a stone cross mounted on top. The horse and buggy stopped just inside the archway.

"Can you wait for us?" Cam asked, the driver nodding in response. "We'll probably be about twenty minutes or so."

It was an old cemetery. Limestone headstones were washed out, their inscriptions faded from weather and time. But there were newer headstones too, and Brooke was drawn to one decorated with a little shrine that consisted of miniature cars, a tiny figurine of Superman, a silver dollar, a golf ball—all neatly arranged on top of the headstone.

"Hey, look at this," Brooke said to Cam. The inscription read: *Christopher Underwood, 1979-2018, Loving Husband & Father. Forever Missed, Forever in Our Hearts.* Cam moved to stand shoulder to shoulder with Brooke and silently read the inscription. "He was loved," Brooke said quietly. "And is still missed. Look at these little offerings." She couldn't help but imagine Christopher Underwood's widowed partner and kids standing before his grave, setting out the little mementos in the hope of reaching across the divide to connect with his departed soul.

"'It is a fearful thing to love what death can touch.' I came across that saying once and have never forgotten it."

"Wow. That's powerful. I think that's what I fear most about death…not for myself so much, but in losing people I love. It's the absence, the finality of the loss, that bothers me most." She still missed her father, who died when she was young, barely twenty. She missed not knowing him as an adult, missed seeing how he might have changed as he aged and whether he would have become softer, more introspective, more present. Had he come to regret not being more spontaneous in his life? Would he have taken the gamble of selling the restaurant, as Brooke had done? And more importantly, would the two of them be friends now? Would he like the woman she'd become? The last thought made her draw in a sharp and painful breath, because in all honesty, *she* didn't much like the woman she'd become.

"Losing someone you love is hard," Cam said softly. "Probably the hardest thing in life to experience. But you're born, you live a life—whatever path that life takes you on—and then, like everything, it ends. If you've loved and been loved, that's what ultimately matters at the end. Not how much money you made or the places you traveled or the degrees in a frame on your wall. They're all part of the pieces that make up a life, but with death, those pieces fall away and you are left with...love. And that is all. That, I've come to believe, is what ultimately matters and is the whole point of living. And you know *why* it's all about love? Because love is the only thing you get to take with you from this world into the next."

It took a moment for Cam's words to take root. Brooke had never thought of life and death in those terms before. "Love, huh? Hey, maybe you should write a song about this stuff."

Cam laughed. "Like, 'Love is the Answer'? Already been done, but even if it wasn't, well, no thank you. Been there, done that."

"Why did you choose being a death doula?" she asked again.

They began picking their way around the cemetery, careful to sidestep puddles from the big storm. They stopped before random tombstones and read the inscriptions. "It was my mom's death that started me on that path."

"I'm so sorry, Cam. That makes me sad." Brooke had met Cam's mom on many occasions, the three of them sharing most of the Christmas holidays during the years she and Cam were together. Ruth Hughes was a lovely woman who was kind, smart, a lot like her daughter. And she cooked the best turkeys. Brining it in water mixed with sugar and salt was her secret, which Brooke had finally managed to bribe out of her with a home-cooked meal of mushroom carbonara. "Was it sudden?"

"Thanks, and yes. It was cancer. Ovarian. She was only sixty-seven. I came home to look after her because, well, I was all she had. Plus I really had nowhere else to go. It forced me to get myself together. Her cancer saved my life, I think. Isn't that ironic?"

"What do you mean?"

Cam turned her face to the gray sky, growing lighter by the minute, and closed her eyes. "I was drowning. I knew I didn't want to be in the music industry anymore, but I didn't know what else to do. I was couch surfing all over the country, drinking too much, smoking too much dope, sleeping around. I was waiting to be rescued, I guess, instead of taking control of my life." She shook her head. "I let way too many outside things control my life. It's good that you're taking control of your life, Brooke, your future. Don't wait until your life has completely fallen apart or for someone to die before you make changes."

Except her life was kind of falling apart and someone *was* dying: Landon. So maybe this was the universe telling her to wake up before it was too late. What she had yet to figure out was if she was capable of making such massive changes. With Cam at her side, even if only for a few more days, maybe she could be like a baby bird that flies from the nest for short spurts at a time, returning to safety until it gains incremental confidence to fly further and for longer periods. What she needed was a friend, but she wasn't good at asking for friendship. *I don't think I can do this without you, Cam.*

"Anyway," Cam continued, "I really took a deep dive into learning everything I could about living with a terminal illness, about death and dying and caring for the sick. I met so many wonderful people—palliative care professionals, patients, caregivers, teachers. It opened my eyes in ways that's hard to put into words. It felt like the path was opening up to me, right before my eyes."

"Tell me what you felt."

A smile came instantly to Cam. "I felt like I'd been born again, almost. I felt like I could see for the first time. And by that, I mean that I could finally see what was important, that I could be so much more useful and so much more fulfilled doing this work. I learned very quickly what a privilege it was to be able to accompany people through a moment of enormous meaning and power."

"So, you finally put that college degree to work, huh?"

College was where they'd first met, at the start of their final year. Brooke was studying a weird combination of English and hospitality. Cam majored in social work, intending for her music to help pay her college bills, only to discover by the time she graduated that she could no longer ignore the call of the stage. Social work never really had a chance back in those days. But Brooke knew that Cam had promised her mom she would get her degree before pursuing music, so as far as Cam was concerned, she'd held up her end of the deal. Over cheap wine, they'd stayed up late into the night many times discussing Cam's lack of guilt for putting the stage ahead of the career she'd trained for.

"Yeah, finally." Cam was still smiling. She'd found her calling, and by all indications, she was damned good at it.

"You always were a people person. You always knew how to talk to people, how to put them at ease. I guess I'm not so surprised about your career after all."

"Nowadays I listen probably more than I talk, but thank you."

They stopped before a handful of bleached white tombstones dating back to the Civil War. Such young men, such young lives lost forever. What had their final moments been like, Brooke wondered. Did they feel as though they'd lived a good life? Were they scared? Did they die alone? Did they have regrets, or were they ready to go when the time came? Had they known love?

"Do you think Landon is ready to go? I mean, is he accepting of his fate?"

"Now, yes, I think so, but there are many stages before you get there. I think he's in the stage of wanting all the people he cares about to be okay without him, to be happy. He won't let go until he feels there's nothing else he needs to do for his loved ones."

Yup, that sounded like Landon, always wanting to take care of others. His attempt to reunite her and Cam, Brooke now understood, was intended as his final act. That he continued to care about her floored Brooke. What had she done to deserve that kind of love and loyalty from a man she was fond of but had never been able to romantically love in return? She'd offered him crumbs when he deserved the whole cake. And here he was, still giving, still loving her unconditionally.

"Oh, Cam." Tears flooded Brooke's eyes. Could she become deserving of his kindness? Was there still time? Admitting her thoughts out loud made her stomach clench, but she sensed Cam would know exactly what she meant. And without judgment. "I don't want to be me anymore."

Cam's eyebrows shot up in surprise, but she said nothing.

"I...I want to be the person I was meant to be."

"All right." Cam was so calm, so accepting, that Brooke felt a sudden rush of love for her. "And who is that, do you think?"

"You. I want to be you." Oversimplified, but basically true.

"What?"

"Strong, loving, kind, wise, accepting, at peace."

Cam flushed deeply. "Brooke, I'm still working on me. I'm a work-in-progress. I mean, don't get me wrong, I'm flattered that you think I'm all those things, but—"

"No. You *are* those things. I want to arrive at that place too. I just don't know where to begin." And that was the hardest part. Like falling into a bad dream, she was suddenly that kid in the classroom who had no idea what the teacher was talking about, while all around her the other kids happily beavered away. Why couldn't she figure this out? "Except maybe for what Maggie told me."

"Which was?"

"To be honest, to be genuine."

Cam nodded. "She makes a good point. If you're authentic, people see that, people are drawn to that. But you can't be authentic until you know yourself and love yourself. Knowing yourself and being authentic make it possible to be seen by others, make it possible to see each other, however we are, whether it's broken, vulnerable, afraid, joyful, happy. Authenticity leads to intimacy."

"But you make it sound so easy!" It couldn't be, could it?
"It's not."

Swallowing the last of her tears, Brooke said, "So where do I start? How do I start?" Was there a goddamned book she could buy? A DVD she could rent? A class she could sign up for?

"Forgiving yourself for not being perfect, forgiving others for not being perfect, is a good place to start. So is treating solitude like a significant other."

The forgiving part she understood. Theoretically she forgave easily, but in her heart, where the truth resided, she was too often stingy. The solitude thing, though? "Huh?"

"Spend time alone. That's what I did after my mom died. I started to figure out how to like my own company, how to be alone and actually like it. Quiet solitude is when I started to figure out what I wanted to do, who I wanted to be. It's about finding a way to letting the noise go." She rolled her eyes. "Believe me, that's not an easy thing when your ego is used to being stroked by thousands of people on a regular basis."

"Wow. And I thought I had it tough." She tried to smile, but the effort was too much. "I don't know if I'm as strong as you, Cam." There it was, the old doubts creeping back in. "I don't know if I can do this."

"You are and you will. And this, the island, is the perfect place for it. I can even give you some meditation tips, if that helps."

"Would you really do that?"

"Of course."

Kurt snorted in the distance, and Cam glanced at her watch. "Someone's getting restless. My last tip of the day is this: be unafraid."

"Unafraid? What do you mean?"

"I mean, don't be afraid of solitude, of being still. And don't be afraid to be vulnerable, to let your true self come to the surface. Don't be afraid to discover new things about yourself, okay? Oh, and after today, I don't want to see you for a couple of days."

"What? Why?"

Cam drew out a teasing wink. "Because you have a crapload of work to do. Alone."

Brooke feigned offense. "Well, a crapload might be a bit harsh, but okay. I'll try." The alone part sucked because she had come to enjoy being with Cam. Cam, who was a stranger, and yet, she was anything but a stranger to Brooke.

Be unafraid.

CHAPTER THIRTY-ONE

Landon is predictably disappointed when Cam calls him and breaks the news that while she and Brooke are going to stay on the island, they won't be continuing with his itinerary.

"But there is one piece of good news." She attempts a cheerful tone. "Brooke never had an affair on me all those years ago. It was all a big mistake."

"Mistake? How does one make a mistake about something like that?"

Cam would prefer to leave it at that, to skip the details because this is between her and Brooke. But if Landon continues to hold out hope that the two of them might reunite, then he deserves the truth. "Our relationship was in trouble, but I was too stupid to notice. I think Brooke was trying to do something dramatic to shake things up. To make me notice. It...kinda backfired, needless to say."

"Wow. Okay. I don't know what to say."

"You don't need to say anything, Landon. We were young and didn't know what the hell we were doing."

"But you two are still talking, yes?"

"Yes." She avoids any more details, tries to distract him by talking about the island's attributes, but his voice recedes with each passing minute, as though he's speaking underwater. Cam asks Landon to pass the phone to Tenley, who confirms that he's getting weaker, isn't eating much. He's alert, he's okay, she assures Cam, but Cam knows that his body is shutting down, his world narrowing until there is only himself, Tenley, his sick bed, his caregivers. She talks a bit longer to Tenley, asks detailed questions, offers to come straight back to Traverse City. "No," Tenley said, "it would break his heart if you cut your trip short. And Becky Neerhof is here a couple of hours every day. It's fine, I promise."

The last of the clouds are disappearing, exactly what Cam doesn't want because their sullenness reflects her mood. She's failing Landon by not being at his side. She's failing him in his quest to see her and Brooke romantically reunited. To Cam, there isn't much worse than disappointing someone who hasn't much time left. And even though it's not her responsibility to perform miracles and grant wishes and make the impossible happen, right now it hurts that she's letting him down.

What am I doing here? I'm taking a vacation when my client has only weeks left.

Except Landon is adamant he doesn't want her to come back yet, and Brooke... Well, who knows if Brooke really wants her to stick around. She can't solve Brooke's problems and she can't solve Landon's right now, either. *Dammit.* What good is she? What is she even doing here, when it feels so self-indulgent?

She rings off and walks down the main street, sidestepping horse poop when she's not hopping over puddles. She has her eye on the bookstore across the street, not because she needs more books but because she can't resist being in the company of those rows of shiny new books with their scent of ink and paper and their stiff spines. There's an entire world in that little bookshop. As she's about to cross the street, she spots Brooke exiting the bookstore, clutching a couple of books under her arm.

Brooke sees her, waves, flashes her a grin as big and bright as the sun. So different from her stone-cold attitude their first couple of days here, and the memory makes Cam smile. She waves back but keeps walking, deciding to skip the bookstore because she doesn't want to enter into a conversation with Brooke. She meant it when she told Brooke she didn't want to see her for a couple of days, but even with the street between them, Cam can feel the bond of mutual appreciation. It's not her imagination that they are actually beginning to like one another again.

O'Doul's looms ahead, and right away Cam notices the For Sale sign in the window. She strolls in, an eruption of jingles announcing her arrival thanks to the antique little brass bell over the door.

"Well, hello there, Cam," Maggie gushes. "It's so good to see you. No Brooke this time?"

"No Brooke this time."

"You're not fighting again, are you?"

"No, we're not fighting. Actually, we're…not really anything except friendly acquaintants, if you want to know the truth."

"Oh, come now, sweetie. You can't fool this old fool."

"Huh?"

Maggie claps a weathered hand on Cam's wrist. "Come with me. Shelly?" She calls out to the teenaged girl who is stocking the freezer. "Woman the fort for a half hour or so? Thanks, honey. I'll be upstairs." She tugs Cam through the Staff Only door and up the stairs to the apartment she shares with her wife. The smell of cabbage soup wafts down the stairwell and Cam's stomach growls. She'd forgotten it's suppertime.

Maggie marches through the door and calls out to Jane, "Look who's here, dear. It's Cam."

Jane, a tea towel over her shoulder, pops her head around the kitchen doorway. "Be right there. How about a bowl of my soup, Cam? Nice to see you."

"I wouldn't dream of saying no to homemade soup."

"Wonderful. It'll be just a few minutes."

The whole place is redolent of cooked cabbage, meat, tomatoes, spices, fresh bread. Cam could plant herself right here for hours and be happy simply inhaling the wonderful aromas. Except she *is* pretty hungry. "Hey, I see the store is officially for sale now?"

"It is." Maggie directs her to the sofa.

The living room is large and airy, a big window looking straight down on the main street. Antiques are everywhere— an etched glass oil lamp, a mahogany wall barometer, an old umbrella stand, a trolley tea cart that probably dates back to the Victorian age. An antique gingerbread clock ticks loudly on the mantel over the gas fireplace. "It's gorgeous up here." The stained-glass transom over the doorway leading to the small dining area catches Cam's eye. It might be an apartment, but it feels like a home.

"Jane's brother is a realtor in Florida, so he's looking for condos there for us. We can't wait to start spending our winters in the warmth and sun. I'd say five decades of cold and snow is more than enough penance."

"I understand, even if I don't fully agree. There's something about taking a walk in the cold that sharpens everything to the bone. If I'm trying to work something out in my mind or in my heart, I love a walk in the cold."

Maggie laughs. "Then maybe *you* should move here full time."

It's Cam's turn to laugh. "Oh, there's lots of winter in Traverse City, trust me. Will you come back and spend your summers here?"

"We're not sure yet. I'd love for us to spend a month or two in Ireland each spring, followed by two or three months here." She lowers her voice to a whisper. "Jane's feet are firmly planted on North American soil, so it's still up for negotiation."

"Ah, okay, I get it."

"So tell me about your fight with Brooke? I can see you two have a lot of chemistry."

"It's not a fight, and we're not a couple."

"But you were a couple."

"We were. Long ago."

"And you could be again if things went a certain way?"

"I doubt it. Brooke has some things she wants to figure out right now. And, honestly, so much time has passed and there are still, I don't know, old wounds that haven't entirely healed. Oh, and did I mention I don't do well with relationships? How they're not really my thing?"

Maggie laughs. "Oh, that old excuse. When it's meant to be, you figure out how to make it work. It's not like we're born to *do* relationships. We learn how to do them, like we learn everything else."

Jane calls them to the dining room, where steaming bowls of cabbage soup and warm, homemade bread await them.

"This is wonderful," Cam says. "But honestly, I didn't mean to invite myself for a meal."

"You didn't," Maggie admonishes. "You're here because we want to share our food with you."

"And," Jane says with a wink, "our infinite wisdom about relationships, if that's what you want to hear."

Cam looks at the two women, sees only kindness and a willingness to help. She can't imagine why she wouldn't tell them everything, so she does.

"So," Maggie says, "it sounds to me like you're torn every which way."

"You still have feelings for Brooke," Jane offers, "and yet you feel like you're wasting your time here when you could be helping Landon. Or at least making his wish come true by reuniting with Brooke."

They've nailed it; Cam can only nod.

"What if," Maggie says, "Landon wasn't in the picture at all. Let's say you happened to come here for a vacation at the same time as Brooke did and the two of you accidentally ran into each other. What would be different?"

"Everything. I'm not sure we would have even spoken to each other if not for Landon. We probably would have pretended we didn't know each other."

Jane winces. "Ouch. Okay, so Landon is the catalyst who got you two at least speaking to each other again. Now his role is done, and you and Brooke have honored that part. The rest is up to the two of you."

"And that's the part that's confusing. I don't know what we're supposed to do now that we've been thrown together on this island. It's not like two people who had an epic breakup eighteen years ago are suddenly going to start seeing fireworks and feeling butterflies in their stomachs because everything is wonderful again. This isn't a Hollywood movie."

With frank inquiry, Maggie says, "Have you forgiven Brooke for ending your relationship the way she did?"

The answer would have been a quick no a few days ago. Now she understands why Brooke did what she did, understands her own role in it all, though it doesn't make the memories of that time any easier. "I have."

In a gentle voice, Jane asks, "Have you forgiven yourself for failing Brooke?"

The question throws her for a minute. For years, it had been easier to pick up the pieces and reinvent herself, to wall off the damage rather than take any responsibility. She swallows against the roughness in her throat. "I'm working on that."

"Well, it sounds to me," Maggie says, "like you're putting too much pressure on yourself. Like Jane said, forget about Landon's wishes. He put the two of you here, and that's it. The rest is up to you and Brooke. And the universe. Now, tell me something. What have the two of you been doing since you got to the island?"

Cam shrugs. "Getting to know one another again. Hanging out. Though it hasn't all been sunshine and roses."

Jane laughs. "Go figure."

"It sounds like getting to know one another and hanging out is exactly the thing to be doing. No need to worry about anything beyond that."

Cam nods at Maggie's advice. It really could be that simple if she let it.

They eat in silence for a few moments. The soup is delicious and so is the bread. Maggie pours them all a glass of wine and says something about closing the store early so they can chat longer. Cam is going to miss their company when she leaves the island.

Maggie disappears for a few minutes to close the store. By the time she rejoins them, Cam, without giving herself time to think about it, has plucked their old guitar off the wall.

"Would you play something for us?" Maggie asks with the biggest puppy dog eyes Cam has ever seen.

Cam fingerpicks a few notes, acquainting herself with the instrument, sharpening her focus. It's amazing how the notes are right there, easily summoned, even though, before the evening of music and dancing with Tenley and Landon, she hadn't picked up a guitar in almost a decade. She closes her eyes and lets herself fall into the sounds the guitar releases, into the way her fingers glide familiarly over the steel strings. She can hear nothing except the beginning notes of "How Sweet It Is (To Be Loved By You)," followed by her voice singing, "I needed the shelter of someone's arms, and there you were." She draws the tune out slowly, sings it like a love song. For once, singing doesn't hurt, doesn't make her sad or anxious. Her mind has yielded to everything but the notes her fingers and the instrument create, the words her voice gives life to. There is only beauty and peace, and for the life of her, she can't remember why she stopped playing and singing. It's like she stopped breathing, and now that she's breathing again, she remembers how wonderful it is.

When the song is over, Maggie and Jane jump to their feet clapping, whooping.

"Girl!" Jane shakes her head in admiration. "You haven't lost a thing! You should be headlining the music festival here this weekend, that's for damned sure."

"Thank you," Cam says. "But I don't ever want to be onstage again." She no longer needs the adoration or the accolades or anything at all from a professional music career. But this, playing and singing for a couple of people, hasn't been nearly as distressing as she feared. It's actually kind of...nice.

"Well, forget the stage," Maggie says. "We're just happy you're sharing your talents with us."

By the time she prepares to leave an hour or so later, Maggie has some parting advice for her. And hands her something in an envelope. "Be yourself, Cam. Shed any expectations that you or

Landon or Brooke might have and just let whatever happens, happen. And be selfish for once."

"For once? Oh, trust me, I got pretty good at being selfish."

"And you probably haven't done a single selfish thing since," Maggie scolds. "It's time. Look after your own needs for a while, child."

The sky shows only a faint hint of the departed sun while lit globes from the ubiquitous lampposts guide Cam back to her hotel. Stores are closing, some of the buildings have gone dark, while others, like restaurants, exude warm light and laughter from inside, the tinkle of cutlery and wineglasses trailing after Cam. She feels lighter after her visit with Maggie and Jane. Lighter because she feels understood. And supported. She thinks about Maggie's suggestion of being selfish. And maybe Maggie has a point. Cam has spent years attending to other people's needs. What about her own?

"I don't even know what I need," she mumbles out loud. Maybe it's time she figured it out.

Back at her hotel, she hears only silence from behind Brooke's door and wonders how she's doing. Inside her room, she opens the envelope from Maggie. Inside is a DVD of the movie *Somewhere in Time*. She's never seen it before, but she's noticed framed pictures of the actors all over town because the movie was shot here decades ago.

She places it next to the television, which, fortunately, has a DVD player built into it. Maybe, she decides, she'll ask Brooke to watch it with her in a couple of days. Maybe it will give them some insight into some of the places they should visit on the island. Or, hell, maybe it's an excuse to spend more time with Brooke, because, hell, she misses her already.

CHAPTER THIRTY-TWO

Brooke cupped the paper coffee cup between her hands and, for about the eleventh time, dipped her head to inhale its delicious aroma of dark roast with a dash of cinnamon and a trace of chocolate. She closed her eyes to more fully appreciate the scent and to enjoy the sensation of the breeze ruffling her hair and dancing across her skin. *Little things*, she told herself. Feel the little things. There was contentment in little things, not just the big things. For years she'd been too busy or too exhausted from being busy to take the time for what she once considered were useless trivialities. Who knew these things could be such a gift?

The lake was finally calm after the storm some thirty-six hours ago, though Brooke supposed that since it was where Lakes Huron and Michigan converged it was not very often that way. The bench she occupied was hard, but after thirty minutes of not moving, she barely registered the discomfort. She inhaled through her nose, held the breath, exhaled through her mouth. Sipped her coffee. Rinse and repeat until her mind emptied and she became only aware of the breeze and the sounds of lapping water in the distance. She decided to focus on other natural sounds around her—gulls, horses, even the distant chattering of people.

It was working, the basic meditation suggestion Cam had emailed to her yesterday. Or at least it seemed to be, if relaxation was the goal. And it was. Brooke couldn't remember a time when her body and mind seemed so uniformly…empty. All she had to do today, she told herself, was breathe. And be. Today mattered, nothing else.

After a while longer she got up and trashed her coffee cup. She decided to walk the mile or so to the Grand Hotel, which was mostly uphill. Once there, she diverged along West Bluff Road, stopping to admire the bird's-eye view of the Straits of Mackinac and the mainland beyond. Trees and water stretched out in miniature before her while the great Mackinac Bridge poked into the horizon, its steel fingers clawing into the sky. Hawks flew in circles above her, surfing the air currents, searching for their next meal. It was so peaceful, so quiet up here. Maybe it was the void of not having any traffic or people. It was blissful.

She strolled past what the locals referred to as "cottages," perched grandly on the limestone cliffs. She remembered seeing them in the distance on the ferry ride to the island. They were Victorian homes, with massive wraparound porches and turrets that lent themselves to imagining a reading room or library inside their domed walls. Cobblestone walkways and gardens of roses and lilies and sculpted hedges added a flair that one usually only saw in magazines. Most of the homes had their own carriage houses, along with their own carriages and horses. Surely not much had changed here in the last century and a half. Only a few hundred people, like Jane and Maggie, lived all year around on the island. Now that was an interesting thought, living here permanently. Winters didn't frighten Brooke; she was a Michigan girl through and through. But if she could feel this kind of peace *here*, could she feel this way all the time? Would she feel it if she lived here?

Forget it, Brooke. She smiled at the preposterous fantasy. It would be expensive living here, and she needed to watch her pennies. Not to mention that good-paying job prospects weren't exactly plentiful on the island, especially during the winter. Ah, well. Vacations always shone a generous light on places and thoughts that the real world kept only in shadows.

Being alone with nothing to do, to Brooke's surprise, wasn't a hardship. When Cam had told her that she needed to treat solitude like a significant other, the idea had confounded her. Alone with her thoughts? Be by herself? No no no. That would only lead to anxiety, self-admonishment, maybe depression. And yet it hadn't. It was as though she had to stop running to see herself clearly.

After another hour of walking, she realized she'd hardly thought of anything at all, or at least she hadn't thought about a single worrisome thing. She understood then that there was no reason to think about responsibilities for the rest of her stay here. Landon, Cam, her unemployment, her house under repair. They were all things she could think and worry about with the unspooling of time, because she liked this Brooke who didn't need to think about anything, didn't need to plan or execute a single thing. There were no expectations on her horizon. There was nothing except herself, the sky, the ground she walked on, the water below. That and air was all she needed this very second.

She looked around her at all the new growth. The foliage on trees, the flowering shrubs, wild columbine, carpets of geraniums and marigolds. Lilacs were everywhere, of course. It was spring—a rebirth of beauty, of hope, of plenty. Which actually, miraculously, mirrored how she felt inside. Possibilities rolled out before her like an endless ribbon of highway, with no right or wrong direction to take. And yet there was also an autumnal feeling in her soul—the curling and dried out husks of life falling to the ground. She was both things at this moment— parts of her drying up, falling away, making room for a riot of new growth.

So, this was what the word *serenity* meant. For the first time in forever, there was a new but calm energy coursing through her. It wasn't born out of a need to be busy or distracted. She'd become so task-oriented, so goal-driven, had developed the habit of measuring time by productivity (oh, how many times had Marcy lectured her to slow down and smell the roses!). It was always about how much could she get done in a day. And if she didn't, it was a failed or incomplete day. She had invested heavily in the science of efficiency, poured more and more time into the less meaningful. And for what? *For what?* If she could accept that what was solid today could be transitory and gone tomorrow, and if she could find space and peace in the recognition that nothing stays the same, then maybe true happiness was achievable.

Brooke had done nothing today but wander around with her head in the clouds, and yet a sense of accomplishment filled her anyway. She took note of the irony of it and did a little fist pump. She couldn't wait to share with Cam how she'd taken her advice to heart and that it wasn't so scary after all. There were no answers to be found, not yet, and that was okay. She didn't need answers today or tomorrow or the next day. Not everything she did needed concrete results. She was her own worst enemy with that voice in her head that said she hadn't done enough, that *she* wasn't enough. That voice needed to be vanquished once and for all, along with the need for external shit to propel her through the day, through her life. Good riddance to that!

Brooke meandered her way back past the Grand Hotel and down the road that led back to town. Horses and their carriages trundled alongside her; people on bicycles glided past. With each step, the noise and bustle of the afternoon reinserted itself into her awareness and the cloak of serenity began to fall away from her. In its place marched in a streak of shame. Shame that over the years she'd let herself become so removed from nature and beauty and contemplation. She had so little in that respect to show for her time on earth so far. With her debts paid, the sale of the restaurant still left her with a sizable bank account. And she owned her townhouse unit outright now. *Oh, bully for you, Brooke. You have no debt anymore and a little nest egg. What else do you have?* Not a lot, if you took away her possessions. What she really wanted was to feel less lonely. There was no one to run her a hot bath and hand her a glass of wine at the end of a long day, to talk with about the things that really mattered, to share glorious moments like today, but also the crappy times. What she didn't have was someone to catch her when she fell. Or even when she merely stumbled.

Her thoughts drifted to Cam, who could have been that person to catch her if only they'd worked on their relationship, persevered instead of walking away because it was too much work, because it was too hard. And she could have been the one to catch Cam, too, if only she had dropped her goddamned ego a few notches. She'd been so stupid and selfish and shameful, the way she'd manufactured an affair instead of being honest about her needs. Why had she been so scared to assert herself, to voice what she needed? Was it because, all these years, she'd secretly judged people like her mother and sister for living lives of following every whim? A secret part of her considered the two of them to be unreliable, self-absorbed, flakey, and other pejorative terms, because they didn't hold down jobs or careers the way most people did. She hadn't wanted to be them, and yet, maybe their habit of taking life as it came wasn't so terrible. Maybe it was...mentally healthier?

All Brooke's life, she'd felt on the outside of happiness—a kid with her nose pressed up against the window of The Happy Store. It wasn't so much that she felt undeserving, but that she rarely allowed herself to indulge in happiness. Not when there were things that needed doing and places she needed to be. Now she had nothing to do, no responsibilities, and she was... unhappy. Not with her lot in life, but with who was. Because with the stripping away of everything else in her life, there was only her.

Up ahead, she noticed Cam exiting a fudge shop with a giant bag of what looked like chocolate-coated popcorn. A sucker for sweets, Brooke began to salivate. "That looks delicious," she called out.

"Are we supposed to be talking?" Cam stage-called back, making her way to Brooke.

"Oh...right." Brooke giggled from behind her hand. "Am I still in my self-discovery purgatory?"

"Well, hopefully it's not that hellish."

"Actually, it's not."

Cam looked surprised. "Really?"

"Really. In fact, I'm off to pick—I mean steal—a fistful of lilacs for my room." Bring a little of this nature indoors to enjoy. Who *am* I? she thought with surprise, because the old Brooke hadn't much use for fresh flowers, not unless they were being carefully placed on the tables at her restaurant.

"Hey, do you…?" Cam broke eye contact. "Never mind."

"Never mind what?" Brooke adored this vulnerable side of Cam. It wasn't new, just new on the island. In the past, Cam had never been afraid to show that side of herself, probably because she easily understood and recognized vulnerability in others. Long before music took over her life, Cam would regularly volunteer for an LGBTQ youth help line, spent every Thanksgiving volunteering at a soup kitchen. She had that natural impulse to rescue strays, whether animal or human, and so it made total sense that she had chosen a career helping people. That she was revealing her vulnerable side to Brooke again was an encouraging sign.

"I, um, was going to ask you to watch a movie with me, but, well, maybe you need more time to yourself. Or, you know, you might want to be alone."

Brooke sighed her impatience. "Cam, I don't want to dance around things anymore. I've been doing it all my life, not being honest when I need to be. So, like, can we make a little pact to not avoid the truth?" It was no empty promise; she would be direct and honest with the people she cared about from now on. She straightened her shoulders to show she was serious.

"Oh. Okay. Absolutely." Cam visibly swallowed, but her shoulders relaxed. "You're sure?"

"I'm sure."

"All right. I can do that. So, do you want to watch a movie with me tonight? It's a DVD. Maggie and Jane lent it to me. It's that movie they shot here a long time ago, the one with Christopher Reeve and Jane Seymour? I don't know much about it."

There was in Cam's imploring eyes that joyful mix of curiosity and satisfaction that a part of Brooke suddenly craved like oxygen. She'd watch *Night of the Living Dead* with Cam if it meant spending a few hours alone with her. "Ooh, you mean *Somewhere In Time?*"

"Damn, am I the only person around here who's never seen it? Or even heard of it?"

"Nope. I never saw it either, but I have at least heard about it." She playfully nudged Cam's shoulder. "And yes. I'd love to watch it with you. I could use a fun distraction." She raised her arms above her head in a stretch and yawned. "All this introspection is exhausting. Hey, are you volunteering to provide the popcorn?"

Cam's grin involved her whole face. "I think I've just been volun-told. Can you provide the wine?"

"Deal."

Standing on the sidewalk, smiling at one another, Brooke felt the years melt away. Could this really be happening?

CHAPTER THIRTY-THREE

Cam's hands go clammy at the knock on her door. It's ridiculous to be nervous. It's only Brooke, here to watch the movie with her. It's not a date. It's nothing at all to be anxious about, yet her stomach is a hive of agitated bees.

"Hi." Brooke holds up two bottles of white wine triumphantly. "Can I throw these in your fridge?"

"Absolutely," Cam says cheerfully. "I'd tell you where it is, but, well, it *is* an identical room to yours."

"You have the nicer view from your balcony."

"No argument there." Across the hall, Brooke's view is mostly of the main street below with a partial water view, while Cam has an unobstructed view of the water. "Want me to complain to Landon on your behalf?"

Brooke's grin vanishes at the mention of his name. "How's he doing? Have you been in touch?"

"I have. Come in, have a seat."

Brooke kicks off her sandals and makes herself at home on the sofa, which is not much bigger than a loveseat. It faces the television, so they'll both have to squeeze onto it to watch the movie. Cam's stomach flutters at the thought, because sitting close to Brooke for a couple of hours, with only the ambient light from the television and the fireplace, would be sort of nice. And sorta thrilling. For now, she moves to one of the wingback chairs and repositions it to face Brooke.

"He's failing," she says plainly, understanding at the same time how vague yet also accurate the term is. "I mean, he's failing faster now. His organs are slowly shutting down. But he's still awake and conscious and eating a bit."

"Does he…have much time?"

"Weeks."

Brooke nods, looks away before she says, "I want to see him before he…goes."

Softly, Cam says, "It's okay to say the word *dies*. Before he dies. And I'm sure he'd like that."

Brooke nods. But there's something different about her—something less rigid, less fearful, more open. Where storms once raged around her, there is tranquility. The transformation is clearly visible, even more so as Brooke's eyes widen in pleasure and a smile lifts her lips. Her eyes always did have that spectacular way of lightening a couple of shades when she was happy. "By the way, I have one rule about tonight."

Cam blinks. "Okay."

"No sadness, no tears, no more serious stuff. The movie, wine, popcorn, hanging out together, that's enough for me."

"Okay," she agrees and marvels at how easy it suddenly is to be with Brooke. Instead of measuring time chronologically, for Cam the lines delineating past, present, and future have blurred, or maybe sharpened, into this moment of quiet contentment. Brooke is right. They don't need to think about anything sad or heavy tonight, because everything is perfect exactly the way it is. They can be present without the past or the future rolling up to their door and pounding on it. "I'll fire up the movie and the fireplace and get the popcorn if you want to open a bottle of wine."

"Sounds perfect."

They sit side by side on the sofa and dive into the popcorn, the opening credits of the movie scrolling along. The early part of the story is set in Chicago, and Cam is anxious for the scenes to move to Mackinac Island. The Christopher Reeve character wants to time travel to meet an intriguing, beautiful woman who has some mysterious emotional connection to him, and it sucks Cam in completely. Brooke seems equally mesmerized.

"Wouldn't that be cool," Brooke whispers, her eyes fixed on the movie, "if we could time travel?"

Cam wants to laugh. It would be another reason or excuse for people to avoid living in the present. Why be here when you can time travel somewhere else? Except she has to admit that the fantasy of time travel is alluring. If she could go back in time to change anything, she'd go back to that day when Brooke fake-confessed her affair. She wouldn't let Brooke off the hook this time, wouldn't walk away from her in hurtful, vindictive fury. Maybe they'd still be together and maybe they wouldn't, but she'll never give up so easily again. Not when it comes to Brooke.

The movie proceeds until, finally, the island unfolds right before them on the large, flat screen TV. And there's The Grand Hotel, a resplendent gem that never seems to change.

"Let's sneak in there and wander around," Brooke announces with the excited anticipation of doing something naughty. "I want to see some of these rooms they're showing in the movie. Do you really think there's a room devoted entirely to artifacts and stuff?"

"Yes and it's probably all artifacts from the making of the movie."

"I'm serious." Brooke lightly smacks Cam on her knee, which is less than an inch from her own.

The touch of Brooke's fingers heats Cam from the inside, and she eggs Brooke on to keep the banter going. "Do we need to dress like ninjas and do this mission at night?"

"No, silly. We'll just go in and act like we're guests."

Cam tosses Brooke a look. "You have something you want to tell me?"

"Like?" Brooke's eyebrows knit in adorable confusion, and the impulse to plant a kiss on her forehead is something Cam has to work at ignoring.

"Like that you're an expert prowler or thief or something? Or that you've at least done this before?"

They pause the movie because Brooke can't stop laughing. She's not drunk, her wineglass is still half full, and Cam loves this mirthful version of her. Her body is relaxed, her leg now resting against the length of Cam's leg, and Cam takes another moment to study her while her eyes are closed and she's still giggling. She's always loved looking at her, whether she was asleep or awake, laughing or spitting out angry words. Brooke rarely ever hid the physical manifestations of her moods, she was always predictable that way, but this new beauty in her is rooted, Cam believes, in some kind of inner peace or acceptance she seems to have discovered. Brooke is more beautiful at forty-eight than she's ever been.

They resume the movie. The characters are falling in love, but the island almost steals it all, and Cam wants to discover more of this place, wants to follow in the footsteps these actors took here more than forty years ago. If Maggie and Jane were hoping the romance bug would bite Cam after seeing this movie, well, they weren't wrong.

"Isn't it perfect," Cam says, "that we're right here, watching this movie, where they filmed it?"

Brooke grins at her. "Hey, let's each ride a horse while we're here!"

"Whoa! I don't think so. My feet like to be on the ground, not dangling from some animal that's four or five times my size."

"Are you wimping out on me, Fos—I mean Hughes?"

Cam feigns indignation. "Never."

"Good. Because I think we should start our own itinerary of things we want to do here and forget about Landon's."

"Okay." But what will Landon think of them forming their own plans? Knowing Landon, he'll be fine with it. After all, his end goal was getting them to spend more time together, and that's exactly what they're doing, even if he isn't aware of it.

"In that case, want to go to the outdoor music festival with me Saturday night?" The words are out of her mouth before she has time to think about how attending her first live music event in years might feel, because being with Brooke is, frankly, more important.

"You mean actually sit and enjoy a concert together? Without you having to go up on stage and leave me somewhere in the audience, watching all the girls go crazy over you?"

"Exactly. Let's watch girls go crazy over somebody else for a change." Cam waggles her eyebrows. This might be fun.

"Ha, maybe *we'll* swoon over someone on stage."

The memory rushes back of the two of them at the Michigan Womyn's Festival in the late 1990s, chasing a rumor as rain fell in sheets and turned the field into an instant mud pit. Cam had already performed her set when the sun was still shining. A rumor reached her that k.d. lang was in the audience, incognito. Well, as much as k.d. lang ever could be anywhere incognito. Cam reminds Brooke of that night, and how, as the inclement weather brought the show to an early close, they took off barefoot in the mud, determined to find k.d.

Brooke moves her hand to rest on Cam's thigh as their voices soar with retelling and reliving that hour they spent looking under practically every tarp and awning and behind every curtained-off or walled-off area, hunting for k.d. Soaked to the bone, they finally gave up but not before stomping and dancing through the biggest puddles they could find, faces and grins upturned to the onslaught from the heavens. They didn't care that they'd failed in their mission, because the mission had become something more pure and thrilling in its spontaneity.

"I love those moments," Cam says, "when something becomes something else that's better than what you planned, you know?"

Brooke nods. Her hand is still on Cam's thigh, occasioning a patch of tingling warmth beneath Cam's jeans. "I'm afraid I haven't had very many of those moments since."

"But you're having one here. This week. Coming to the island, right?" There's the urge to wrap her arm soothingly around Brooke's shoulders, the way she used to without being asked. And then the fantasy of pulling Brooke onto her lap fills her vision, and it's almost more than she can bear.

"You're absolutely right." Brooke ponders in silence. "I thought this was going to be something else completely, when I first came here." She rolls her eyes. "Oh, how I fought it. And fought it hard."

"You did. Correction, we both did. But I'm glad we're not anymore."

"Me too. I…like it here."

Brooke's face is suddenly inches from Cam's. Cam can smell the wine and popcorn on her breath. Has the intense desire to taste it on Brooke's lips. Intense enough that she draws in enough breath to fill her lungs to try to stifle the urge. And then the moment is gone as Brooke turns back to the television, and so does Cam. They're still touching along the length of their legs, though, and Brooke's hand continues to rest on Cam's thigh, as if it's been forgotten, except it isn't forgotten. Not by Cam, because from Brooke's touch comes the soft, slow ignition of want through Cam's body, ambushing her. The surprise comes not because it's Brooke who still has the power to turn her on, but that she is turned on at all. Cam has done a tremendous job over the years of convincing herself that she doesn't need anyone.

The movie ends, not a happily ever after, unless you consider reuniting in eternity as a happy ending. Which is fine with Cam, she's a big fan of eternity, but at the same time, she craves a happy earth ending at the moment. A silly, unrealistic, happy ending—the kind that makes you cry from joy that is completely and utterly embarrassing.

Brooke's head droops onto Cam's shoulder. Soft snores soon follow. Cam finishes her glass of wine and lets Brooke sleep against her for a few more minutes before she carefully removes herself and shuts the television off, clears away their empty glasses and the bits of popcorn. Brooke isn't budging, isn't even lifting an eyelid as Cam whispers to her that the movie is over. She's completely out. *Now what?* At least the last time she put Brooke to bed, it was in Brooke's own room.

Cam slips into the bathroom to wash her face and brush her teeth, hoping that Brooke will wake up on her own. No such luck. Cam lifts Brooke's arm, but it's floppy and uncooperative. "Brooke? Brooke? It's time to wake up."

Nothing. Time for Plan B, which is to let Brooke sleep right there on the sofa because it's late and Cam doesn't feel like fighting anymore to wake Brooke up. *Shit.* The sofa is too small for Brooke's lanky figure to sleep on without throwing her neck or back out, so Cam braces herself, throws her arm under Brooke's shoulders, wraps another arm around her waist, and hauls her as carefully as she can onto the king bed. There's lots of room for both of them...room enough that they won't need to touch each other. Room enough that she won't even know Brooke is there. *Right?*

CHAPTER THIRTY-FOUR

The light slanted into the room at a weird angle as Brooke slowly opened one eye. Where the hell was she? This wasn't her room because the French doors to the balcony were…not where they were supposed to be. Something immovable was up against her too, something warm and soft. Reluctantly she opened another eye, afraid of what she'd find until she remembered. She was in Cam's room. She must have fallen asleep last night after the movie. Why didn't Cam wake her up and make her go back to her own room?

Unless…

Wait. Okay, she was still clothed beneath the blanket Cam must have placed over her. She stole a look at the slumbering Cam beside her, also fully clothed. Nothing had happened between them. Which was…kind of disappointing, because Brooke wouldn't have minded a kiss or two or three. For old times' sake. Or, you know, to see how it felt kissing Cam after all these years. A little experiment, that's all.

"Hi," Cam croaked. "I'm sorry. I hope this is okay."

"Okay that you took care of me again?" Brooke smiled, touched by Cam's generosity.

"Something like that. You fell asleep. I couldn't wake you up. A girl could get a complex, you know."

"What? Why?"

Cam laughed. "You always seem to fall asleep on me."

Brooke felt her face flush, because Cam was right. What was it about that? It wasn't boredom. Could it be because she felt so relaxed around Cam? So...*herself*? "Sorry. I'm not usually this much of a drag on a d—" Shit, she almost said date. "I do appreciate you not letting me sleep on that tiny sofa. My back thanks you, that's for sure."

Brooke rolled onto her side and Cam did the same until they faced one another. Neither said anything for the longest moment, the weight of those soulful green eyes landing on Brooke with their golden flecks and warming her from the inside. There was no script to follow, nothing to guide either of them forward in this unusual situation. Had Landon been onto something, coaxing them back together? Had he seen or come to know something they didn't? Did dying give him some special insight into matters of the heart? Maybe. Or maybe this was simply how things happened when you let them.

"Cam?"

"Yes?"

"I think you're the best person I know." Brooke reached up before she could stop herself and gently brushed a lock of hair from Cam's cheek. "Landon too. I'm not sure what I've done to deserve either of you, but whatever it is, I'm grateful."

"You're not so shabby yourself, you know."

Brooke desperately wanted to believe Cam, but there was so much to work on. If Cam thought she was getting there, getting to a place of an open mind and heart, then that was something, wasn't it? "Thank you," she whispered, emotion cracking her voice; she so wanted to believe in Cam's faith in her. More than that, she wanted to deserve it.

"For what?"

"For being here. For being you. For being patient with me and believing in me."

"Oh, Brooke. I always believed in you. Even when I doubted myself, I never doubted you. But I didn't express that to you, did I? I was too damned busy trying to be a rock star."

"It's okay. I was too damned busy dreaming of being a culinary star to worry about believing in anything or anyone else. Our world wasn't big enough for our two egos, was it?"

Cam shook her head. "I think sometimes people aren't ready for a certain person in their lives at a particular time. Opportunities don't always have a good sense of timing."

"No, but we do. Humans, I mean. I know I blew some opportunities, and I'm ashamed of that. I'd like to think I won't be as stupid the next time."

"You won't be. Now, we have a mission today. Shall we shower and grab breakfast? Ninjas need fuel, you know."

Brooke giggled. She'd almost forgotten about their agreement to sneak into The Grand Hotel and roam around like brazen tourists. Or brazen trespassers, take your pick. "You want to start in the shower first before I join you?" She waggled her eyebrows in jest. No harm in a little innocent fun.

Cam rolled off the bed, her eyes bright and warm and teasing. "A ninja needs all her focus and concentration for the mission at hand without the distraction of a beautiful woman. So how about we each shower in our own rooms and meet downstairs for breakfast?"

"Spoilsport." Brooke chuckled and dragged herself off the bed. God, she remembered the showers they used to take together, when they couldn't get enough of one another. She could still see, in her mind's eye, Cam's perfect naked body, wet and glistening and chapped red from the hot water and ohhh… *Stop it Brooke, or you'll get all hot and bothered. Ooh, too late for that.*

Two hours later, they scampered through a back door of the hotel as a guest was exiting, Brooke striding through like she owned the place. "I'm a hospitality expert," she whispered to reassure Cam, who lagged behind and, Brooke feared, might bolt at any second. "I know what I'm doing."

Cam uttered a noise of disbelief but gamely followed Brooke down the hall on the dark brown, plush carpet and past pale green walls, and it was as if they were inside a mint chocolate cookie. At an elevator, Brooke randomly pressed the button for the third floor. Down another hall they went, past closed doors, until Brooke pulled up short with a squeak. A door to one of the rooms opened and a chambermaid exited, leaving the door ajar as she headed to a supply closet around the corner.

"Let's go," Brooke urged, tugging Cam along.

"What? Where?"

"Into that room that's open."

"No way."

"I just want to peek inside."

Brooke edged her way in, prepared to say she'd accidentally entered the wrong room if challenged, but it was empty. Empty and spectacular. She whistled softly between her teeth as her eyes took in the décor, the view, the ambience. The entire room was steeped in 1800s Victorian tradition. It really was like stepping back in time.

"What?" Cam's curiosity seemed to have triumphed over her reluctance. In seconds she too was inside the room. "Wow. Cool."

It was decorated in rich blues and golds—textured flower motif wallpaper, luxurious draperies, thick carpet. But the showstopper was the massive mahogany four-poster bed with creamy satin curtains and matching bedspread. The ceilings were twelve feet high, the furniture was blond wood, a chandelier sparkled. The wall sconces looked antique. Brooke was sure the view from the window was equally spectacular, if only she could—

"Excuse me, ladies. Are you supposed to be in here?"

A massive woman in a maid's uniform, hands on her generous hips, stood at the open door. Brooke recoiled at being caught. Her mouth clamped shut, her feet frozen in place. She totally deserved this, but... Now what?

"So sorry," Cam butted in. "Wrong room." She grabbed Brooke's hand and tugged her. Hard.

"Did you know," Brooke said to her once they'd scampered far enough away from Attila the Hun, "that they have a presidential suite and a governor's suite?"

"Don't even think about it." But Cam was laughing and, still clutching Brooke's hand, jogged with her the rest of the way through the hotel and back out the door they'd entered, running and laughing and holding hands like a couple of kids who'd got caught raiding the cookie jar.

Breathless and hyped from their adventure, Brooke gushed, "What's next? That horse ride we talked about?"

"Oh God, you were serious?"

"Yup."

"And you swear you're not trying to kill me?"

"Oh, ye of so little faith. Come on. There's a stable not far away where we can hire a horse."

"A horse *and* a driver," Cam mumbled.

Brooke flashed a devilish grin. There'd be no driver.

CHAPTER THIRTY-FIVE

Even though her horse ride lasts no more than twenty minutes before the beast suddenly bolts and heads back to the stable like its butt is on fire, Cam's legs are rubber and her ass is sore from the saddle. *Hallelujah!* She can give up horses now, bloody temperamental things. Except the stable hand is insisting that they're paid up for ninety minutes and there are no refunds. Take a two-person carriage together, he says. It's simple, and, he promises, he'll assign them Edith, the stable's oldest and most passive horse. Even a child can handle Edith, he declares, his promise more like a dare. Brooke (of course!) takes the bait. Before Cam knows it, Edith is being hitched to an open carriage and Brooke is climbing aboard like she's an old hand at this.

Visions of Edith galloping off, trundling them over hill and dale as they scream for her to stop, keep Cam occupied as Brooke, reins firmly in her hands, urges to Ethel to get going.

"See?" Brooke shoots her a smile that says she's got everything under control. "Nothing to worry about."

"Humph. Easy for you to say." Cam pretends to sulk, but she's having way too much fun to be seriously annoyed as she watches Brooke competently steer Edith down the street and around the corner. Brooke's expression adorably alternates between *I've got this* and *Oh shit.* "Where are we going, anyway?"

Brooke shrugs. "No idea. It's part of me learning to take things as they come, remember?"

"I like it." Cam settles back in the seat, which isn't a whole lot softer than a bag of rocks, but she's not complaining. She slides her arm around the back of the bench seat and studies Brooke. The way she accepted the role of carriage driver without hesitation, how she's a study of fierce concentration with her pinched brows, it's not a stretch to conclude that Brooke would be stellar at running a restaurant. "Do you miss it yet?"

"What's that?"

"Your restaurant."

"Not really, or maybe not yet. But I miss the people. The regulars, my staff. Like, there's this little old couple, Lorraine and Jim, who would come in every Friday night for dinner, insisting that their little table candle be lit while they held hands and stared at their menus, even though they always ordered the same thing." Brooke shakes her head. "The pandemic changed everything. I haven't seen Lorraine and Jim since it started. I don't even know if they're okay, and that bothers me."

"It was rough for me too. I had to wear all kinds of PPE to keep seeing my clients. They couldn't have many visitors, and when they did, they all had to dress in hazmat suits. Kinda hard to be touchy feely in all that gear. I don't think I understood how much loneliness was out there before the pandemic."

"It's epidemic, don't you think?"

"What, loneliness?"

"Yes."

Brooke guides the horse and carriage into the dirt parking lot of a little stone church. The horse stops in front of a hitching post as if it's been ordered to do so.

"Without people," Cam says, "the world isn't much worth living in, don't you think?"

"I can agree with that. I think we forget that sometimes. Hey, isn't this church the cutest?" She hops down and expertly ties up the horse to the post.

"Where'd you learn how to be so good at this horse thing?"

"I'm actually not good at *this horse thing* at all. It's called bluffing from watching a lot of westerns when I was a kid. And luckily, Edith here is letting me off the hook. I'm sure she knows I'm a tourist playing at cowboy and she's letting me have some fun because, hey, maybe she thinks I'm trying to impress you."

"Well, you definitely are." Cam jumps down from the carriage and follows Brooke.

The double wooden door is open and there's no one inside. The nave and sanctuary are no bigger than a tennis court, but the ceiling, tall and angled and held up with massive oak beams, make it seem much grander. The round, stained glass window above the altar takes Cam's breath away, and Brooke too is staring at it. Slashes of blue, purple, and gold send jagged splinters of sunshine toward their feet.

"Wow," Brooke gushes. She heads to the front pew and sits. "It's so pretty in here. And peaceful. I think I could sit here for hours."

Cam wordlessly sits down beside her.

"Did you...are you religious now, Cam, since you became a death doula?"

"Not really. Spiritual, yes, although I had to learn a lot about different religions so that I could understand some of my clients' needs better. I don't counsel them on religious matters, there are people I can call for that, but I've found it helpful to at least have a working knowledge of most of the common religions."

"What about Landon? He's a lapsed Catholic. Is he still lapsed?"

"I'm not sure, we haven't discussed it much yet. But I did notice recently a couple of rosaries lying around his room. Even a lapsed religion can bring people comfort in their dying. I think it helps them to accept that they haven't been perfect, that their life hasn't been perfect, and that it's okay. They're forgiven and loved as they are, and they will take that love and acceptance with them on their transition. It really comes down to inner peace, and if religion can help with that, then so much the better."

"But how can you be peaceful when you know you're dying? That you're going to die soon? I'd fight like hell if it were me."

"Oh, believe me, my clients do fight like hell. They don't want to die. But there comes a point where fighting is hurting them, is keeping them anxious or afraid, is keeping them at arm's length from accepting what's happening to them. They want to reach in and find that part of them that is forgiving, that is loving, that is pure, because they want to die with dignity, with serenity. They want to be at peace before they die. I know it sounds like a cliché, but it's true."

"But peace is a state of mind. How do you reach that state in the chaos of dying and fear and loneliness?"

"Believe me, it is possible to find peace in every death, no matter how chaotic." Cam has been by the side of clients who had no choice but to die in a hospital with machines beeping and whirring, amid the noisy hardware and bustling staff whose job is to keep them alive until they're not. And sometimes there are distraught or argumentative family members who bring their own brand of turbulence to the situation. "The trick to finding peace is to remove everything else. When you release your anger, hatred, or unresolved feelings—when none of that is left—you are at peace."

Brooke lets out a long breath but doesn't speak for a few minutes. Finally, she says, "How come we're so conditioned to think that happiness is beyond the next hill?"

"Probably because it feeds into consumerism. There is a vested interest in leading us all down that garden path, and as long as we keep searching for happiness somewhere else, it keeps us distracted from doing the hard work of finding our own happiness from within. For me, it was always the next album or the next concert that was going to make me happy."

"It didn't work, huh?"

"Nope, not by a long shot. My life was falling apart in spite of my Herculean efforts to find happiness from outside—from things, from other people, from substances. I didn't see it until I had almost nothing left. I was living in the past or in a future that didn't exist yet and doing everything I could to avoid the present."

"I think I get that now. Right before the pandemic, I was actually considering starting a chain of small Italian restaurants in southern Michigan. Nothing big, just a couple of other locations to start, but it was like I didn't know how to be happy if I didn't have a challenge. Ugh, I'm so glad I didn't go through with it. And I'm so glad I've started to figure out that you can't accumulate your way to happiness. How could I have been so stupid all this time?"

"You haven't been stupid. Look at the billion-dollar industry of self-help and enlightenment books. It shows you that we're all trying to figure it out, that we've all been there at some point. So no, you're not alone."

"Thank you," Brooke says.

Cam looks at her in surprise. "For what?"

"For not judging me. For not making me feel like I'm stupid or inferior because, I don't know, I'm such a newbie with all of this."

"You're doing fine. Better than fine." In a bold move that might even be unwelcome, Cam takes a chance and slides her hand between them, then slowly slips her hand into Brooke's. "I like this new Brooke."

Brooke squeezes back, and shining in her eyes is something that looks an awful lot like peace.

CHAPTER THIRTY-SIX

Brooke took her time getting ready. A little eyeliner and lipstick, a sundress she bought earlier in the day because she couldn't bear to put on something old, something from before, plus a new set of silver earrings, one a spoon and one a fork (they were adorable and she'd been unable to resist the culinary theme to them). She wanted to look different, to match the kind of different she felt inside. Whenever she found herself wondering if she'd be able to sustain these new feelings and thoughts after leaving the island, she tried to dam up the stream of doubts. She would need to work on herself every day through meditation, spending time alone, finding joy in simple things, being in the now.

She could do this. Look at Cam. Cam had found a way to discard the things that were dragging her down. She'd found a way to live her life more simply, doing something with her life that brought her so many rewards. If Cam could change her life, so could Brooke. Already she felt lighter, less anxious, less wanting to control and construct every part of her existence.

Fear of the future drove her anxiety, she understood that now, and it was all the more reason to start living in the present.

But these new epiphanies came at a cost. Landon was losing his life. Cam would soon go back to her work, three hundred miles away from where Brooke lived. And what was waiting for Brooke when she went back to Ann Arbor? What was she to do next?

Stop it. Just stop it. This is not living in the now, she told herself, feeling the old patterns tethering her again. *Stop worrying about the future.*

A knock on her door was perfect timing. She opened it to find Cam, holding a single pink rose. She handed it to Brooke.

"Thank you. It's beautiful."

"Beautiful rose for a beautiful woman."

"Oh, Cam. You don't have to butter me up." *But please don't stop.*

"I'm not. You *are* more beautiful now. I can see the changes in you."

"Really?" She studied Cam's face for signs of insincerity or sarcasm, but there were none. "Why, thank you. I sort of do feel more beautiful, if that doesn't sound conceited."

"It doesn't, not from you. New dress? And I love your earrings. They're cute."

A blush warmed Brooke's cheeks. Not because Cam had noticed these things, but because of the approval in her eyes. "Thanks. And yes."

"You look terrific, Brooke."

"You look damned good yourself." Casual but neat in sandals, Capri pants, and a scoop neck shirt that nicely showed off her neck and shoulders, Cam was a gorgeous sight. She clutched a sweater in her hand.

"You going to be warm enough in that dress?" Cam asked.

"I think so. It's been such a warm day, I'm sure it will be fine." Cam stuck out her elbow, and Brooke took the cue, tucking in her hand. It occurred to her that Cam might find the concert uncomfortable and was only going along with this *date* for her sake. "You sure you're okay going to this? I mean, will it bring back painful memories or make you uncomfortable? Because we can skip it, you know."

"No, I'm fine, but thank you for asking. I haven't been to a concert in a long time, but I think maybe I'm ready to change that."

"What about singing and playing again? In front of people?"

"That part is still difficult for me." Her smile was a valiant attempt. "I'm working on it. So far no more than an audience of two."

"Sounds like a start to me."

Outside, Cam hailed a horse and carriage taxi for the ten-minute ride to the Mission Point resort, on whose grounds the festival was being held. It took only a few minutes of navigating through the crowd to spot Maggie and Jane, who were joining them for the evening. They'd spread two large blankets on the ground, one for them and the other for Brooke and Cam.

Maggie beamed at them. "We're so glad you two made it."

Brooke still clutched the rose in her hand; she'd forgotten to leave it in her room. "Thanks for letting us join you."

Jane's grin couldn't be any wider if she tried. "I see you two are getting on fabulously." She flashed them a thumbs-up. "Come, take a load off. The music is about to start."

Dusk had crept in, but the flick of a switch instantly bathed the stage in yellow, blue, and red—a kaleidoscopic beacon in the growing darkness. The sensation coursing through Brooke was one of warm nostalgia, a pleasant anticipation that reminded her of the many concerts where she watched Cam perform. All those years of blame and resentment over those damned concerts—it wasn't fair, she could see that now. The truth was, she had loved every minute of watching Cam perform—the way she owned the audience with her talents and the visceral way she connected with them. But it was also true that the stage had too often turned Cam into a monster—a moody maestro who came to treat everyone else as though they were her subjects. It wasn't the healthiest time in their lives, but they could at least be thankful that those years were behind them. That period certainly didn't need to define their future—well, if they had any sort of future together, that is.

A female duo strode on stage first with acoustic guitars slung over their shoulders. They began playing a folk tune, their harmonizing spot on. Original work, mixed with covers, including "If I Were Your Woman," followed. Brooke edged a little closer to Cam on the blanket, wanting to feel her warmth, her softness, wanting her to also remember that it was one of their favorite songs.

As if reading her mind, Cam turned to Brooke and grinned. "They're good, huh?"

"Sure are. But not as good as you."

"Aw come on, you don't have to stroke my ego, I promise. I'm okay with this, Brooke, I really am. I know I'm a good musician, but that's over for me. Now I can just be like every other music lover and enjoy the music for its own sake."

"All right. But does that mean you might start singing and playing regularly again? For your own pleasure, I mean?"

Cam nodded slowly, her eyes moving along with her thoughts. "I think it's a good possibility, yes. But never like this. Those days are done."

Brooke threw her head back and screamed a silent *Yes!* As long as Cam didn't completely bury her love for music, it was all good. Small was good, even if it was only an audience of one or two.

"Hey," Maggie shouted over the music. "Before it gets any darker, I want to take a happy picture of you two."

"Oh!" Brooke said with a nervous glance at Cam. "Sure. I mean, if Cam doesn't mind."

"I don't mind." She beamed up at Maggie, ready for the photo.

Jane interjected. "No, wait, that won't do. Scoot closer."

Brooke inched closer, but only a little. It was Cam who closed the gap between them and boldly threw her arm around Brooke's shoulders with affectionate exuberance. Yes, that was more like it, she thought, as they grinned for the camera.

Maggie snapped a few photos with her phone. "Perfect. I'll text you these later." She turned her phone around to show them. And the photo really was perfect. The flash lit up their smiling faces...smiles that went right to their eyes. They looked like old friends. Or new lovers. The dawning that something was happening inside her brought a lump to Brooke's throat. It was not only her growing peace, her learning to love herself, but what she was feeling for Cam. It wasn't nostalgia, it wasn't the imprint of the past reinserting itself. This was something new, something tender, something that filled her up with lightness and wonder and other things she couldn't name. She wondered if Cam felt these things too.

"I don't want to send this picture to Landon," she whispered to Cam, wanting to keep this moment, captured so perfectly in the photo, for themselves.

"Okay. Are you chilly?" Cam asked, taking her sweater without being asked and carefully draping it around Brooke's shoulders.

"Thanks." Brooke shivered a little, unaware until now that the night air had developed a distinct chill. The growing moonlight and Cam's presence had made her forget everything practical.

A dance floor had been set up in a corner of the grassy field, its outline demarcated by a border of twinkling, multicolored lights embedded in the ground. Jane and Maggie made a beeline for it as the songs lowered in pace and volume. The new band on the stage was singing Don Henley's "Heart of the Matter."

Brooke tamped down her insecurities, stood, and held out her hand to Cam in invitation. In the dark, she could see Cam's lips lift in a smile as she slipped her hand into Brooke's and followed her. There was electricity where they touched, and the sensation traveled pleasurably up Brooke's arm and straight into her chest. It was all she wanted, to feel Cam's arms around her under the beguiling moonlight while they swayed to the music. She hadn't wanted something so intimate in so long, she'd forgotten intellectually what that kind of want was like, but her body snapped to attention. Oh yes, her body had no trouble remembering and relishing that warmth in her blood, the intensifying fullness in her chest. Even the nervous tension in her stomach was something to be treasured.

They began to dance, inching closer as the song played on. Cam's body was strong but also supple against Brooke, and it was so Cam…solid and capable, but also soft and safe. Neither noticed when the song segued into a slow rendition of "I Put a Spell on You."

"*You*," Cam said a low voice that sent a rumble through Brooke, "feel so good in my arms. I'd forgotten how good dancing with you felt."

Wisps of warm breath against her cheek, Brooke pressed closer against Cam, caught sight of the full moon over her shoulder—a bright, gold disc. She internalized its shimmering glow, imagining that same glow lighting her from the inside. These ten days were turning out to be the biggest and nicest surprise of her life. "So do you," she replied, wanting to keep talking because maybe it would smother the urge to turn her face to Cam's and kiss her. And she wasn't ready to take that risk. Not yet. "I feel like we could stay here and do this all night. Isn't it wonderful?"

"It is. It feels…right. It feels good."

"How do you make a moment last forever, Cam?"

Cam paused. Brooke could feel her slow, even breath against her neck. "You breathe it in, feel it in your whole body, appreciate it, enjoy it. And then you breathe it out and let it go. That's the trick, because the moment doesn't last forever. Nothing does. But you can make the *feeling* last forever."

Brooke liked that—making feelings last forever by keeping them in your heart, in your memories. She breathed in long and deeply, closed her eyes, and let her body relax while feeling every movement, every touch. By feeling the moment as intensely as she could, she found she could let it go when it was time, because her body would forever remember being in Cam's arms on a glorious, moon-drenched evening.

By the third song, Maggie and Jane had left the dance floor.

"You okay?" Cam asked.

Brooke could only nod. A knot of emotions, all of them good, had taken up residence in her throat.

"Come on," Cam said, heat infusing her voice. "Let's get out of here."

Brooke followed Cam, their hands locked together like they might lose each other in the crowd. Or lose one another again. They didn't stop to say goodbye to Jane and Maggie, and somewhere lost was the rose from Cam. Maybe someone else falling in love would find it.

The carriage ride back to the hotel was quick and silent, the two of them nestled on the bench seat beneath a blanket the driver had helpfully left folded on the seat for them. Brooke shivered. Cam put an arm around her shoulders the rest of the way, and it felt safe. And something more. It was like a new level of happiness was opening to Brooke whenever Cam was near.

"I'm sorry," Cam said as they ascended the stairs of their hotel. "We could have stayed if you wanted."

"I don't. I didn't. Want to stay. I mean, I loved it, don't get me wrong. It was perfect." The electricity between them hadn't stopped pulsing through Brooke's fingers as she turned to Cam at the top of the stairs, in the hallway near their rooms, and hugged her. She didn't want Cam to leave, so she kept her arms around her. "Thank you for tonight."

"You're very welcome." Cam's cheek brushed against Brooke's. A soft, subtle declaration that perhaps Cam didn't want to go either.

We don't have to end the evening yet, Brooke dared to think. Things were progressing a bit quickly, maybe even prematurely, but it wasn't like they hadn't been together before. They were Bette and Tina. Well, Brooke and Cam now. New, but not new. Cam's warm hand circling her back sent a powerful streak of want through Brooke, reminding her that they had always had a magnetic physical attraction to one another. In the early part of their relationship, they'd spend hours in bed together, exploring each other's bodies, pleasuring one another. Even out of bed, they rarely stopped touching or kissing. She almost missed a final exam because she couldn't pull herself out of Cam's arms, Cam's bed. She could still remember the cocky grin on Cam's face as Brooke finally managed to extricate herself from their bed, barely in time to write her exam. Cam was warmth and light and Brooke wanted only to be near her—a planet revolving around the sun.

Blinded by her hunger for Cam, Brooke gently pushed her against the wall, right outside the doors to their rooms. Her mouth found Cam's, their lips pressed together, and they kissed as if they were pouring themselves into each other. The taste of Cam's mouth, the smell of her skin, her hair, was a nuclear bomb to Brooke's senses. Even the air crackled with heat, and Brooke had the silly thought that she might not survive this, yet she didn't want it to end, even if it killed her. Which it wouldn't, she assured herself. As Cam's hand floated down to her hip, her touch featherlight but warm, arousal flamed to life in Brooke's belly. And then Cam's mouth moved down her neck, down to her collarbone, left bare by the sundress.

"Oh, Cam," Brooke mumbled. "Don't stop."

But it was the wrong thing to stay because Cam did stop. Her face hovered next to Brooke's, her eyes full of doubt where there had been desire seconds ago. "Brooke, I'm not sure this is a good idea."

Brooke didn't want to have to think, not with her brain a morass of hormones. "We could have tonight. Couldn't we?"

Cam shook her head, more snuffing out of Brooke's red-hot desire. "No. Not tonight." She leaned her forehead against Brooke's as a form of apology, enfolding her in a hug that was affectionate but no longer sexual. "I loved being with you tonight, every second of it. But I need to go, okay?"

"Are you sure? I mean, are you okay? Are *we* okay?"

A lopsided smile, so familiar, reassured. "Yes. We are. But we need to go slow and talk about this okay? And not right now. Talk, I mean. Or…anything else."

Disappointment slumped Brooke's shoulders, but Cam was right. They weren't a couple of sex-crazed, hormonal teenagers. They were adults who needed to figure out how not to screw things up between them. Again. "Okay. Buy you breakfast tomorrow?"

"You're on."

One last kiss, this time on the cheek, before Cam turned to her own door and slipped the key into the lock.

CHAPTER THIRTY-SEVEN

The next morning, Cam is still unable to forget about the kiss. Or rather, the blinding heat behind the kiss. Another minute of making out in that hallway and they would have ended up in one of their rooms. Closing her eyes, she can picture the desire in Brooke's eyes, in her parted lips. The way Brooke had felt in her arms, first while they were dancing under the stars and then in the hallway outside their rooms, had tripped every circuit in her brain. It was familiar, wanting Brooke so much, but new also. Different. They went through years of being together and then years of not being together and now they're no longer a couple of twentysomethings and... Her head feels like it might explode. Her wanting Brooke again might have been part of Landon's big plan, but it was supposed to be folly, designed to make a dying man feel better, not a thing that might actually come to fruition. It's weird, when something isn't close to being on your radar and then, bam, you can think of nothing else. The exhilaration in her chest, the pleasant buzzing in her brain from the memory of every detail from last night—the world is painted in a much brighter shade today. It's because of Brooke.

Cam had left for the restaurant ahead of Brooke, wanting to walk alone through the downtown to clear her head. But really it was to immerse herself in the blood rush of those same feelings she'd felt pressed up against Brooke last night outside their rooms. And yet it wasn't only a sexual thing, a physical need for Brooke's body. Brooke was…different. Not only was she not the young, headstrong woman of decades earlier, she was not even the same person she was almost a week ago during their forced lunch date, when she looked ready to throw Cam off the nearest dock and into the water. This introspective, more tranquil Brooke, who's also curious and thoughtful and adventurous, is fun to be around. But maybe Cam too has changed over the past week. She has been smiling more, she realizes. Has been thinking of things other than death and dying for a change, too. She's been more present, more spontaneous, doing things like long bike rides and sneaking into hotels and kissing a woman and…

Cam suppresses a grin as she walks past the big ceramic pink horse over the door and into the Pink Pony restaurant. She asks for a table on the back patio, overlooking the marina, then orders two mimosas so that Brooke will have something to sip on when she arrives.

Yeah, Cam tells herself, *you've definitely developed a thing for your ex.*

She's smiling again and then her brain goes into a full meltdown as Brooke walks through the door and onto the patio, propping her sunglasses onto her head as she glances around for Cam. Cam should signal her or call out, but she wants to admire Brooke for a few more seconds. Brooke has never stopped being beautiful, but there is something more layered, more nuanced about her beauty now. Her newfound tranquility cloaks her in a certain grace and poise that can't be faked. Cam knows what a person at peace looks like; it's a quiet, contented confidence evident in their eyes, in the set of their mouth, in their posture, and in the ease of their smile. It's as though they have all the time in the world, and yet they're fully, extraordinarily aware of everything going on around them. There's strength that comes from living one's life in the moment, and Cam can so clearly see it in Brooke at this moment. She wonders if she looks that way to others and if Brooke notices it herself when she looks in a mirror.

Brooke's eyes find her, and the smile on her lips is as bright as a noon sun hijacking the day. She tracks through the busy jumble of tables and diners to sit across from Cam, and the breath Cam has been holding leaves her in a ragged exhale.

"I…" Doubting herself suddenly, about to check her words, Cam realizes she's tired of working so hard at being mindful of every word she speaks. Self-editing is no way to be with Brooke if they want a chance at starting something new. She clears her throat. "I've never seen you look more beautiful, Brooke."

"Oh, Cam." Brooke's eyes fill with a surprising number of tears.

"I'm sorry. I didn't mean to—"

The server delivers their mimosas, interrupting the moment.

When he's gone, Brooke says, "No, I'm fine. Really." She takes a sip of the mimosa and smacks her lips in pleasure. "Oh God, this is exactly what I needed. Thank you."

Cam decides to press Brooke. "It's not usually a good sign when I make a woman cry."

A raise of one eyebrow. "You have experience in making women cry, do you?"

"Ha, no. You have to be in love in order to break someone's heart. Or for someone to break yours. I haven't exactly been in that position since…well, since you." With every woman she's slept with in recent years, except for Nora, there's been an implied agreement that it was only sex, a transitory companionship. The delineation has always been clear in her mind that her empty spaces could never be filled from that type of coupling.

A quiver in Brooke's chin. "Oh, Cam, I'm so—"

"No, no. It's okay." She does not want Brooke's apology, because with it comes judgment that Cam has been unhappy or broken all this time. No. Her wounds may have left scars, but they've healed. "Can we talk about Landon?"

The server announces his return. Would they like to order food?

"I'm famished," Brooke announces, quickly scanning the menu before closing it.

Cam is hungry too. Perhaps the mind-numbing kisses from last night burned a lot of calories. They each order spinach and feta omelets with a side of sausage.

"Did something happen to him that I don't know about?" Brooke asks. "Because I need to see him before he…dies?"

"You will. He's still okay for now." In a few days Cam will see Landon, which also means there are only a few more days before the island becomes a memory and Brooke goes…home, she supposes. *Don't get ahead of yourself, Cam, stay in the moment.* "But… Okay, I'm trying to be delicate here, so I—"

"Please don't." There are no more tears in Brooke's eyes, just a clear-eyed anticipation of a frank discussion. This is not someone who's fearful of the truth or who can't handle it. This version of Brooke is so much braver.

Cam rubs her hands nervously over her thighs. "I'm not judging. I just want to understand."

"It's okay, Cam. You can spit it out. I promise I can handle it."

Cam doesn't beat around the bush when she's talking to her clients, yet she's so tongue-tied around Brooke now that she can only blame last night's kiss for this crack in her composure. She breathes in, breathes out, dives in. "All right. Why did you marry Landon? I mean, you said earlier that he was kind, he was safe, he was a good man, and you needed someone like that in your life. I get that. But… Why a man? Does it mean you're bi?"

It seems a lifetime before Brooke answers. "I'm not sure what it means if I'm totally honest. It wasn't even something I considered until I met Landon, and then, well, it seemed unimportant to spend much time dissecting or analyzing it. It just…was."

"Okay. That's good. I want you to be honest. I want us to be honest with each other."

"Does my answer change anything between us? Or your opinion of me?"

"No." Until reconnecting with Brooke, it never occurred to her that Brooke might choose a man. She assumed…so much, as it turns out. Maybe they should have talked about this sort of thing when they were a couple. They should have talked about a lot of things. "I'm only asking to help me understand you. I want to know you. And you know what? I think now that I didn't know you as well as I should have all those years ago. And I apologize for that. And, hell, Landon's a great guy."

Brooke's expression softens. "Oh, Cam. We both have a lot to be sorry about, don't we?"

"We do. But I don't want to get stuck in the potholes of the past. Recognize where mistakes or shortcomings were made, then either fix them or vow to do better if they can't be fixed, and move on. Or at least try. I don't like things in my life being unresolved, and I realize now that you were a big part of my unresolved past." Brooke has always been the missing link.

Brooke holds Cam's gaze with a quiet challenge. "Now that we're resolving some things…does it mean you're ready to move on? And what exactly does that mean to you, moving on? What is it that you want, Cam?"

Cam smiles at the balls it took for Brooke to ask those questions. She's proud of her, and it only increases her desire to take their new friendship, or whatever it is, further. The welcome arrival of their food allows her time to consider her answer. It's not that she doesn't know what she wants, it's that she wants them to want the same thing and she's afraid Brooke doesn't.

She waits until they've both eaten a few bites before she answers, knowing the wait must be killing Brooke. It's killing her too, not being able to predict Brooke's response. "What I want is to see where things go with us. I want to date you, Brooke."

Brooke's mouth falls open. "And here I thought you were going to dump me."

"You did? Why would you think that?"

"Because you're a million miles ahead of me in the personal growth department. Because I wasn't sure you could ever truly forgive me for what I did to you. Because I treated you like crap when I first realized it was you here on the island. Let's see, what else? Oh, there's the fact that I live six hours away from you. And that I don't have a job anymore." Laughter bubbles up from Brooke. "I'm not doing a very good job of selling myself, am I?"

"You don't need to. I said I want to date you and I mean it. I realized this past week that there's a reason I loved you all those years ago. Well, more than one reason."

"But I'm not the person you loved back then. I'm not Bette anymore."

"And I'm not Tina anymore." Cam rolls her eyes to lighten the moment. "Thank God. Look, I'm attracted to you. The chemistry between us is still off the charts. And I don't want to fall in love with Bette or with the old Brooke."

"You don't?"

"No. I'd like to fall in love with the new Brooke. I mean, if you'll give me that chance."

Brooke looks close to tears again. "I don't know why I keep deserving people like you and Landon in my life."

Cam reaches across the table and takes Brooke's hand in both of hers. "Stop doubting. Accept what I have to offer, okay? And start believing that maybe you have a lot to offer others as well."

"Can I make a confession?"

"Can my heart stand one?"

Brooke smiles. "I still sleep in one of your old T-shirts occasionally."

"You do?"

"Remember that women's music festival in Saginaw?"

Cam nods. "It was the summer of 2001." She closed down the show with her rendition of the Koko Taylor blues song, "I'm a Woman." It was a month before 9/11, when the cruel tides of the world were gathering *en force* while the blissfully ignorant danced and sang and made love.

"Your name is among the artists on the back. I never gave it back after we broke up."

"I always wondered what happened to that shirt."

"You did?"

Cam laughs, shakes her head. "Actually, no, I'd forgotten about it. But I'm glad you kept it. It means you—"

"Never got over you."

Cam knows she's got her best cocky grin on display, but she doesn't care. "So I guess that means you'll date me?"

Brooke leaps up from her chair, rounds the table to Cam's side, and hugs her from behind. "When can we start?"

"I think we sort of did. Last night."

"Ooh, yes, it certainly felt like a date." Brooke returns to her chair, but she hasn't stopped smiling. "Should we go on another date tonight?"

"I would like that. But I have a rule."

"You and your rules are going to kill me."

"Ha! It seems you've had a few rules here yourself. Remember your rule that you didn't want to spend all your time with me, that you wanted your own time?"

"Oh, right. Hmm. Can I have a do-over with that one?"

The banter, the laughter, the honest talk about their feelings leaves Cam marvelously light-headed. This is nothing at all like the old Brooke and Erica, and yet there's a recognition in their souls that makes the chronology of time irrelevant. They've each grown into better versions of their former selves.

"You'd make me a very happy woman if you altered that little rule of yours. But I want to do this right. I want to go slow. I want to start from a place where there's no baggage bringing us down. I want us to—"

Brooke's blazing eyes shut Cam down mid-sentence.

"What's wrong?"

In a stage whisper, Brooke says, "Does that mean no sex? No making out?"

"Oh, well, I suppose going slow means…ahem, waiting for sex?" Seems like a reasonable assumption.

A pout, a fierce shaking of her head. "I was afraid of that."

"Wait, I didn't say… I mean, we could…" What does she mean? Of course she wants to make love to Brooke and the sooner the better. The bedroom has never been their problem.

But she doesn't want sex to take over, to be the engine that drives their relationship. "How about the going slow part is whatever we decide it looks like?"

"Now that's an answer I can live with." Brooke's grin is infectious, and soon they're giggling above their empty plates.

CHAPTER THIRTY-EIGHT

The forty-foot catamaran sliced through the chop with a whoosh, allowing for the experience of sailing while its double hull provided more stability than a traditional sailboat. Which was a good thing or else the champagne in Brooke's glass would have sloshed onto her comfortable shoes numerous times by now. She kept one hand on the railing and the other firmly around her glass, however, so as not to tempt fate.

"What do you think?" she asked, nervous but eager for Cam's answer. Earlier this afternoon, she'd slipped away to book the private charter as a surprise, knowing how much they both loved the water.

The horizon, shot through with streaks of pink and gold and orange and blood red as the sinking sun presented its departing gift for the day, made it hard to tear their eyes away. It was a glorious sunset. If Brooke only had one more sunset left in her life, she would want it to be this one. Cam's gaze too had barely left the horizon, except to settle over Brooke with a look of mildly startled appreciation, like she couldn't quite believe they were here together. She looked content, full of introspective joy. Really, Brooke didn't need an answer as to what Cam thought of their date. All she had to do was look at her.

"It's wonderful, Brooke. Perfect."

A surfeit of feelings rippled through Brooke. Cam was right about the evening being perfect. The temperature was pleasant, the straits weren't too rough, and ice-cold bubbly and warm hors d'oeuvres were being served by their own personal server. The five-hundred-dollar price tag was totally worth it to watch Cam lap up the view, the breeze ruffling the thick waves of her chestnut hair, her face bathed in the rapidly fading golden light. Brooke would gladly pay that kind of money every day to see Cam look like this. "You look beautiful. And happy."

"Oh, Brooke. You look beautiful and happy too. Is this really happening?"

A spray of water, shockingly cold, hit Brooke squarely on the face. She laughed. "Yes. I think it really is happening. I have a wet cheek to prove it."

Cam wrapped her arm around her and planted a kiss on her cheek. "You're right, it is wet. And soft. And..." She leaned in closer, her eyes dropping to Brooke's mouth, and kissed her on the lips. It was a sweet, lingering kiss that nearly made Brooke drop her glass of bubbly and made her toes curl at the same time. The thing about kissing Cam was that it could be totally hot or totally sweet, and sometimes, without warning, one seamlessly melded into the other. Regardless, Cam's kisses echoed in every cell of Brooke's body; she could kiss her all day long.

The server was a young woman (from Trinidad, she'd told them) who smiled at catching them in the act of kissing, her dark eyes twinkling at them above her tray of warm brie and crackers. "Kissing can work up an appetite," she said with a wink, offering up the tray.

"You're so right," Cam replied. "That means your timing is perfect. Thank you."

The brie melting in their mouths, Brooke brought up the summer following college graduation when they took a week-long sailing course. They'd both ended up in the water numerous times, sometimes due to their incompetence, but more often because one of them would mischievously jostle the little boat until it tipped and they were both soaked. They were unceremoniously kicked out of the course before they could complete it, the instructor telling them to come back when they were serious about learning to sail.

"I don't think I'm serious about learning to sail yet," Brooke joked.

"Me either. But I think you'd have a pretty tough time trying to tip this sucker."

"Yeah, not going to happen. Besides, my days of ending up in the lake as a form of fun are long gone."

"We did have a lot of fun, didn't we?" Cam's eyes shone with memories, good memories that had, for too long, been overshadowed by their ugly breakup.

"We did. Remember that road trip we took to visit my mom, who was down in Utah staying at some commune for the summer? Down to our last fifty dollars coming home and the only motel available that final night had that creepy guy who wanted to rent us a room by the hour?"

Cam threw her head back and laughed, mimicking the guy's pervy voice as he said, "We have zee back r-r-room by the hour for intercourse."

Brooke mimicked puking. "Ugh. At least we had the car to sleep in. The room probably had one-way glass or something."

"Or cameras hidden in the ceiling." Cam shivered. "And dirty sheets. Yuck!"

Their server, Savitri, returned with a bottle of Veuve Clicquot to top up their glasses.

"Between the waves and the wine," Brooke said, "I might have to stumble my way back to the hotel."

"That's okay," Savitri said. "I can radio in and have a horse-driven cab meet us at the marina."

Brooke held out her glass. "In that case, fill her up, Savitri. Thank you."

"I'm so glad," Cam said after Savitri left, "that we can remember the good times. It became too easy to convince myself that all of our time together was shit, but I know now that's not fair. There would have been no pain in breaking up if there hadn't been a lot of good things about us."

Brooke had also done a bang-up job of painting their time together as terrible, figuring, she supposed, that doing so would provide the justification for her to move on without guilt. But lies, including the invention that their entire relationship had been total crap, never made for a good foundation on which to build anything.

"There was always love, I do remember that. But when you're young and trying to figure out your life, love doesn't always feel like enough. When you think it's holding you back from what you really want to be doing, it feels like a prison. I realize now how wrong that was." How could they have been so stupid, not to realize that love, in the end, is the only thing you get to hold onto, just like Cam said. Not the career, not the trips or the house or the parties or any of it. Love shouldn't be a prison. Love should embolden. She understood that now.

"Agreed," Cam said softly. "We didn't understand what we had."

Funny that Landon knew all along that what she felt for Cam was special and not something that the passing years could diminish. "Landon was right, you know."

"About what?"

"That I never stopped loving you."

"Really?"

"Really. I've never stopped, and I'm not going to pretend I don't still love you."

Cam squeezed her hand tightly. "I've never stopped loving you either, Brooke. And I think that's why I was never successful in a relationship after you. Not because I was bitter and broken…well, I was, but I healed. It's because I knew I still loved you, and trying to love two people that way at the same time never works."

"Tell me about it. That's why Landon and I never had a chance."

"Was he hurt badly?"

"He was hurt. I mean, who wouldn't be? But he never blamed me. He knew the score when we got together. He hoped I would change my mind, but he wasn't stupid." Brooke laughed lightly. "The man is actually a saint."

"I wish I'd known him then."

"You like him, don't you?"

"We could be good friends, I think, if we'd met under other circumstances. I can see why you married him."

Tears filled Brooke's eyes. "It should have been you I married."

Cam gave her another squeeze. "Let's make a deal right now. No more beating ourselves up about the things we did. Or didn't do, in this case. It's too much of a time waster, living in the past."

Well, that made sense, especially coming from someone who was a death doula. Cam saw people at the end. For those people, there was no going back to the beginning or even to the middle. There were no do-overs. The end was all that was before them, was the only place to put their remaining energies. If Brooke was going to start living her life in the now, it was time to put the past to bed. For good.

"All right. I'll make that deal with you."

The catamaran made a wide turn to head back to the marina. Savitri came by to collect their empty glasses and plates and to warn them the cruise would be over in less than fifteen minutes. The sun was barely above the water now, only a few pale streaks of light illuminating the inky blue sky. At the boat's railing, Cam put her arms around Brooke's waist from behind, rested her chin on Brooke's shoulder as they watched the sun disappear into the lake.

Brooke placed her hands over Cam's. There were so many questions crowding her mind. How would this work between them? Where were they going from here? And where was she going with her career? Her life wasn't a dumpster fire anymore, but she was still a long way from figuring things out. Then there was Landon. She wanted to see him, to be there for him (if he wanted her to). What was all that going to look like?

Don't, she told herself, remembering Cam's advice while they danced together at the music festival, when she had asked Cam how to hold onto a moment.

She closed her eyes, took a deep breath, and let her body imprint in her memory what joy felt like.

CHAPTER THIRTY-NINE

Cam drapes her arm behind Brooke's chair and stretches out her legs beneath the table. They're out for dinner with Maggie and Jane at the Seabiscuit Café, and Cam has already wolfed down her grilled asparagus and fried macaroni cheese balls. She was hungry, but she also wants them to wrap things up and get out of here before the karaoke starts. Karaoke bars make her break out in a rash. Unfortunately, they'd already ordered their food before she noticed the karaoke sign.

Cam tries to catch the server's eyes to signal for the bill, but it's crowded and he has at least four other tables to look after. Cam nudges Brooke's foot with her sandal to try to get her to stop asking the forty-nine questions she seems to have of Jane and Maggie about what it's like to live on the island full time. But Brooke's not taking the hint. Now she's asking how the island's five hundred or so full-time residents celebrate Christmas, and Maggie is only too happy to describe the giant decorated Christmas tree that gets plunked down in the middle of Main Street and how there are carols sung around it every evening for the twelve days of Christmas. On and on she goes, but Cam stops listening because someone on the tiny stage begins to fumble with cords and dials on the sound system. *Aw shit.*

"It's karaoke time!" The young man has stopped turning dials and plugging in cords. He holds the mic like he's Mick Jagger about to swallow it and starts singing "Super Freak." He bounces around the stage, camping it up, and every time he sings "she's a super freak" he screeches into the mic and twirls around, then dips the mic stand, finishing with a Michael Jackson moonwalk. His antics have everyone's attention, and Cam joins in the collective laughter and applause.

Maggie and Jane are captivated, which means a fast exit is now out of the question. A middle-aged man and woman get up next and start singing Elton John and Kiki Dee's "Don't Go Breaking My Heart." They're incredibly serious, singing like it's their job, even starting over after the woman muffs a line. Cam wants to laugh, but her laughter dies in her throat when Maggie and Jane crank up the pressure and start urging her to sing a song. Like the turning of a dial on the sound system, her throat tightens. Singing to Landon and Tenley or to Maggie and Jane is one thing. *This* she cannot do.

"I think we should leave," she whispers urgently to Brooke, hoping her eyes convey her desperation. To Maggie and Jane, she says, "Thanks for the vote of confidence, but the stage isn't my place anymore."

"But you're so good," Maggie implores. "I don't understand."

No, they wouldn't, Cam supposes. They wouldn't get that her drive to be successful on the stage put her in an unhealthy place. No, screw that. The truth was, that life had cost her dearly. And not just in losing Brooke. After the breakup there'd been too many nights on stage and too many festivals she couldn't even remember, thanks to the miasma of booze and marijuana and one-night stands. Superficial adoration was something she wanted no part of again, but this wasn't the time or place to enlighten her new friends.

Jane turns on the puppy dog eyes. "Just one song?"

Brooke's hand finds Cam's thigh and gives it a reassuring squeeze, as if to say, you don't have to if you don't want to, but

I've got your back if you do. Grateful, Cam places her hand over Brooke's, gives it a squeeze, and stands up on slightly wobbly legs. Maybe if she gets this monkey off her back, she can finally banish the anxiety that punches her in the gut every time someone asks her to sing.

From the stage, she surveys the crowd. Okay, it isn't big, maybe thirty-five people in total, and half of them are chatting to their tablemates or riveted to their phones as they eat. Easy-peasy. She can sing one song and not for Maggie and Jane or even for Brooke. But for herself. She can get it over with and find out that it's not so terrible anymore. Right? The little teeny tiny crowd is nothing, she tells herself. Like singing in the shower.

She punches in her choice—Linda Ronstandt's soulful version of Smokey Robinson's "Ooh Baby Baby"—without giving it much thought because the last thing she wants to do is stand up there fumbling around with selections while people gape at her or grow impatient. At the saxophone intro, nobody pays her any attention. As she sings the intro, "Oooooh, la-la-la-la", the room begins to quiet. They're noticing her voice, noticing that this is something different, something special. Curious heads swing in her direction, conversation fades then stops altogether. Other than her voice and the saxophone in the background, there is absolute silence. Not a utensil or a clink of a glass or a sneeze. "I did you wrong…my heart went out to play," she croons. She's got them now, they're all hers, and the adrenaline from the power that comes with holding an audience captive begins to propel her through the song, just like old times. The muscle memory of performing has shown up, and her voice burbles up from deep in her chest, like it has a memory of its own, growing stronger with every note. She's standing still but belting out the song, her hands cupping the mic tenderly, like a lover's face.

There is a quiet buzz in the room, like the humming of electrical lines. The confidence building in Cam's chest sends her deeper into the song, deeper into herself to express the emotions behind the song. She opens her eyes long enough to see Brooke grinning at her as tears course down her cheeks. Maggie and Jane are smiling and giving the thumbs-up like they've won the lottery or something. Two women near the stage stare at her with their mouths silent O's. A couple of others pull their phones out to snap a photo or take a quick video of the performance. There isn't one head in the room that isn't turned in her direction. She closes her eyes again because the visual onslaught is too much, but the song...the song is beautiful and she knows she's killing it and she knows the audience knows she's killing it. It's the one moment about singing that she truly enjoys...losing herself and knowing the audience is also losing itself in an unspoken alliance of giving and receiving, an acknowledgment that they are all united on this ride.

The song is in its final notes and already the audience is clapping, at least half of them on their feet. Cam gives a little bow, mumbles thank you, steps back and ignores an encore call. She is done, she has survived. And it's...sort of awesome. There's a cleansing feeling coursing through her, a scrubbing of the fear and the nerves because, dammit, she's still freaking good and people still love to hear her sing. And that's good enough for her. She still has it; she doesn't need more.

Back at the table, Brooke throws her arms around her neck and gives her a searing kiss. "Darling, that was incredible. I think your voice is even better than it was twenty years ago. And it was pretty damned incredible then. God, Cam. Do you have any idea what you do to me?" Visible is the shiver streaking through Brooke.

"No," she whispers in Brooke's ear, but she'd love to hear more. The urge to touch her is irresistible and she raises a palm to Brooke's cheek, cupping it lightly. "Why don't you show me."

There's gravel and smoke in Brooke's voice. "Let's get out of here."

Cam doesn't need to say anything. There's a slow burn in her stomach; she knows it's yearning. She stands up, takes Brooke's hand in hers. Cam slides a hundred-dollar bill into Maggie's hand to pay for dinner, shoots them a knowing wink, and in the next moment she and Brooke are practically sprinting out the door with a handful of people yelling after Cam, begging her to stay and sing. "Who was *that*?" Cam can hear distinctly before the door swings shut.

"Whew, we escaped!" Cam is laughing as she and Brooke make haste back to their hotel, holding hands. It feels like at any moment a tribe of new "fans" might round a corner and chase after them, but the street is quiet. They're alone, the stage a memory now.

"Are you okay? I mean, from the karaoke? How do you feel?"

She tickles Brooke's fingers with her own. "I'm fine. It wasn't as bad as I expected. Funny how it all came back so fast—the singing, the timing. But honestly? I don't miss it. I don't crave that stuff anymore. It was fun, but I couldn't care less if I don't do it again for another decade."

They walk the rest of the way in silence, but as they ascend the stairs of the hotel to their rooms, Brooke says, "I'm actually kind of relieved that the karaoke hasn't reignited your interest in a music career. It's…not an easy life, is it?"

"Nope. Not for me, not for you." They halt outside their doors, and Cam feels a pinch of guilt. Brooke was there for her in those early years, rarely missing a concert, consoling her after a deal fell through or a record fell flat, celebrating her victories, giving her honest feedback when she wrote songs or as she listened in at rehearsals. "I put you through a lot, didn't I?"

"Shhh." Brooke presses her lips to Cam's for a soft kiss. "We made a deal, remember? No more beating ourselves up over the past. It's over, Cam. We both survived it. And now we've found one another again."

Tears prick at the back of Cam's eyes as the truth hits her: she's felt alone for a long time. Solitude she's okay with, but the loneliness cuts deeper and isn't soothed by her work, rewarding as it is, or the distraction of friends. She got good at telling herself she didn't need anyone, long after she thought she needed everyone. Maybe the truth lies somewhere in the middle: she needs a few good people in her life—people like Landon and Tenley, Maggie and Jane. And Brooke, of course.

As for the stage, tonight has reminded her that it can be its own form of loneliness—up there apart from the crowd, even though the crowd feeds her ego. An old music teacher once told her that adulation was like eating a piece of chocolate cake. "It fills you up and tastes sweet, but two hours later you're starving again. Your ego gets fat, but your soul becomes anorexic." It took her a few years to understand the advice, more to actually believe it. And then it took more years and a hell of a lot of introspection to work on fattening her soul and starving her ego.

"I like where I am," Cam blurts out. "And where I'm going. And I like that you're here with me, Brooke. I don't feel alone when I'm with you."

"Stay with me tonight?"

Cam's heart leaps. She wants like crazy to stay, to kiss and make out with Brooke, to make love to Brooke. Is it too soon? Aren't they supposed to be going slow? Last night's date on the catamaran ended, again, with a goodnight kiss in the hallway. Which felt totally right. But this is different. This time she's turned on like crazy, and her body doesn't want to say no. She's excited by Brooke, excited by the prospect of how the rest of the night might unfold. Her belly is a cauldron of nerves. Will being with Brooke be like it was before? Or will it be different now, because *they're* different? She smiles to herself. *You won't know until it happens.* She looks at Brooke and hopes she can't hear her madly beating heart. "Kiss me?"

"Gladly." Brooke pulls her against her chest, stroking her face with infinite tenderness. Gently, she lifts Cam's chin. Her finger grazes Cam's jaw, her touch inciting tiny electrical shocks along Cam's skin that rush straight to her head.

Brooke kisses her. Deeply. Thoroughly. Sweetly. Her tongue sweeps over Cam's bottom lip, her teeth tugging it gently, before she goes back in for more kissing, and all Cam can think about is…nothing. Her mind is one big delicious black hole, but her body certainly isn't. Every part of it has awakened and is throbbing with want. She shudders, pulls her mouth away from

Brooke's even though there's nothing she wants more than to keep on kissing Brooke.

They look into each other's eyes for a long moment—gauging, measuring, evaluating. Do they both want this? Will there be regrets later? Is this the right time?

"Yes," Cam says with the resolve of a woman who knows exactly what she wants.

Brooke grins, unlocks her door, and pulls Cam inside.

CHAPTER FORTY

Fully clothed and lying on Brooke's bed, they kissed until the world seemed to collapse around them. It might have been minutes or hours, for all Brooke could figure. Or care. They made out like a couple of teenagers with only the soft glow of a corner lamp painting faint shadows on the walls. And it was... spectacular. More than once, Brooke had to force herself to slow down, to enjoy every moment of the foreplay. Or at least, she sure hoped it was foreplay. If it didn't end with sex, she was going to climb the walls in frustration, but she would survive. The last thing she wanted was to spook Cam or do anything to mess up this fledgling romance, but, oh God, she wanted Cam to touch her. Just the thought of it made her ache all over.

In another moment Cam's hand, the one that rested on Brooke's belly, began a slow crawl up her body, brushing the underside of her breasts. "Reading minds now, are you?" Brooke gasped.

Cam stopped kissing her long enough to smile. "I have quite a few talents, you know."

"Oh, trust me, I know." Her body was well versed in the gifts of Cam's talents.

Cam's mouth found hers again, then grazed her jaw before kissing a wet trail down her neck. Her hands got busy too, stroking Brooke's breasts through her shirt. And that was all Brooke could take of keeping that damned shirt on. She needed Cam's hands on her bare skin. Now. Rolling over, she yanked the shirt off and tossed it to the floor.

"I like a woman who knows what she wants," Cam teased.

"And since you can read minds, you already know what I want."

"That's very true." Cam's eyes, half-lidded and smoky with lust, dropped to Brooke's breasts. It wasn't hard for Brooke to read Cam's mind, either.

Brooke held her finger up to Cam for a brief timeout. Reaching behind her back, Brooke unclasped her bra and flung it to the floor alongside her shirt. She watched as desire flared in Cam's eyes. It was clear they both wanted this, but Brooke needed to ask one last time. Sex was like a train speeding downhill; after a certain point, there was no way to stop it.

"Before we get swept away—"

"I already am."

"Oh, Cam." Emotion tickled Brooke's throat. This was one of those moments she wanted to memorize forever—there were so many of them this week with Cam. "You've never looked more beautiful than you do right now. In my bed. With me. But I need to make sure that we're both...sure."

"I know. I understand. And I am sure. Brooke, I never stopped loving you. But now that I understand you better, now that I know who you really are, or rather, who you've become, I don't want to stop this. I don't want to stop discovering you, and I don't want to stop moving toward a future with you. I know we still have a lot to talk about, but I don't want to do any more talking, okay? Not tonight."

Brooke's lips twitched into a flicker of a smile before she kissed Cam. She didn't want to do any more talking tonight either. Her actions would say everything that needed to be said.

And with that, she pulled Cam's hand onto her bare breast and held it there.

"You like this?" Cam brushed her nipple, now taut with desire.

Brooke shuddered, squeezed her eyes shut. It was almost too much, Cam's touch. "No...more...talking...remember?"

"Right. Silly me."

Cam's mouth took the place of her hand, and she was ravenous—sucking, licking, teasing, stroking. Her other hand crept up Brooke's thigh—still encased in denim—and grazed the fabric with her nails, drawing soft circles. It was driving Brooke wild, shooting rockets of pleasure through her. She needed to be completely naked. Needed both of them to be completely naked.

"Please," she whimpered.

She felt Cam's grin against the skin of chest. "I think I've tortured you long enough."

"Remember, darling. The torture can go both ways."

Cam shot up and hastily released Brooke's button and zipper, then pulled her jeans off. "About time" were the only words that popped into Brooke's head. Cam palmed her through her panties, rubbed softly, and oh, Brooke was so drenched down there. So incredibly turned on.

"Naked," Brooke ground out from between clenched teeth. "We need to be naked. Oh, and did I mention that foreplay is overrated?"

Cam laughed; she understood Brooke's need. "Let me." She slid Brooke's underwear down her legs. Like the slow opening of a gift. Cam sucked in an audible breath as she surveyed Brooke's body with eyes that had gone a dark sea green. For a moment, it was as though Cam were afraid to touch her.

Brooke whispered, "I won't break."

"Sorry. I can't stop looking at you. You're so wonderful. So beautiful."

"Older now, Cam. I'm almost twenty years older. Which means your mind is being tricked into thinking back to—"

A finger pressed against Brooke's mouth. "I'm not talking about then. I'm talking about what I see before me. Which is a beautiful woman. Who also looks very turned on, by the way."

Propping herself up on an elbow, Brooke let her eyes wander critically over Cam's fully clothed body. "Somebody needs to join me in the naked department. And fast."

"Yes, ma'am!" Cam mock saluted her, but it was only a couple of seconds more before she tore off her own clothes with warp speed and jumped back into bed.

She was simply gorgeous. Yes, not as tight or as trim as she was in her late twenties, but who was? Cam looked like a woman who had matured, who took care of herself, who was satisfied and confident with her life, with herself, and made no apologies about it. She was everything Brooke remembered and more. She was everything Brooke admired in a woman.

Slowly, Cam lowered herself over Brooke. Skin on skin, there were little sparks of fire everywhere they touched. It was familiar, this uniting of their bodies. So familiar. And yet it was also breathtakingly new and exciting. Brooke closed her eyes. She wanted to remember with her body how this moment felt. Their hips found a light, steady rhythm, and it was like bobbing on a warm wave together where they were safe, warm, caressed. And damn, it felt good.

"Kiss me," Brooke said, opening her eyes long enough to see the hunger in Cam's, but also the love.

Warm breath caressed Brooke's jaw before Cam kissed her slowly. Their bodies writhed together, the tension gathering, building to a crescendo. Brooke's hands gripped Cam's ass, and Cam's hand moved to Brooke's center, teasing, cupping, meeting wetness and heat and an insistent invitation for Cam to go inside her.

"Is it okay if I—"

"Yes!" Brooke practically screamed.

As Cam's finger slipped inside, Brooke's hot anticipation was met with relief as instant as the flipping of a switch. The strokes were perfect, achingly beautiful, and so were the kisses Cam rained on her jaw and neck, then her collarbone and breasts.

Brooke moaned against her tensing muscles, seeking relief in her thrusting hips, her own moan sending a streak of fire through her veins. Her hands left Cam and fisted the sheets, the pleasure tide beginning its thundering journey up her legs, cresting in time to the quickening pace of Cam's hand.

"I've got you, babe," Cam whispered. "Come for me."

Brooke cried out, her body shuddering violently as she held on and rode her orgasm. Her arms reached around Cam, and with each new ripple of pleasure, she pulled her closer. Was there a way their bodies could be fused into one? Could they stay in this little cocoon of joy for, oh, about a thousand years? She felt a rush of love for Cam that was as strong and as powerful as the tallest waterfall.

Cam rested her cheek on Brooke's chest. "I feel your heartbeat."

"It's a little fast right now, huh?"

"About a million miles an hour."

"That's your doing, you know. It's all you, darling."

"I'm good with that. And Brooke?" Cam's head tilted to look at her.

"Yes?"

"It's been…a while for me. As in, years. Was this… Was I okay?"

"Oh, sweetie." Brooke encouraged Cam to lie down beside her. "You were wonderful."

"I have more things in my repertoire, you know."

"Oh, do I ever." Sex had never been their problem. Brooke adored sex with Cam. "And I look forward to getting reacquainted with what's in the rest of your toolkit. But right now, it's time for you to relax and enjoy, ahem, a few of *my* tricks."

Cam's eyebrows quirked up in the most adorable way, and then her dimples burst through and that was the end of Brooke. She was a goner. She surrendered to the thrill of fresh arousal and moved on top of Cam. Cam's skin smelled the same…mint and something citrusy. She wanted to worship that body with first her hands, then her mouth. She heard Cam's breath hitch as she found her breasts. Her lips followed the same path as her hands, kissing Cam's pebbling nipples, drawing wide circles around them. She was lost in Cam's breasts, she always did get lost there, and it wasn't until Cam's hips began to twitch and demand more attention that Brooke shifted gears.

She smiled as she slowly kissed her way down Cam's body. When they were young, sex was like a horse race. Fast, thundering, sweaty…an explosive sprint to the finish line. This time it was every bit as intense, but the ride was more measured, more nuanced, more protracted. Which took nothing away from the sexy sensations. If anything, it only intensified their intimacy.

"Brooke," Cam rasped, "you turn me on so much. I want to come for you."

"Yes," Brooke replied, sliding a finger through Cam's silky wetness. "But not yet."

Brooke's hand found Cam's pleasure points, and she watched as Cam's face alternately tightened and relaxed with each stroke. Her breath deepened. Her legs twitched. But Brooke didn't want Cam coming yet. Not until she tasted her. She moved her mouth to the inside of her thigh, where she nipped lightly, then licked and kissed the tiny bruise she'd created. Cam's moan grew greedy, which only emboldened Brooke. She exhaled her breath over Cam's center. Oh, she was going to enjoy this! She ran her tongue softly over her glistening arousal, tasting the salt, thrilling when a sharp gasp escaped Cam. Hands tangled in Brooke's hair, urging her to keep going, and Brooke did. She increased her pace, alternated between sucking and licking, until Cam's legs began to spasm and she cried out, calling her name.

Brooke kept at it until Cam's body began to still. With a final kiss, she slid her way up, kissing her way there, halting suddenly when she saw that Cam's cheeks were wet.

"Sweetie. Are you okay? Did I do something wr—"

"No! Oh, you were perfect, Brooke. And… I'm sorry. God. I'm a blubbering fool."

Brooke lay beside her and pulled a blanket on top of them. "Tell me what you're thinking. What you're feeling."

"Happy. I'm feeling happy." Cam looked at her. Her cheeks were drier now, but her eyes were glistening still. "I feel, I don't know, almost like a new person. Different. More complete, maybe. It's hard to explain."

"Sure that's not the sex talking?" Brooke smiled to make it a joke, but inside, she worried. What if it was just the sex that had them feeling so close right now, making them feel so happy together? What if this all splintered into a million pieces in the light of day?

"No. Absolutely not the sex talking." Cam turned on her side, facing Brooke, and stroked her cheek with the tip of her finger. "But we should talk. Tomorrow. After we get some rest."

"Rest? We're supposed to sleep now?" Brooke supposed, in the abstract, that she was tired, but her body throbbed with the insistent afterglow of sex. She was pretty sure that she could be aroused and ready to go again in under a minute.

"Well," Cam said with a suggestive eyebrow dance. "I suppose we could try. Or not."

CHAPTER FORTY-ONE

Cam is starving and can't stop thanking Brooke for slipping downstairs and bringing them back coffee, juice, and breakfast sandwiches. "You can have my firstborn. Fair tradeoff, don't you think?"

Brooke throws her arms around her and kisses her before setting the food and beverages out. "I think it's a little late for you to have a firstborn, sweetie. But since you did work up an appetite, rewarding you is the least I can do."

"You worked up an appetite too, or have you forgotten?"

The blush on Brooke's face is adorable, but there is a note of triumph in her grin. "How many rounds was it? Four?"

"Three-and-a-half. We got sleepy, remember?"

"Ah, yes. And for some mysterious reason, I'm still tired."

"Me too." Cam drags herself out of Brooke's embrace—only because there's food and coffee. She makes a lunge for a breakfast sandwich and a cup of coffee. "Is it weird that in some ways, I feel like it's about 1999 again? Like we've been transported back in time?"

"It feels like that to me, too. Except without all the angst and drama."

"Cheers to that." They pretend to clink their Styrofoam cups in a toast. "I'm all about the simple things these days." Like this. Could there be anything better? Though she supposes they should try to be adults, which means not spending the entire day lounging (and doing other things) in this room. "What do you want to do today?"

Brooke shoots her an are-you-for-real look. "Nothing, if it entails leaving this room."

"We only have today and tomorrow left on the island. I thought maybe—"

"Come here."

Brooke sets her breakfast sandwich down and opens her arms. Cam doesn't think twice before she's in those arms again, holding tightly and being held even tighter. It seems impossible that in less than ten days, she's gone from a solitary existence to being in love. And she is in love with Brooke. Has never really *not* been in love with Brooke, but so much time has passed. Time where she thought she'd never see Brooke again. Time where she never expected to discover their breakup was built on a spectacular lie.

"How about a compromise?" Cam suggests. "Let's spend the rest of the morning hanging out here, then break for lunch and...go golfing."

"Golfing?" Brooke scrunches up her mouth and stares at Cam as though an alien as taken over her body. "Are you kidding me? Since when is either of us a golfer?"

"I thought we could handle that eighteen-hole executive putting course."

"Okaaaay. If you prefer that to being in this bed with me."

"Oh, trust me, I don't. But I want to take a cute selfie of us golfing and send it to Landon."

"Oh, right, he still thinks we're fighting, doesn't he?" Neither of them sent Landon the picture Maggie took of them at the concert, looking particularly cozy. He's still in the dark about their budding relationship.

Cam pulls out of the embrace to tackle the rest of her breakfast sandwich. Breakfast of champions. Or of the over-sexed, anyway. "We could send him the picture," she says as she chews. "And nothing else. Let him and Tenley figure it out."

"Right. That way it's not a total surprise when we tell them about us for real."

Their sandwiches consumed, Cam brings her coffee to her side of the bed and crawls in, her back against the headboard, and stretches her legs out in front of her. "You want to see him. He'll want to see you. We'll go back and stay at my place in Traverse City." A worrisome thought occurs to her. What if Brooke plans to go back to Ann Arbor as soon as they leave here? Or right after she sees Landon? What exactly is the plan once they get on that ferry for the mainland? Because one thing Cam knows for sure, she needs to get home to be with Landon and Tenley. She's been checking in with Becky, her replacement, every day. Landon is weakening, and so following Brooke back to Ann Arbor is not an option right now. "If you want?"

Brooke settles in beside her, cradling her cup of coffee like the prized possession it is. They're both morning coffee addicts. "Of course, I want to see him. If you're okay with putting me up?"

Cam clutches her chest. "Oh, the hardship."

"I can cook, you know."

"I remember. And since you've owned an Italian restaurant, I'm thinking you're even more magnificent in the kitchen than ever."

"Cooking for one has never been very inspiring, but at the restaurant, sure. I can cook a pretty mean creamy gorgonzola gnocchi. And a vegetarian ravioli to die for."

Cam's mouth is watering. "Please stop, or I'm going to orgasm right here."

Brooke's eyes brighten as she grins. "Can I watch?"

Cam swats her playfully. "Into voyeurism, are you?"

"Nah. I'm more into participating, if you get my drift."

"Oh, trust me, I get your drift. I love that you're not a sidelines kinda gal." The heat is intensifying between Cam's legs, but they need to settle some things first. "I have to warn you, when we get to Traverse City, I'm going to be spending quite a lot of time with Landon and Tenley, probably several hours a day at this point. Plus I'll be on call during the night."

"That's fine. I won't get in the way. I'll come around as much as Landon wants. Or if he doesn't want me to, that's fine too. He's... He doesn't have much time left, does he?"

"It's hard for me to know until I get back there and can see him for myself, but no, not much."

Brooke gets a faraway look in her eyes. Cam has no idea what she's thinking about until she blurts out, "I can't stop thinking about what it would be like to live here full time."

"On the island?" Where is Brooke going with this? Surely, she doesn't—

"Yup. Right here." There is awe and excitement in her eyes, just as there was when she was in her twenties and she would talk about her dream of owning a restaurant one day. But there's a rock-solid determination now built on the confidence of success—a component that was absent in Brooke two decades ago. Cam knows that with fewer years ahead of them than behind them, they're at the point in their lives where the abstract either becomes action or it dies. "I want to, Cam. I want to move here. I love it here, and I think I'm actually brave enough to handle their winters. Not to mention the scariness of doing something so different from anything I've ever done before."

"Wow. Okay. I didn't see that coming."

"Me either. But I think this is me now. You know, not overthinking, not over-planning, not over-angsting everything to death. I thought it started here, this new spontaneous me, but it didn't, Cam." She sets her coffee on the nightstand, takes Cam's hand, and settles their joined hands in her lap. "Selling the restaurant, taking Landon up on his mysterious proposition to come here... I think somewhere inside I was preparing for this. For changing my whole life. It feels like the universe is telling me I need to go big if I'm going to turn everything upside down." She rolls her eyes and laughs. "I sound just like Marcy."

"How is Marcy these days?"

"Kooky as ever. Drives me nuts, but I love her to death."

Yup, sure sounds like the Marcy Cam remembers. A good person, but she has a tendency to take up all the air in a room with her presence.

The breakfast sandwich Cam has eaten feels like a rock in her stomach. Just when they've found each other again, Brooke wants to move to the island. While not nearly as far away from Traverse City as Ann Arbor is, Mackinac Island is still a two-hour drive away. What would that look like for them as a couple?

"I…" Cam pauses, not wanting to say the wrong thing and discourage Brooke, but some clarity would be good. "That's actually kind of a neat idea. And I guess you'd be a little closer. I mean, you'd be two hours away instead of five. So that's an improvement, right?"

The look on Brooke's face is inscrutable—another stab of worry for Cam. If Brooke doesn't want a serious relationship with her, well, okay. She will be absolutely fine, like she's been for a long time now. She can do alone. Well, maybe not as well as before, but, hell, she can get a dog if that will help.

"Cam, wait." Brooke squeezes her hand. "Come with me."

"What?"

"Here. Move here with me."

"Brooke, I… Seriously?"

"Seriously. You've helped me see that life is short, that I should take life as it comes. Embrace new adventures. So that's what I'm doing, and I think you should, too. Come on, sweetie. Will you at least think about it?"

Cam is floored, not with the idea of being with Brooke, but with moving so suddenly. "It's not quite that easy for me. I have my business, my clients. I'm not ready to retire. Hell, I can't retire. I need to work a few more years and…"

Cam is grasping at excuses because…what the hell? Pick up and move here? With no job prospects? She looks at Brooke and sees a kid at Christmas morning, with her new toys and a mountain of wrapping paper beside her who can't stop grinning. Now who's the one afraid of change? Afraid of embracing new adventures, new opportunities? Of living her best life with the woman she's loved for, like, forever.

Brooke, patient, tilts her head as she listens to Cam verbalize a laundry list of roadblocks. Finally, she says, "I understand. But I only care about loving you and being with you for the rest of my life. That is the most important thing to me, Cam. If it means we live part time here and part time in Traverse City, then fine. We'll figure it out. Just don't give me a blanket *no* right now, okay? Please? But take all the time you need."

Cam smiles and pulls Brooke into her arms. "I don't think I know how to say *no* to you. Don't you understand that yet?"

"Good, because I hate that damned word."

Cam laughs, kisses Brooke on the mouth. She tastes like coffee. "So you won't say *no* to me if I suggest certain...things right now?"

They fall onto the bed and Brooke pulls the sheet over them like a tent. "Like I said, *no* doesn't exist in my vocabulary with you."

CHAPTER FORTY-TWO

The golf course was so cute and tiny, yet perfectly manicured, just like a real eighteen-hole golf course. The only club they were given was a putter, thank God, because with only one club to figure out, Brooke at least had half a chance of not making a complete fool of herself.

"Your legs look spectacular in those shorts," she said right as Cam took her shot on the final hole.

"Argh! Look what you made me do." Cam's shot veered dramatically away from the hole. She threw up her hands in pretend outrage, added a glare for good measure before breaking out in a grin. "Be careful, little girl. Two can play that game."

Brooke shrugged. "I'm not scared. Bring it on!"

Cam sprinted over to Brooke and gave her a kiss on the lips and a quick squeeze of her ass. "How am I ever going to concentrate on a shot again if I know you're staring at my legs?"

"Not only staring, but dreaming up all the things I'm going to do to you later. With those legs wrapped around me."

"Oh, that's so not fair!" Cam had that devilish spark in her eyes, like she was dreaming up her own sex fantasies or was about to beg Brooke to drag her back to their hotel. Instead, she said, "Hey, let's take that selfie for Landon before we're done." They were on the eighteenth hole, so it was now or never. Cam pulled out her phone, slung her arm loosely around Brooke to strike a pose, and snapped a photo.

Too staged, too boring. "Wait," Brooke said. "That won't do. Do another one."

"All right." This time, as Cam was about to take the photo, Brooke dove in and planted a big sloppy kiss on Cam's cheek. *Click.* "Hey! You didn't warn me you were going to mug for the camera."

"Of course not. What fun would that be? Okay, now send that to Landon. We wanted to give him a hint that things have, shall we say, thawed between us?"

"Right. That ought to get their chins wagging." Cam sent the picture, then pointed at Brooke, her putter, and the hole. "Your turn, Hot Shot."

"Yeah, yeah, watch an expert at work, will ya?" Brooke lined up her putt, bent her knees, and wiggled her butt furiously until she heard Cam break into fits of laughter behind her.

"A few more wiggles and you're guaranteed a hole in one."

"Nah, the wiggles are for your benefit. I've got my fabulous hand-eye coordination for the hole in one."

"Well, keep wiggling, cuz the wiggles will get you a hole in one with *me.*"

Brooke doubled over in laughter, her putter slipping out of her hands. "Did you really just say that?"

"Um, I guess I should have used my inside voice?"

More laughter. God, it felt so good to laugh with Cam. Brooke picked up her putter, though now her thoughts traveled to a different kind of hole in one, thanks to Cam's raunchy comment. "How am I supposed to hit this stupid ball when you've got me all aflutter?"

"Aflutter, huh? I like that. Even rhymes with putter. How about we aflutter back to one of our rooms after you're done with your putter?"

"Oh, you're such a romantic, my darling. Not to mention a poet. Or something."

"Hmm, okay. I shall make you all aflutter later with my romantic side, okay? Or, like, write you some poetry or something."

Brooke batted her eyelashes. "Promise?"

"Promise."

"In that case, let's get this damned game over."

They watched her ball roll toward the hole, slowing, then picking up speed as it started its descent. With one last roll, it perched on the edge of the cup, wobbled, then dropped in with a soft thunk.

Brooke leapt in the air. "Holy shit, I did it! I actually did it."

Cam hugged her, spun her around, and they danced a little celebratory jig next to the flagpole. "Oh baby, look at you! You just needed the right inspiration, that's all."

Cam's phone dinged. "Landon," they said in unison with matching grins. Sure enough, it was a text from him.

Brooke hates golf, which can only mean one thing: my plan is working after all! Have you two picked a date yet? ;)

Landon always was a smart guy. Brooke watched over Cam's shoulder as she typed:

Don't get ahead of yourself, buster. It's called a truce.

"Good," Brooke said. "Keep him guessing a little. He deserves it after throwing us on this island together without warning."

"Agreed. We can't let him think he won." Cam's fingers typed.

You up for a visit from both of us in a couple of days?

A smiling emoji was followed by two thumbs up.

"I think that's a yes," Cam said, tucking her phone away.

"Good. But, jeez, I'm nervous. I haven't seen him in a long time and…he won't look the same, he won't…you know. It'll be different."

"It will. But beneath the illness, he's still Landon. He's still the man you remember, and that's the way you need to play it. Be yourself. Be his friend. Treat him the way you've always treated him, but don't avoid the elephant in the room. He's dying, and if you don't acknowledge that, it's like rejecting the most important thing that's ever happened to him."

"I can do that." It was never uncomfortable when she and Landon were together; they were always able to talk freely. Even when she had finally admitted she wasn't happy being married to him, he simply took her into his arms while they both cried together. He admitted he wasn't happy either, that he would love her always, but not as a spouse. "We will be what we were always meant to be…good friends," he'd said then, in his typical display of generosity and insightfulness and acceptance.

After dropping off their putters at the kiosk, Brooke and Cam held hands as they walked down the street. Cam was unusually quiet.

"What are you thinking about?" Brooke ventured.

"About how quickly my life has changed over the last eight days. I mean, I work with the dying, I know how fast life can change course. It's a lot to take in."

Brooke's throat ran dry. "Are you having second thoughts?"

Cam's eyes widened. "What? No! Not about you, about us. I'm marveling at it, to be honest. I thought that chapter in my life was over for good. It wasn't a stretch to think I'd be on my own forever. And now…" She shook her head, lost in her own thoughts again. "It's kind of unbelievable."

"I know. It's a lot to take in for me, too. You know, shortly before coming here, I literally swore off relationships forever."

"Uh-oh. That could have been very bad timing for me."

"Don't worry. You changed my mind in record time. But I feel like, for the first time in forever, it's okay to not have the answer to every question, to not have a road map of my life. The ground beneath me might be shifting, but it's solid, dammit. With you. And I don't ever want to be apart from you again."

They stopped in the middle of the street and clutched each other. Pedestrians, horses, bicycles—island traffic naturally wove around them, like a river parting for rocks. A voice calling their names finally pulled them apart. It was Maggie, on the steps outside of O'Doul's, wearing her ubiquitous green apron with the clover leaves on it.

"Hey, you two lovebirds. How much longer are you here for?"

"We leave the day after tomorrow," Cam said.

A deep frown engraved its way onto Maggie's face. "Well, can't you two stay for the summer? Or forever?"

Brooke exchanged a secret wink with Cam. "You never know, Maggie. You just never know."

"Come for brunch tomorrow. Jane and I will want to see you both before you go. What do you say? We'll even close the store for a couple of hours if we have to. Think of it as a culinary sendoff."

Brooke's stomach growled in anticipation. She didn't need to be asked twice. "We wouldn't miss it for the world."

CHAPTER FORTY-THREE

Cam stuffs herself. The table overflows with stacks of sausage and pancakes, bowls of fresh fruit, maple syrup from the Upper Peninsula, as well as a big fat bowl of whipped cream for topping the pancakes. Brooke immediately goes for a mountain of sugary goodness piled on top of her stack of pancakes. There's a river of coffee and juice to wash down the scrumptious food. Maggie and Jane could run a course on how to be the perfect hosts. And their cooking skills are even better.

Cam listens as Brooke asks them more questions about the island. Her idea of moving here isn't idle talk; she's serious. It had come as somewhat of a shock to Cam yesterday but today it intrigues her. What would it be like living here full time? Is it even possible for her? She needs to work at least part-time to make ends meet, and she suspects Brooke will need to as well. Which is fine, except working as a death doula is Cam's career; she can't fathom doing anything else. Is there enough work here for her? She does a calculation in her head, and it's not reassuring. The island's full-time population of five hundred or so is not enough. Not even close. On the other hand, the mainland is a twenty-minute ferry ride, with access to another 3,500 residents between Mackinaw City and St. Ignace. Okay, that might be enough for part-time work in her field at least, though the ferries shut down for a couple of months in the winter, which would leave her stranded on the island. But it's do-able, and it gives her some measure of hope. And relief. Moving here actually is a possibility for them, if that's what they decide.

Maggie's eyes light up as if she's been reading their minds. Or tea leaves, which is a real possibility, knowing Maggie. "Have you two ever thought of moving here? To the island? You both seem to love it so much—the pace of life here, its natural beauty, the people."

"We've sure loved it here," Jane adds. "Don't think that just because we want to move to Florida for a few months of the year and sell the business, that we're giving up on this place. It gets in your blood. We're islanders forever."

"Well," Maggie says on a laugh. "I've always been an islander, having grown up in Ireland. Which…" She looks pointedly at her wife. "…is where I want us to spend at least a month of the year from now on."

Jane rolls her eyes, but the gesture is no match for her smile. "All right, all right. Six months in Florida, a month in Ireland, and five months here. Sounds about right to me."

"Actually," Brooke confesses with a nervous glance at Cam, "I would love to move here. I've been giving it a lot of thought the last few days."

Jane looks from one to the other. "Not both of you?"

"Working on that," Brooke says and squeezes Cam's knee beneath the table.

"It's something I'd consider," Cam finally says, purposely vague, because it's a conversation that needs to continue privately between her and Brooke. And there's still a lot yet to get her head around. She has her home, her clients, her routines. And yet maybe her routines and entrenched way of living has her stuck. Where has her sense of adventure gone? Agreeing to come here has been the most outrageously adventurous thing she's done since a friend out west got her drunk enough to try bungee jumping. And that was a lifetime ago, not to mention dangerous and stupid. This was neither of those things. Wasn't she supposed to be taking her own advice and living her best life? Was she being a hypocrite? Something shifts inside her. She understands that the pandemic has guaranteed that life is never going to return to the way it was. That's the thing about change. As soon as something big changes, a million smaller changes flow from there until almost nothing looks the same again. Reuniting with Brooke has been a seismic change that guarantees her life will never go back to the way it was. Change means…changing everything.

"What is it," Jane asks Brooke, "that makes you want to live here?"

"Somehow it feels so real here. There's so much natural beauty, but it's a rugged beauty with all the rocky outcrops and the powerful currents of the straits." Brooke grows more animated. "For two centuries, people found a way to make a life here, under what I imagine were awfully trying circumstances. I love the idea that, especially once the tourists are gone, people here have to rely on one another. I'm sure it takes everyone pulling together to keep this place going."

Maggie smiles. "That's the nature of island life, the incredible sense of community that comes with that."

Brooke nods. "And no motorized vehicles. It's like stepping back in time, back to a simpler time. More time to reflect on what's important, I suppose. More time to appreciate the small things. And that really appeals to me right now."

Jane's laugh is steeped in sarcasm. "It's simple here, all right. Sometimes the Internet can go down for days if there's a bad storm."

"Power too." Maggie shrugs her shoulders. "But we get by. Like you said, we have each other here. People help one another."

"I think I'd actually be okay with that, being without power or the Internet for short periods." Brooke glances at Cam with a self-deprecating smile. "I haven't always been the most rugged person, but I'm willing to learn."

The three of them take turns sneaking curious glances at Cam, as though they're waiting for her to jump on board any minute. To change the subject a little, she says, "Any prospective buyers for your store come forward yet?"

"Nothing yet," Maggie says. "These things can take months. Sometimes years, to find the right buyer."

"Wait," Jane says, wagging her fork excitedly at Brooke. "You've got a restaurant background. Which I know isn't the same thing as running a general mercantile, but...have you considered the idea of taking over the store?"

Brooke's face colors. "It... No, I hadn't thought of it. Though I'll need something, some kind of work. I mean, I don't know. It's a big responsibility and so busy in the summers, which means there wouldn't be time for me to actually enjoy the summers here." She passes a glance at Cam, and Cam can see the wheels turning behind those gray eyes.

It's all happening so fast, she thinks. Like, everything is suddenly racing ahead of her and she hasn't caught up yet. But she loves Brooke, so she squeezes her hand under the table. "Honey, you'd be great at it if that's what you decide you want to do."

Something is cracking wide open, and in rush excited voices as Jane, Maggie, and Brooke talk about the store. The word partnership is thrown around. Maggie and Jane offer to help share the load in the summers, it's really the winters they're trying to escape, and the business is starting to be too much for them on their own. A partnership could be the ideal solution, they decide. And just like that, Cam is on the outside of this three-way alliance. And that's okay with her. She doesn't need to jump into anything. She has to see Landon through his last journey, then she'll decide what she's going to do.

"Will you come back soon?" Maggie asks them. "So that we can talk more about this?"

"Definitely," Brooke says, with a glance at Cam. "I see lots and lots of talking in my future."

She says it with a smile in her voice, and the absence of drama and any sort of pressure is so refreshing that Cam is famished again and takes another helping of sausage and fruit. Brooke knows what she wants. And she'll do it, with or without Cam by her side. But she has made it clear she'd prefer that Cam goes with her, and that's enough for now.

Cam leans close to Brooke and whispers in her ear, "I love you."

CHAPTER FORTY-FOUR

The sun was beginning its descent as Brooke walked down to the beach with her empty coffee cup and the children's sand buckets she'd picked up at the island's only toy store. Much of the shoreline consisted of pebbles and limestone, but there were a few sandy patches, which she'd noticed on the disastrous tandem bike ride she and Cam had taken last week. Sand was exactly what she needed for this little exercise.

She left a note taped to Cam's door asking her to join her here—she could have texted, but she purposely left her phone in her room after making her call to Marcy earlier. She didn't want Marcy texting or calling her back right now, not when the sun was quickly going down on her last night on the island and there were sandcastles to build.

"Oh, Marcy," she said out loud, plunking herself down on the empty patch of sand. "Smug, smug Marcy." Well, not at first. Brooke had been the smug one, announcing all of her news on one long stream over the phone that kept Marcy speechless. Once Marcy found her voice again, she declared that she'd always known Brooke was far braver than she gave herself credit for. Of course, she had to toot her own horn too, prattling on about how her influence had finally gotten through to Brooke. Brooke didn't take the bait, and Marcy followed up with the usual why-didn't-you-call-me-sooner crap. It was a personal revelation of the best kind that Brooke didn't need Marcy's permission or approval. She had never needed it. She'd been too scared until now to believe it.

She dropped to her knees. With her hands, she scooped water onto the sand, then packed her bucket. She was flipping her second bucket upside down when she felt a pair of eyes on her. Cam's voice, warm and deep, called out. "Okay if I interrupt the artist at work?"

"Some artist. But yes, please." One of her turrets unceremoniously collapsed.

"Let me help." Cam plopped down on her knees and began filling another bucket. They did this for several minutes, working in companionable silence.

"You really like it here," Cam said, her voice neutral.

"I do. If I'm going to start over in my life, why not here? I want simple. I want the outdoors. I want to be part of a community." She turned to Cam, her heart in her throat. "But none of it will mean much of anything if you're not here with me."

"Brooke—"

"No, wait. Let me finish. I feel like *me*, for the first time in decades. The pandemic wasn't enough to teach me to be happy with the small stuff, to slow down, to learn to like myself. But this place, seeing you again…" Tears clouded her vision. "Landon dying. All of it is like the perfect storm. I didn't listen before, but it's like the universe has taken me by the shoulders and shaken the crap out of me. And I'm listening now, Cam. I'm listening. But if I go back to Ann Arbor, it's all going to disappear. All of it, including you." She began to cry big sloppy tears. Watched them drip onto the sand. "And I don't want to go back to the way I was before. I want to hold onto this feeling. I want to hold onto you. And I want to hold onto everything I've discovered here about myself." It felt like she finally had all the pieces she needed in her life but had absolutely no idea how to hang onto them all.

Cam pulled her into her arms and held her close. "You've got me, I promise."

Brooke sniffed back her tears. "Does that mean…"

"I've no intention of losing you again, now that I've found you. It's time for me to follow you, just like those years you used to follow me around."

Brooke held up a hand. "No. I don't want anybody following anybody. This time, we walk side by side." When Brooke looked up, tears were streaming down Cam's face—past her dimples and around her smile, and it was the most beautiful sight Brooke had ever laid eyes on.

"Now that is a deal I can't refuse."

Brooke looked at Cam and met her future in one glance. She'd been prepared to give up this fantasy of living here and move to Traverse City, if that was what Cam demanded. But this…this was much more than she could have expected. "I found myself here. And I found you here."

"Then that makes this place about perfect, in my mind."

"I couldn't agree more." Brooke moved to sit between Cam's legs, the sandcastle forgotten, and leaned back into Cam. Strong arms tightened around her.

"It's our last night here," Cam said, her breath warm against Brooke's ear.

"For a while."

"Right. For a little while. What do you want to do?"

"I want to sit here and finish this damned sandcastle with you and watch the sun go down."

"Then that is what we shall do."

"But not for a few more minutes. I'm not ready for this moment to end yet."

"Good. Neither am I."

CHAPTER FORTY-FIVE

Cam spends the morning with Landon and Tenley, catching up and assessing Landon's condition. Before seeing them, she spent an hour going through Becky's detailed notes from the last ten days. Landon is on morphine now for increased pain and his appetite is almost non-existent. Protein shakes and the occasional piece of fruit are his only intake. Another scan while she was away offers nothing but poor news: his cancer has metastasized further.

"You look happy," Landon observes from his hospital bed in the library. "I can see it in your eyes, yes?"

Tenley brings in tea for herself and Cam—Landon doesn't want any. "Did you and Brooke patch things up on the island? Please tell us that you are indeed as happy as you look. And as happy as you both looked in that picture you sent us from the golf course."

Cam won't keep them in suspense. She'd rather most of the details come from Brooke, since Landon has known her longer and more intimately, but Brooke is back at Cam's house. They decided it was best for Cam to come alone to see Landon today, not only to make sure it's still okay for Brooke to come by, but to resume her doula duties.

"We did manage to patch things up quite nicely, thank you. I won't lie, it didn't look good for a while."

Landon waves a hand in the air, his digits as bony as a leafless tree. "Figured that. But you persevered."

"We did."

"And?" Landon wants more, and Tenley is on the edge of her seat too, curiosity filling her eyes.

Cam beams, because she can't not smile when she talks about Brooke, and then she catches herself—she doesn't want her happiness to appear insensitive. It's not unusual for the living to feel guilt for, well, living, so her hesitation swamps her for a minute. *Oh, what the hell.* The man orchestrated this whole thing and he wants to make sure his matchmaking scheme worked. "We found each other again and we couldn't be happier about it. We owe this to you, Landon, and to you, Tenley. Thank you for something that I consider is nothing short of a miracle."

Landon wipes a tear from his eye, but he can't stop smiling. "I can't believe it actually worked. But it was the two of you who made it happen. Tenley and I just threw you both onto the same piece of rock for a few days."

A look of guilt washes over Tenley's face. "I'm sorry we sprang it on the two of you the way we did. We honestly figured it was the only way to get you both to go."

"Well, you weren't wrong. I'm pretty sure that if we had known of your plan ahead of time, we wouldn't have gone through with it. There were a couple of days where we weren't very happy with the two of you. Or with each other." Cam studies Landon. She's confident she knows the answer, but says, "Has our reunion made you happy?"

"Yes, you've made a dying man very happy. Brooke was too damned stubborn to see her way to happiness. You, I'm not too sure about. It was either stubbornness too or an extreme sense of pessimism where love is concerned."

"Well, I'm grateful, Landon. Thank you."

"No. Thank *you*." He closes his eyes, looking like he's asleep, but a smile creeps onto his lips. "That was my only piece of unfinished business."

Wendy the dachshund comes bounding into the room, her little stub of a tail wagging furiously. She stands on her hind legs in front of Tenley.

"My cue," Tenley says, "for putting her on the bed with Landon."

Landon makes room for the dog, who immediately curls up beside him and falls asleep. "You brought me Wendy," he says, grinning, "and I brought you Brooke."

Cam can't resist. "Fair tradeoff?"

Landon strokes the dog. "Absolutely."

Cam tells them both more about her visit to the island, and the three of them reminisce about the place until Landon starts nodding off again.

"When is Brooke coming?" he asks out of nowhere.

"Is tomorrow okay?"

"Yes. I want to see her."

Tenley says, "And I'd like to finally meet her."

"She'll like that."

"Good," Landon says. "One more thing. We…" He looks at Tenley and waits for her to nod. "We're ready for you to tell us what's going to happen to me. At the end. What will my dying look like, Cam?" His eyes survey Cam in that frank, no bullshit way of his that she's come to know and respect.

Cam holds nothing back. We'll manage the pain, she promises, but when the end approaches, Landon will sleep more frequently, have less energy and fewer moments of conscious awareness.

"Sometimes when the dying appear to be asleep they are actually unconscious, yet when they wake up they say they had a good sleep. We don't seem to notice when we become unconscious. At the very end, you see, as a person's organs are shutting down, they are unconscious all the time. And then their breathing starts to change. Sometimes it's deep and slow, then it can be shallow and rapid, then there are longer gaps between breaths. Very gently the breathing slows and then stops altogether."

Watching her mother die was the first time Cam had experienced the ending of life. She knew what to expect, the hospice staff had prepared her well. Living, she decided then, was a hell of a lot messier and more complicated than actually dying.

"So I won't even notice that I'm hardly breathing?"

Cam shakes her head. "No pain, no panic, just peacefulness before you slip away."

"Thank you," Landon says. "For telling me the truth."

Tenley takes it all in with quiet resignation. She's a strong woman, but Cam knows that even the strong have weak moments. It's clear that Tenley keeps her weakest moments for when she is alone.

"And I'll be here the whole time, for both of you."

"Sorry. Last question," Landon says weakly. He can barely keep his eyes open. "Remember…a while back…I said home is a place…where your soul can rest. Did you…find home? With Brooke?"

Cam reaches across the bed and takes Landon's hand in both of hers. There are tears in her eyes and she has to focus on keeping her voice from dissolving into sobs. "Yes. I found home. With Brooke."

A smile settles on Landon's lips as he falls into a deep sleep.

CHAPTER FORTY-SIX

Breakfast this morning held no appeal for Brooke, her stomach a churning mess in anticipation of her visit. It would be her introduction to Tenley, and she would get to see Landon for the first time in more than a dozen years. Cam had done her best to prepare her, but it would be its own unique experience no matter what. Nothing about any of this was normal.

Be strong be strong be strong.

The door was answered by Tenley. To her surprise, Brooke was immediately enveloped in a hug. Wordless, these two women who'd both loved Landon held each other for several minutes. And it didn't feel weird at all. It felt serendipitous and their way of acknowledging the bond that tied them together.

Cam was staying away so that Brooke and Landon could have some alone time, though now that she was here, Brooke wished she had her lover's hand to hold. But Cam was right; she and Landon needed their own private closure.

"He's in the library," Tenley said, leading the way. "Can I make you tea or coffee?"

"I'm okay, thanks. A bit too nervous to drink anything."

Tenley turned and with a watery smile said, "I understand." With a quiet snick, she closed the library door after her.

Inside, a Tiffany lamp and two antique oil lamps were lit, providing the room with a warm glow that was both inviting and comforting. Soft shadows from the flickering flames of the oil lamps danced on the ceiling, a reminder that the flames were a living, breathing thing. Brooke remembered the blue glass oil lamp from when she was with Landon, and seeing it now made something click in her mind. Landon was still Landon, not some dying stranger she needed to fear.

The lamps reminded her of Landon scribbling a poem on an empty page at the back of the book he'd been reading, while they sat one night and enjoyed the light from the blue oil lamp. She'd never forgotten his spontaneous little poem.

My love is alive.
Like the dance of a flame,
Hot, it burns a lovely light
As I whisper your name.

Oh, Landon, she thought with a heart that was melting one drip at a time. *You were always too good for me.*

He was lying in his hospital bed, his eyes closed, looking as frail as a small child. His hand moved to beckon her closer. Though she hadn't said a word yet, he knew she was there. A wheelchair and walker had been shoved into a corner. A table nearby was full of pill containers. There was a box of adult diapers on the floor—the detritus of the dying. She turned her attention back to Landon.

"Oh, darling," she whispered. "I'm so sorry, Landon. I'm so, so sorry about all of this."

A weak smile was all he could muster. "Brooke. You came."

"Cam told me she'd kick my ass all over Michigan if I didn't."

"Wrong." It took effort for him to speak, his chest rising and falling with each word. "It was Tenley who would have...kicked your ass."

Brooke laughed. "I don't think I want to get on the wrong side of Cam *or* Tenley."

"Me either."

And just like that, their union was renewed. They were Brooke and Landon again. Not like they were. Not anything like they were. It was the way, Brooke knew, that it should have been all along—their souls connecting in friendship, not in romance.

"You've always been my friend," Brooke said, pulling the chair as close to the bed as she could and carefully placing Landon's hand in hers. It was like holding a baby bird. "And I've always been so thankful for your friendship."

"As have I. Can we be...completely honest?"

"I wouldn't want it any other way, especially now."

"Especially now." Landon rolled his eyes but with a smile. "This sucks, doesn't it?"

"God, does it ever."

"You know... I knew the minute the words *I do* came out of my mouth...that our getting married...was a mistake."

There was nothing hurtful in his tone. Brooke sensed that no words of a condemning nature would be spoken in this room. This was Landon's sacred nest, the last place that would know his existence. There was only honesty here. And love. "Turned out your instinct was right."

Landon nodded. It was clear that words would not be plentiful. "I regret...it didn't work out...but...I never regret having you in my life. I...don't regret...any of it."

"I feel the same. You're a good man, Landon. The very best. And I'm honored you chose to invest part of your life in me. I'll never forget our time together. Or our friendship." Small, shallow breaths helped Brooke keep her composure. She did not want to fall to pieces in front of him, but it was hard. So damned hard. She didn't have the experience of saying goodbye to her dad when he died—it had happened too suddenly.

"You're...a good person too. Don't ever forget. But...tell me... Why did you lie to Cam? Why did you tell her...you had an affair?"

If Brooke could have a do-over for one thing in her life, it would be that. But there were no wizards anywhere handing out wishes and do-overs. It was a useless fantasy.

"I was unhappy at the time, and I didn't know how to fix it." She can still remember her thirty-year-old self as full of impatience and indignation, easily bruised emotionally, in a hurry to get on with her own priorities. "I thought I had to blow it all up with Cam—Erica then—and see where the pieces fell. I thought I needed to do something dramatic to change the way we were together. Except I realized—too late—that sometimes when you blow something to smithereens, there are no pieces to pick up. Sometimes it's just…gone. Incinerated."

Landon grew quiet, either sleeping or thinking, Brooke couldn't be sure which. After several minutes, he said, "No, not gone. Though the radioactivity of nuclear waste eventually decomposes, it…takes thousands of years."

Brooke laughed. "Luckily in this case it didn't take quite that long. Hey, how did you know there was still a chance for Cam and me?"

"Because that kind of love…never goes away. It's…like the secret rings inside a tree trunk…or the vein…that runs through a rock. Might not…see it on the outside…but it's there."

"I wish I'd figured that out a long time ago."

"No, stop having…regrets. No time. Love. Gratitude. Friendship. Generosity. Those… Only those."

"You're right. Thank you for reminding me. You always were two steps ahead of me. And Landon? Thank you for bringing Cam back into my life."

"I did it…for me, too. I wanted…something good to come… out of all…this."

"I know. Plus you're an incurable romantic."

That earned her a smile. "Guilty."

"Tenley's a very lucky woman."

Landon shook his head. "Me… Lucky. Three…beautiful women…surrounding me."

It astounded Brooke that Landon could still find his sense of humor. "I brought you something from the island." She dug around in her pocket and pulled out a stone she'd collected on the beach. It was the size of half dollar, polished smooth by centuries of water, and with so many rings around it, it resembled a tiny planet. Rings on stones were supposed to bring good luck. Maybe luck would accompany Landon on his next journey. Gently, she folded it into his hand and made a silent prayer.

"Thank you."

"Landon? I'm so sorry I hurt you." Brooke hiccoughed a sob, quickly covered it with her hand.

"You also loved me. One you meant...to do... The other... you didn't."

Brooke brought his hand—the one curled around the stone—to her lips and kissed it. Then she looked straight into his half-lidded eyes. "Landon, have you had a good life?"

There was no hesitation. "The very best."

EPILOGUE

Four months later

There's something about the fall that lends itself to reflecting, to taking stock. Which is why it's Cam's favorite season. Beauty isn't always at its zenith with the noon sun and the fullness of summer's bounty. She likes finding it in sunsets, in the curling leaves that have fallen from trees and their riot of colors before they go. The dying have taught her a lot about finding beauty in things that others miss.

She looks at Brooke, playing fetch on the beach with Wendy, and it's like looking at the sun. There is a streak of love for Brooke that is both familiar and new—spring and fall converging. They are building something good together, right here on the island, and she knows with every cell in her body how right Brooke was in insisting they move here, that this was the perfect place for them to start over. And yet, for all the newness that shapes their lives now, there is, always, time to reflect on where they've been and how far they've come, an appreciation for the circuitous routes of their lives. And mostly, a cherishing for their lives having intersected again.

Wendy's little tail rotates around like the blades of a helicopter as she chases the stick again. Tenley rounds into view, clapping and encouraging the little dog. Tenley and Wendy have joined Cam and Brooke on the island for a few days for the scattering of Landon's ashes and because they've vowed to stay friends. They spend their time exploring the island together and, in the evenings, over a glass of wine and in proximity to the light from Landon's antique blue oil lamp, they swap stories about the man who brought them all together. After Landon died, Tenley insisted they keep the blue lamp to remember him by.

"You two really are happy together, aren't you?" Tenley looks at them like she still can't believe how brilliantly the matchmaking turned out.

"Yes," Cam says. "And it's been the most incredible surprise." She should be familiar by now with the power and frequency of surprises in life—another thing the dying have taught her.

They've set everything out for a picnic on the beach, and though it's chilly, the breeze is tranquil and the sun is providing them with a scintilla of warmth.

Brooke joins them, Wendy at her heels with her little tongue hanging out. "Sorry, Ten," Brooke says brightly, "but we might have to dognap Wendy when you're not looking."

"Oh no you don't. But she'd be happy to visit for a week or two every year. As long as I can come too."

Cam says, "You know you have an open invitation. We'd love you to visit any time. And to stay as long as you like. That's why we chose a two-bedroom place, you know, so there'd be room for guests." It's only been three weeks since they closed on a two-bed, two-bath coach house that was converted years ago to a year-round cottage, and they love it. Its high-beamed ceilings and thick walls provide exactly the kind of rustic charm that suits living here. And it has a yard big enough for a patio and a small veggie garden and room for potted flowers.

"Well, in that case, I'd be happy to be a regular guest. And it kind of feels like I'm visiting Landon at the same time."

Brooke, not Cam, is the first to reach over and hold Tenley's hand. "I miss him, too."

The three of them are quiet. It still feels strange not to have Landon among them. For three weeks, it was the four of them—Brooke and Cam and Tenley sitting vigil as Landon actively died. It was beautiful and terrible, loving and heartbreaking. An end but also a beginning. They spent hours reminiscing at Landon's bedside, even after he slipped into a coma. Right up until the end Cam sang his favorite songs, Tenley daubed his favorite whiskey and his favorite ice cream on his lips, Brooke lit the lamps and put cold compresses on his head when he spiked a fever. They are always accessible, those memories from those final days and final minutes of Landon's life—they don't need to speak about them now.

"What will you do, Tenley?" Cam says softly. "Any decisions yet going forward?"

Tenley's eyes skim across the horizon. She's taken the fall semester off from teaching, but beyond that, she's made no plans. She will likely stay in Traverse City. It's the place she's lived all her life and the place where she built her life with Landon. "You've got me thinking. If you two can start your lives over in another place, why can't I?"

Brooke shrugs. "You could always retire here one day. And if you got bored, you could come work at the store a couple of days a week for me."

Tenley looks from one to the other. "That's very kind of you. But really, now every option is on the table, with absolutely no hurry to choose a single one of them."

"It's wise to take your time," Cam offers.

"Well, you two give me hope that the idea of change doesn't have to be scary. Or daunting. I'm so proud of you both. Brooke, running the store. And Cam, expanding your death doula business to include music therapy. Was it very hard to get yourself established here?"

"Not really. Everyone around here has been surprisingly open to both avenues of my work." Two months ago, Cam jetted off to a week-long conference in British Columbia for a refresher on using music to work with those on the autism spectrum and for the brain injured. She'll take some online courses over the next year, but her music therapy business is off to a promising start.

"And now your own home," Tenley adds. "It's all coming together beautifully, isn't it?"

"Just about," Cam says, leveling a surreptitious wink at Tenley.

Last night, when Cam and Tenley took Wendy for a walk while Brooke stayed back and cooked them a tasty lasagna dinner, Cam confessed that she was going to ask Brooke to marry her. Cam knows Tenley isn't a fan of the institution of marriage, but she had to tell someone before the excitement ruptured her spleen.

"When?" Tenley asked with excitement, her smile crinkling her eyes.

"This weekend, after you and Wendy have gone."

"Landon would love knowing you were going to propose to Brooke."

"It's actually something I wanted to do a very long time ago. I even had a fantasy of how I wanted to do it. And now I actually get to do it."

"Well, there's no doubt of the answer, I can tell you that. Please call me right afterward so I can be the first to congratulate you both."

"I will." Maggie and Jane would be the second call she and Brooke would place.

And now Cam sneaks a glance at Brooke, knowing that tomorrow night, she will get down on bended knee, right here on this private beach. She will sing a song she wrote for Brooke, tell her that she's the love of her life and that she can't imagine spending the rest of her life without her biggest inspiration by her side, then ask Brooke to marry her. For good measure, she pats the little box in her jacket pocket that contains the engagement ring she bought last month.

Tenley returns the wink before opening a bottle of Dom Perignon that she had insisted on splurging on. It's for toasting

Landon one final time. It's also for a secret toast to the forthcoming proposal.

Brooke raises her glass. "To Landon. He gave us ten very special days in May that we'll never forget and will be forever grateful for."

Cam clinks flutes with Brooke and then Tenley, but halts before taking a sip. "No, wait. He gave us much more than that. He gave us the one thing he didn't have. He gave us the gift of time."

The three clink again and sip the bubbly, and it's the most exquisite thing Cam has ever tasted.

Bella Books, Inc.

Women. Books. Even Better Together.

P.O. Box 10543
Tallahassee, FL 32302

Phone: 800-729-4992
www.bellabooks.com